LIMIT

Limit: Volume 5

Translation: Mari Morimoto
Production: Risa Cho
Tomoe Tsutsumi

First published in Japan in 2011 by Kodansha, Ltd., Tokyo
Publication for this English edition arranged through Kodansha, Ltd., Tokyo
English language version produced by Vertical, Inc.

Translation provided by Vertical, Inc., 2013
Published by Vertical, Inc., New York

Originally published in Japanese as *Limit 5* by Kodansha, Ltd.
Limit first serialized in *Bessatsu Friend*, Kodansha, Ltd., 2009-2011

This is a work of fiction.

ISBN: 978-1-935654-65-0

Manufactured in the United States of America

First Edition

Vertical, Inc.
451 Park Avenue South
7th Floor
New York, NY 10016
www.vertical-inc.com

Fashion Forward

Ai Yazawa's breakthrough series of fashion and romance returns in a new 3-volume omnibus edition, with a new translation and a new gorgeous trim size. Relive this hit all over again, 'cause good manga never goes out of style!

All volumes available now
280-320 pages each, Color plates, $19.95

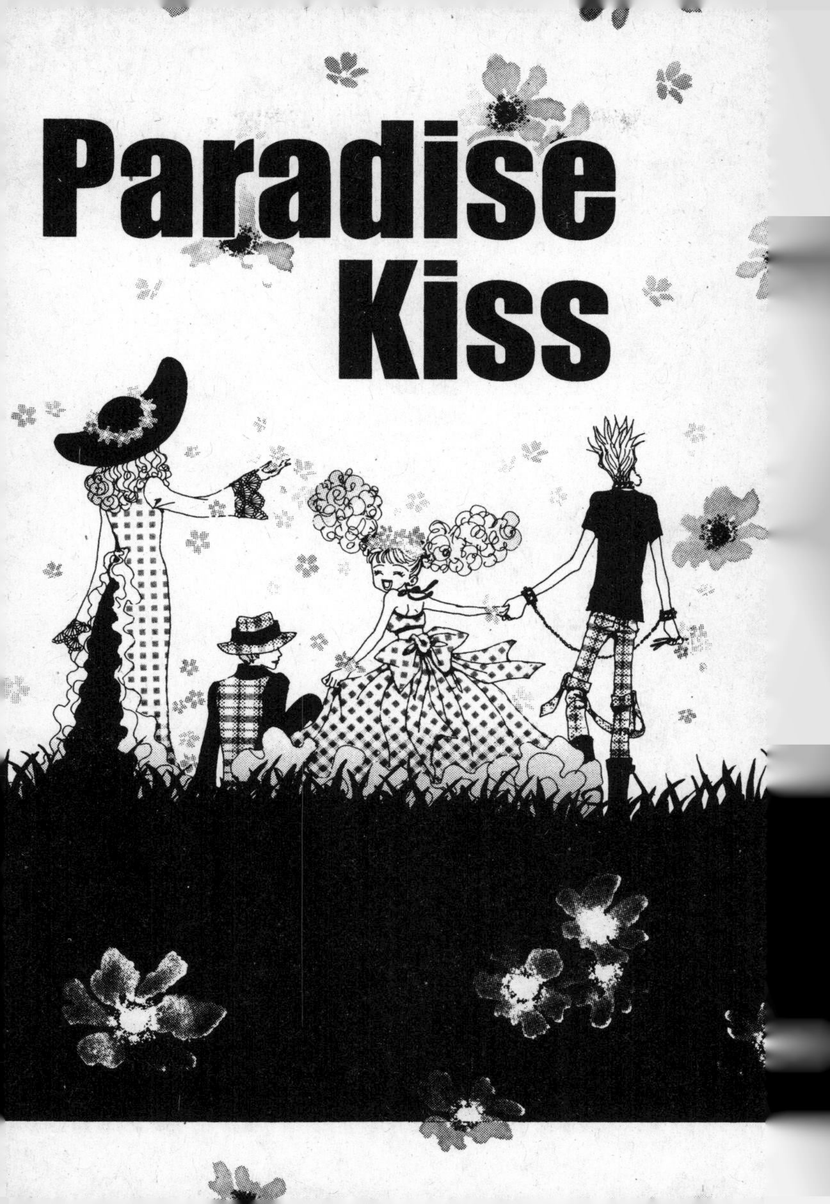
Paradise
Kiss

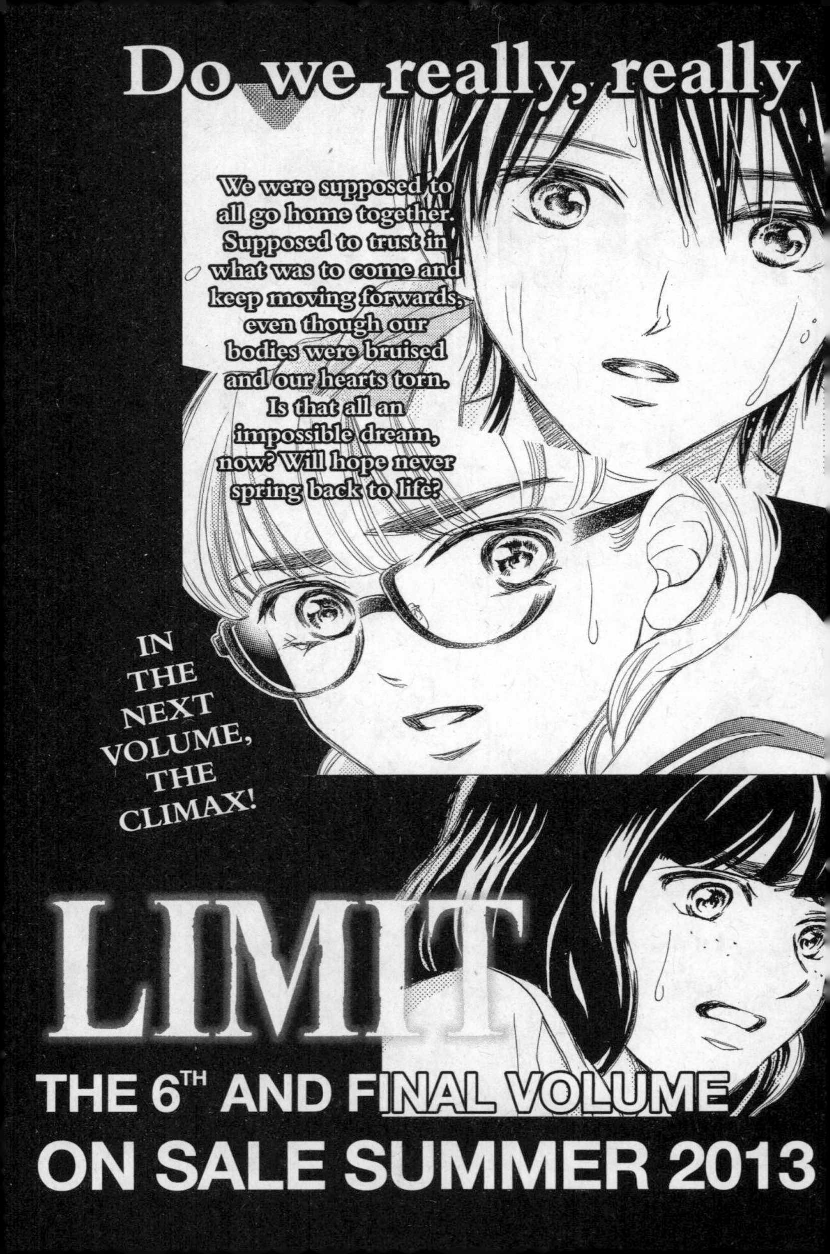
Do we really, really
We were supposed to all go home together. Supposed to trust in what was to come and keep moving forwards, even though our bodies were bruised and our hearts torn. Is that all an impossible dream, now? Will hope never spring back to life?
IN THE NEXT VOLUME, THE CLIMAX!
LIMIT
THE 6TH AND FINAL VOLUME
ON SALE SUMMER 2013

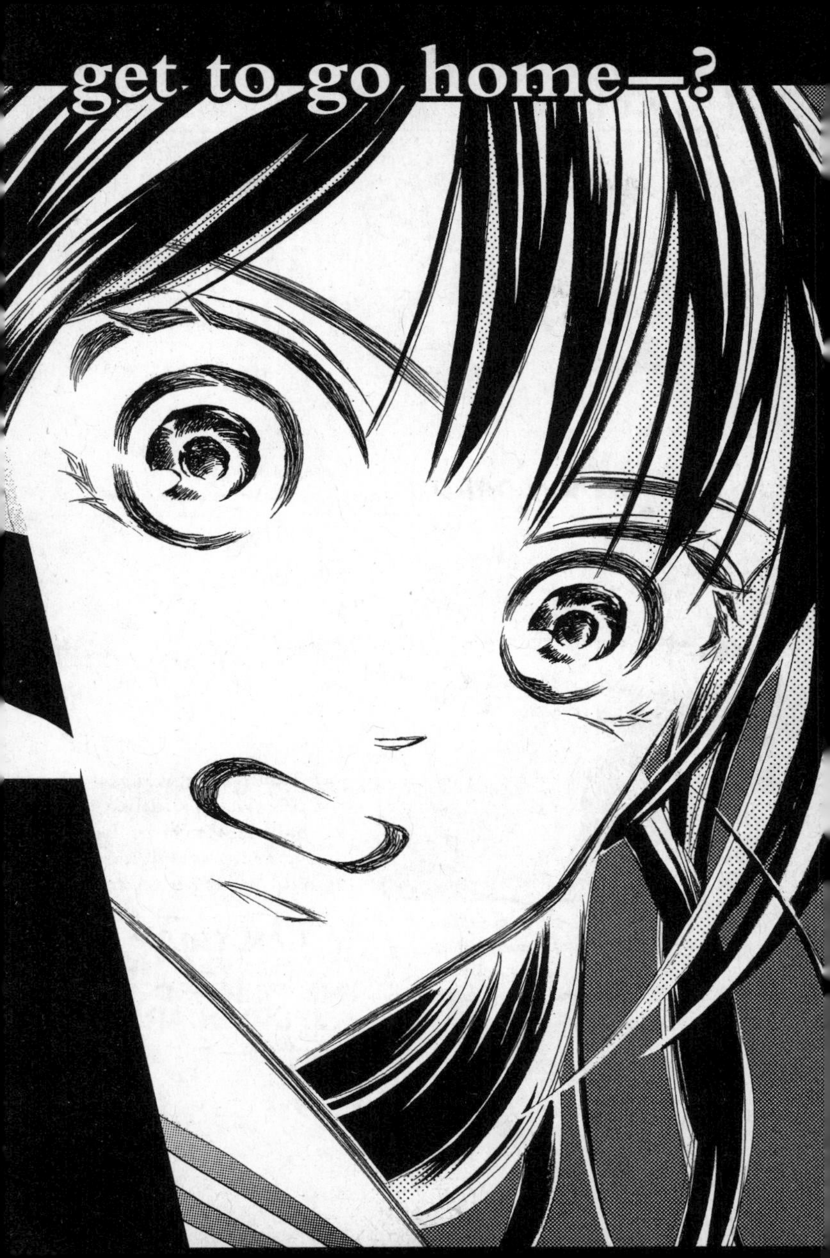
get to go home—?

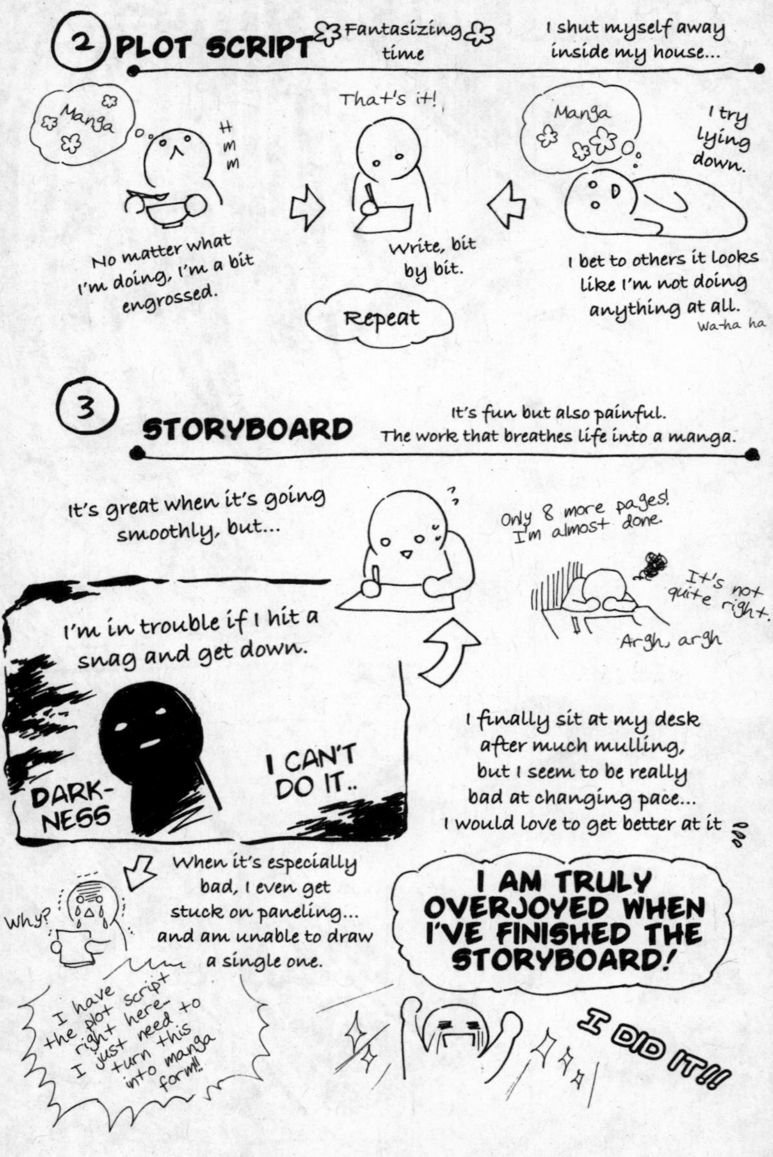

2 PLOT SCRIPT
Fantasizing time
I shut myself away inside my house...
I try lying down.
Manga
I bet to others it looks like I'm not doing anything at all.
Wa-ha ha
That's it!
Write, bit by bit.
Repeat
Manga
HMM
No matter what I'm doing, I'm a bit engrossed.
3 STORYBOARD
It's fun but also painful. The work that breathes life into a manga.
Only 8 more pages! I'm almost done.
It's not quite right.
Argh, argh
It's great when it's going smoothly, but...
I finally sit at my desk after much mulling, but I seem to be really bad at changing pace... I would love to get better at it
I'm in trouble if I hit a snag and get down.
I CAN'T DO IT..
DARK-NESS
I AM TRULY OVERJOYED WHEN I'VE FINISHED THE STORYBOARD!
I DID IT!!
When it's especially bad, I even get stuck on paneling... and am unable to draw a single one.
Why?
I have the plot script right here... I just need to turn this into manga form!!

MY WORKROOM

~ BEFORE A STORY COMES TO LIFE ~

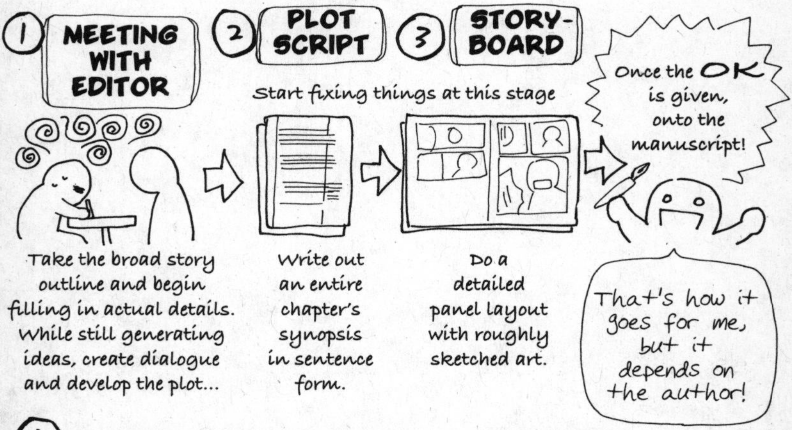
1 MEETING WITH EDITOR
2 PLOT SCRIPT
3 STORYBOARD
Start fixing things at this stage
Once the OK is given, onto the manuscript!
Take the broad story outline and begin filling in actual details. While still generating ideas, create dialogue and develop the plot...
Write out an entire chapter's synopsis in sentence form.
Do a detailed panel layout with roughly sketched art.
That's how it goes for me, but it depends on the author!

1 MEETING WITH EDITOR

Production meetings for LIMIT often take place at a café. One that has a nostalgic, somehow familiar feel to it.

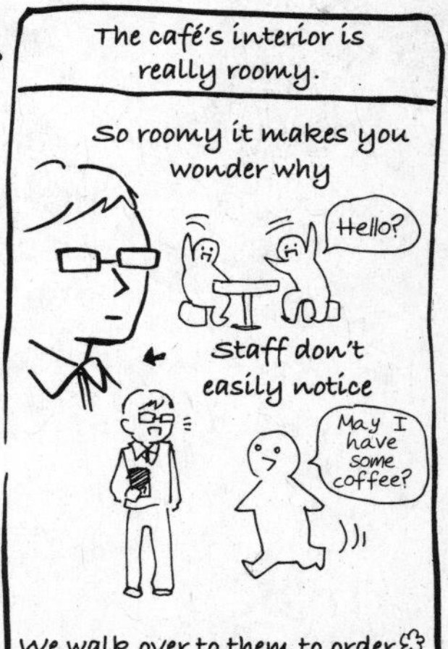
The café's interior is really roomy.
So roomy it makes you wonder why
Hello?
Staff don't easily notice
May I have some coffee?
We walk over to them to order

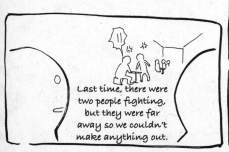

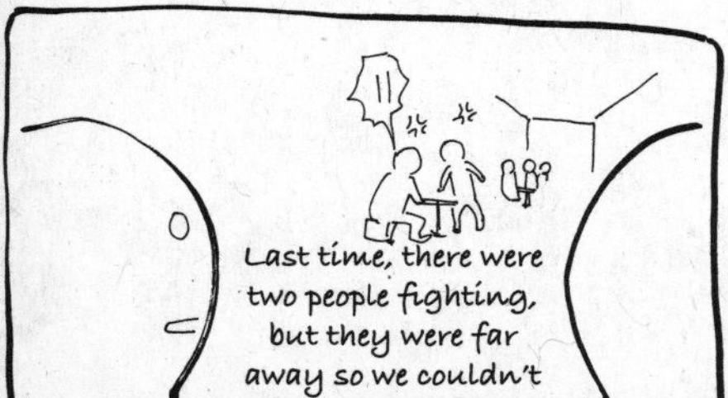
Last time, there were two people fighting, but they were far away so we couldn't make anything out.

To be continued...

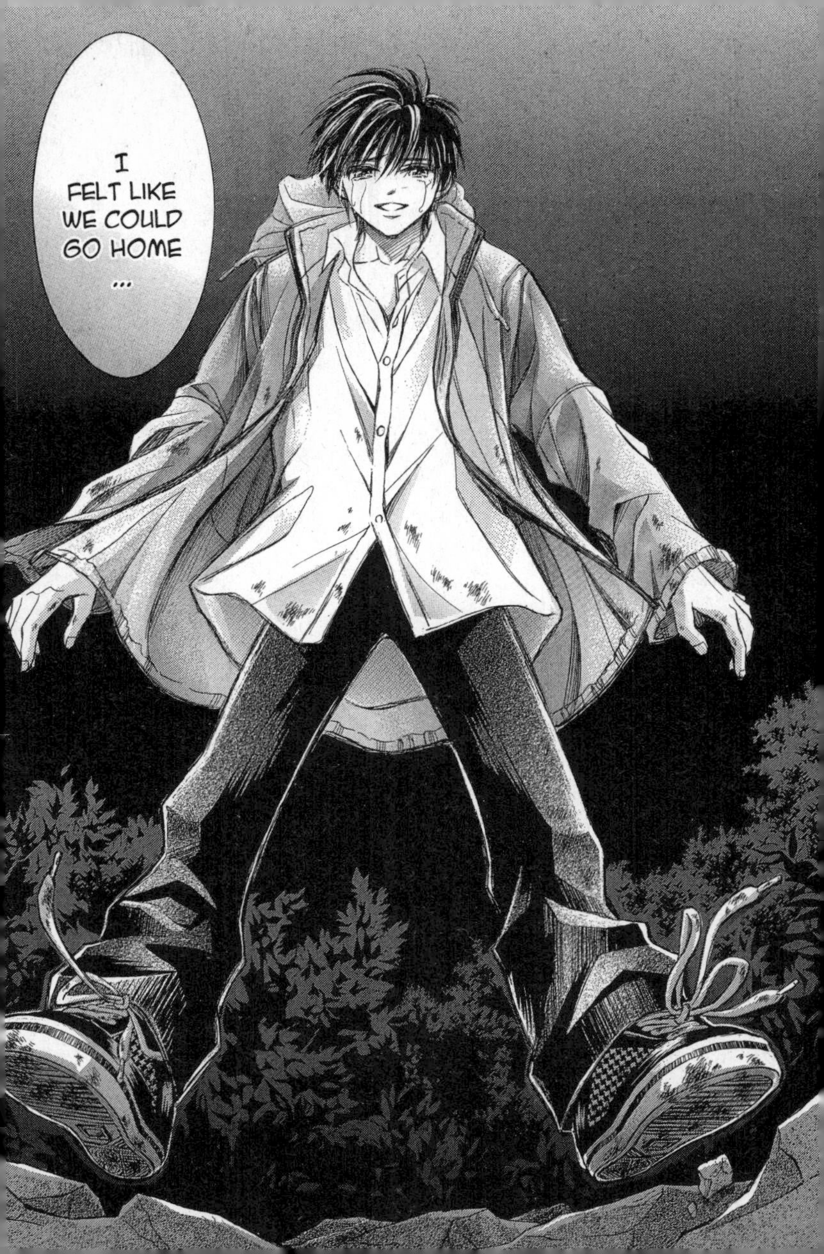
I FELT LIKE WE COULD GO HOME ...

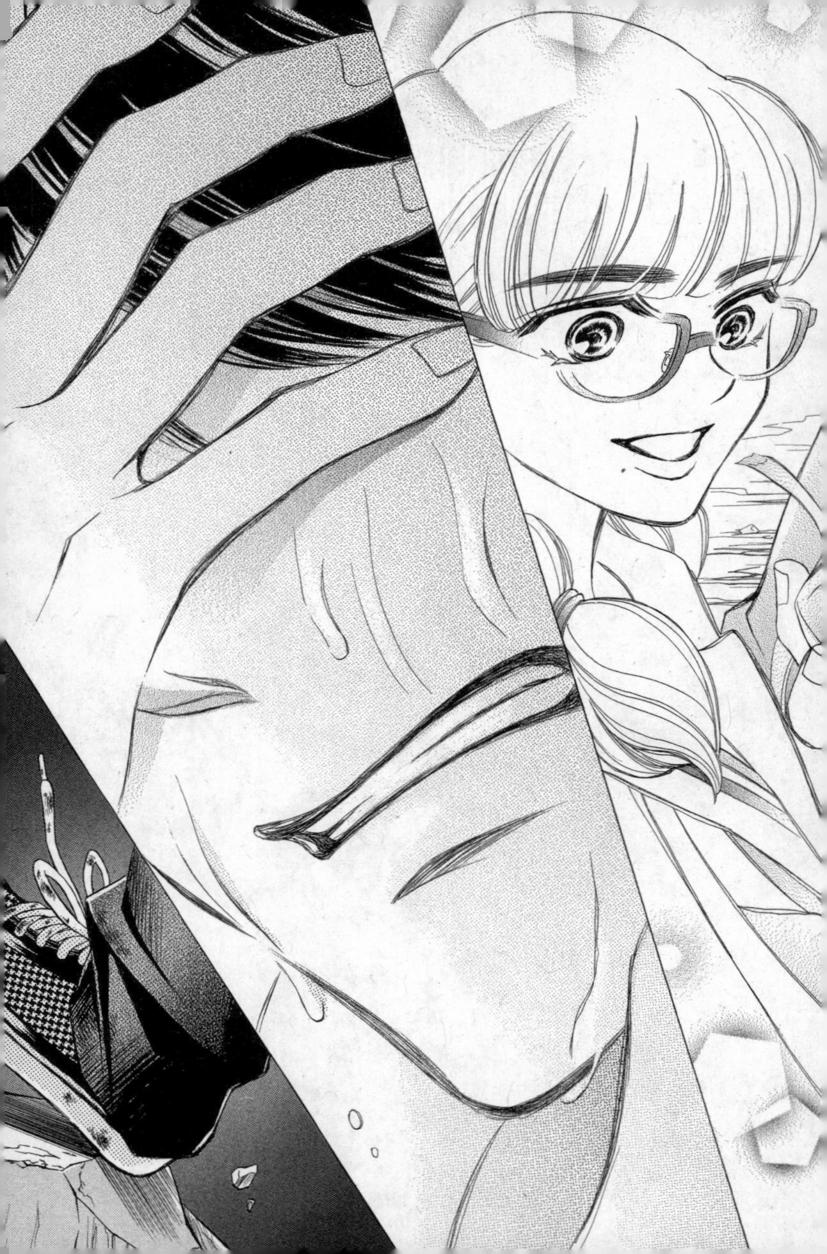

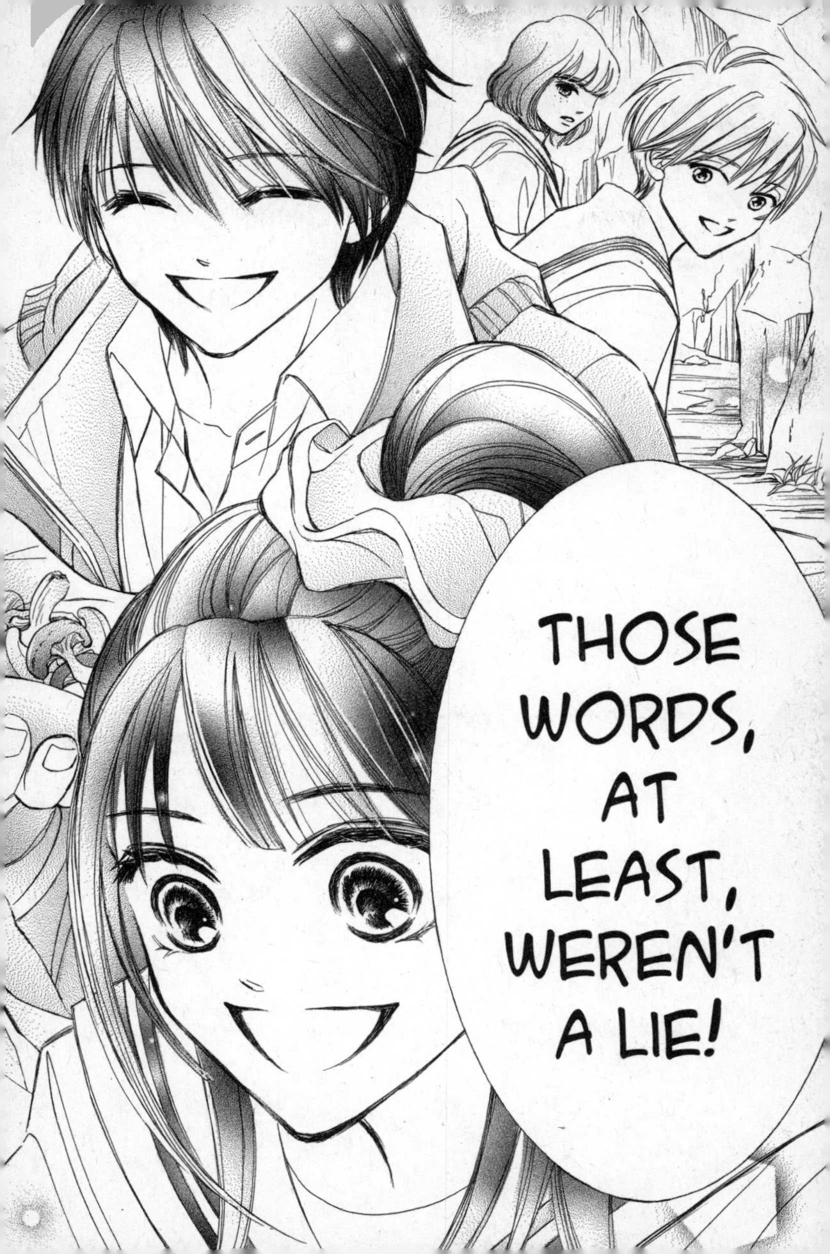
THOSE WORDS, AT LEAST, WEREN'T A LIE!

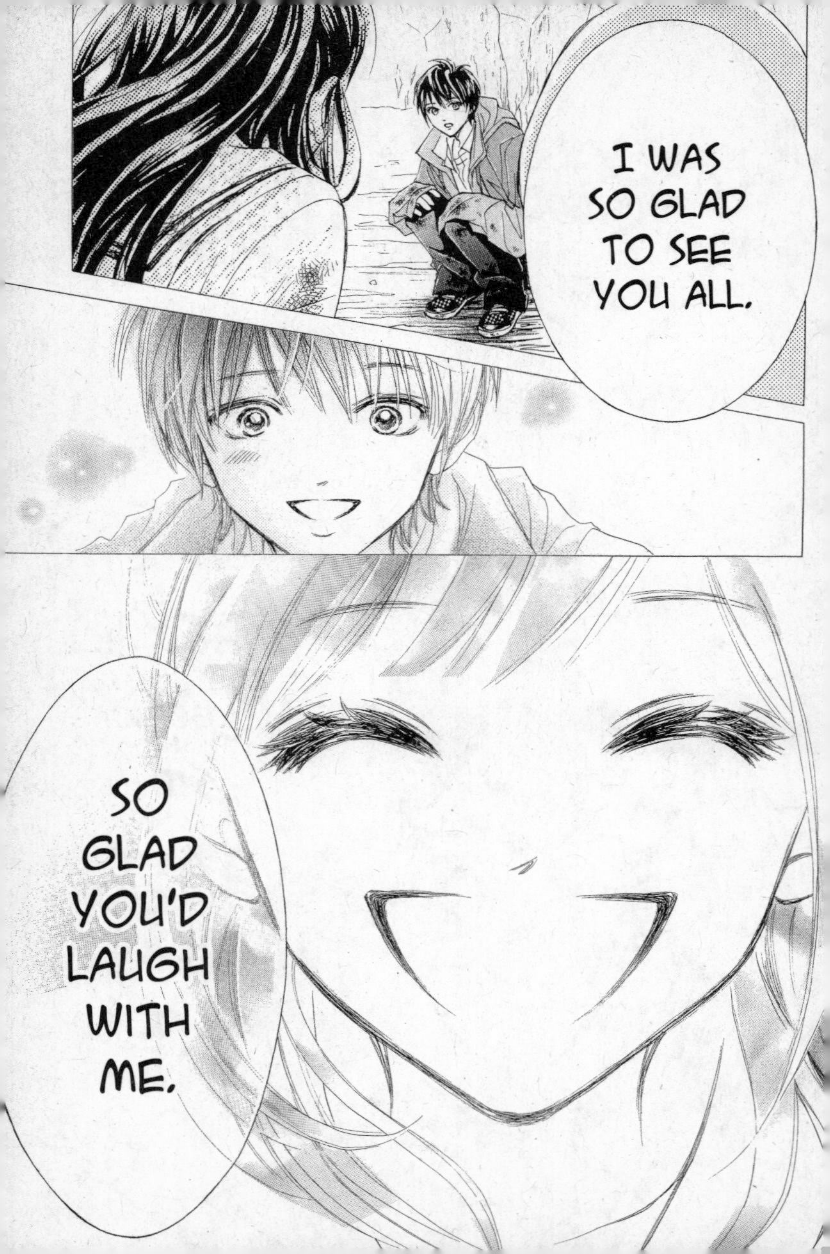
I WAS SO GLAD TO SEE YOU ALL.
SO GLAD YOU'D LAUGH WITH ME.

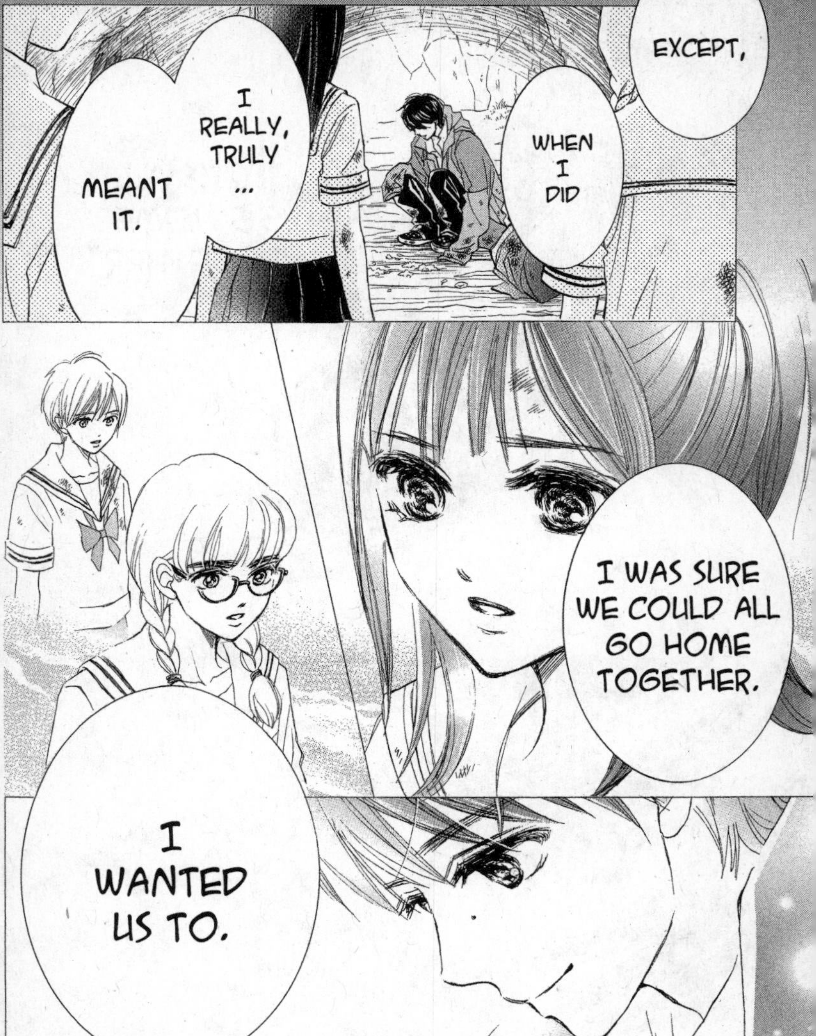
EXCEPT,
WHEN I DID
I REALLY, TRULY ...
MEANT IT.
I WAS SURE WE COULD ALL GO HOME TOGETHER.
I WANTED US TO.

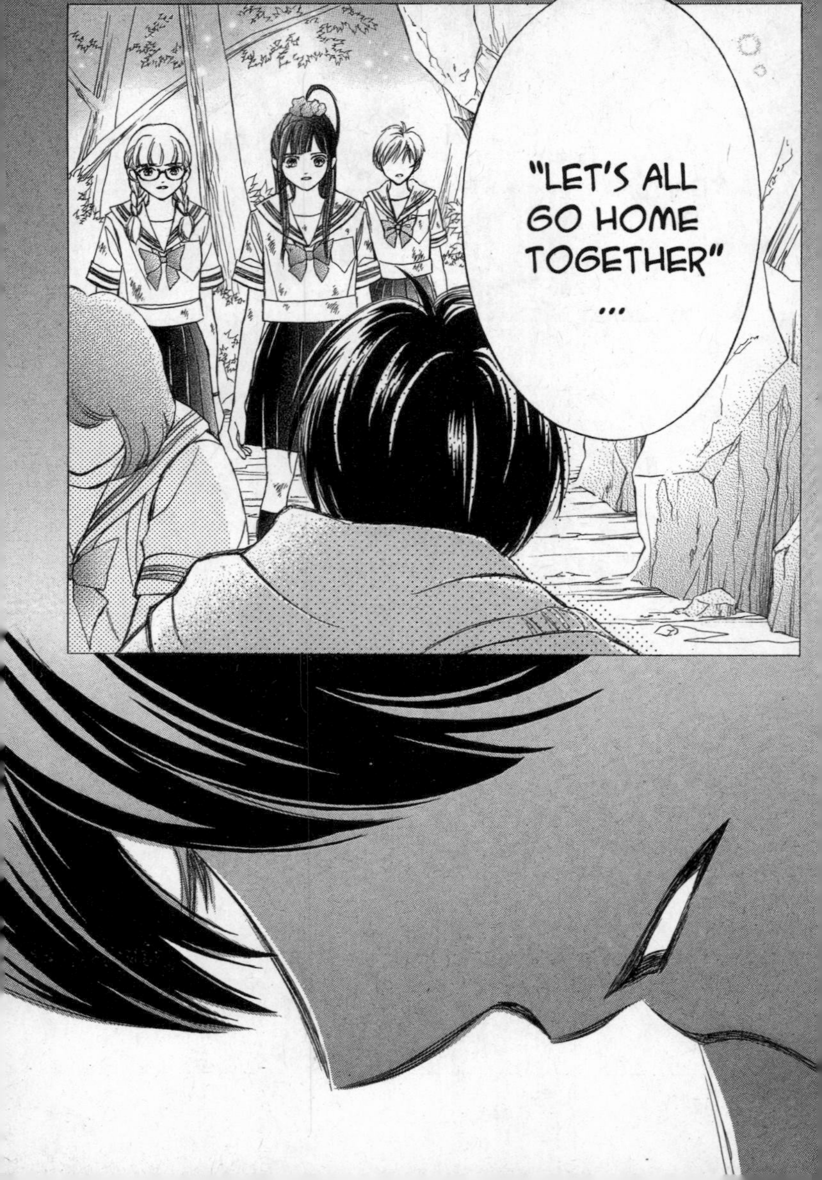
"LET'S ALL GO HOME TOGETHER" ...

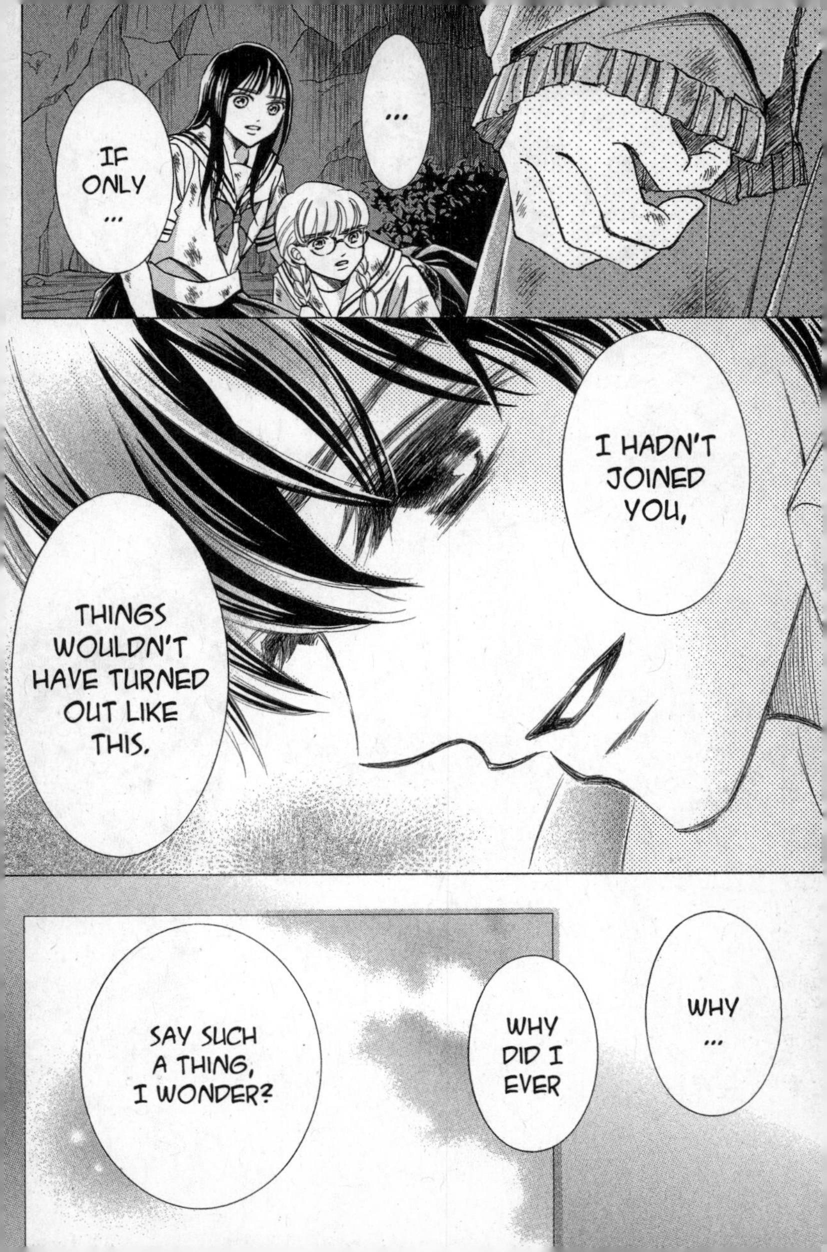
...
IF ONLY ...
I HADN'T JOINED YOU,
THINGS WOULDN'T HAVE TURNED OUT LIKE THIS.
WHY ...
WHY DID I EVER
SAY SUCH A THING, I WONDER?

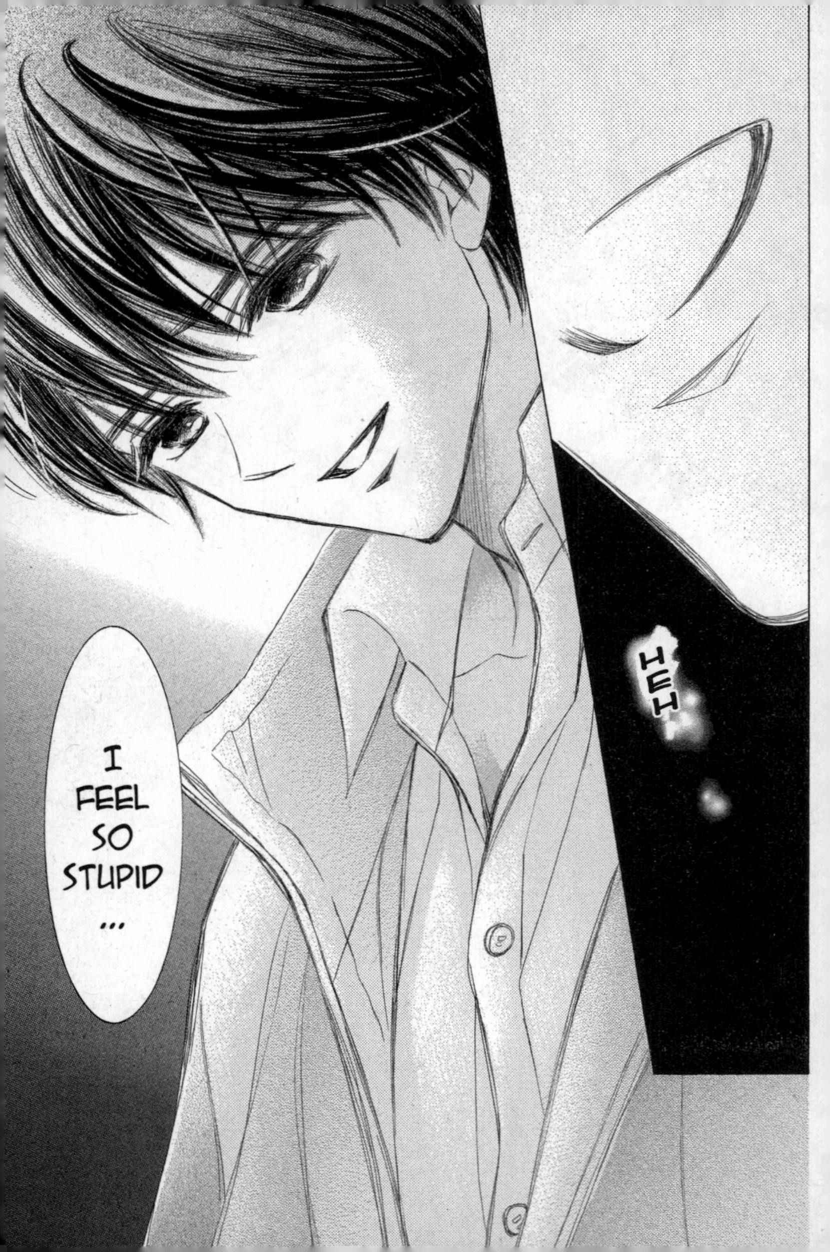
HEH
I FEEL SO STUPID ...

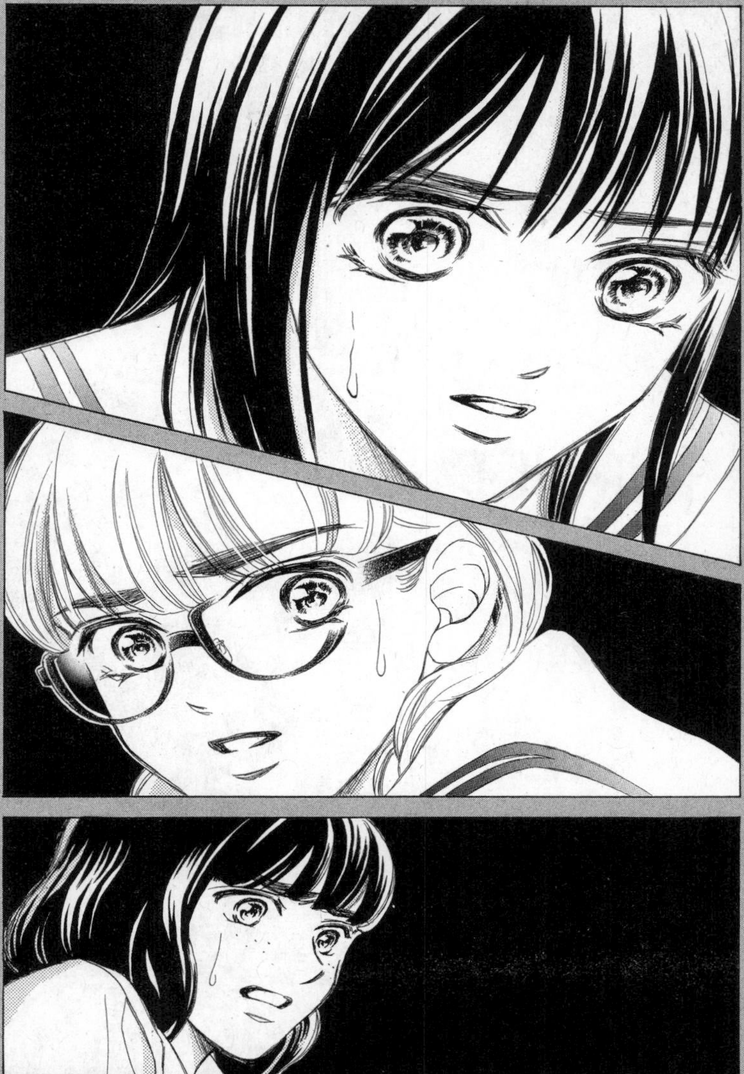

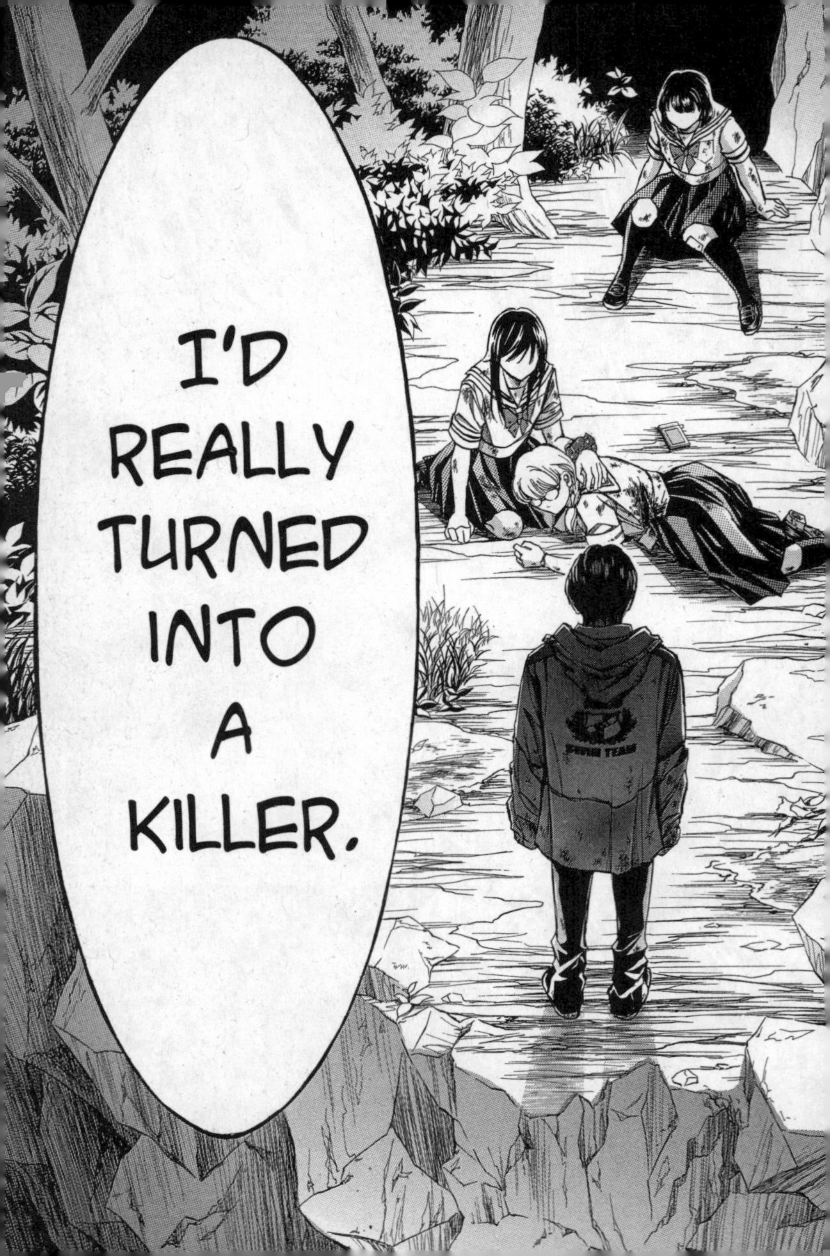
I'D REALLY TURNED INTO A KILLER.

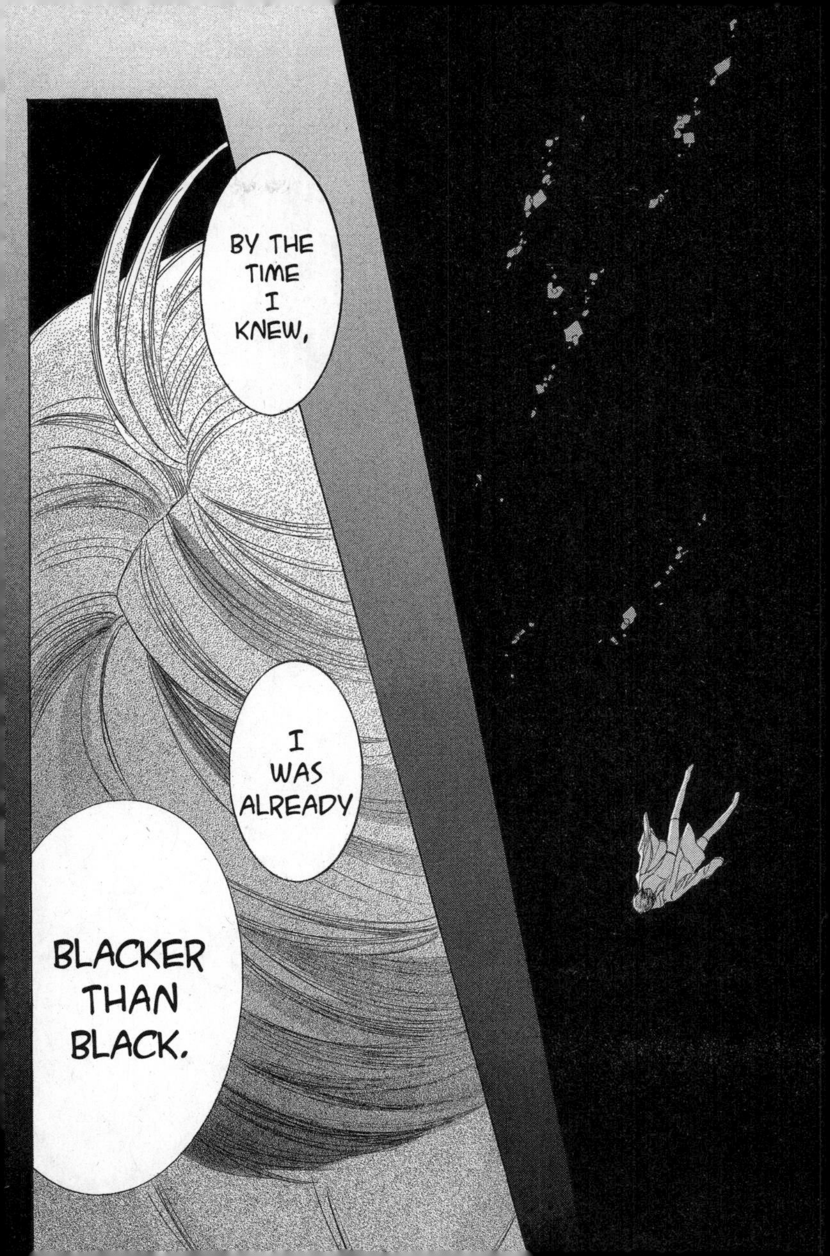
BY THE TIME I KNEW,
I WAS ALREADY
BLACKER THAN BLACK.

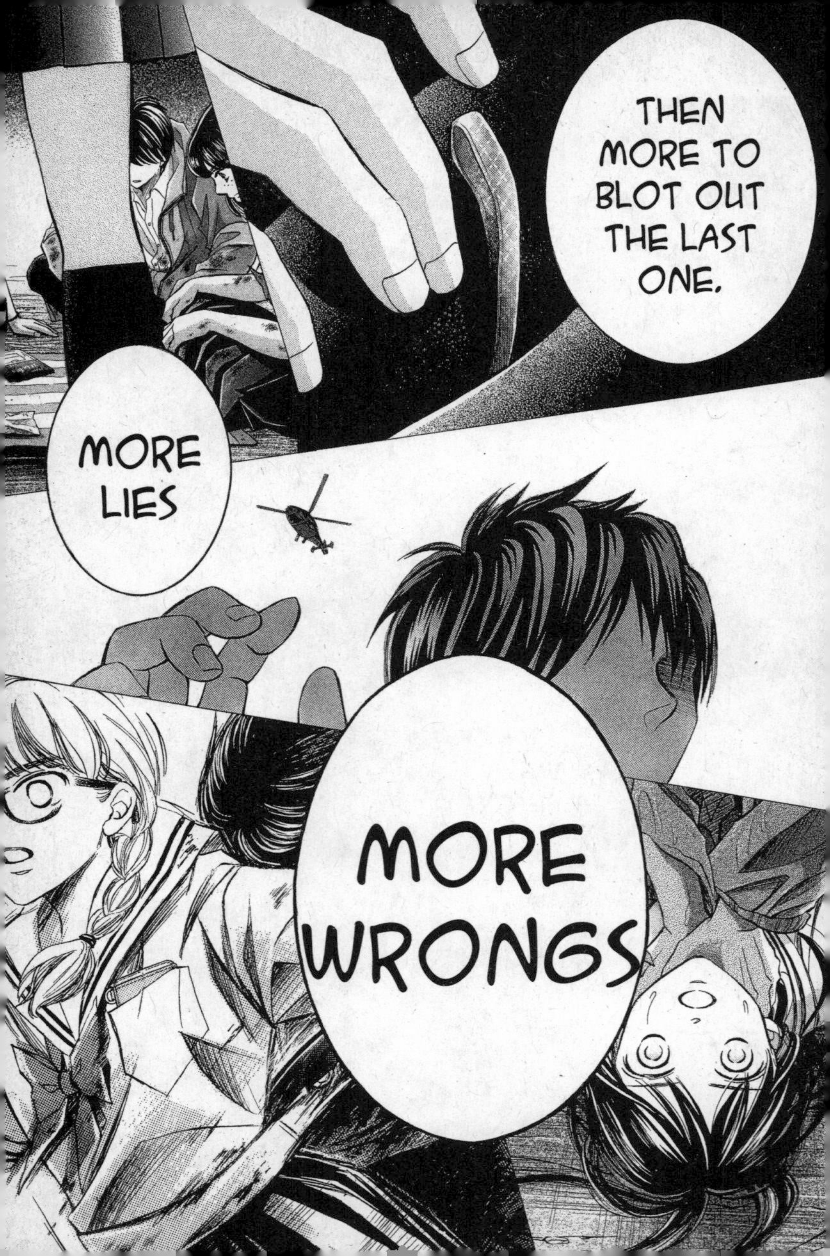
THEN MORE TO BLOT OUT THE LAST ONE.
MORE LIES
MORE WRONGS

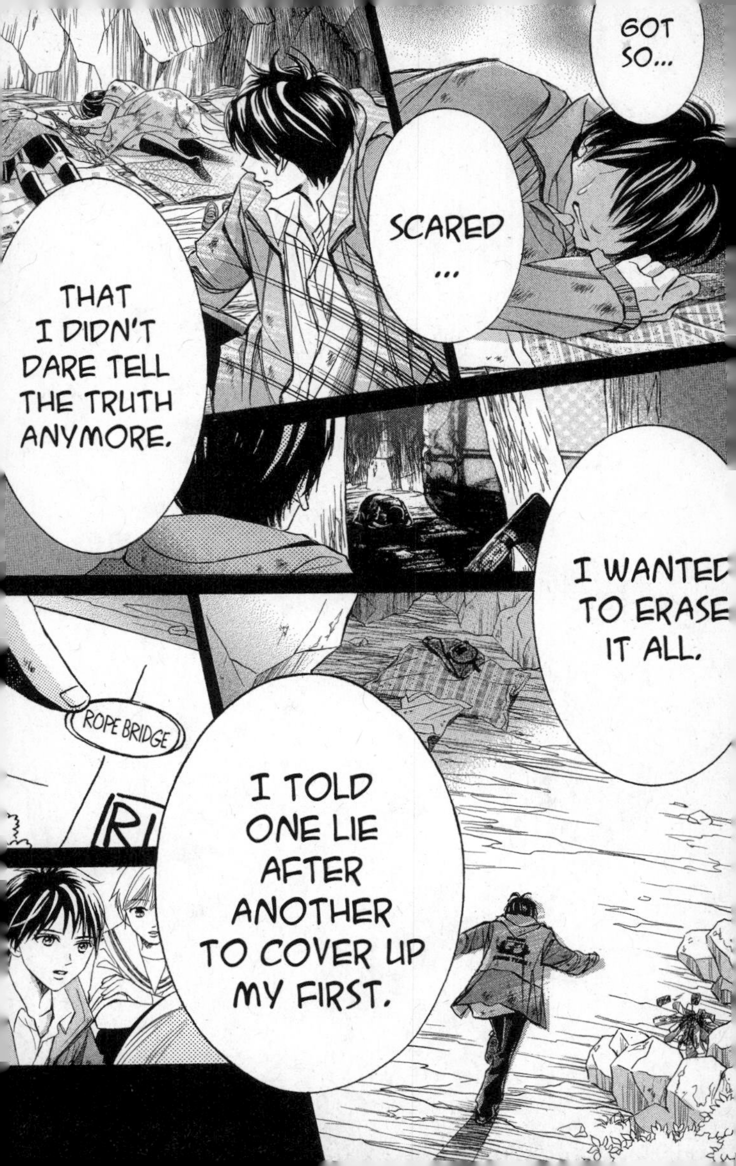
GOT SO...
SCARED ...
THAT I DIDN'T DARE TELL THE TRUTH ANYMORE.
I WANTED TO ERASE IT ALL.
ROPE BRIDGE
I TOLD ONE LIE AFTER ANOTHER TO COVER UP MY FIRST.

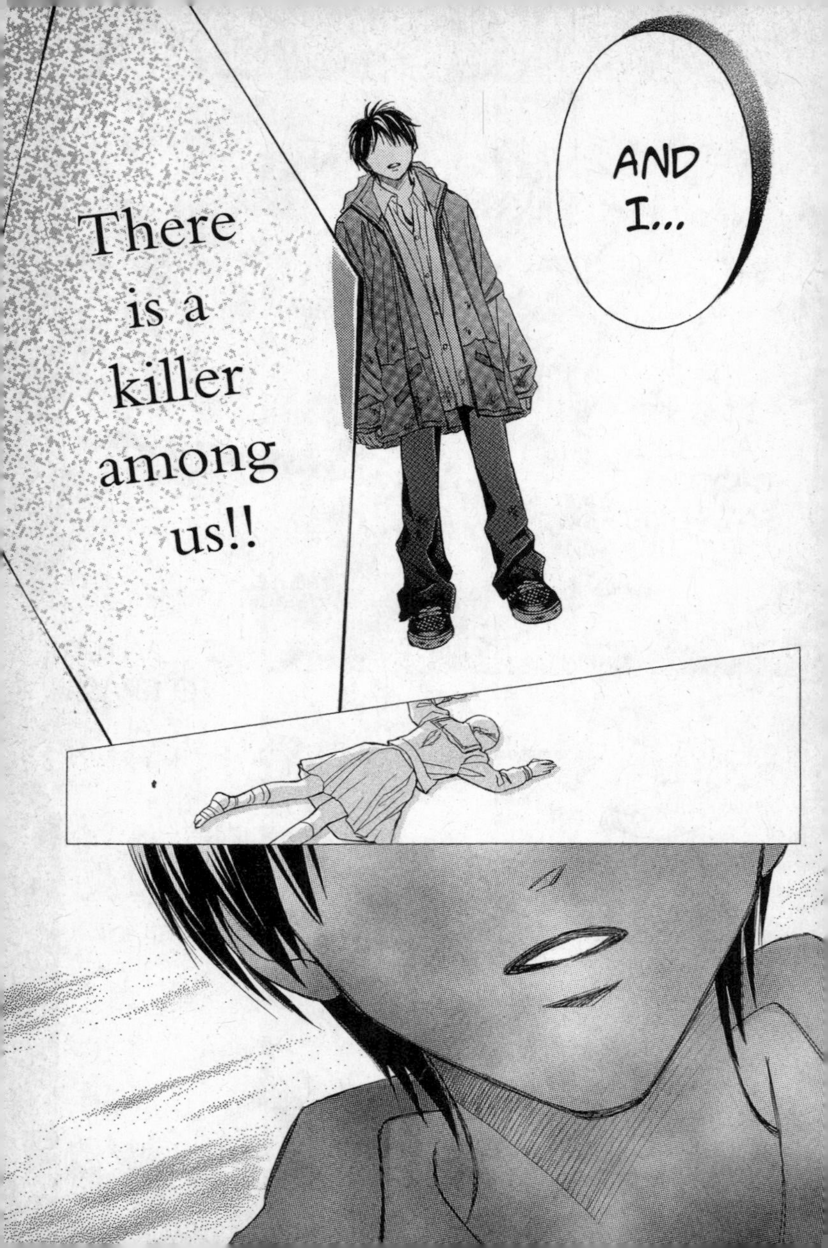
AND I...
There is a killer among us!!

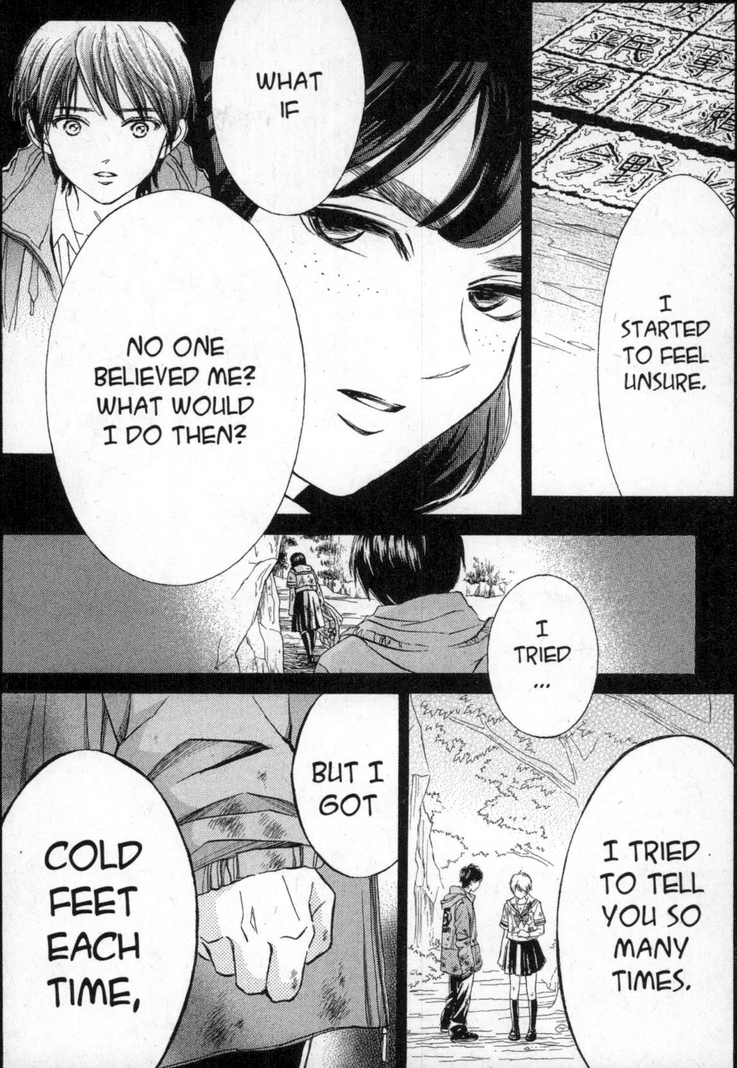
I STARTED TO FEEL UNSURE.
WHAT IF
NO ONE BELIEVED ME? WHAT WOULD I DO THEN?
I TRIED ...
I TRIED TO TELL YOU SO MANY TIMES.
BUT I GOT
COLD FEET EACH TIME,

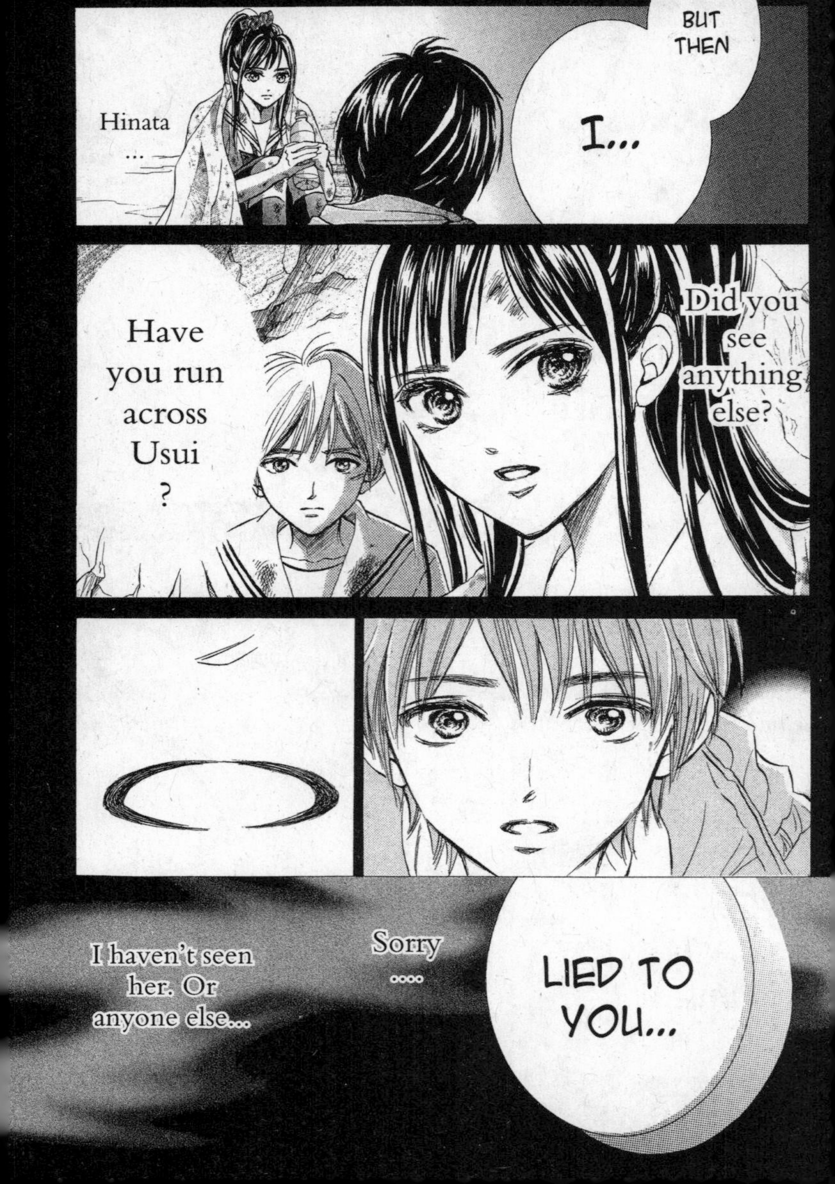
BUT THEN
I...
Hinata ...
Did you see anything else?
Have you run across Usui ?
LIED TO YOU...
Sorry ....
I haven't seen her. Or anyone else...

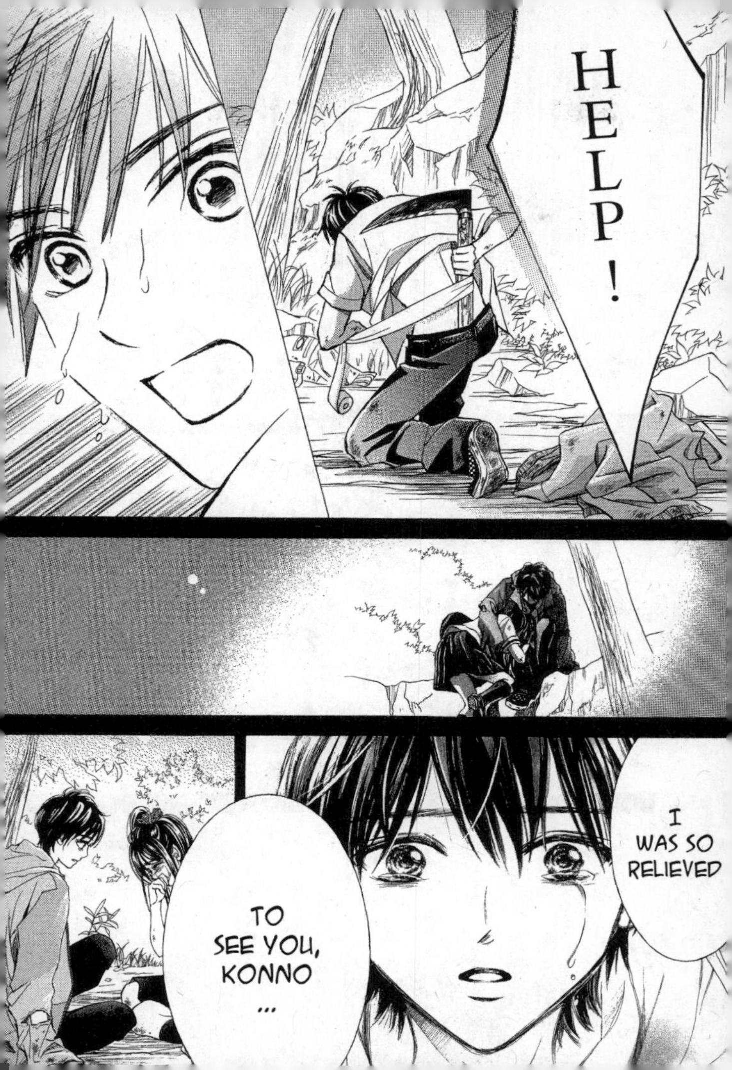
HELP!
I WAS SO RELIEVED
TO SEE YOU, KONNO ...

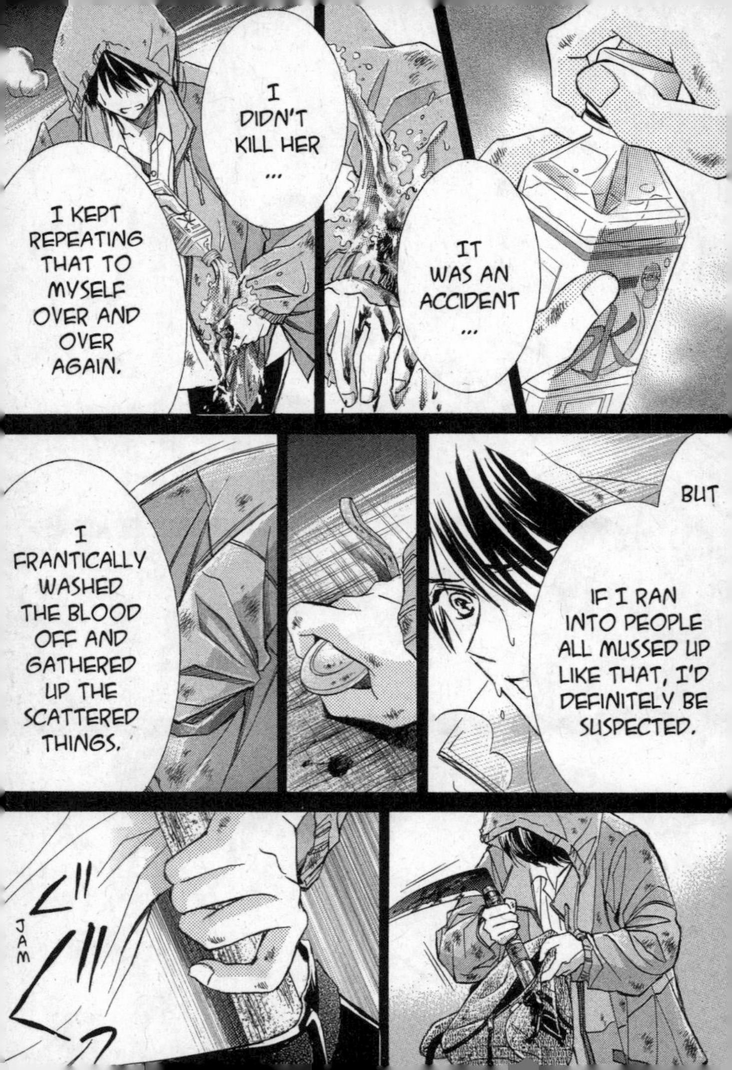
IT WAS AN ACCIDENT ...
I DIDN'T KILL HER ...
I KEPT REPEATING THAT TO MYSELF OVER AND OVER AGAIN.
BUT
IF I RAN INTO PEOPLE ALL MUSSED UP LIKE THAT, I'D DEFINITELY BE SUSPECTED.
I FRANTICALLY WASHED THE BLOOD OFF AND GATHERED UP THE SCATTERED THINGS.
JAM

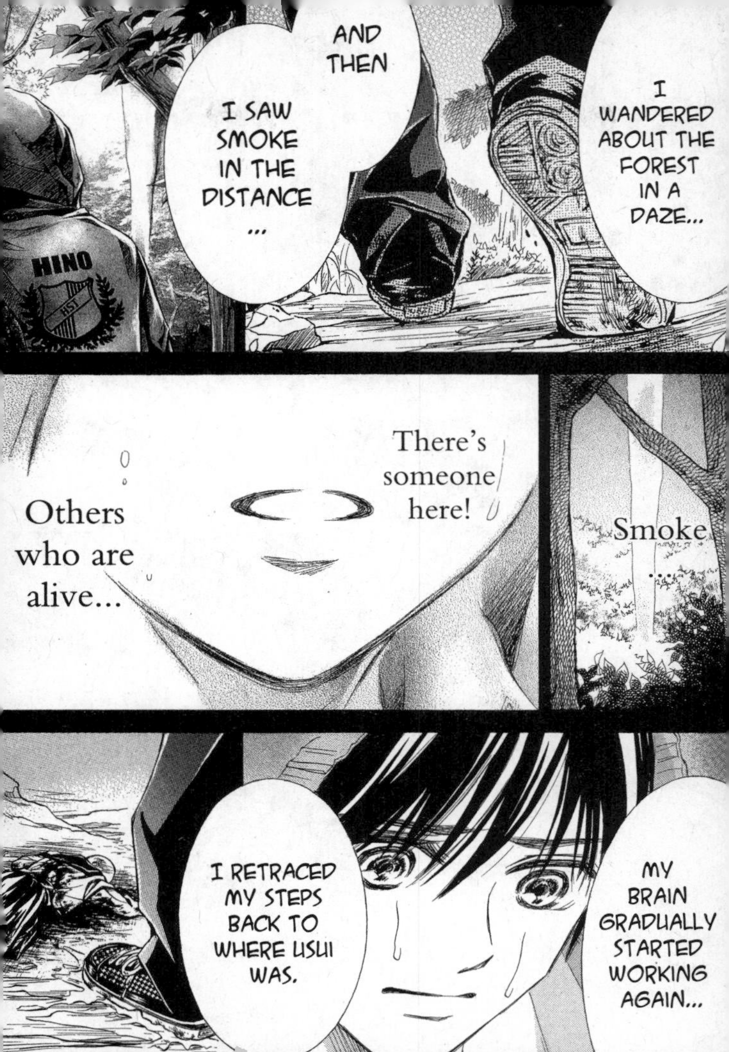
I WANDERED ABOUT THE FOREST IN A DAZE...
AND THEN
I SAW SMOKE IN THE DISTANCE ...
HINO
Smoke ...
There's someone here!
Others who are alive...
MY BRAIN GRADUALLY STARTED WORKING AGAIN...
I RETRACED MY STEPS BACK TO WHERE USUI WAS.

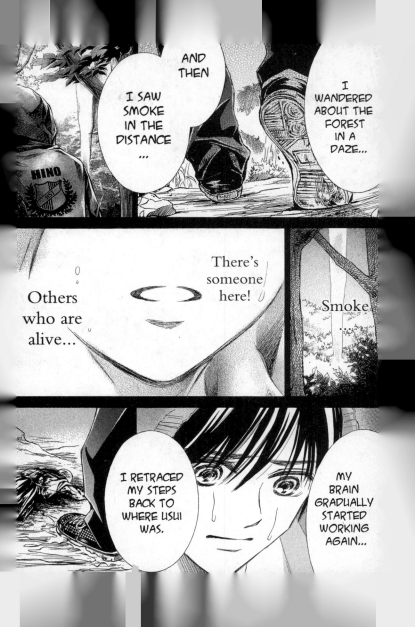

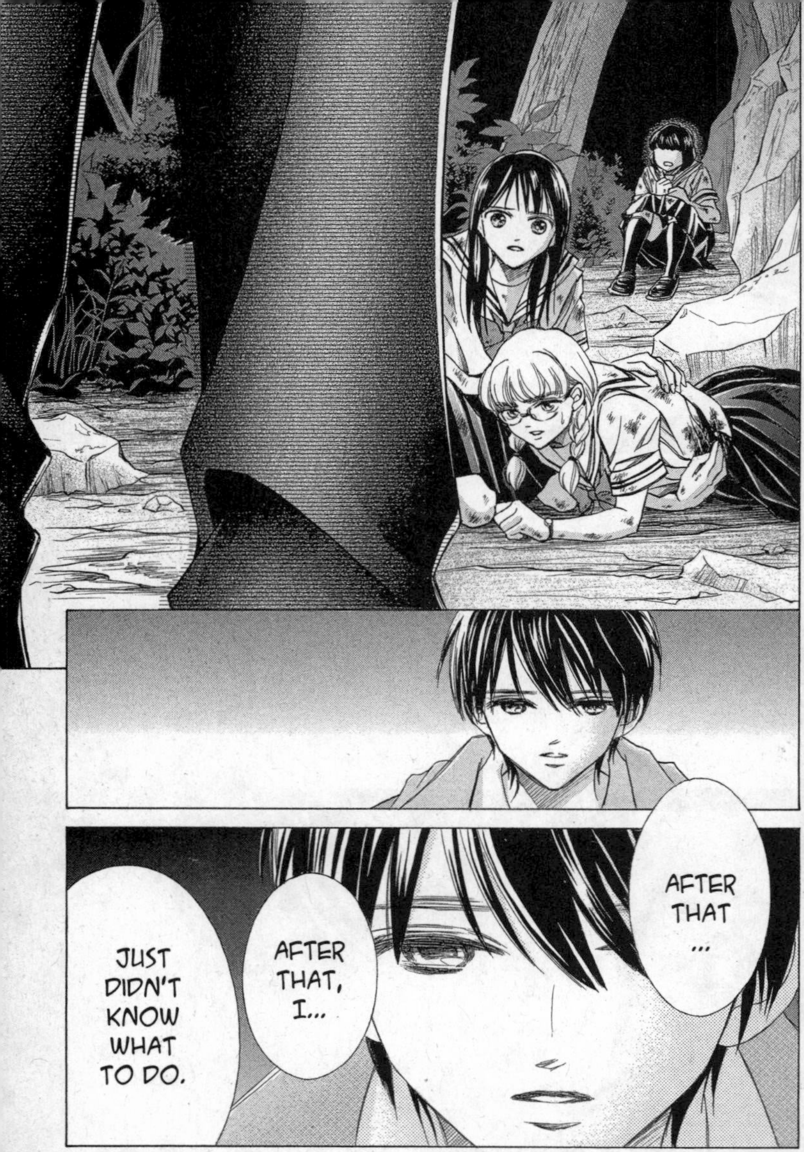
AFTER THAT ...
AFTER THAT, I...
JUST DIDN'T KNOW WHAT TO DO.

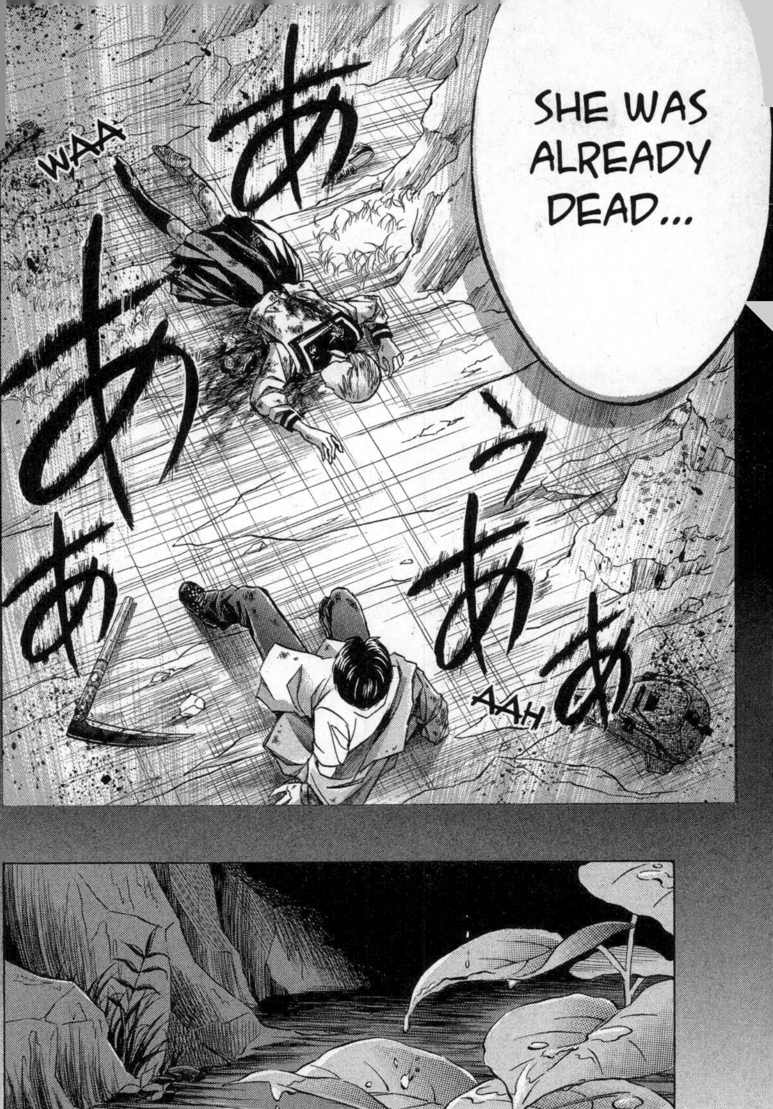
SHE WAS ALREADY DEAD...
うあああ
AAH
あああ
WAA

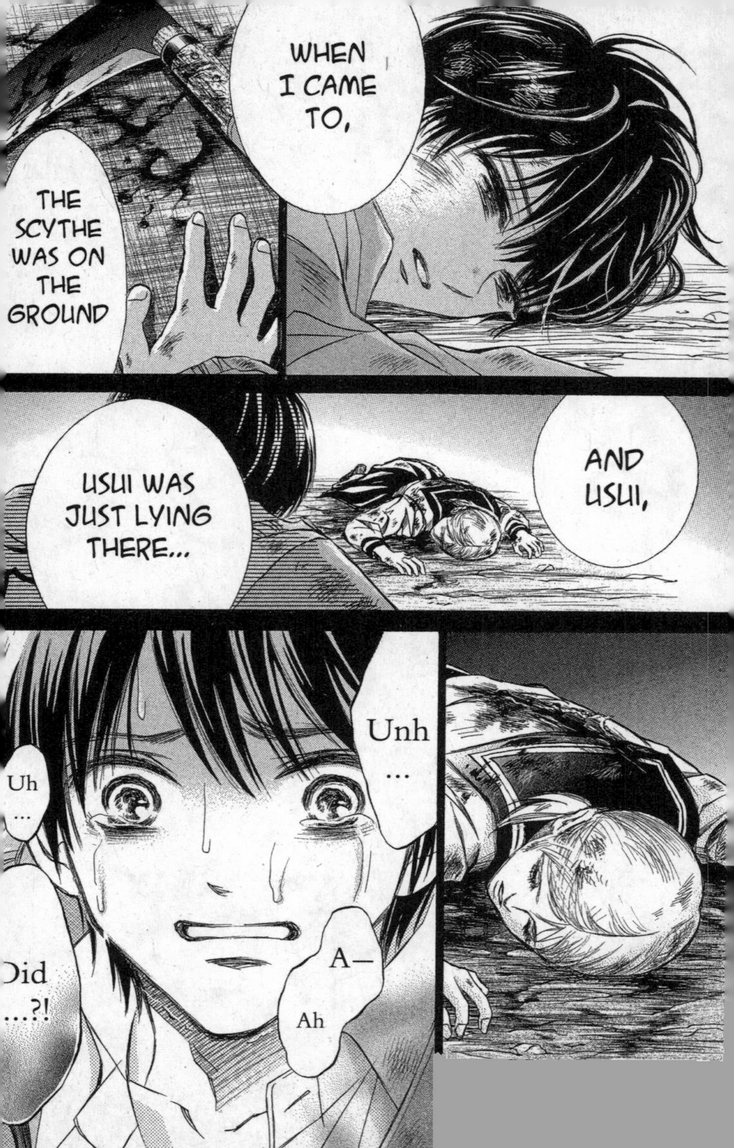
WHEN I CAME TO,
THE SCYTHE WAS ON THE GROUND
AND USUI,
USUI WAS JUST LYING THERE...
Unh ...
Uh ...
A—
Ah
...?!

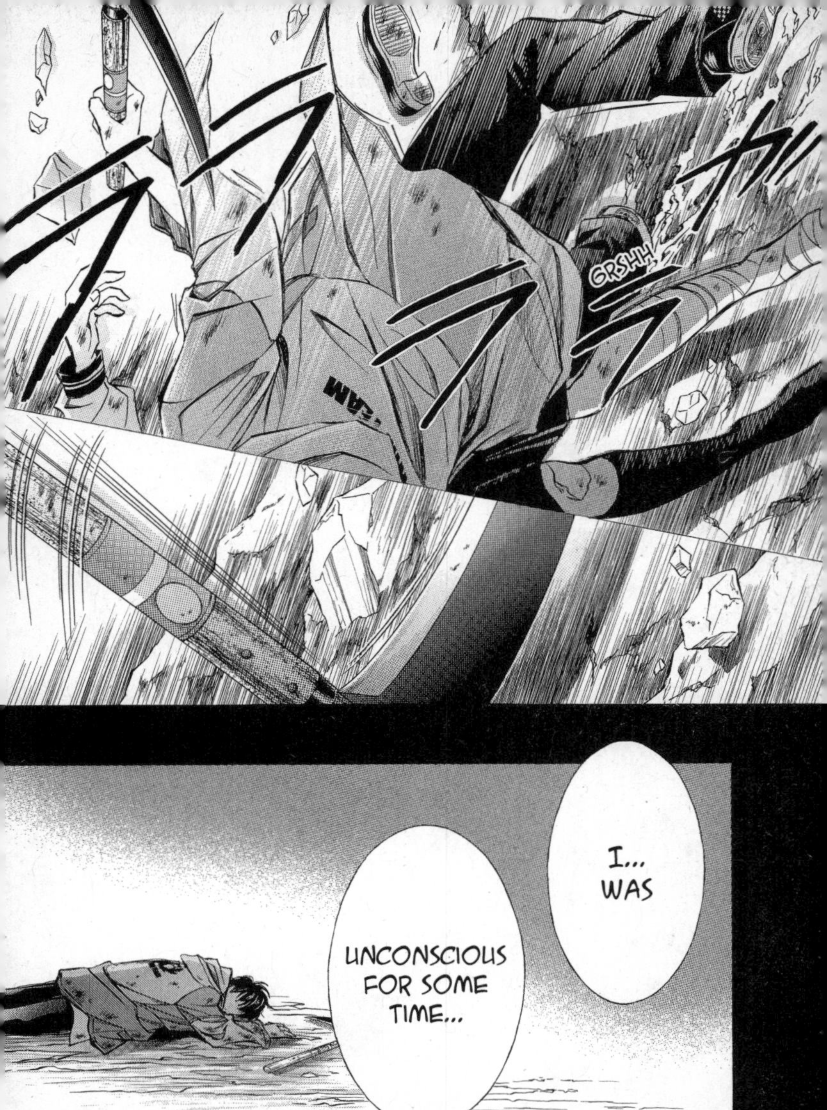
GRSHH
I... WAS
UNCONSCIOUS FOR SOME TIME...

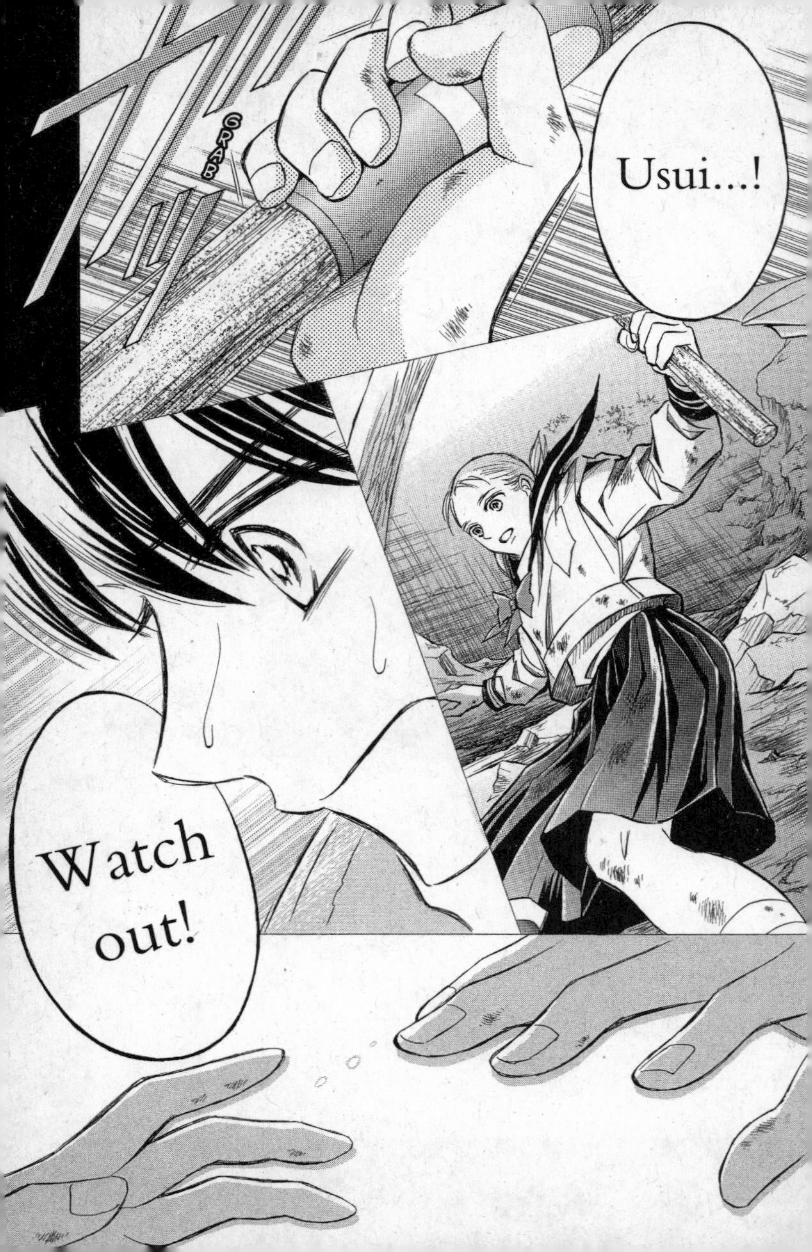
Usui...!
GRAB
Watch out!

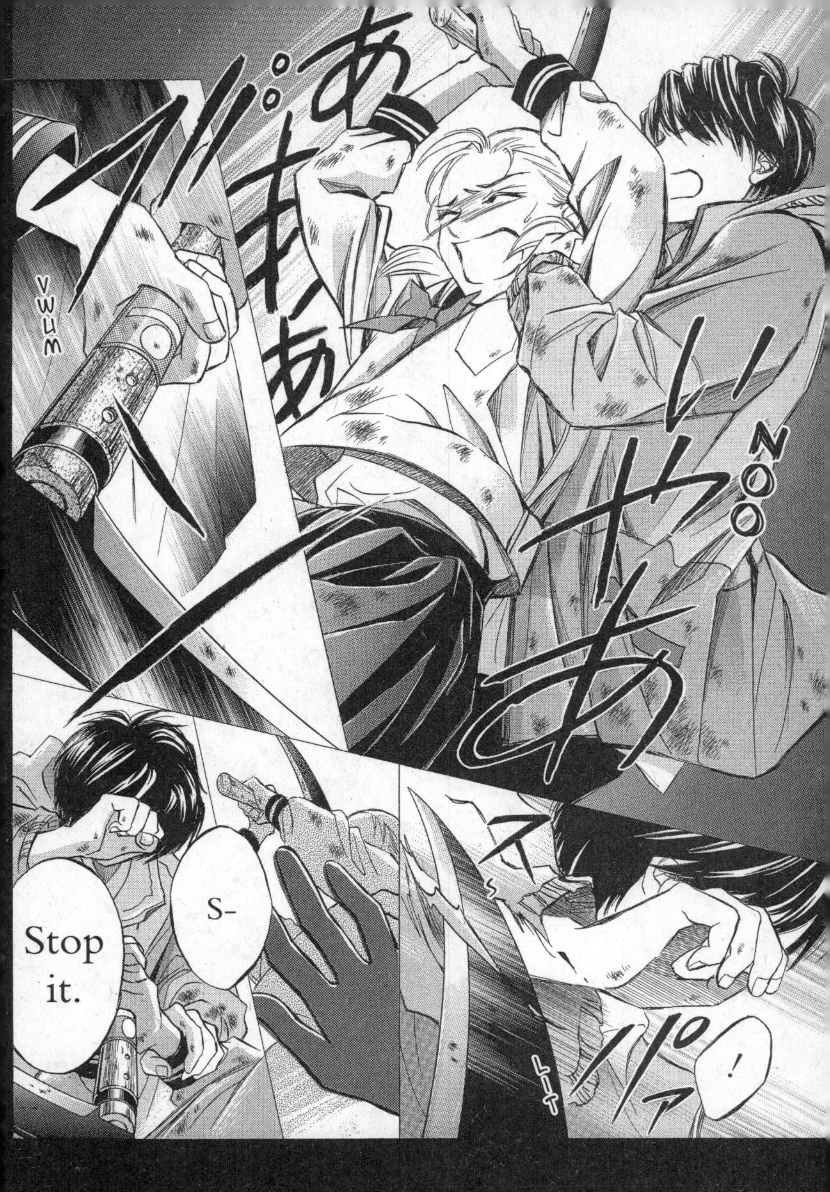

NOOO
VWUM
!
LIT
S-
Stop it.

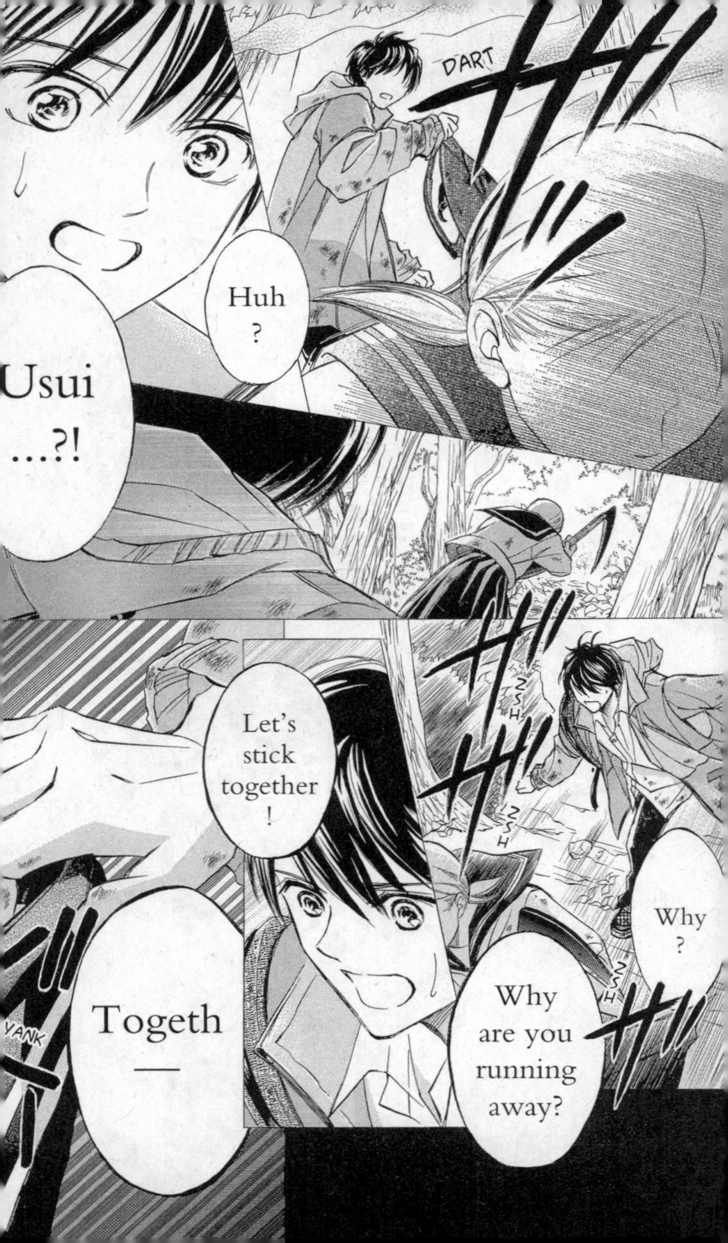
DART
Huh?
Usui ...?!
ZSSH
ZSSH
Why?
Why are you running away?
ZSSH
Let's stick together!
Togeth—
YANK

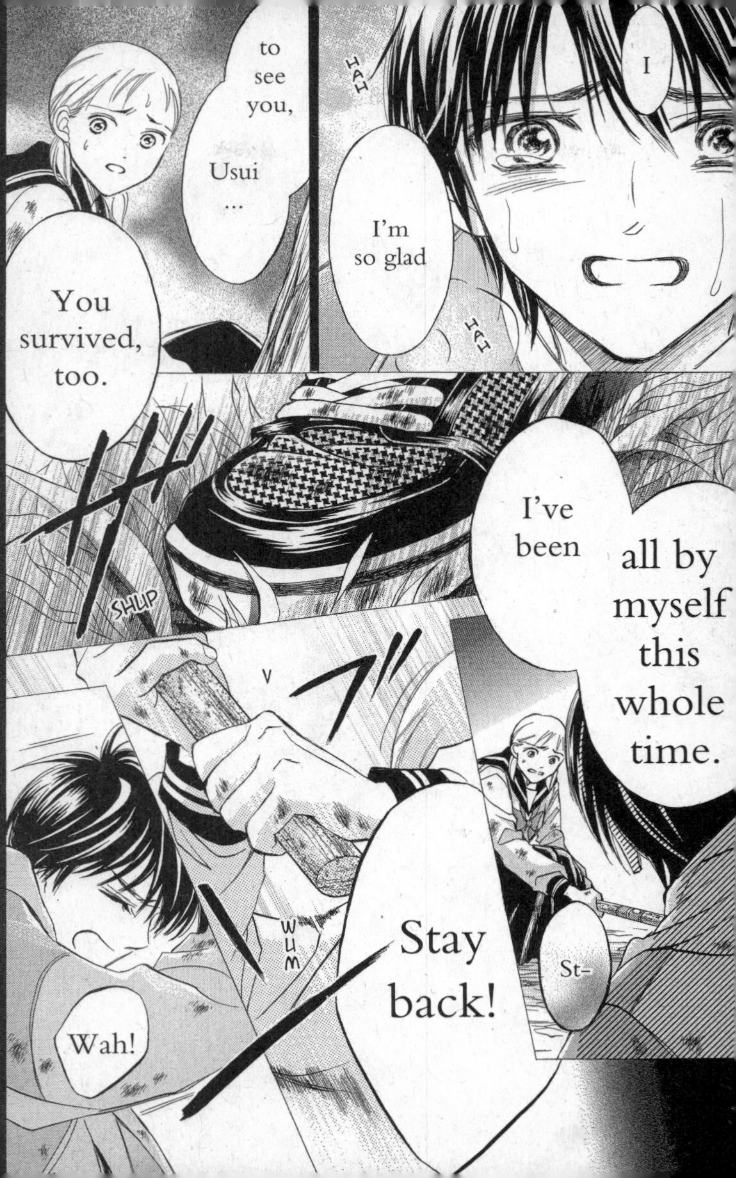
I
HAH
I'm so glad
HAH
to see you, Usui ...
You survived, too.
I've been
all by myself this whole time.
SHUP
St-
ブ
V
Stay back!
WUM
Wah!

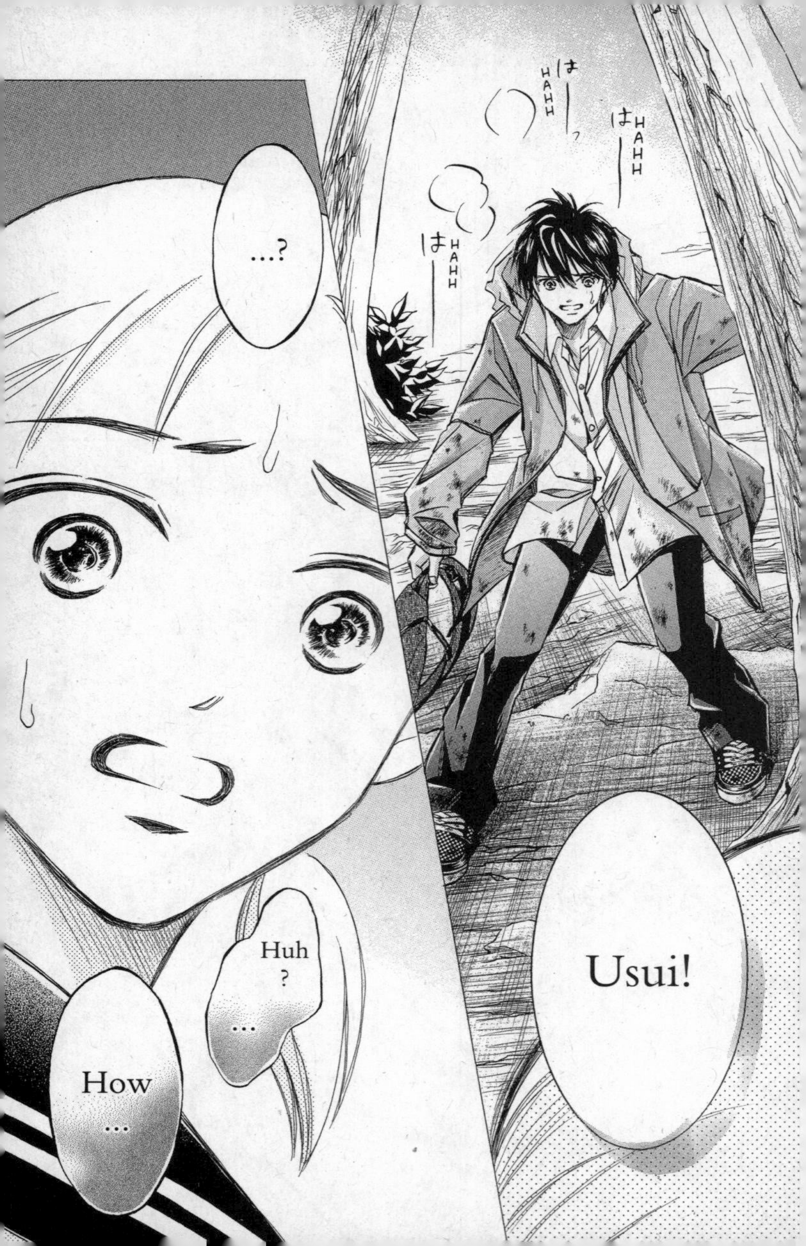

はーっ HAHH
はー HAHH
はー HAHH
Usui!
...?
Huh? ...
How ...

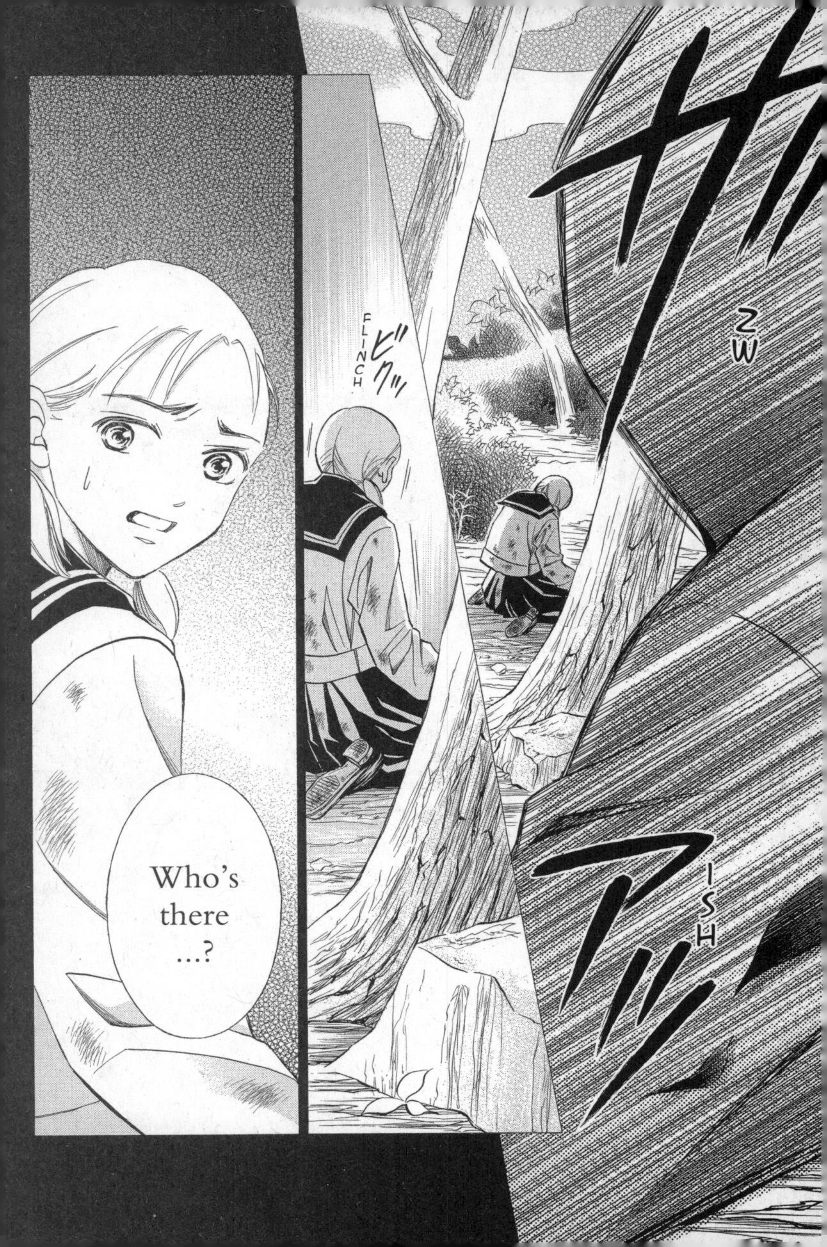
ZW
ISH
FLINCH
Who's there ...?

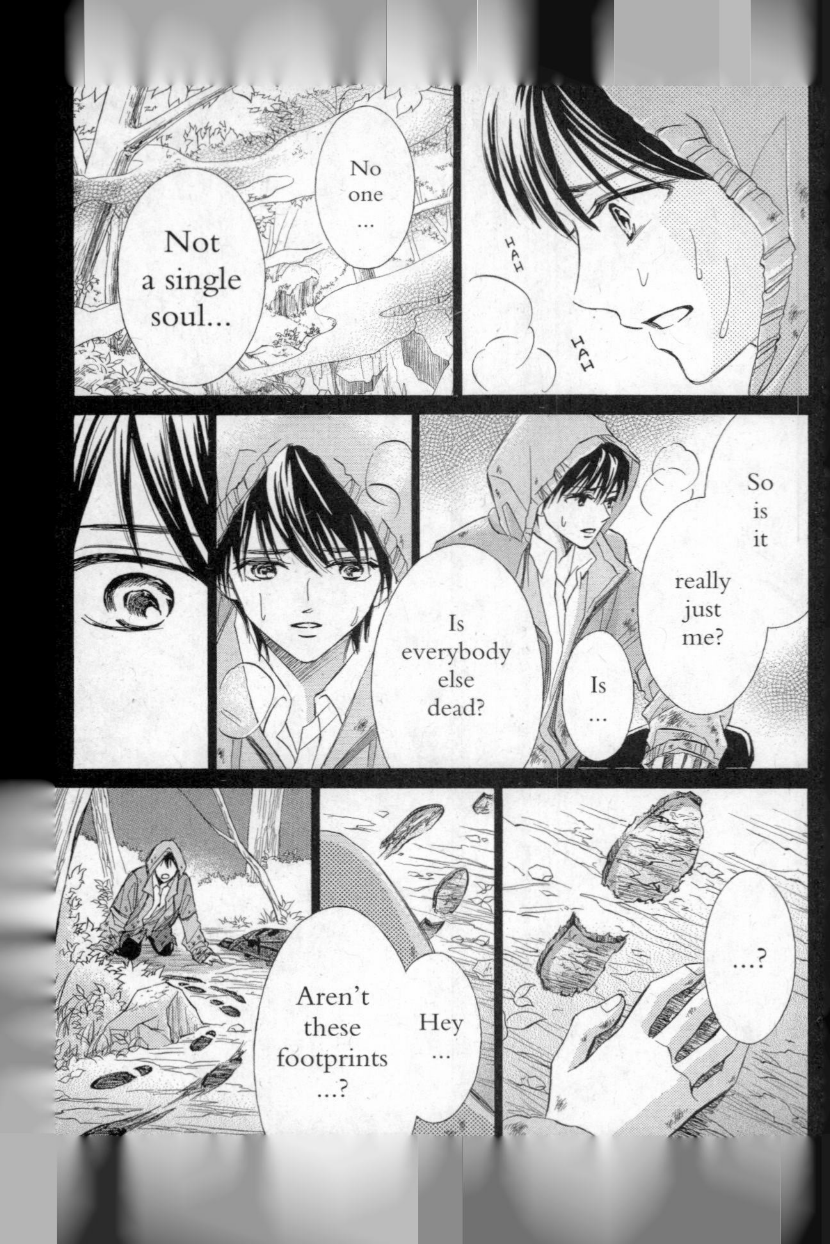
HAH
HAH
No one ...
Not a single soul...
So is it really just me?
Is ...
Is everybody else dead?
...?
Hey ...
Aren't these footprints ...?

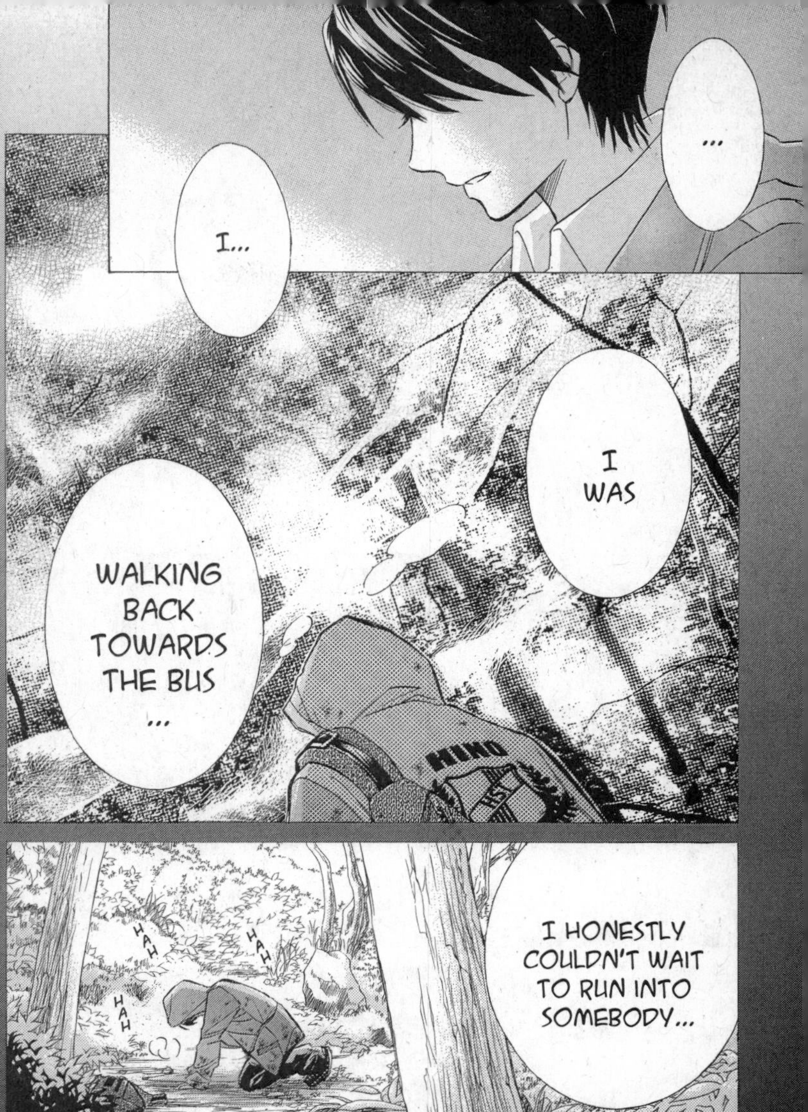
...
I...
I WAS
WALKING BACK TOWARDS THE BUS ...
I HONESTLY COULDN'T WAIT TO RUN INTO SOMEBODY...
HAH
HAH
HAH

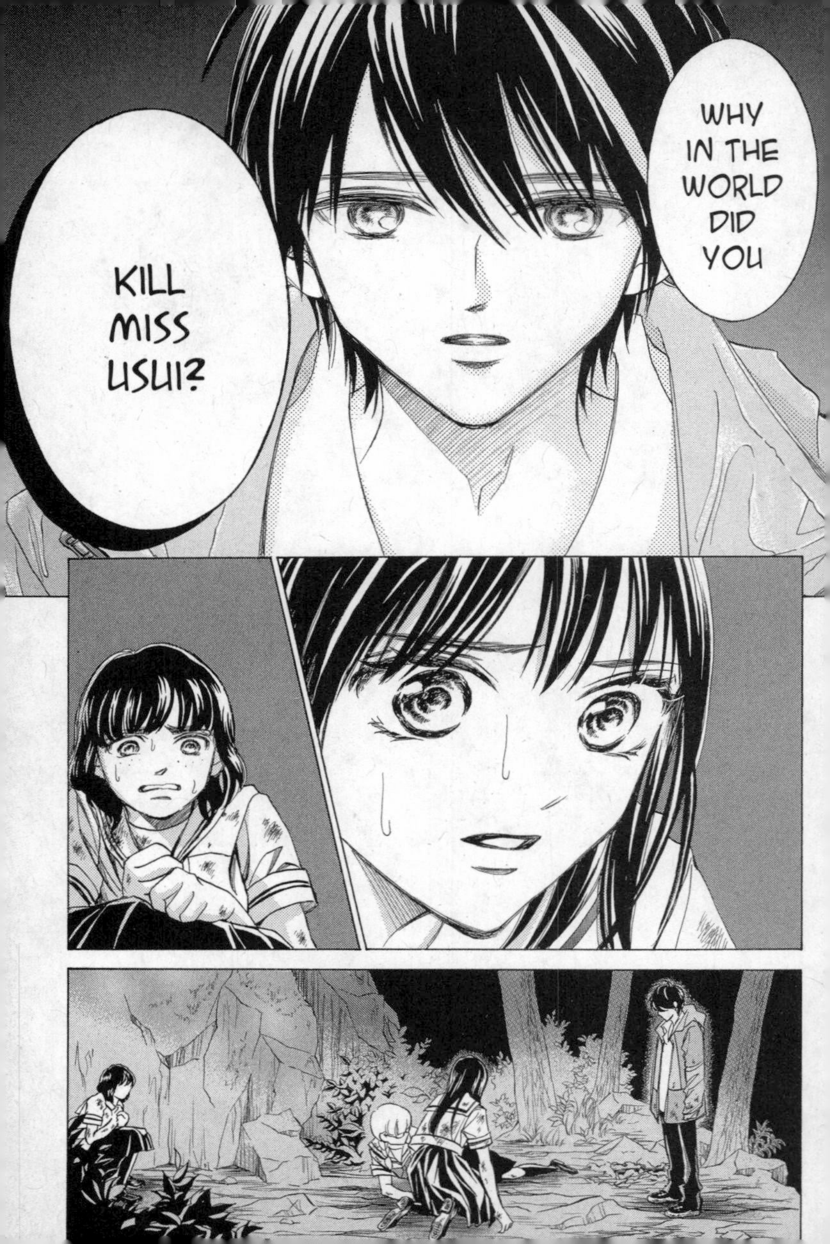
WHY IN THE WORLD DID YOU
KILL MISS USUI?

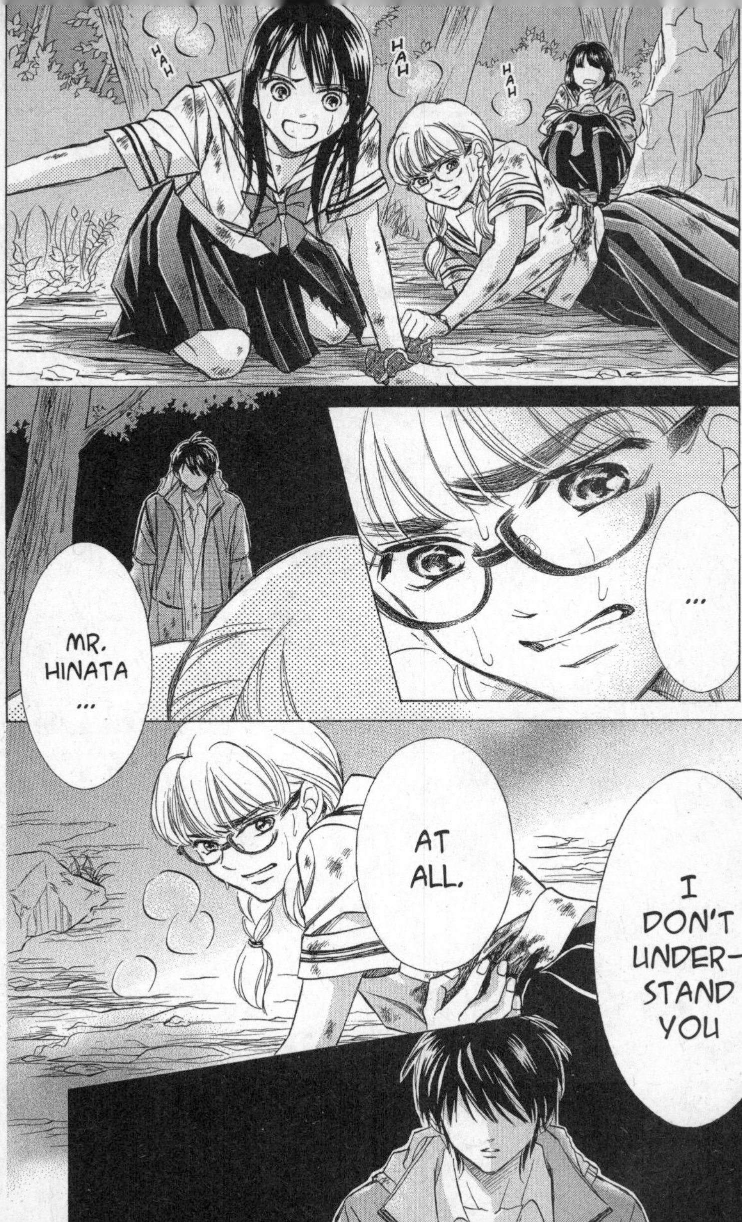
HAH
HAH
HAH
...
MR. HINATA ...
I DON'T UNDER-STAND YOU
AT ALL.

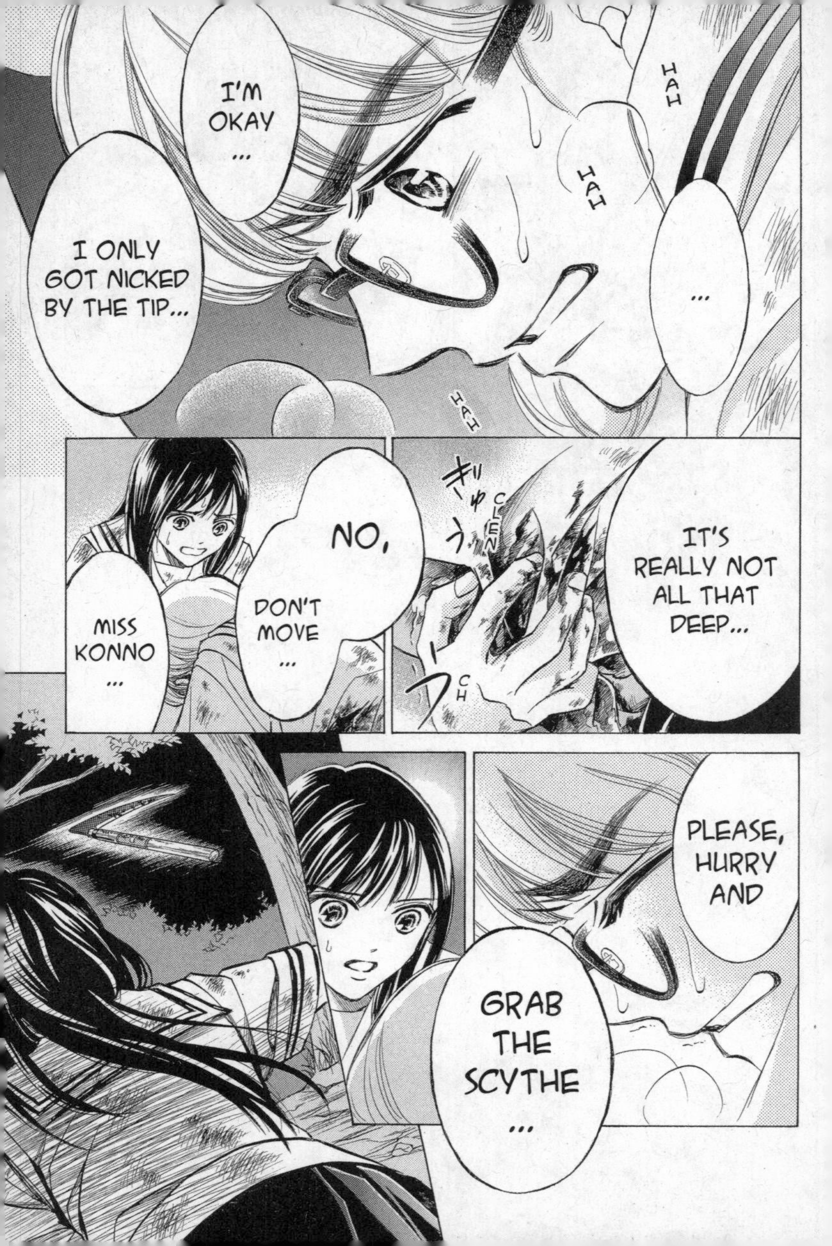
HAH
HAH
...
I'M OKAY ...
I ONLY GOT NICKED BY THE TIP...
HAH
IT'S REALLY NOT ALL THAT DEEP...
CLENCH
NO,
DON'T MOVE ...
MISS KONNO ...
PLEASE, HURRY AND
GRAB THE SCYTHE ...

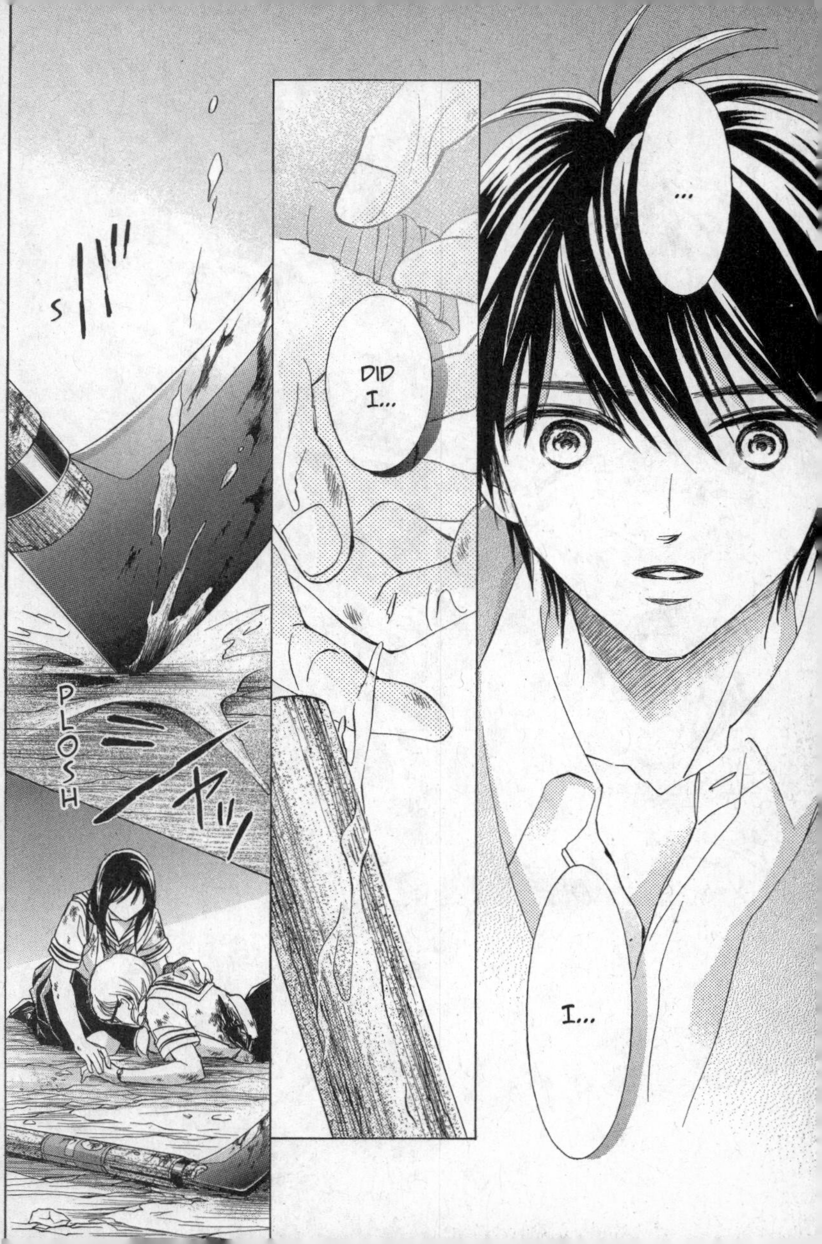
...
I...
DID I...
S
PLOSH

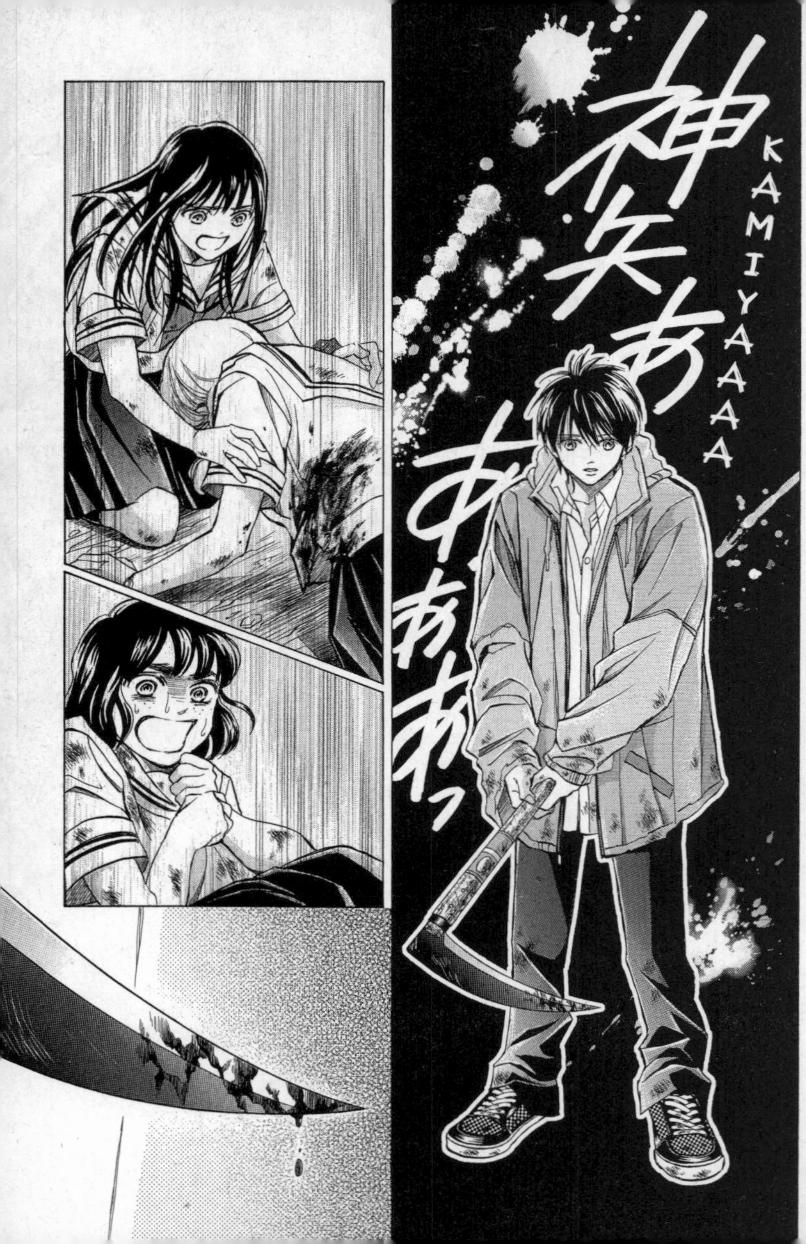
神矢ああああっ
KAMIYAAAAA

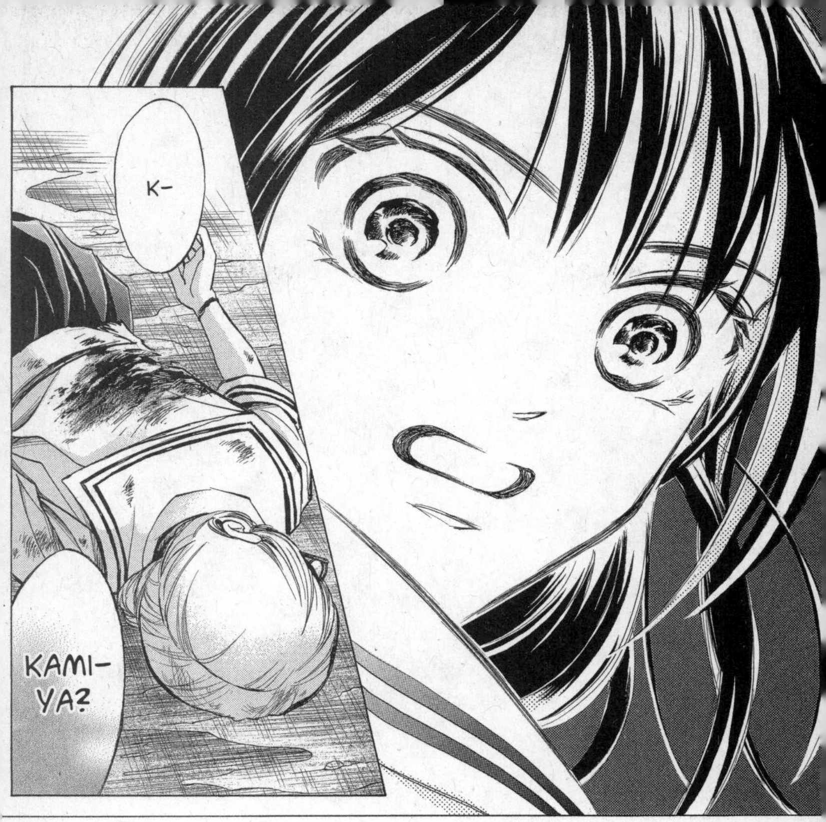
K-
KAMI-YA?

LIMIT

Scene.19 Confession

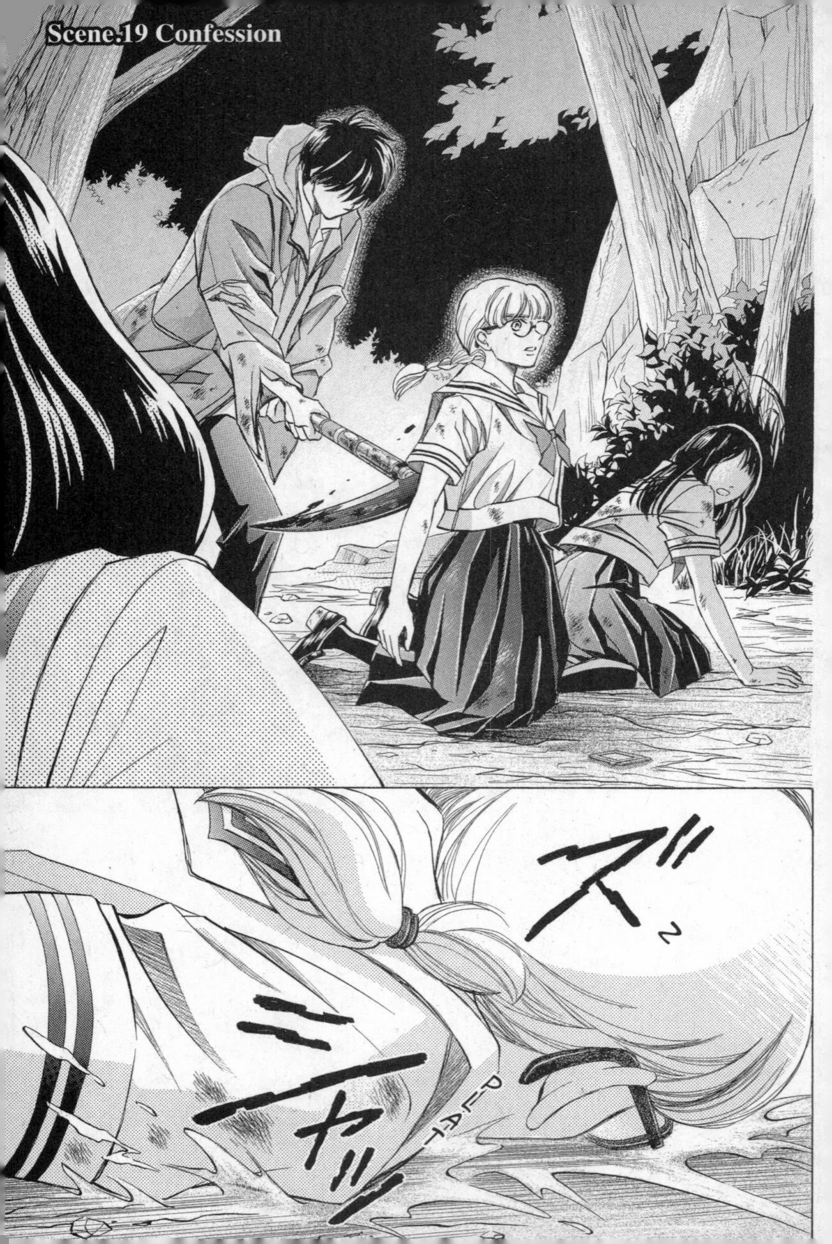
PLAT

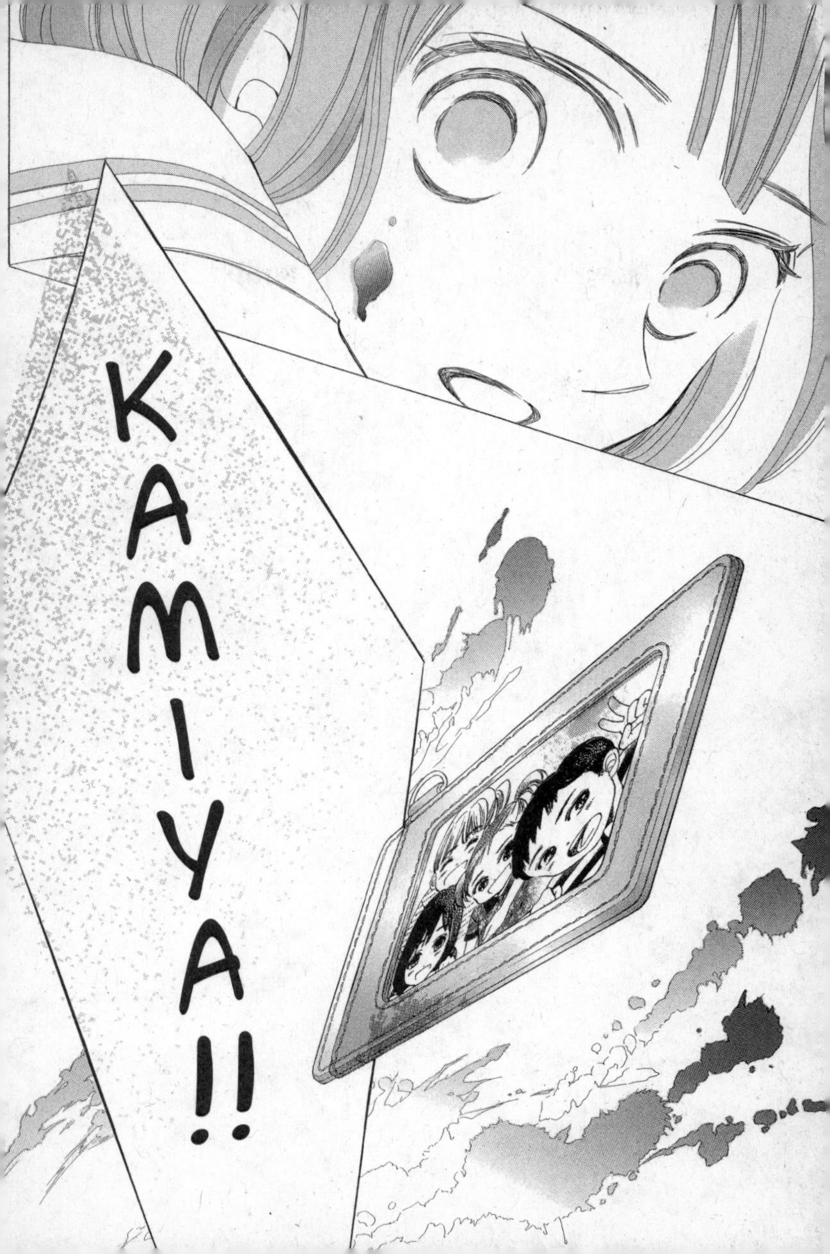
KAMIYA!!

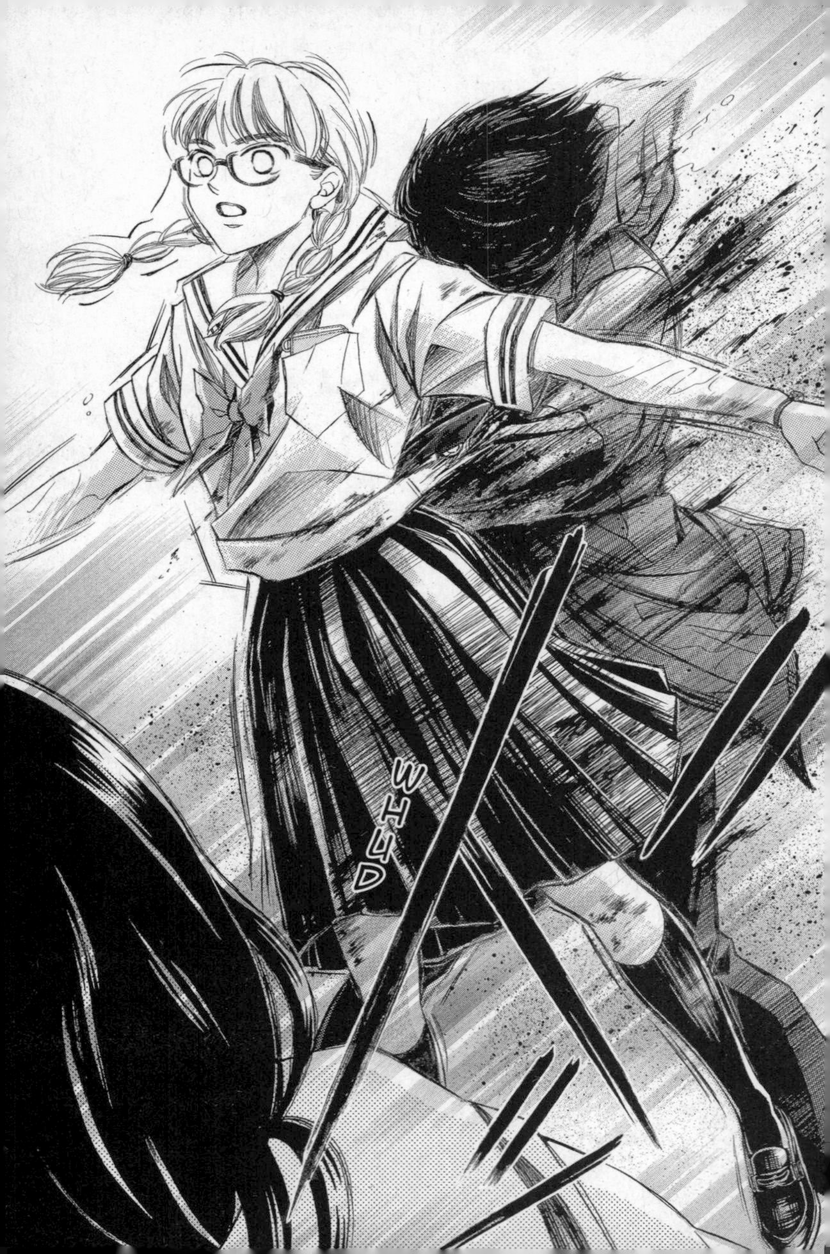
WHUD

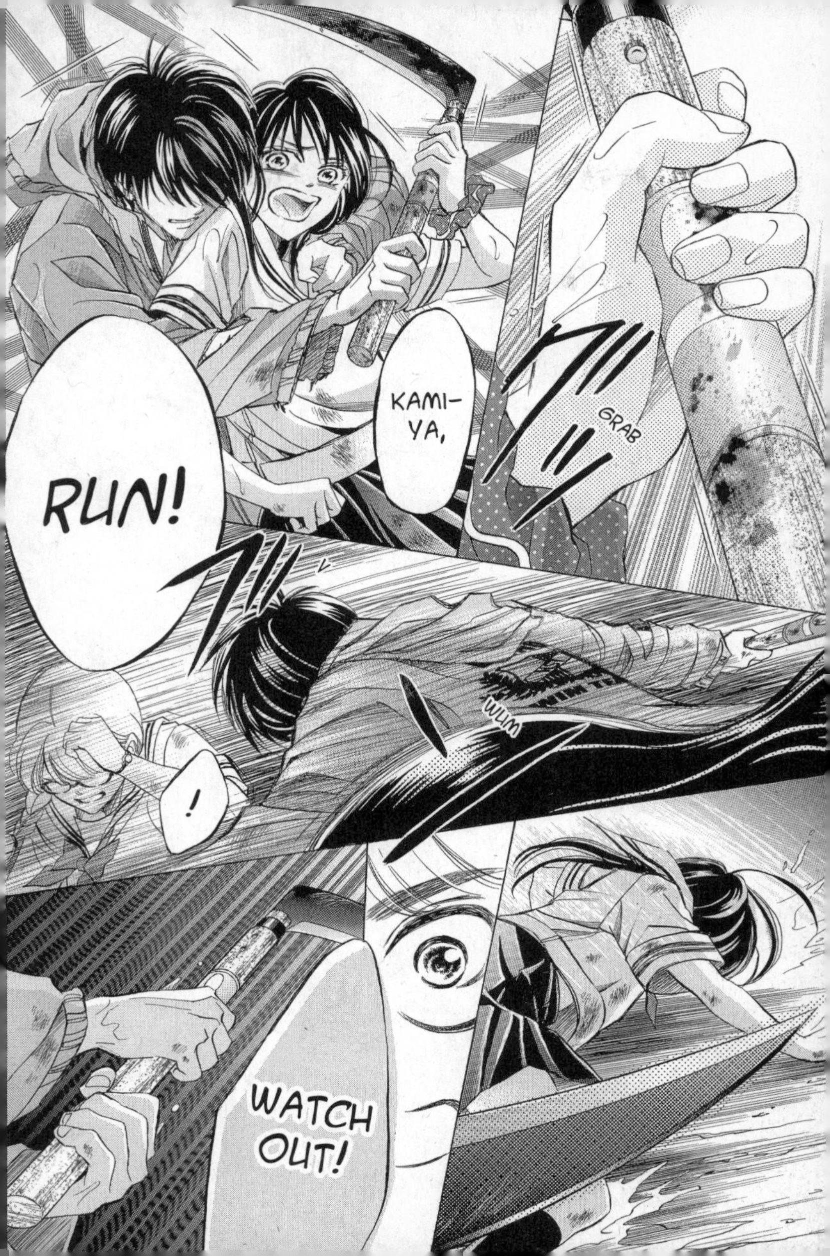
GRAB
KAMI-YA,
RUN!
WUM
!
WATCH OUT!

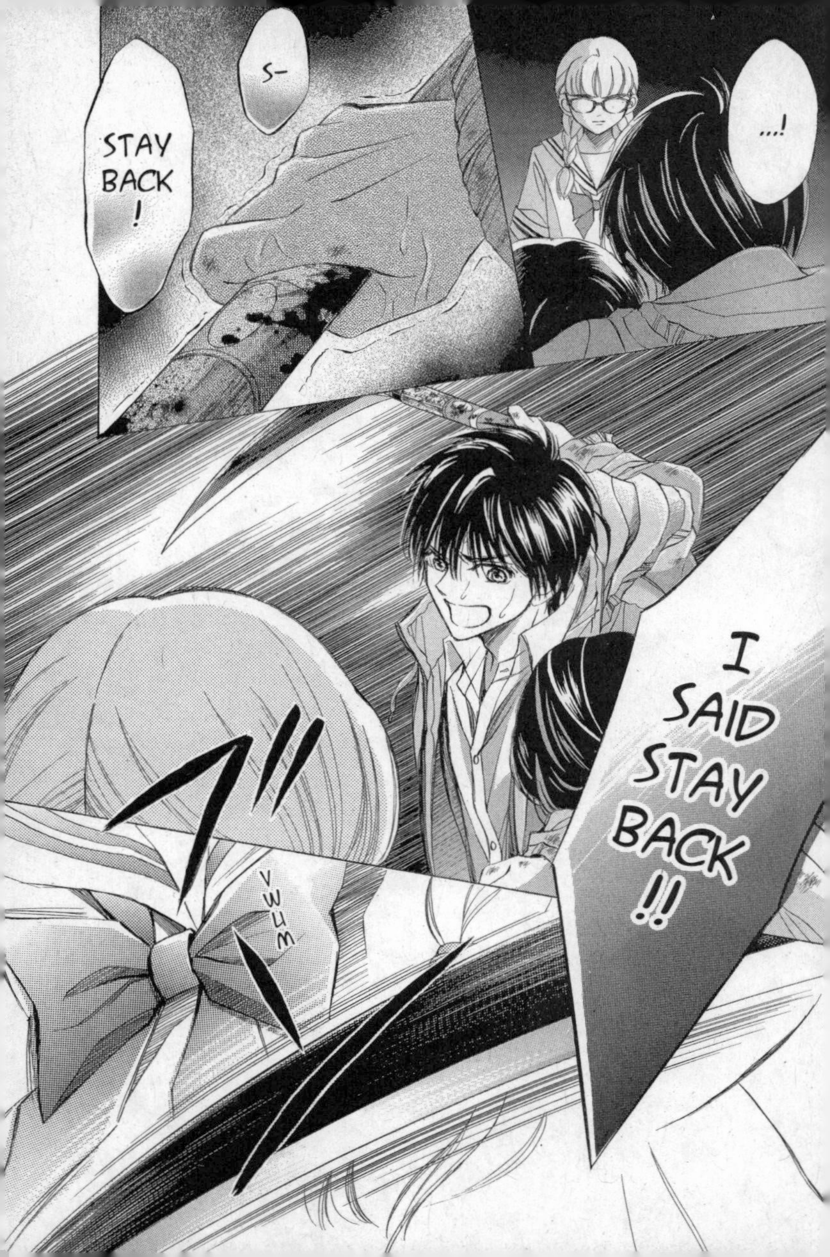
...!
S-
STAY BACK!
I SAID STAY BACK!!
VWUM

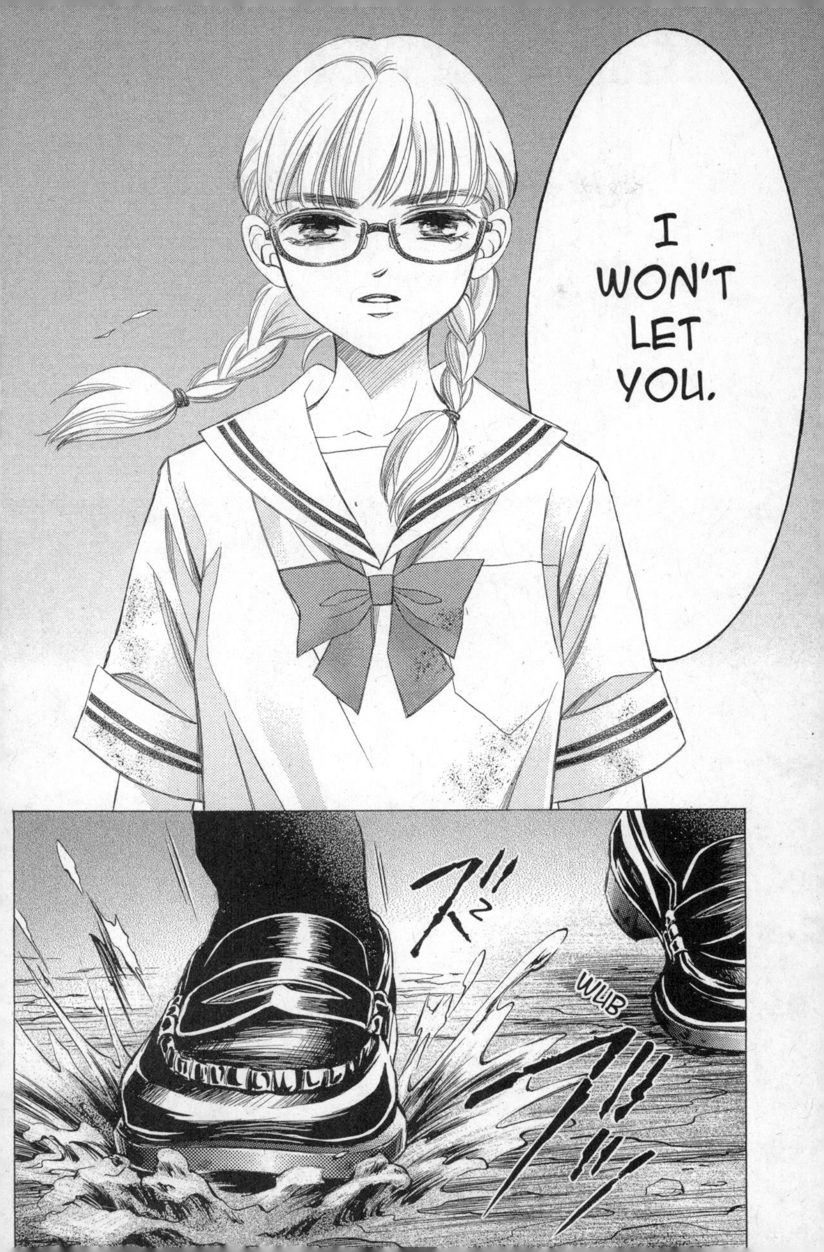
I WON'T LET YOU.
WUB

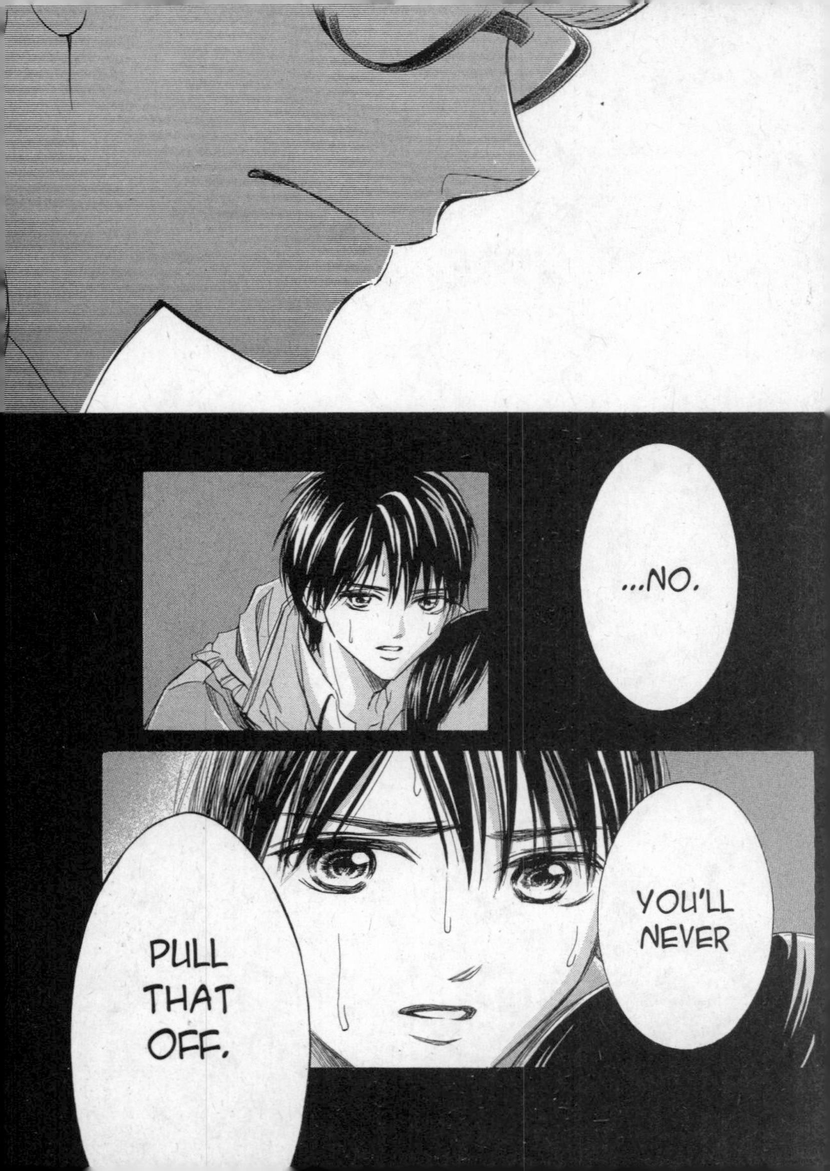
...NO.
YOU'LL NEVER
PULL THAT OFF.

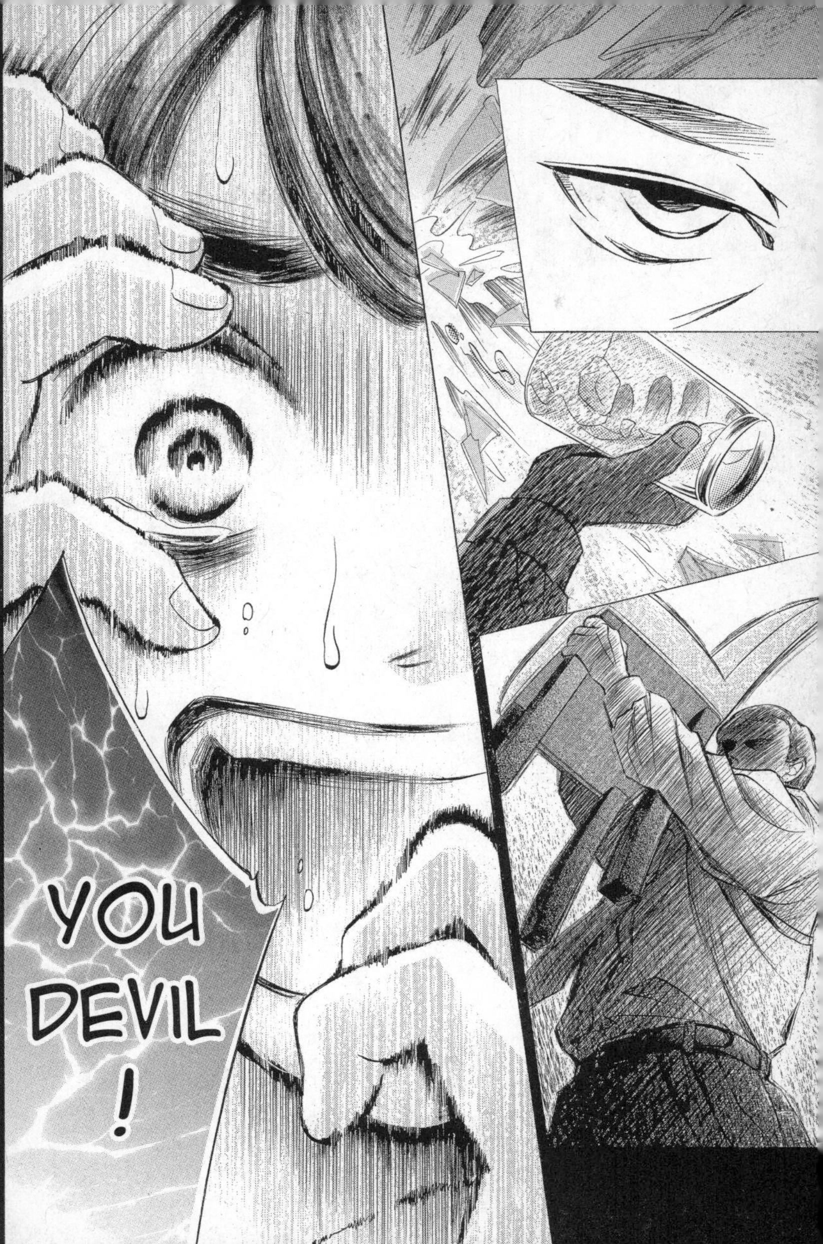
YOU DEVIL !

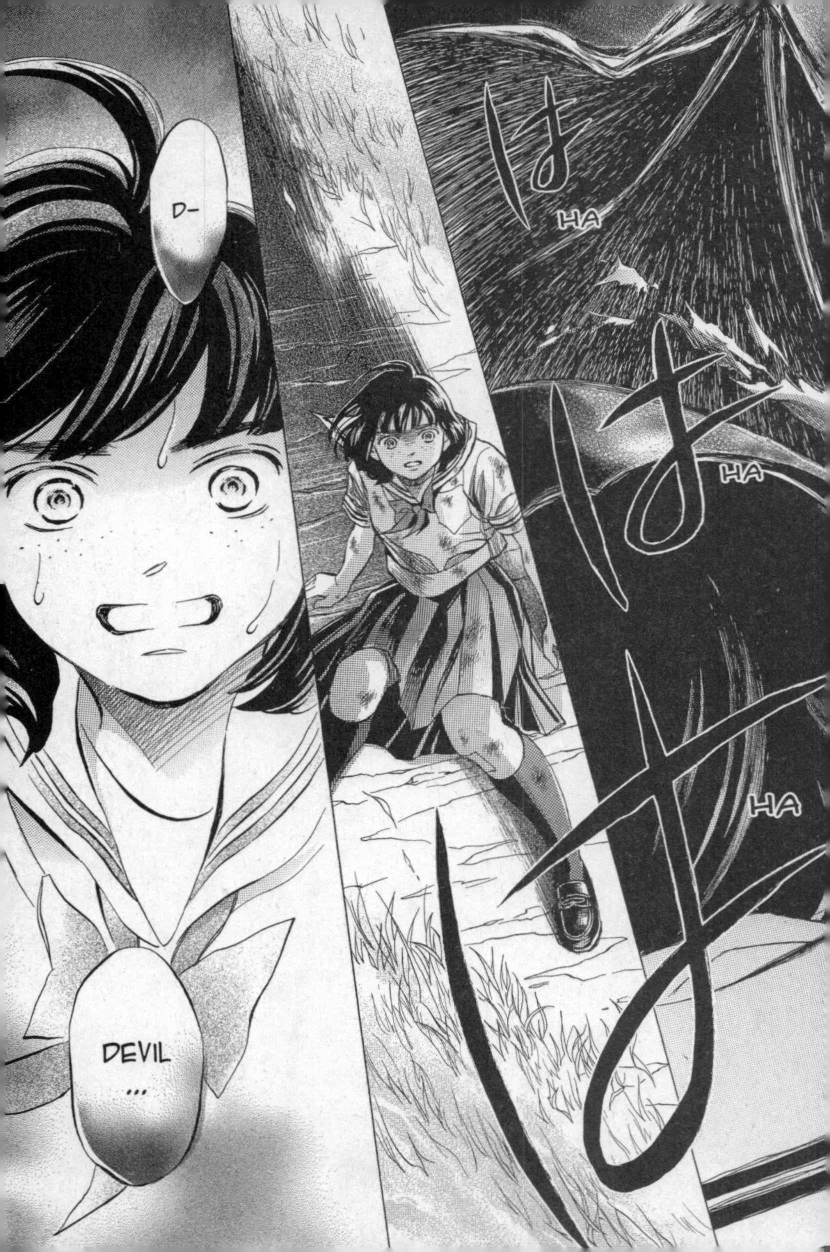
は
HA
は
HA
は
HA
D-
DEVIL
...

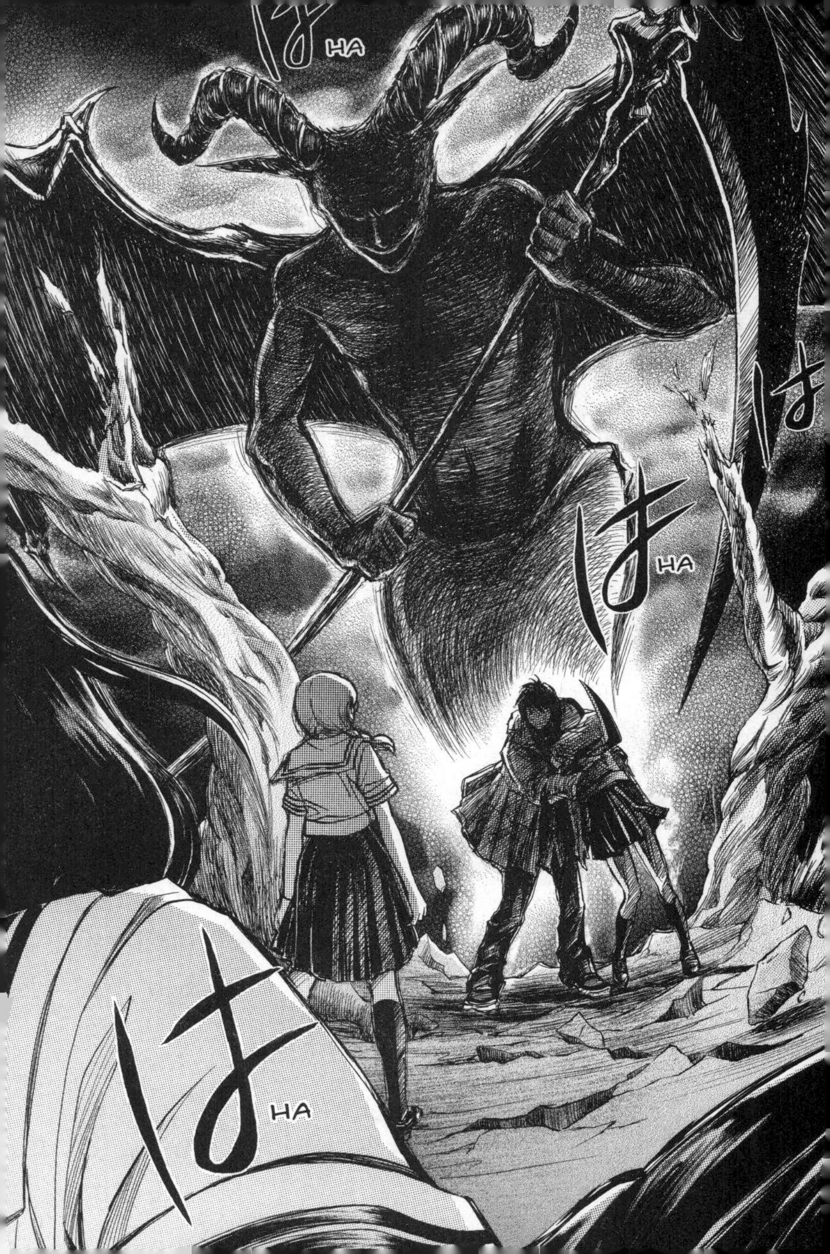
は HA
は
は HA
は HA

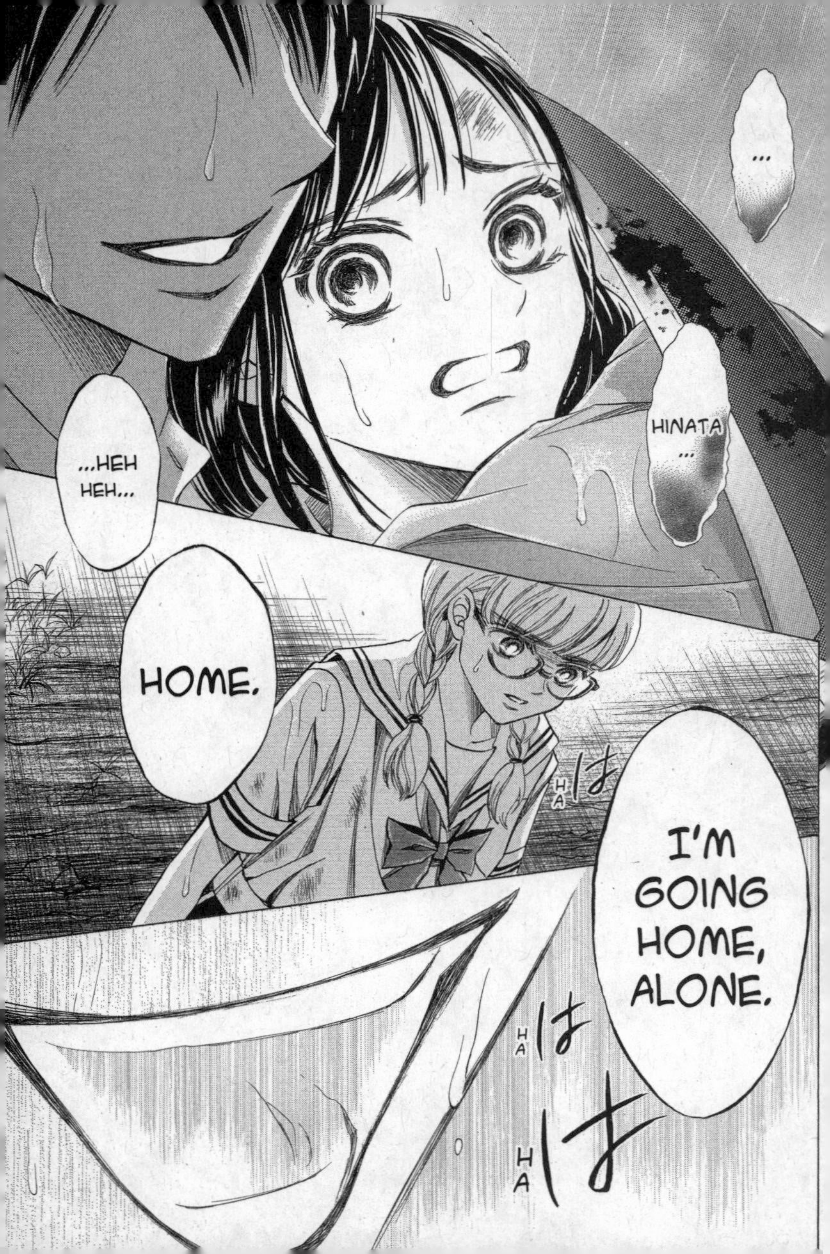
...
HINATA ...
...HEH HEH...
I'M GOING HOME, ALONE.
HOME.
は HA
は HA
は HA

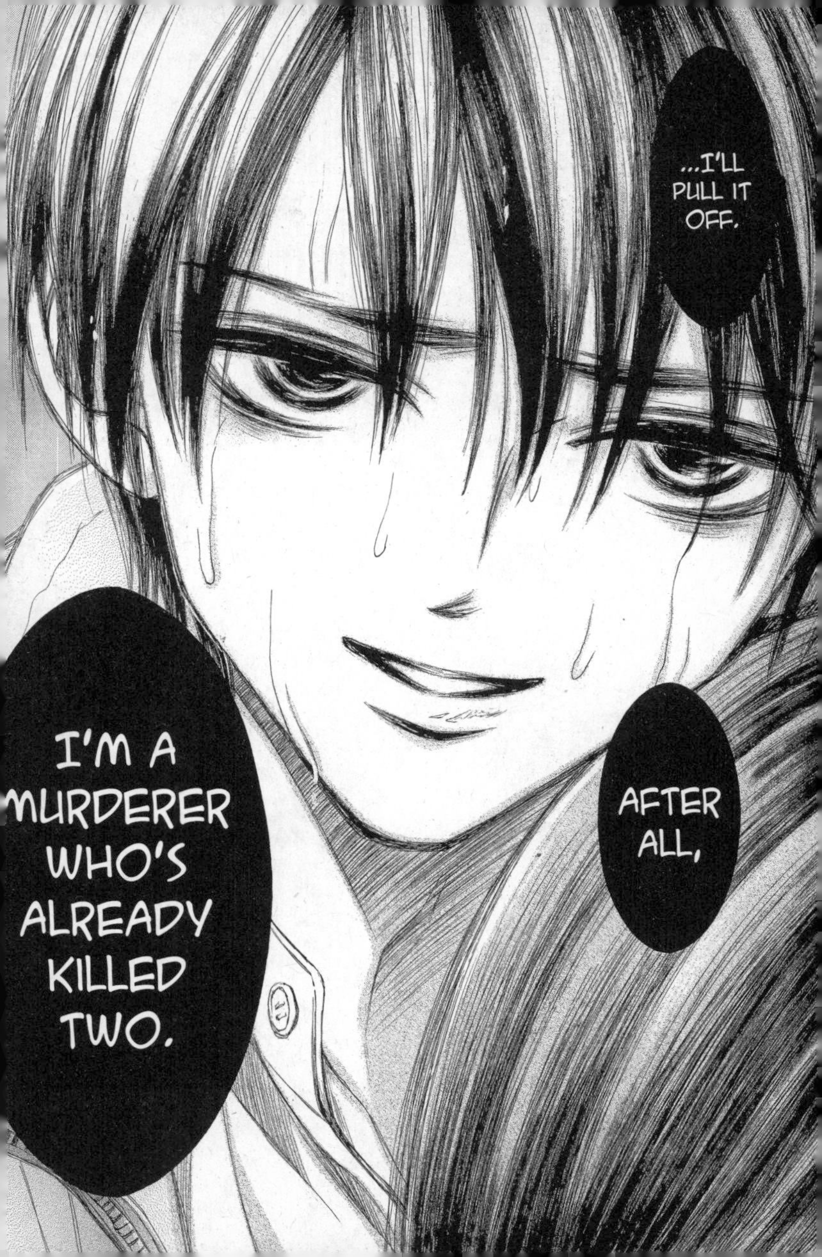
...I'LL PULL IT OFF.
AFTER ALL,
I'M A MURDERER WHO'S ALREADY KILLED TWO.

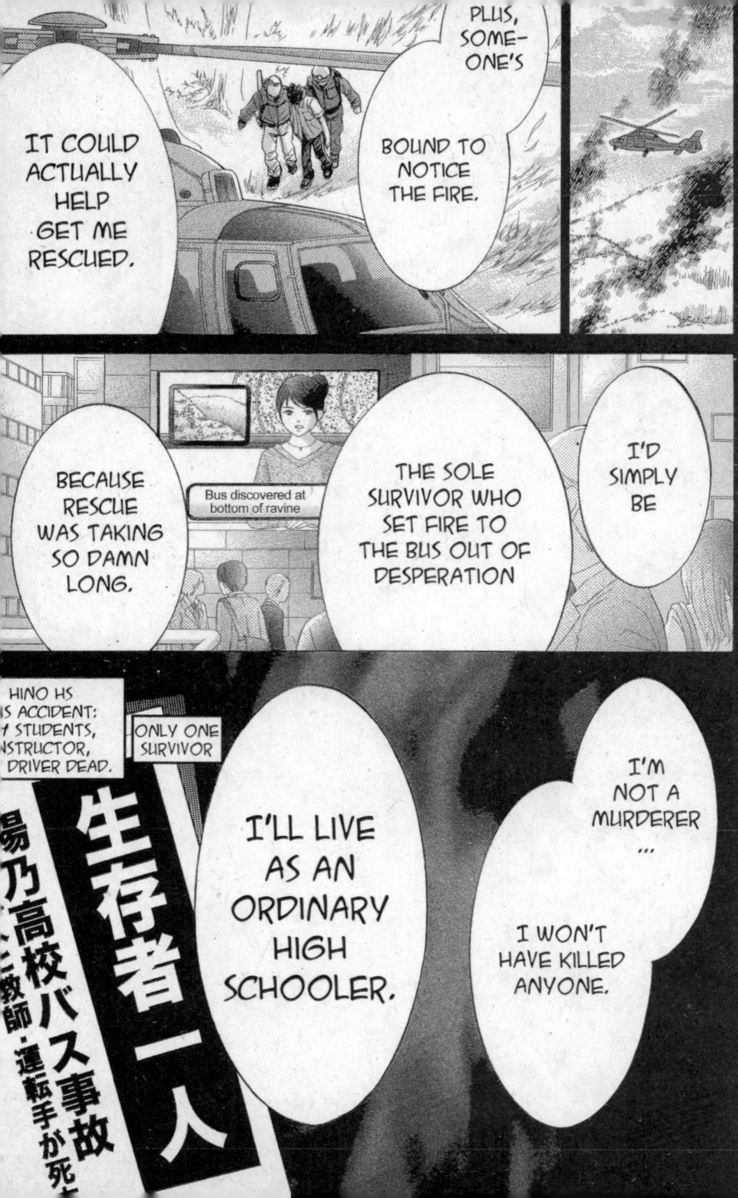
PLUS, SOME-ONE'S BOUND TO NOTICE THE FIRE.
IT COULD ACTUALLY HELP GET ME RESCUED.
I'D SIMPLY BE
THE SOLE SURVIVOR WHO SET FIRE TO THE BUS OUT OF DESPERATION
Bus discovered at bottom of ravine
BECAUSE RESCUE WAS TAKING SO DAMN LONG.
I'M NOT A MURDERER ...
I WON'T HAVE KILLED ANYONE.
I'LL LIVE AS AN ORDINARY HIGH SCHOOLER.
生存者一人
ONLY ONE SURVIVOR
湯乃高校バス事故
教師・運転手が死
HINO HS
S ACCIDENT:
STUDENTS,
NSTRUCTOR,
DRIVER DEAD.

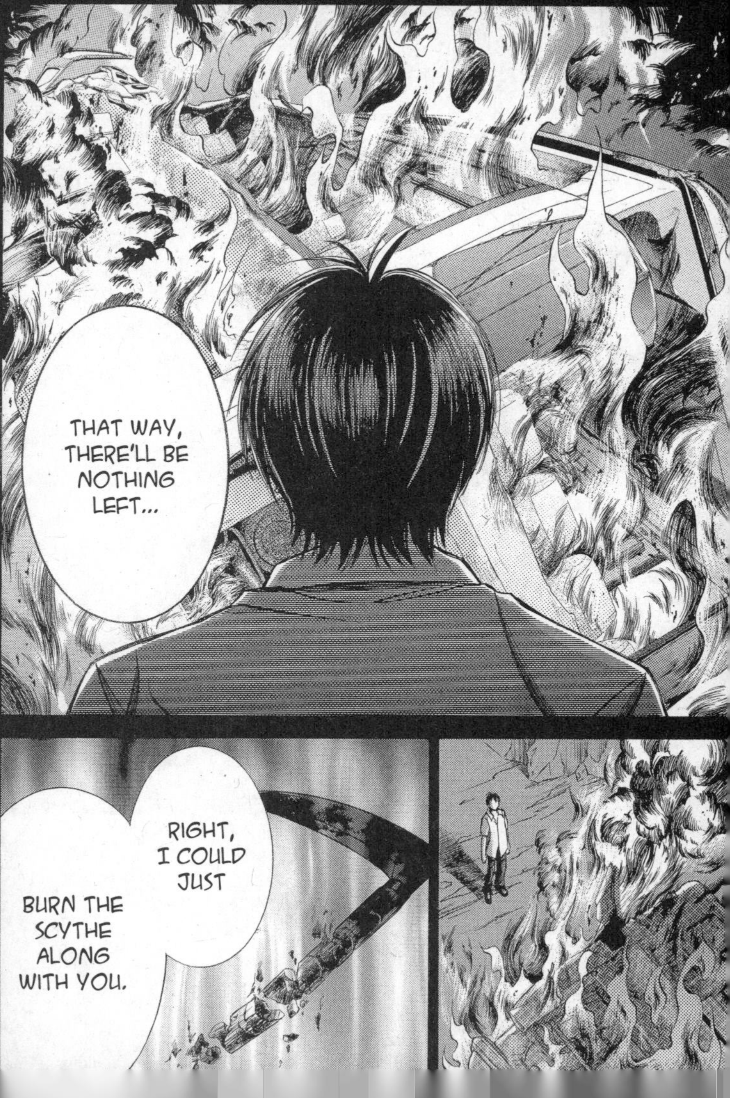
THAT WAY, THERE'LL BE NOTHING LEFT...
RIGHT, I COULD JUST
BURN THE SCYTHE ALONG WITH YOU.

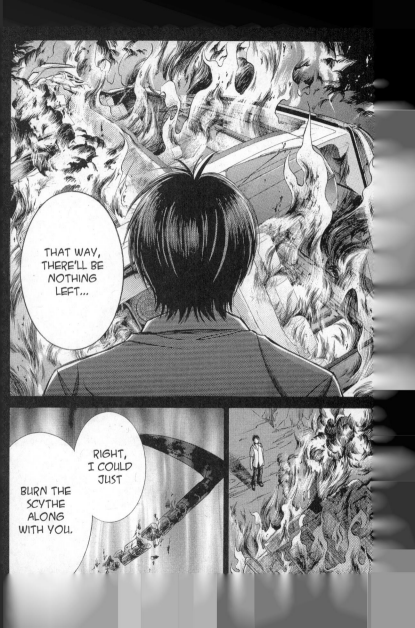

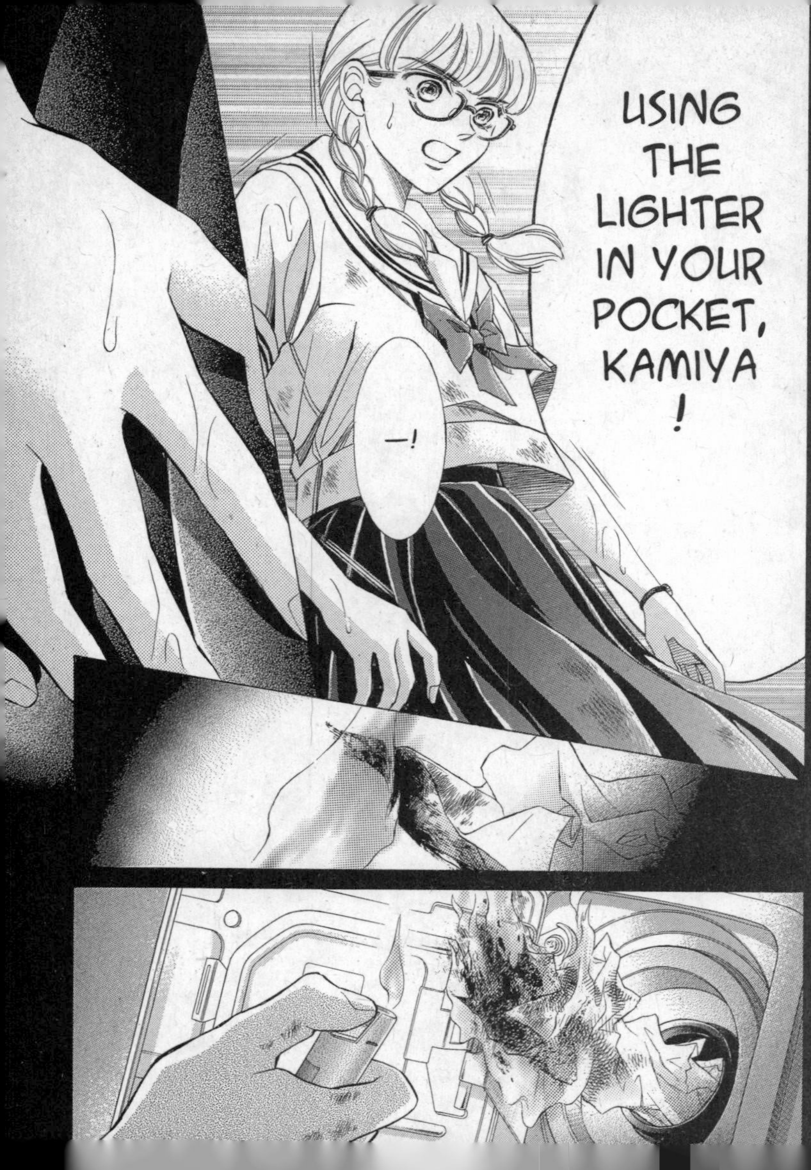
USING THE LIGHTER IN YOUR POCKET, KAMIYA!
—!

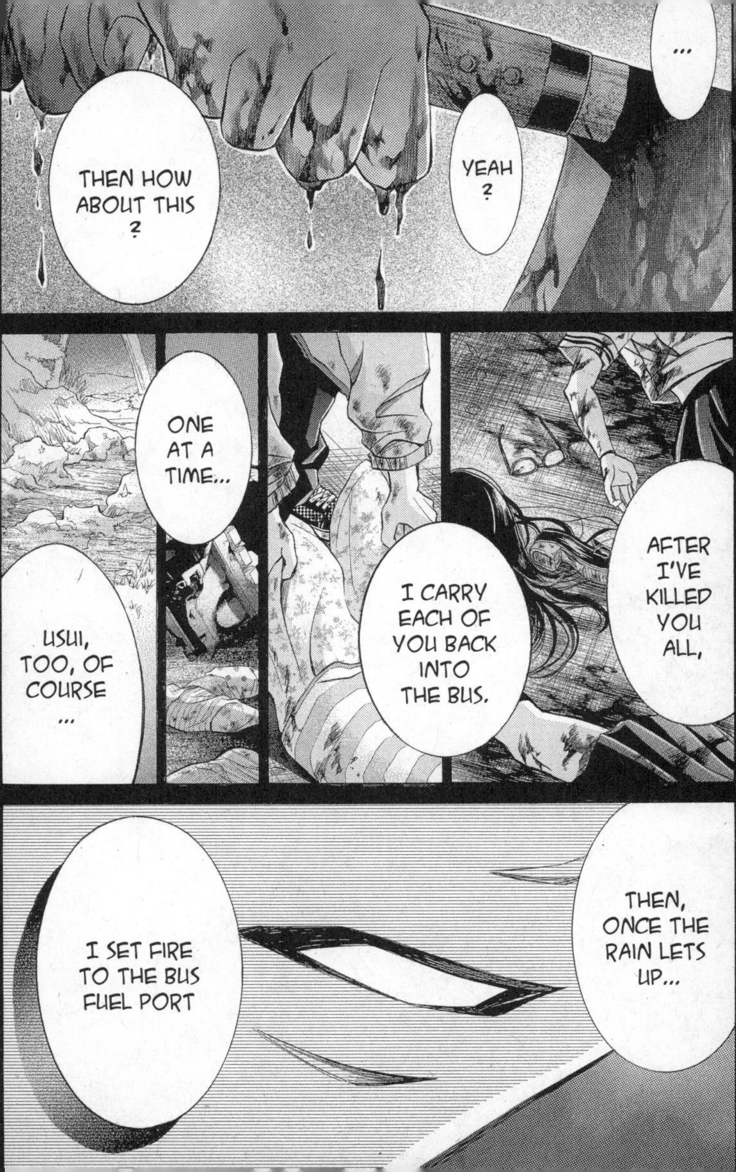
...
YEAH?
THEN HOW ABOUT THIS?
AFTER I'VE KILLED YOU ALL,
I CARRY EACH OF YOU BACK INTO THE BUS.
ONE AT A TIME...
USUI, TOO, OF COURSE...
THEN, ONCE THE RAIN LETS UP...
I SET FIRE TO THE BUS FUEL PORT

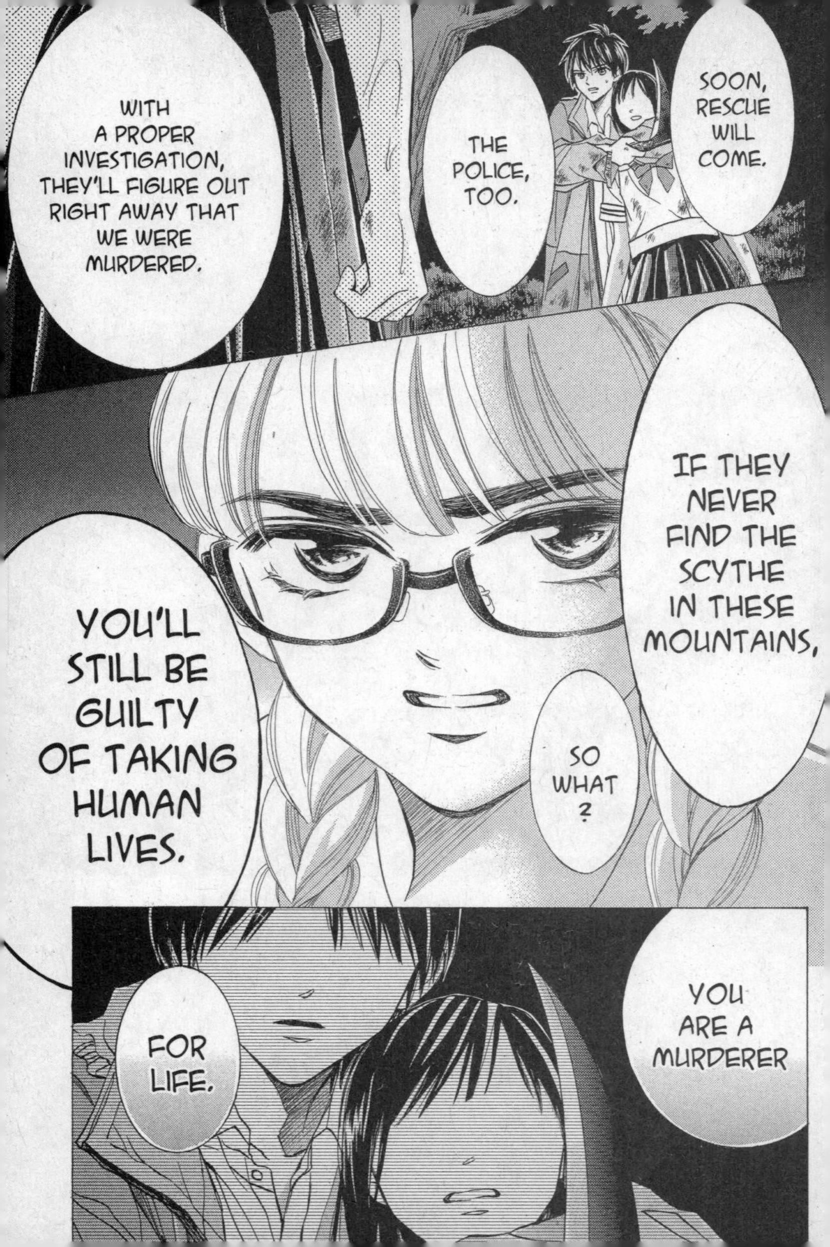
SOON, RESCUE WILL COME.
THE POLICE, TOO.
WITH A PROPER INVESTIGATION, THEY'LL FIGURE OUT RIGHT AWAY THAT WE WERE MURDERED.
IF THEY NEVER FIND THE SCYTHE IN THESE MOUNTAINS,
SO WHAT?
YOU'LL STILL BE GUILTY OF TAKING HUMAN LIVES.
YOU ARE A MURDERER
FOR LIFE.

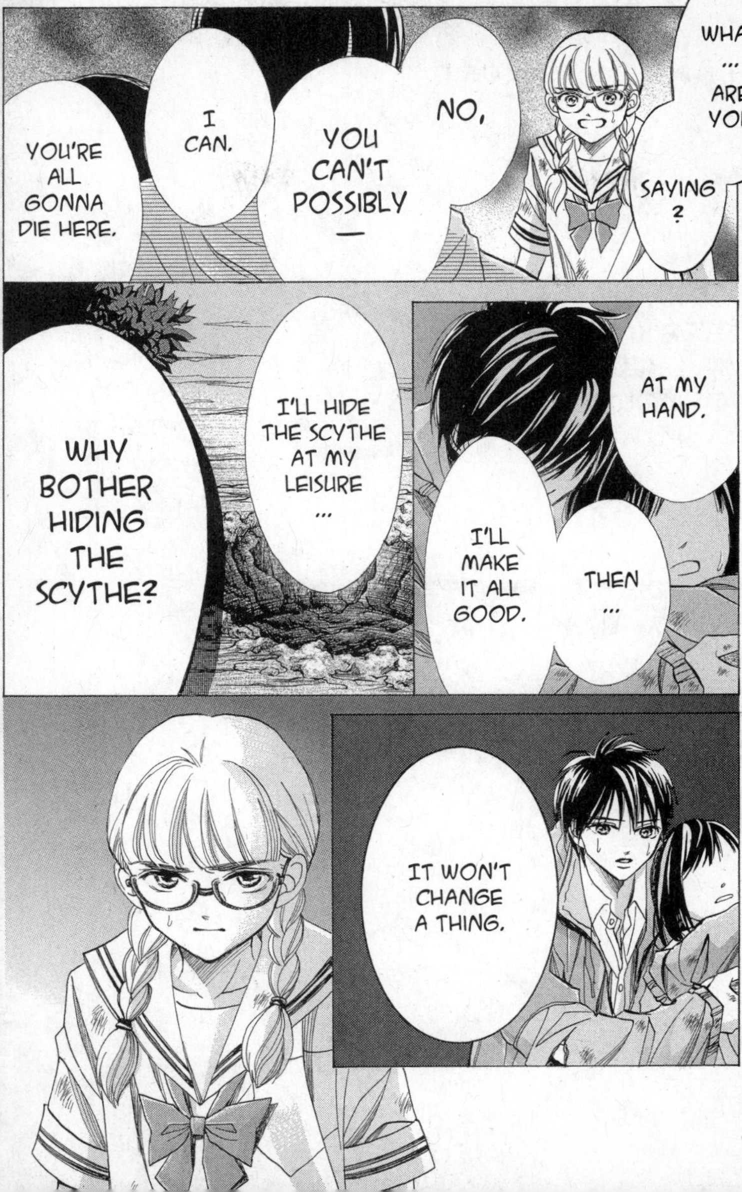
WHAT ... ARE YOU
SAYING ?
NO,
YOU CAN'T POSSIBLY —
I CAN.
YOU'RE ALL GONNA DIE HERE.
AT MY HAND.
THEN ...
I'LL MAKE IT ALL GOOD.
I'LL HIDE THE SCYTHE AT MY LEISURE ...
WHY BOTHER HIDING THE SCYTHE?
IT WON'T CHANGE A THING.

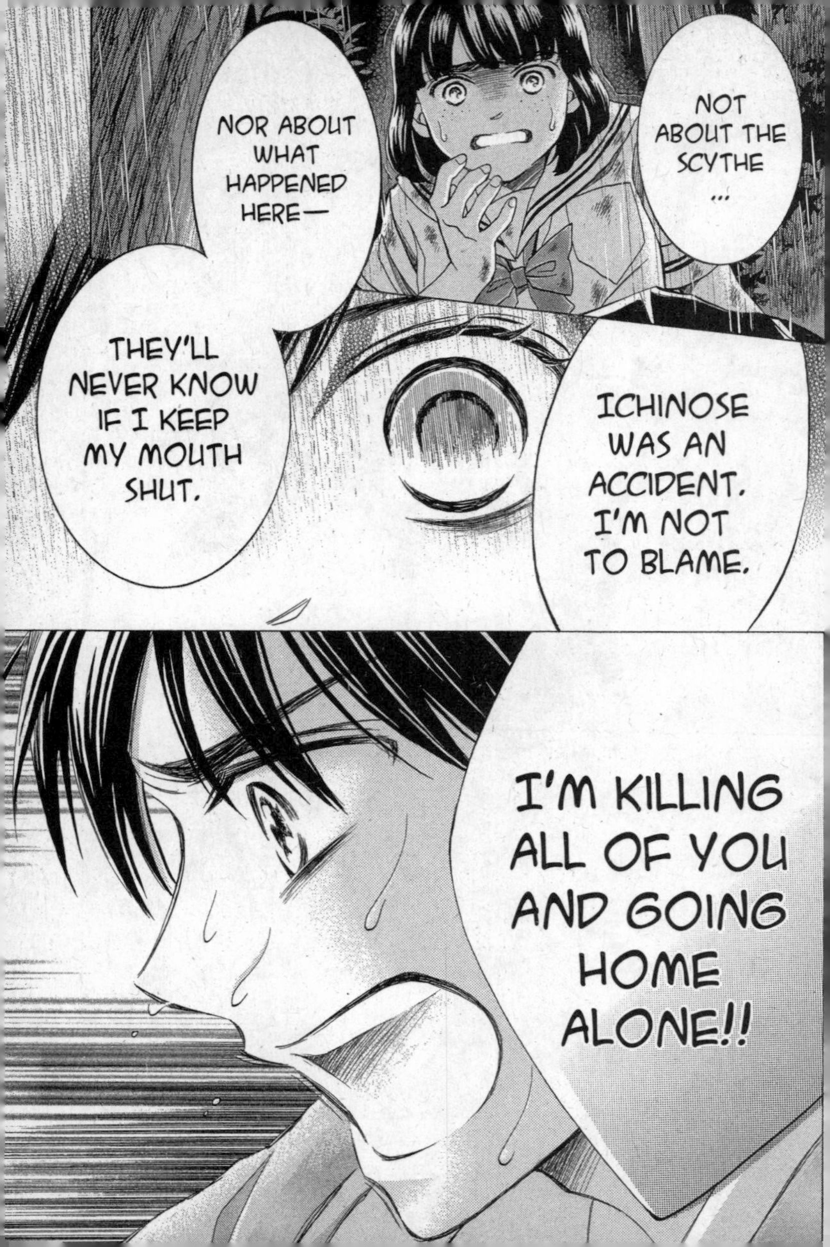
NOT ABOUT THE SCYTHE...
NOR ABOUT WHAT HAPPENED HERE—
ICHINOSE WAS AN ACCIDENT. I'M NOT TO BLAME.
THEY'LL NEVER KNOW IF I KEEP MY MOUTH SHUT.
I'M KILLING ALL OF YOU AND GOING HOME ALONE!!

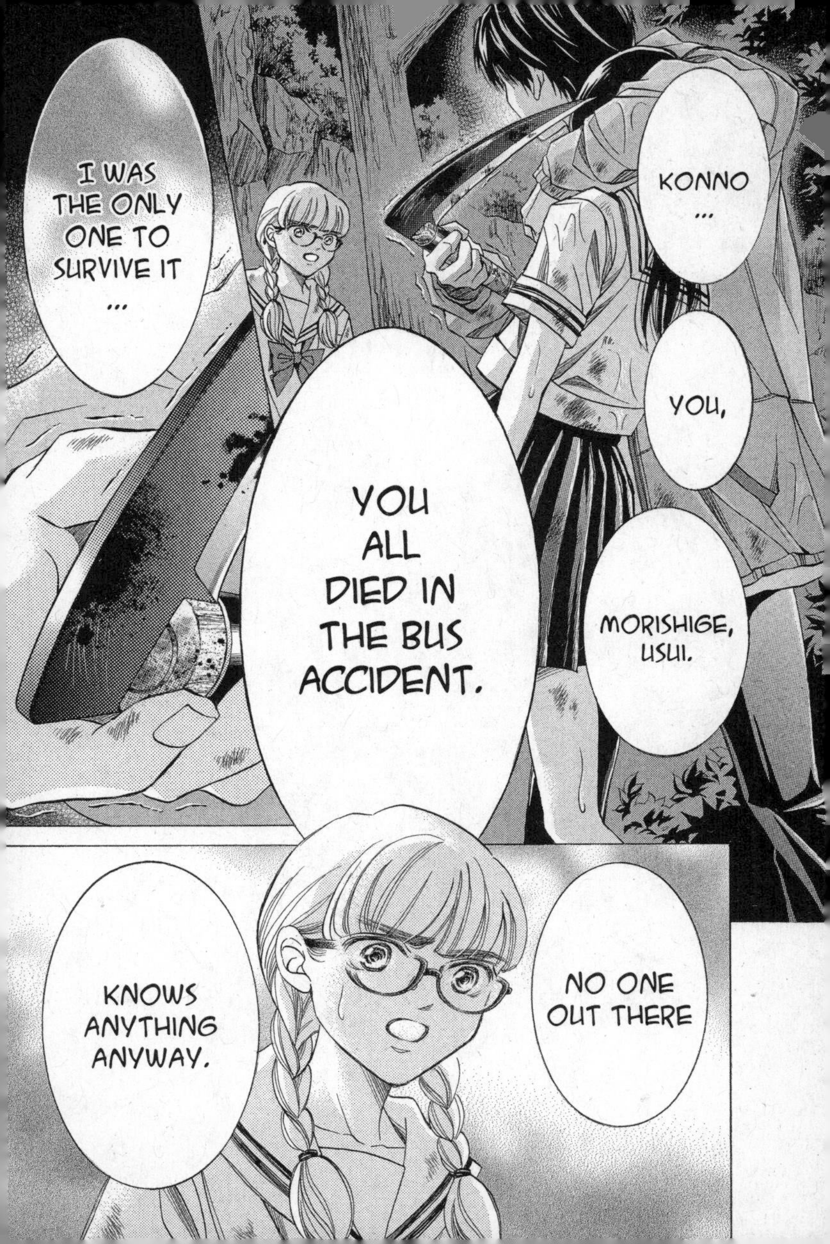
KONNO ...
YOU,
MORISHIGE, USUI.
YOU ALL DIED IN THE BUS ACCIDENT.
I WAS THE ONLY ONE TO SURVIVE IT ...
NO ONE OUT THERE
KNOWS ANYTHING ANYWAY.

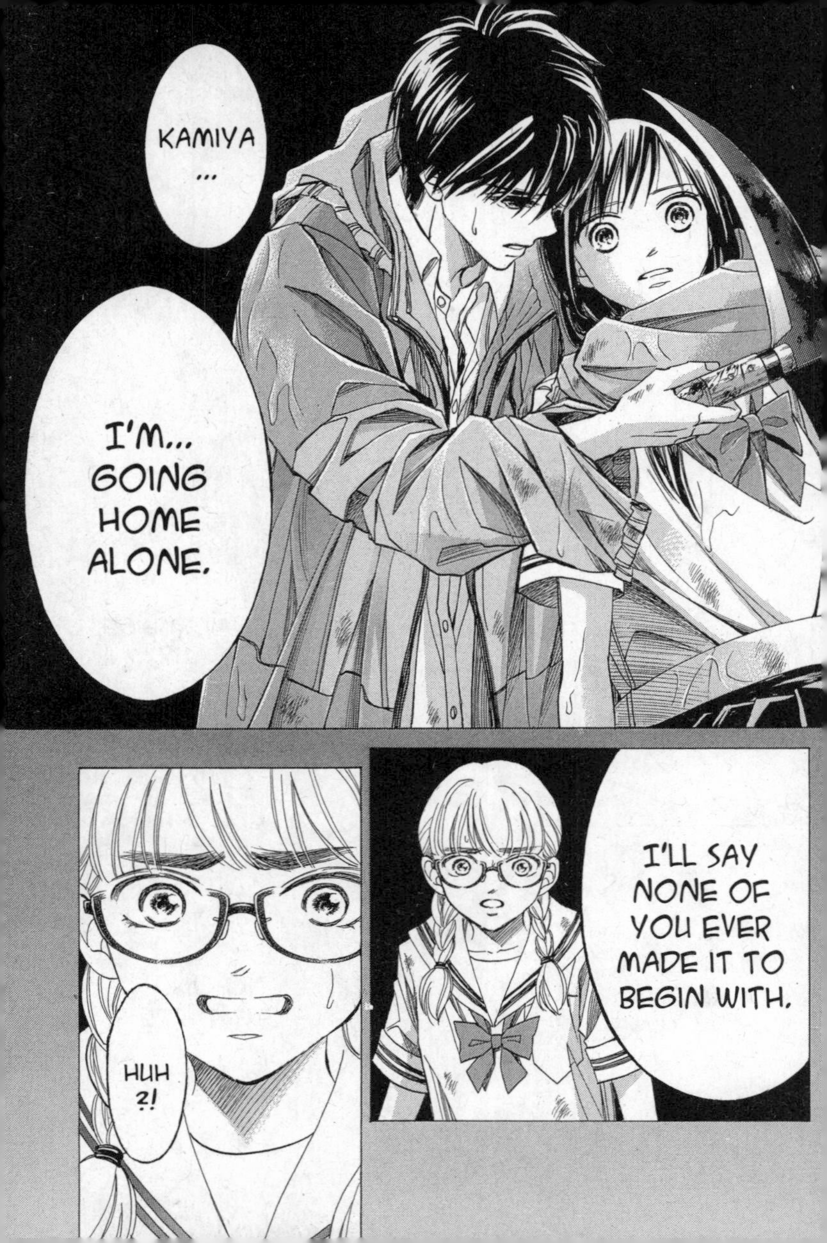
KAMIYA ...
I'M... GOING HOME ALONE.
I'LL SAY NONE OF YOU EVER MADE IT TO BEGIN WITH.
HUH ?!

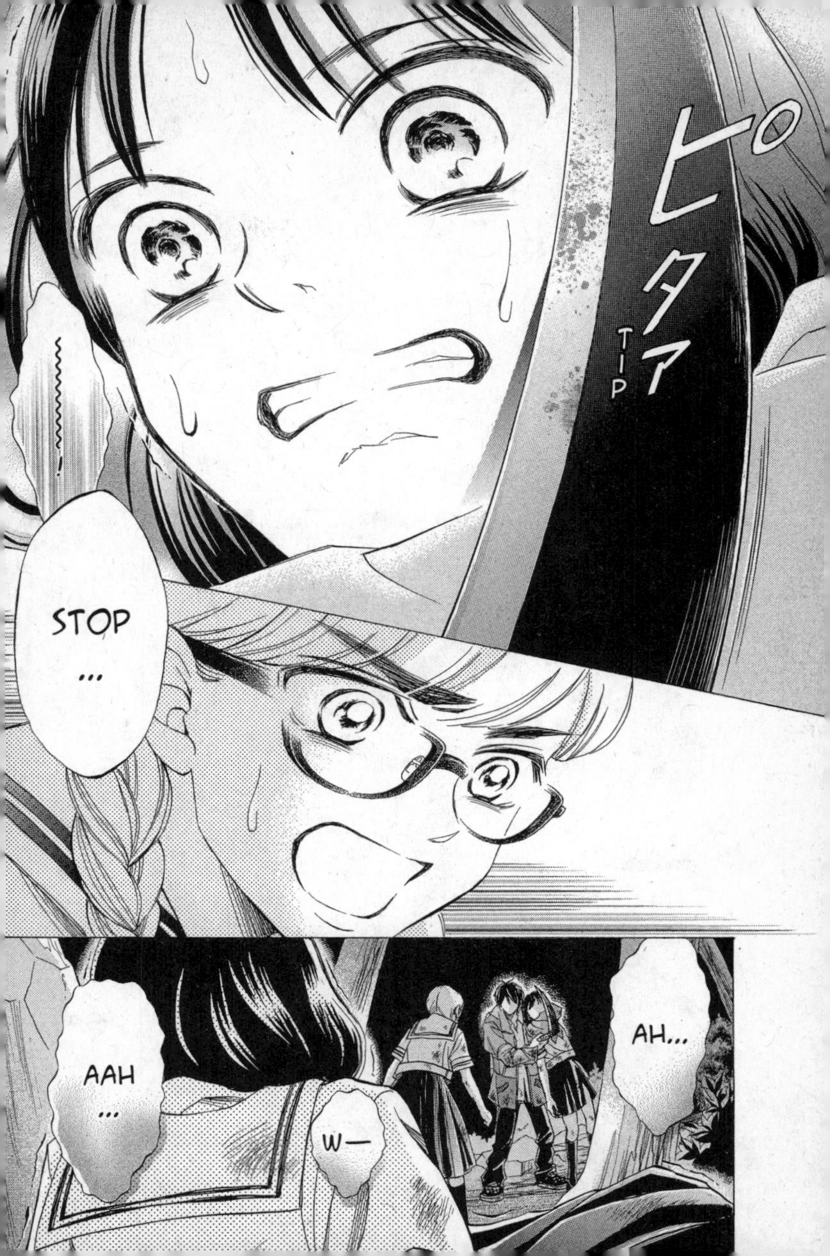
ピタァ
TIP
STOP ...
AH...
W—
AAH ...

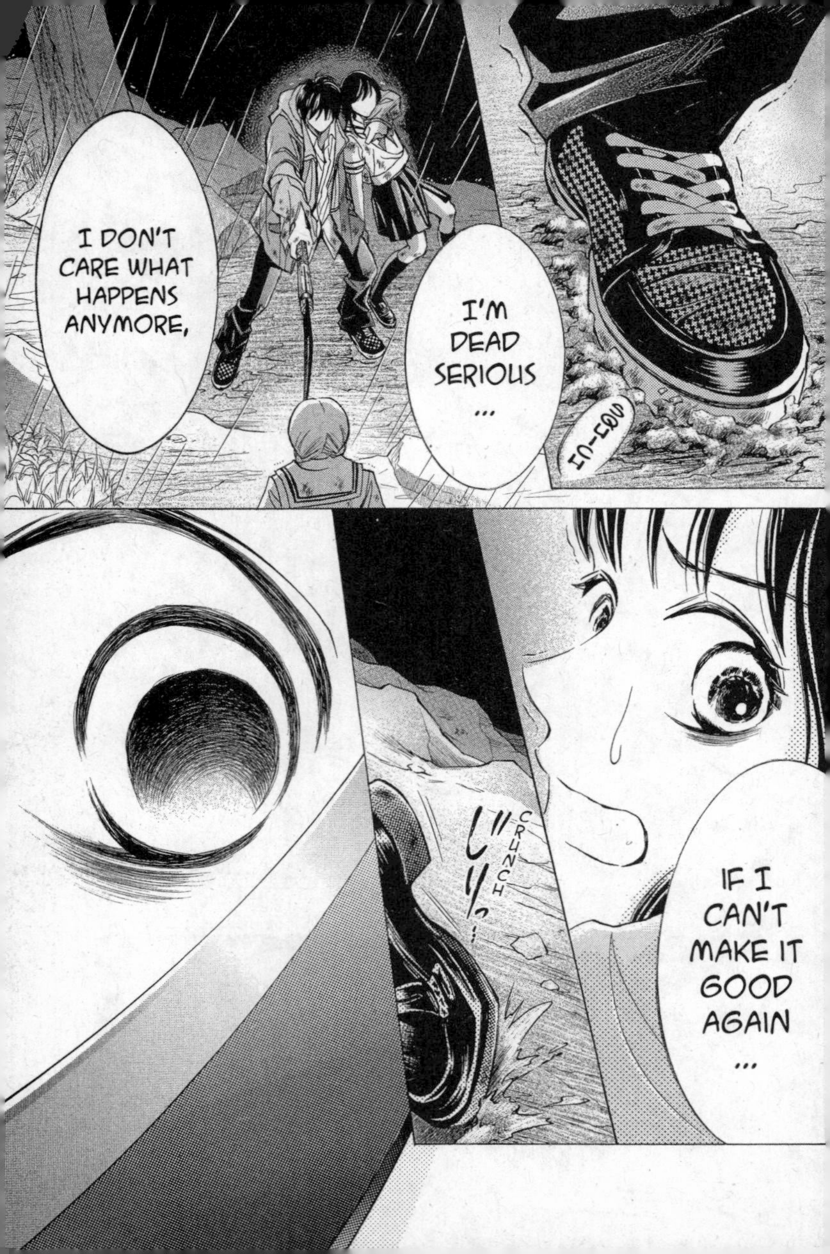
I DON'T CARE WHAT HAPPENS ANYMORE,
I'M DEAD SERIOUS ...
IF I CAN'T MAKE IT GOOD AGAIN ...
CRUNCH

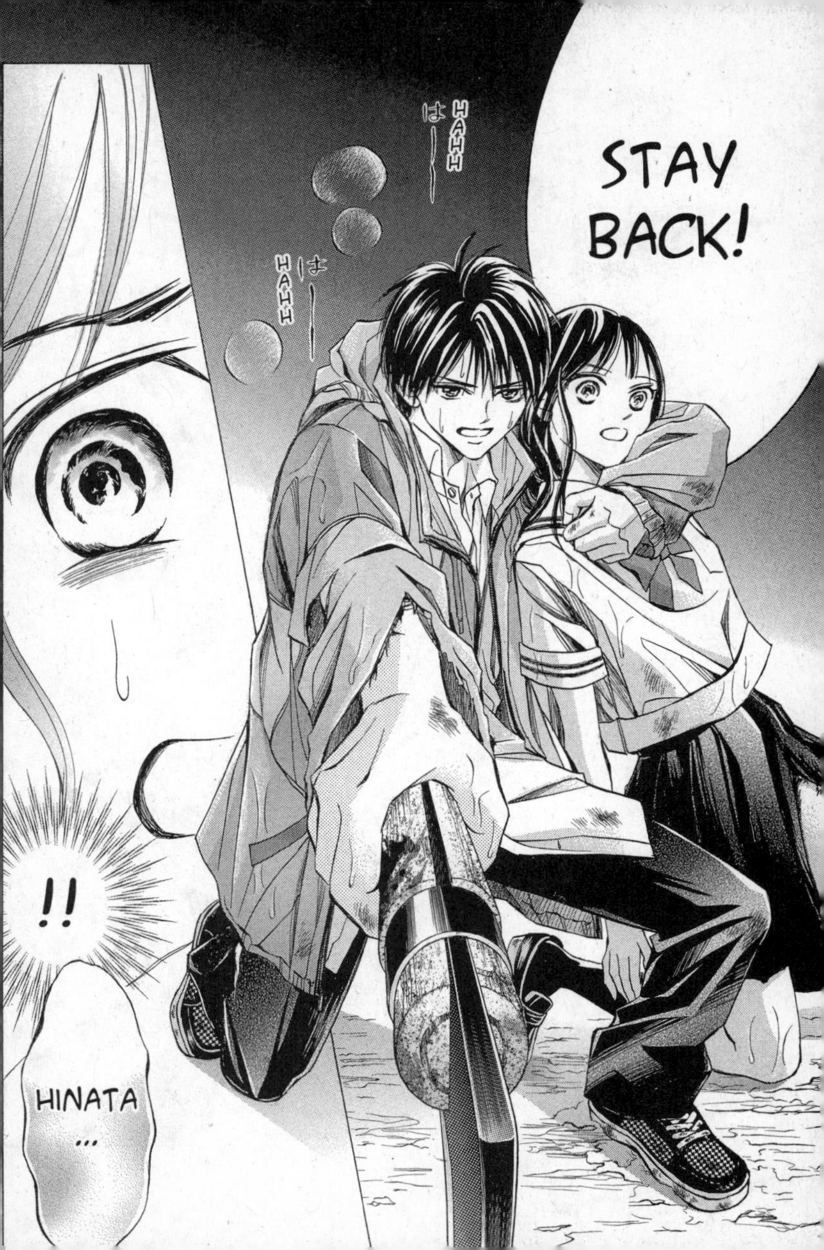
STAY BACK!
はーー HAHH
はーー HAHH
!!
HINATA ...

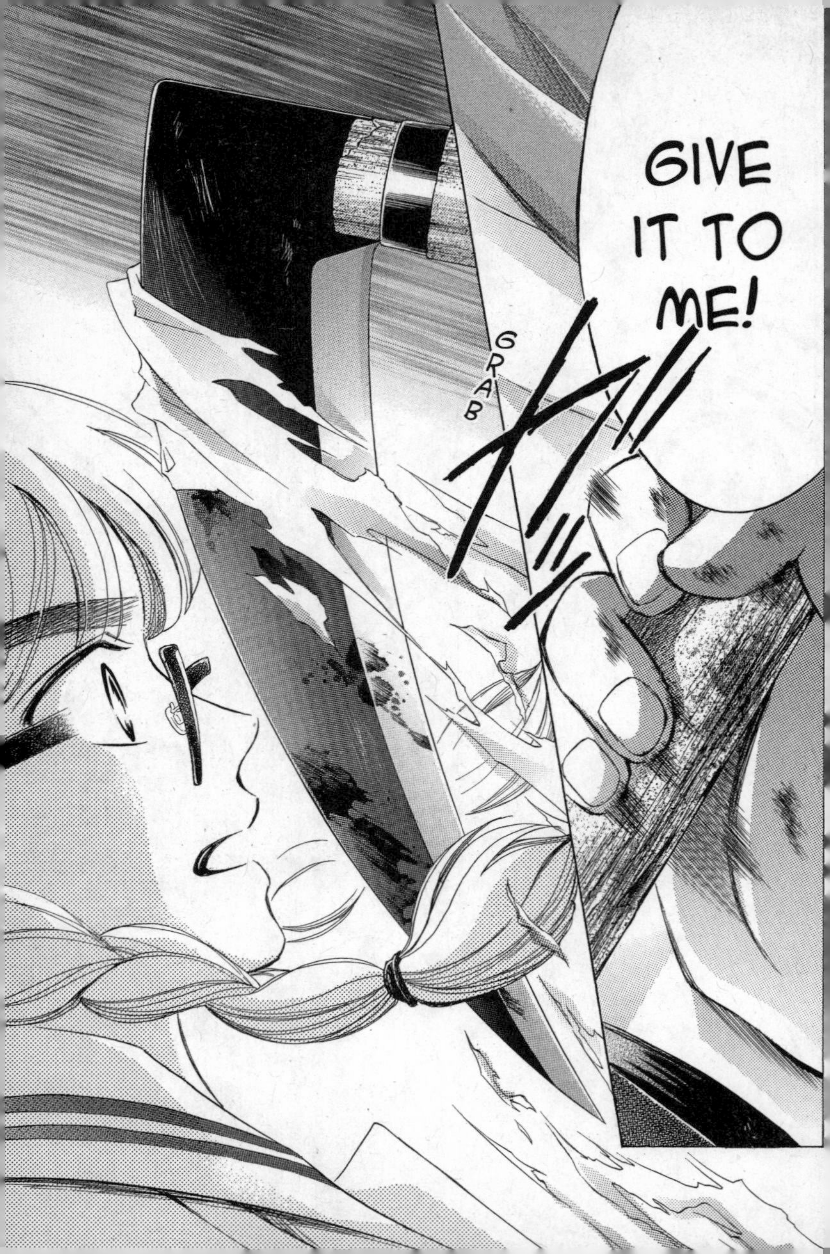
GIVE IT TO ME!
GRAB

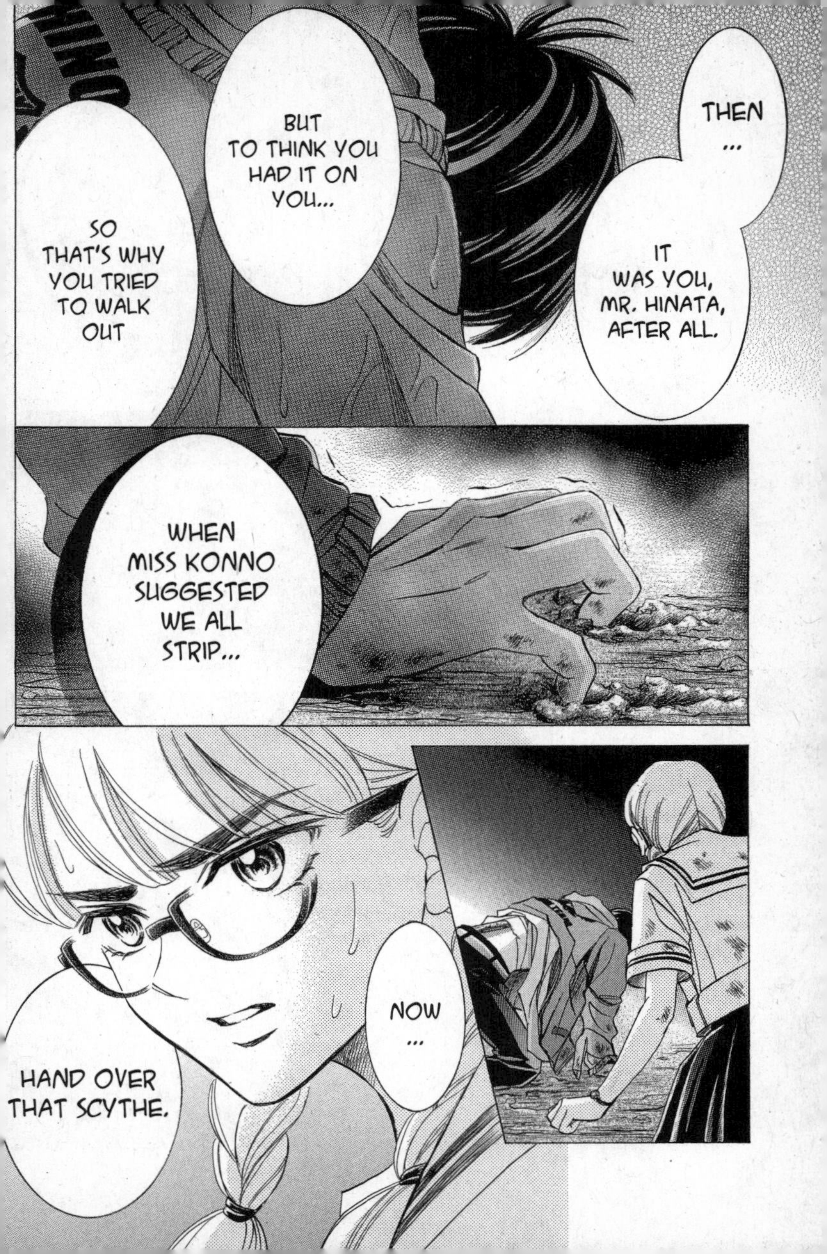
THEN ...
IT WAS YOU, MR. HINATA, AFTER ALL.
BUT TO THINK YOU HAD IT ON YOU...
SO THAT'S WHY YOU TRIED TO WALK OUT
WHEN MISS KONNO SUGGESTED WE ALL STRIP...
NOW ...
HAND OVER THAT SCYTHE.

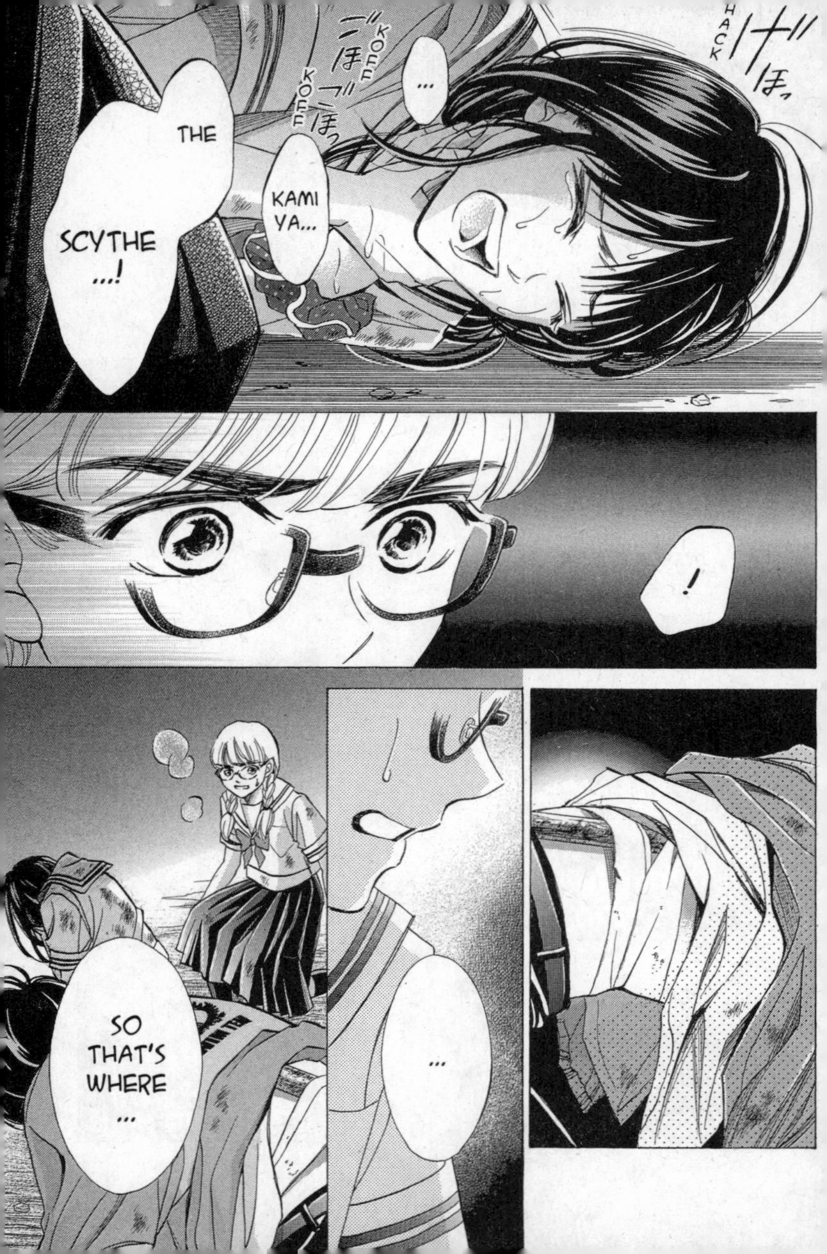
HACK
げほっ
...
KOFF KOFF
ごほっごほっ
KAMIYA...
THE SCYTHE ...!
!
...
SO THAT'S WHERE ...

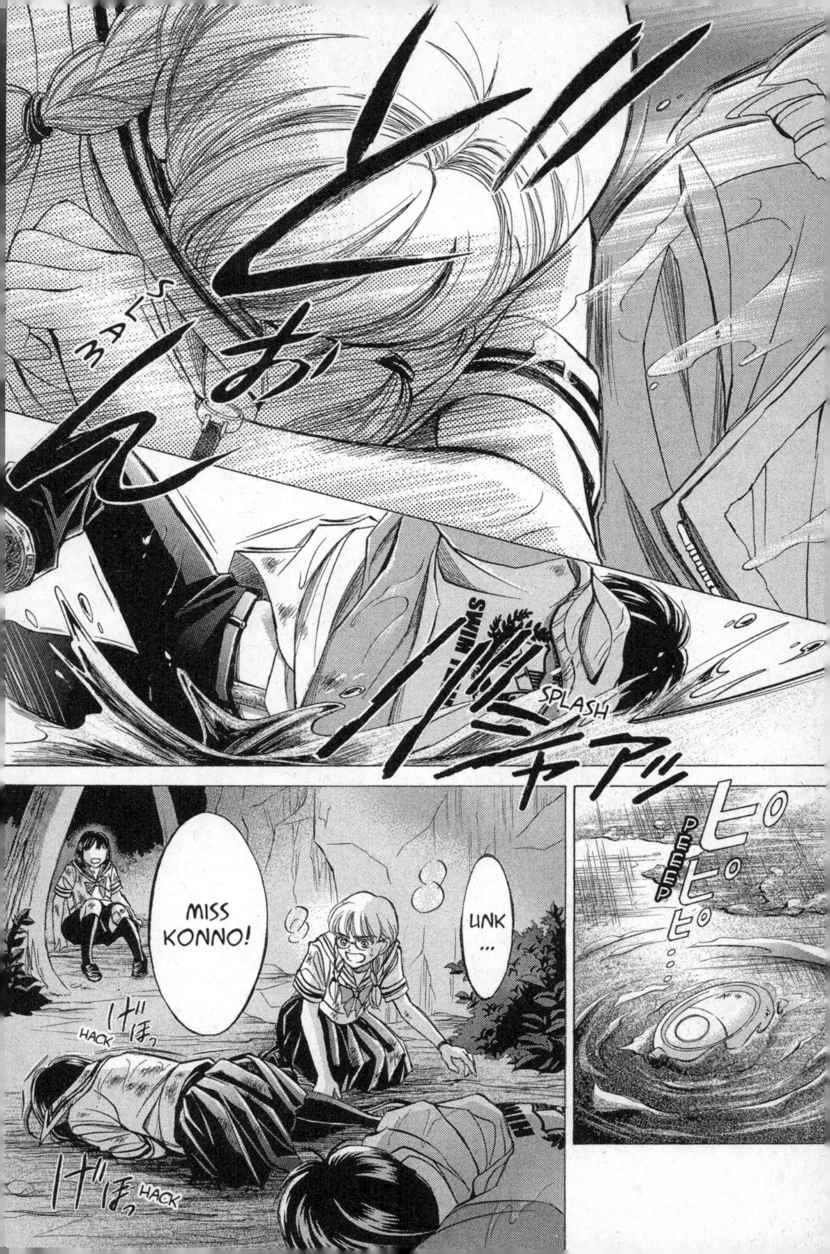
SWISH
SPLASH
ピ。ピ。ピ。ピ。
PEEEEP
UNK
...
MISS KONNO!
げほっ
HACK
げほっ
HACK

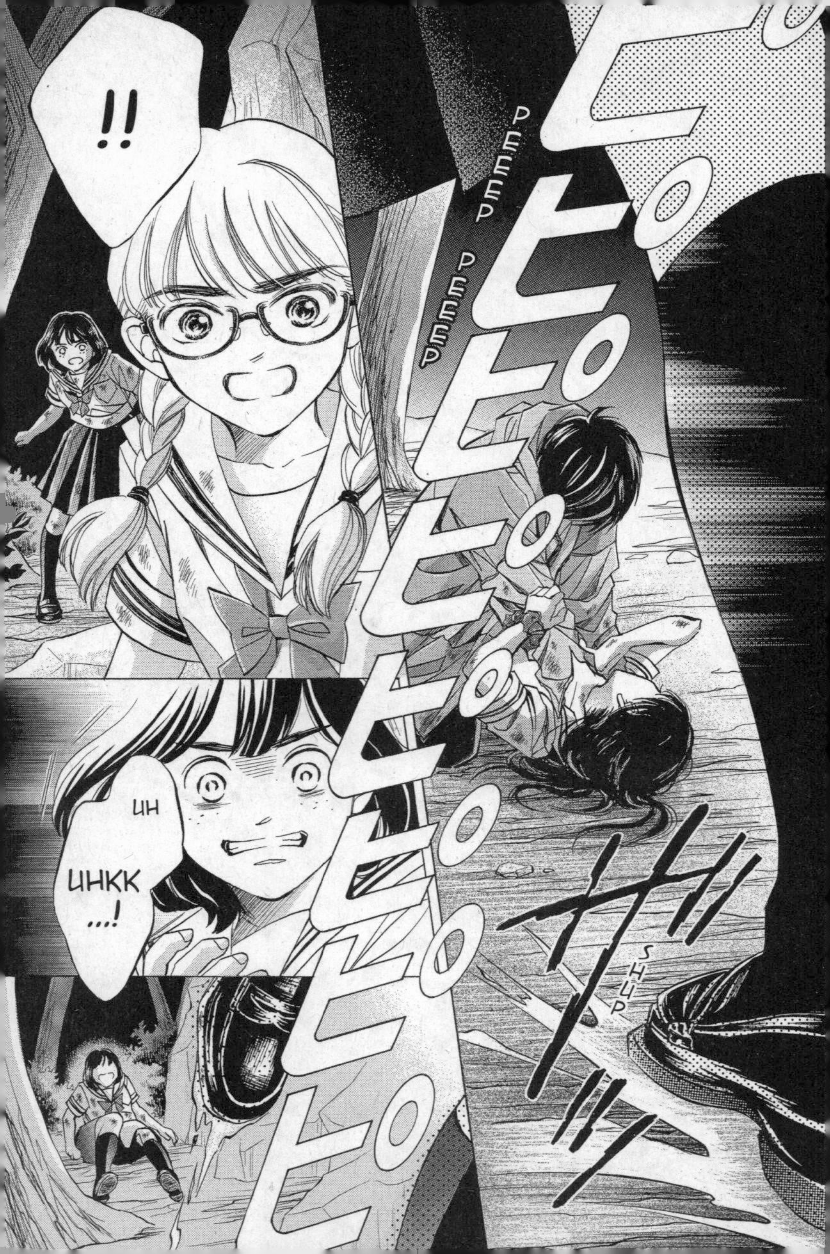
PEEEEP PEEEEP
!!
UH
UHKK
...!
SHUP

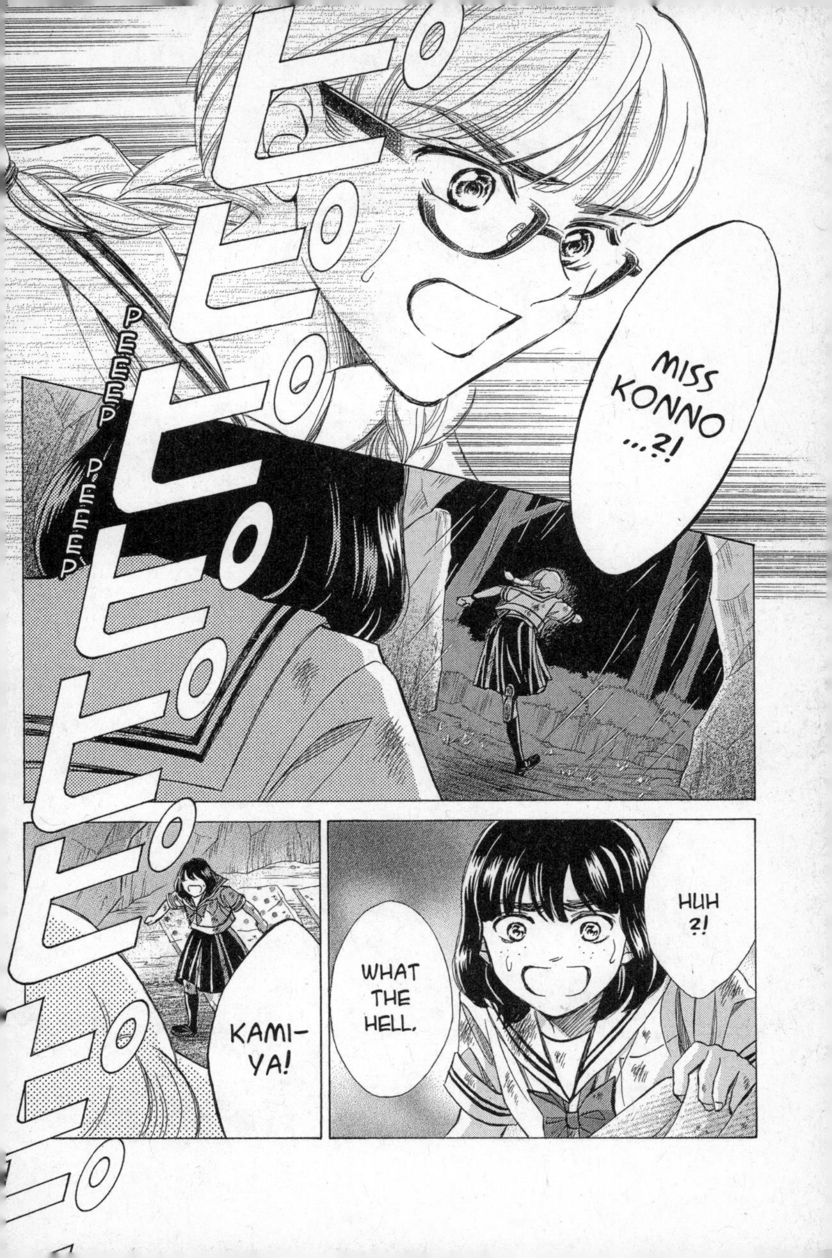
MISS KONNO ...?!
PEEEEP PEEEEP
HUH ?!
WHAT THE HELL,
KAMI-YA!

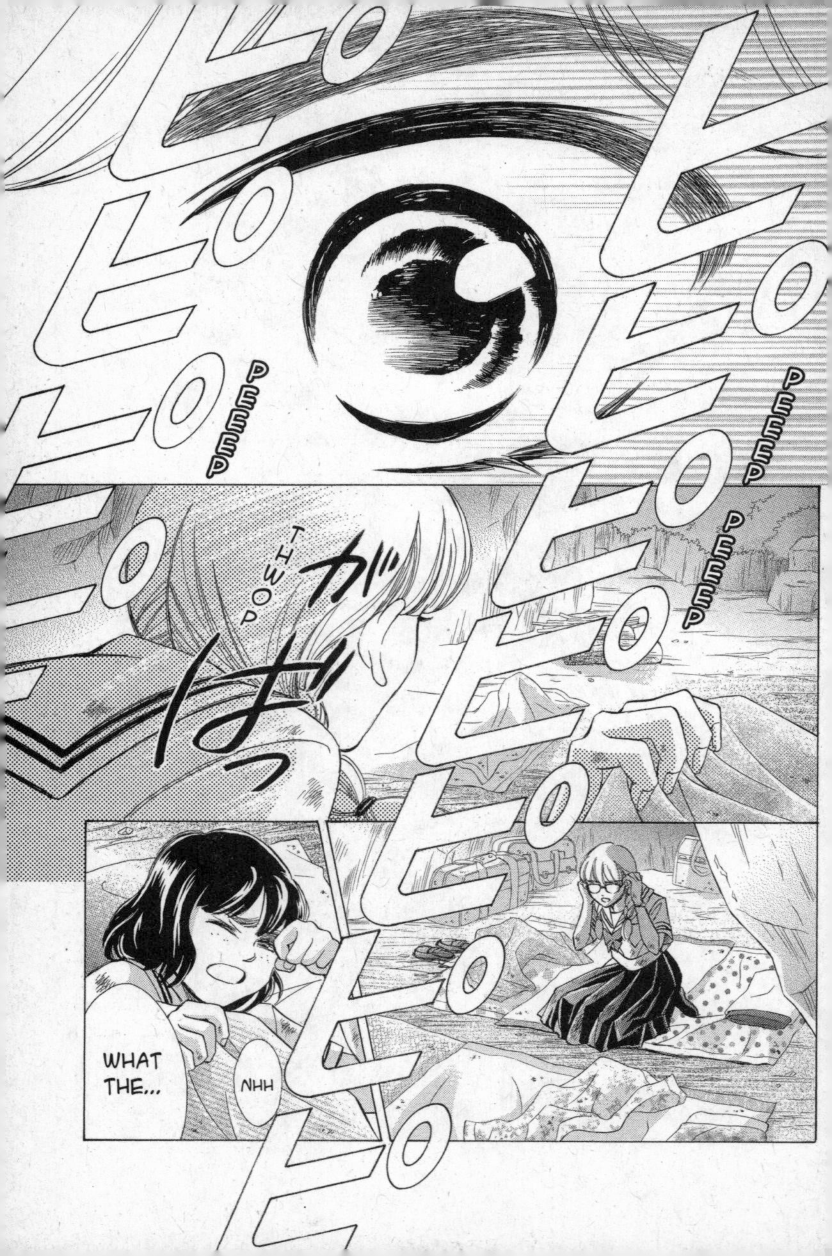
PEEEEP
PEEEEP
PEEEEP
THWOP
がばっ
NHH
WHAT THE...

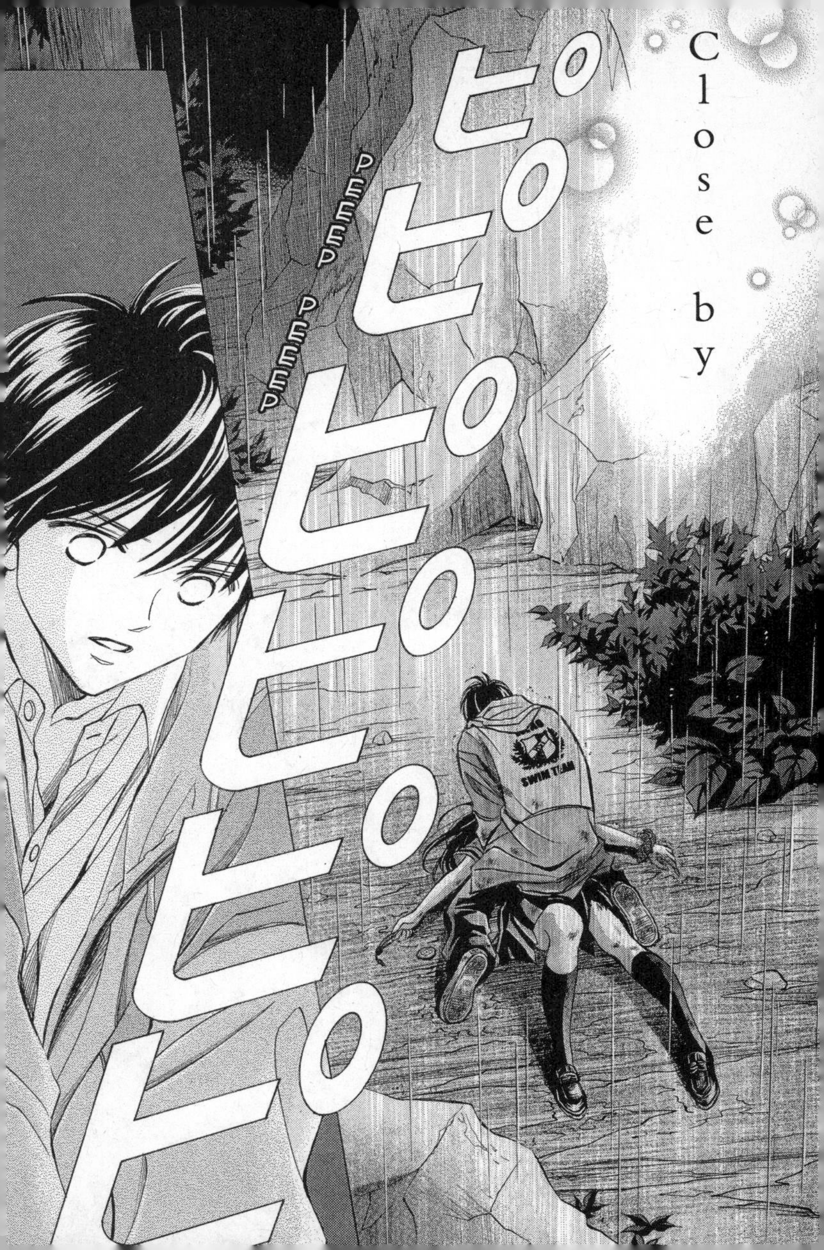

Close by
PEEEP PEEEP

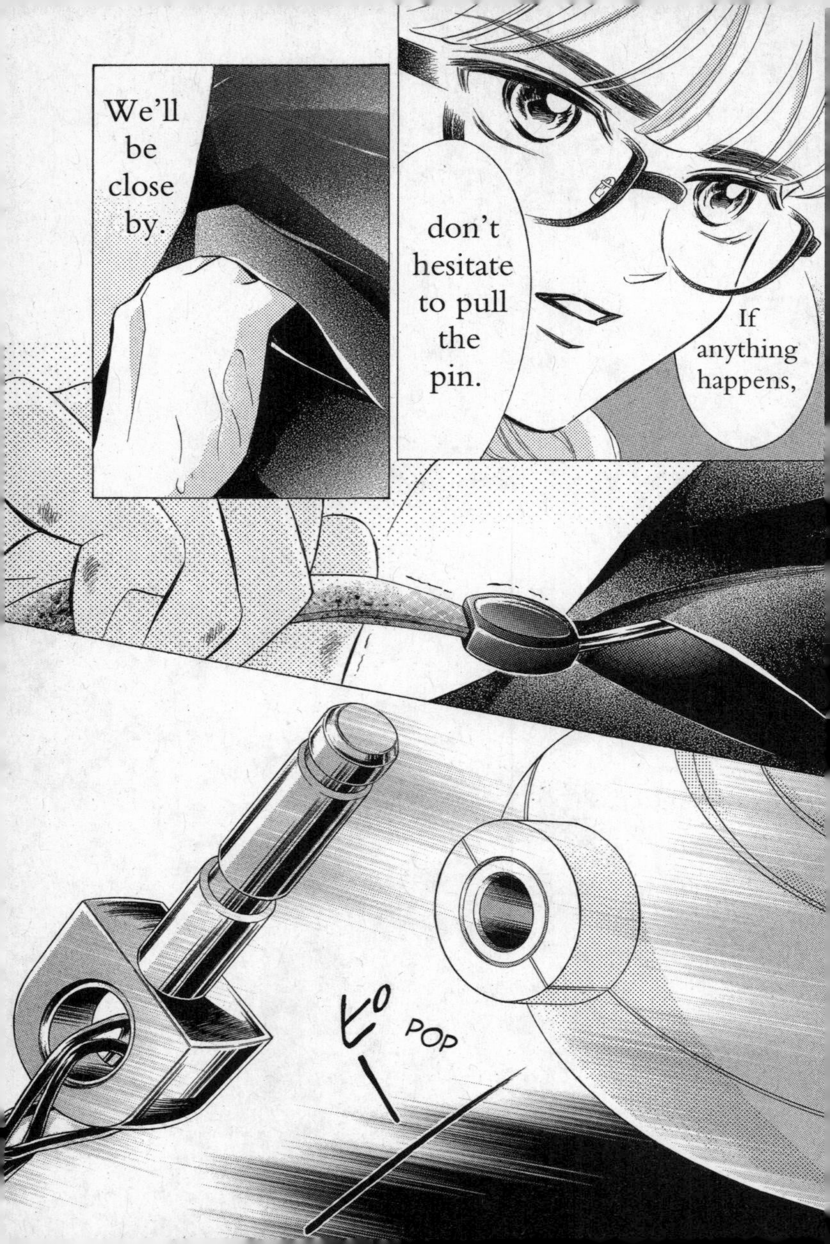
If anything happens,
don't hesitate to pull the pin.
We'll be close by.
POP

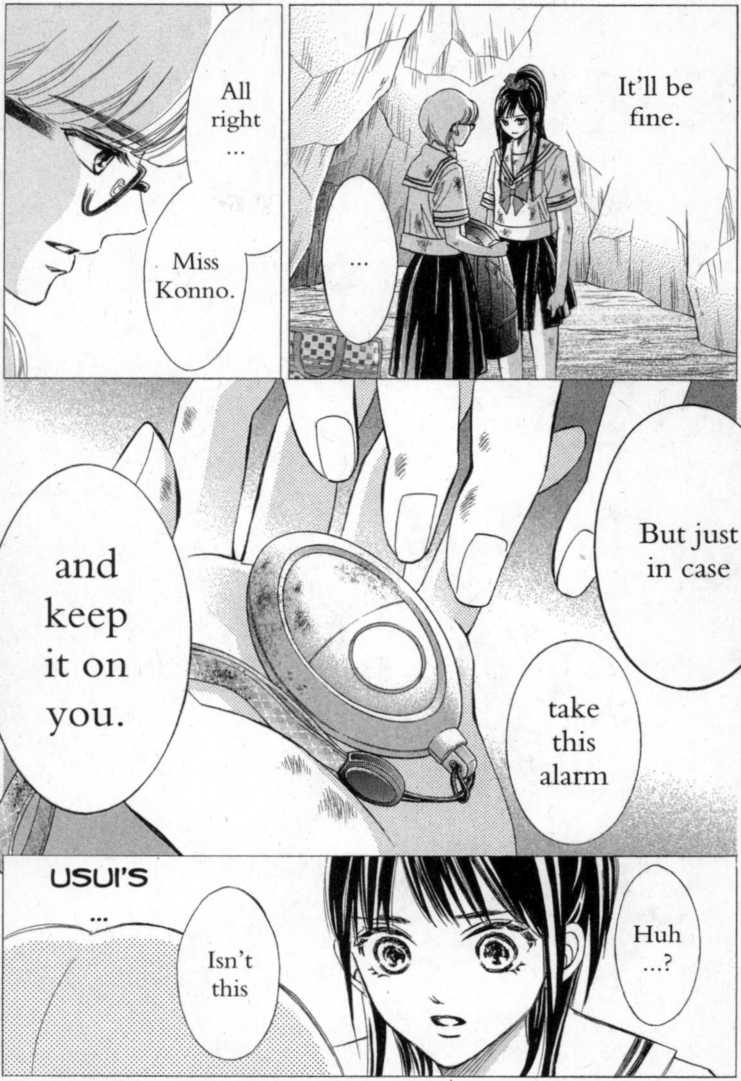
It'll be fine.
...
All right ...
Miss Konno.
But just in case
take this alarm
and keep it on you.
Huh ...?
Isn't this
USUI'S ...

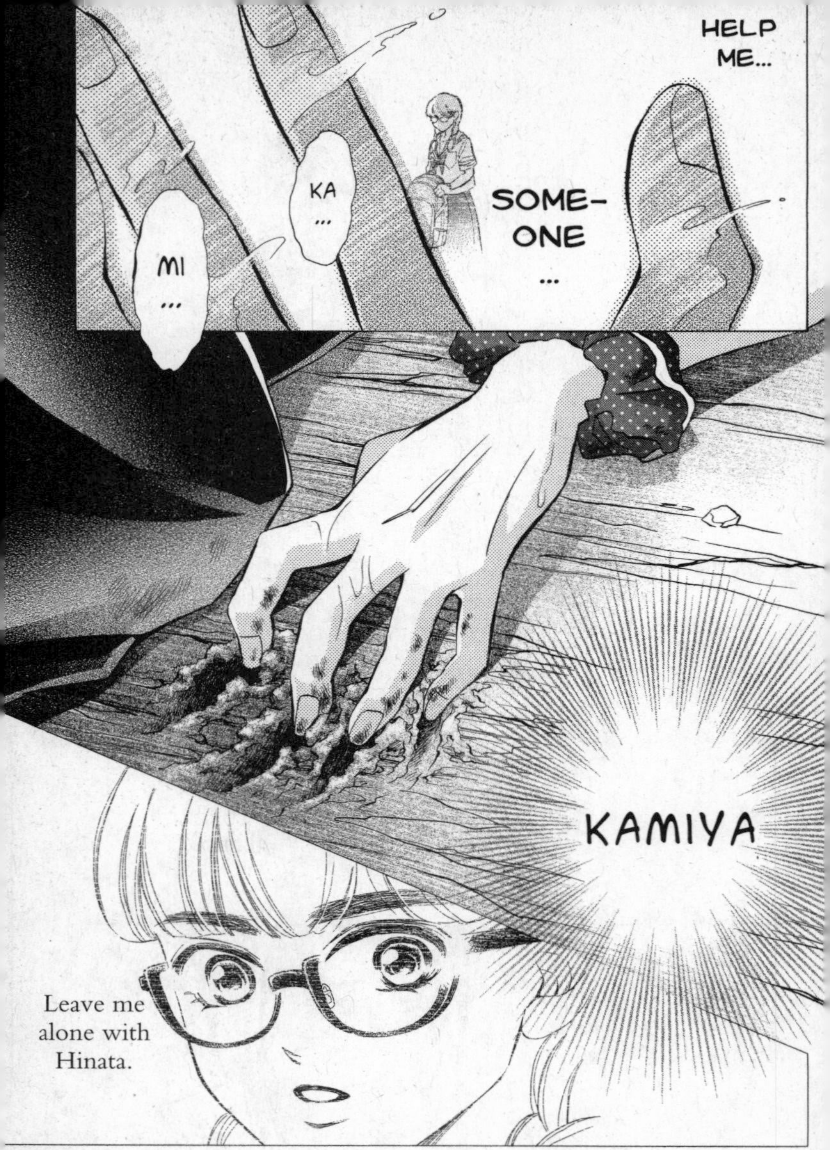
HELP ME...
SOME-ONE ...
KA ...
MI ...
KAMIYA
Leave me alone with Hinata.

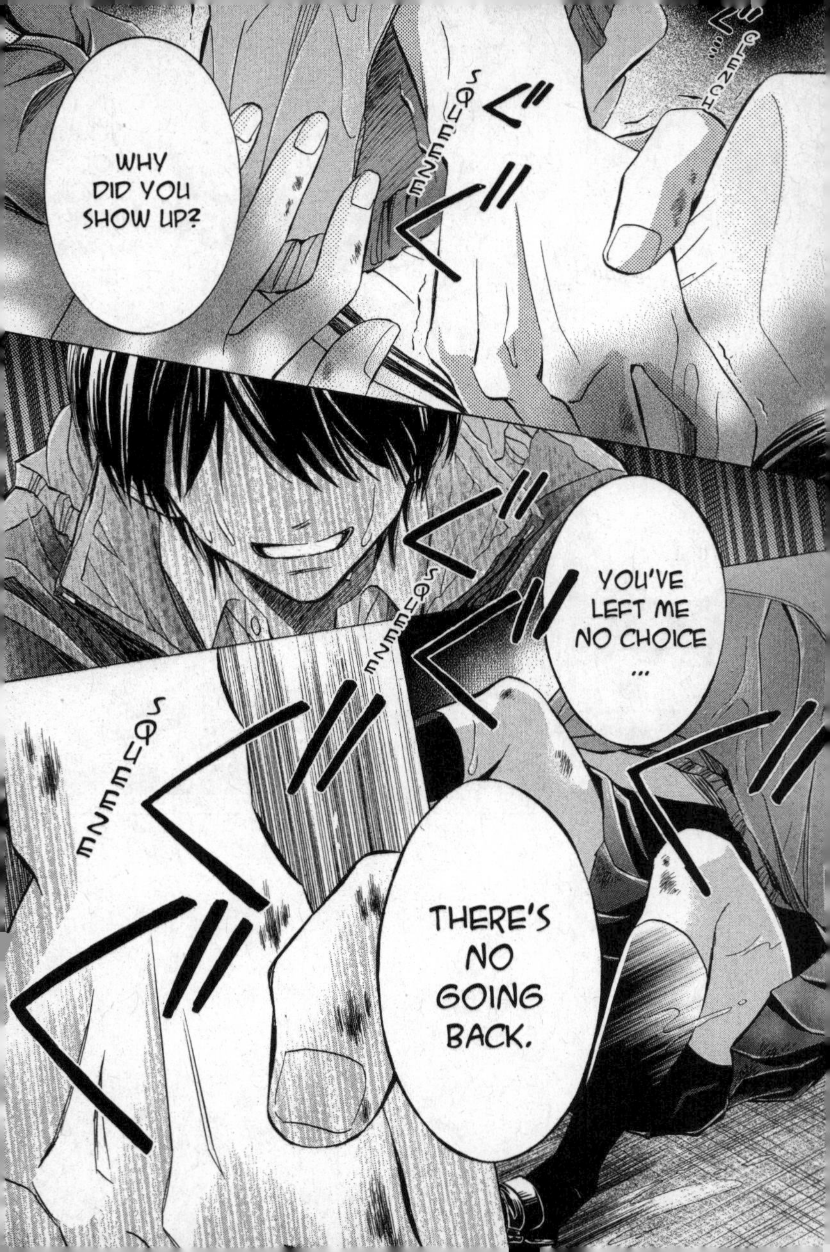
CLENCH
SQUEEEZE
WHY DID YOU SHOW UP?
SQUEEEZE
YOU'VE LEFT ME NO CHOICE ...
SQUEEEZE
THERE'S NO GOING BACK.

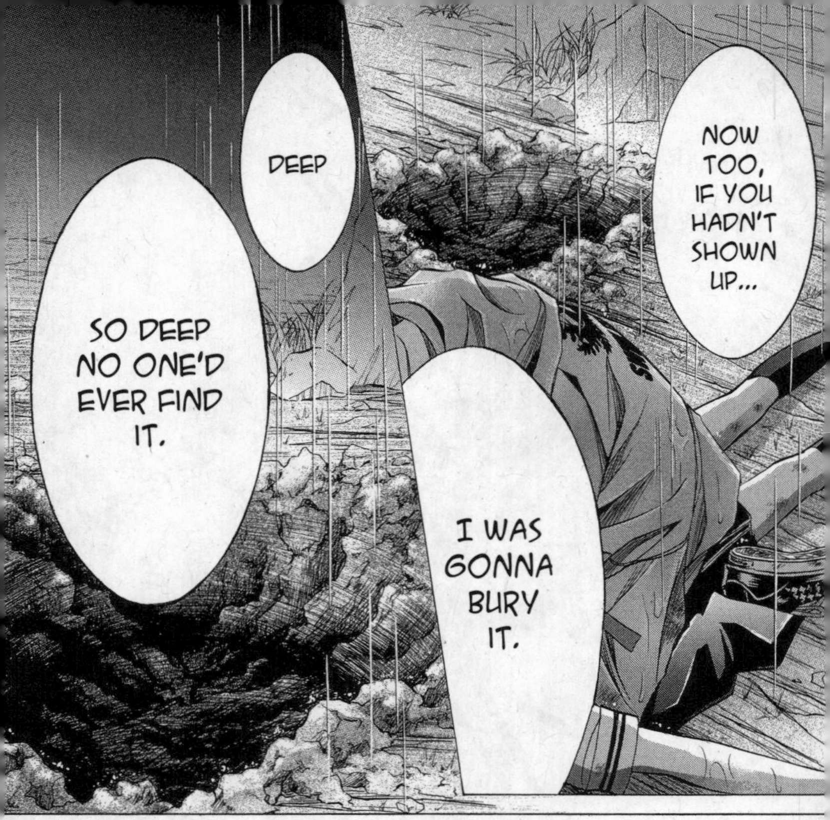
NOW TOO, IF YOU HADN'T SHOWN UP...
I WAS GONNA BURY IT.
DEEP
SO DEEP NO ONE'D EVER FIND IT.

LIMIT

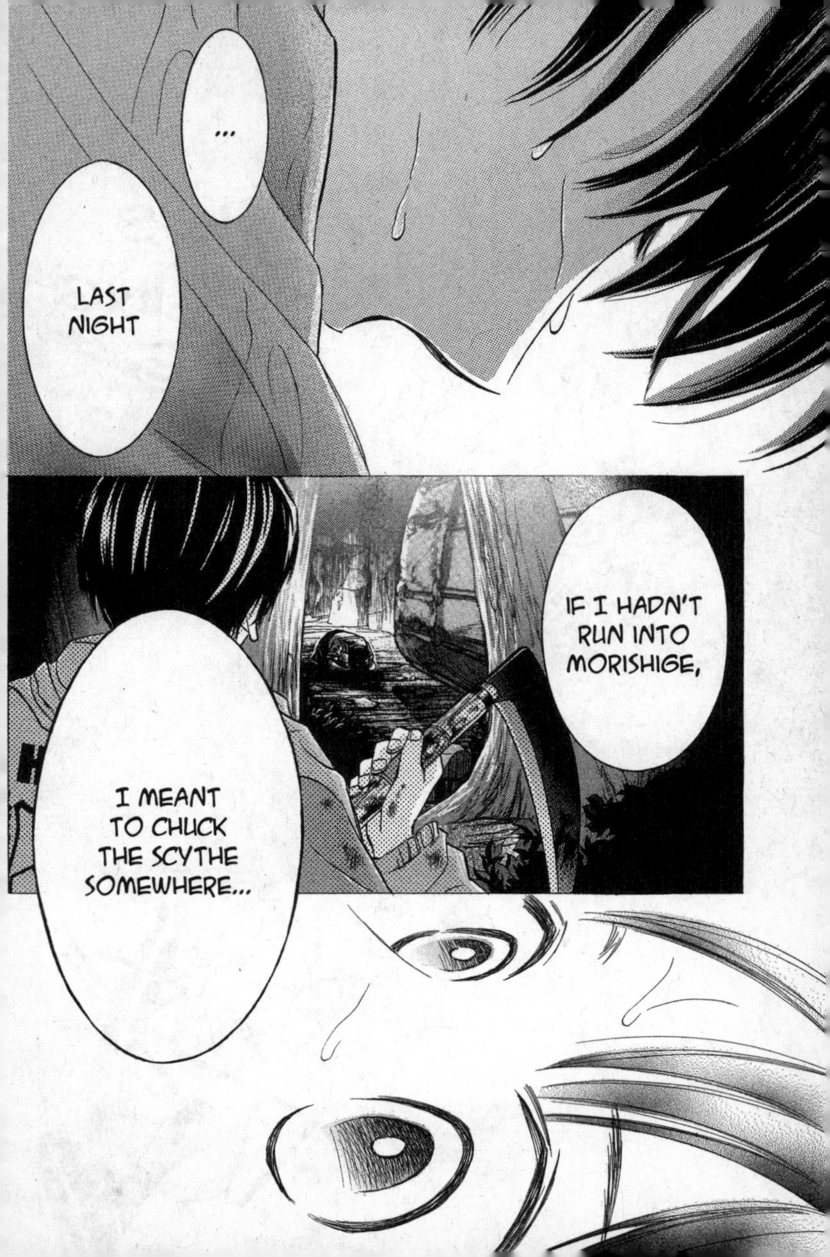
...
LAST NIGHT
IF I HADN'T RUN INTO MORISHIGE,
I MEANT TO CHUCK THE SCYTHE SOMEWHERE...

Scene.18 – The Whereabouts of the Blade

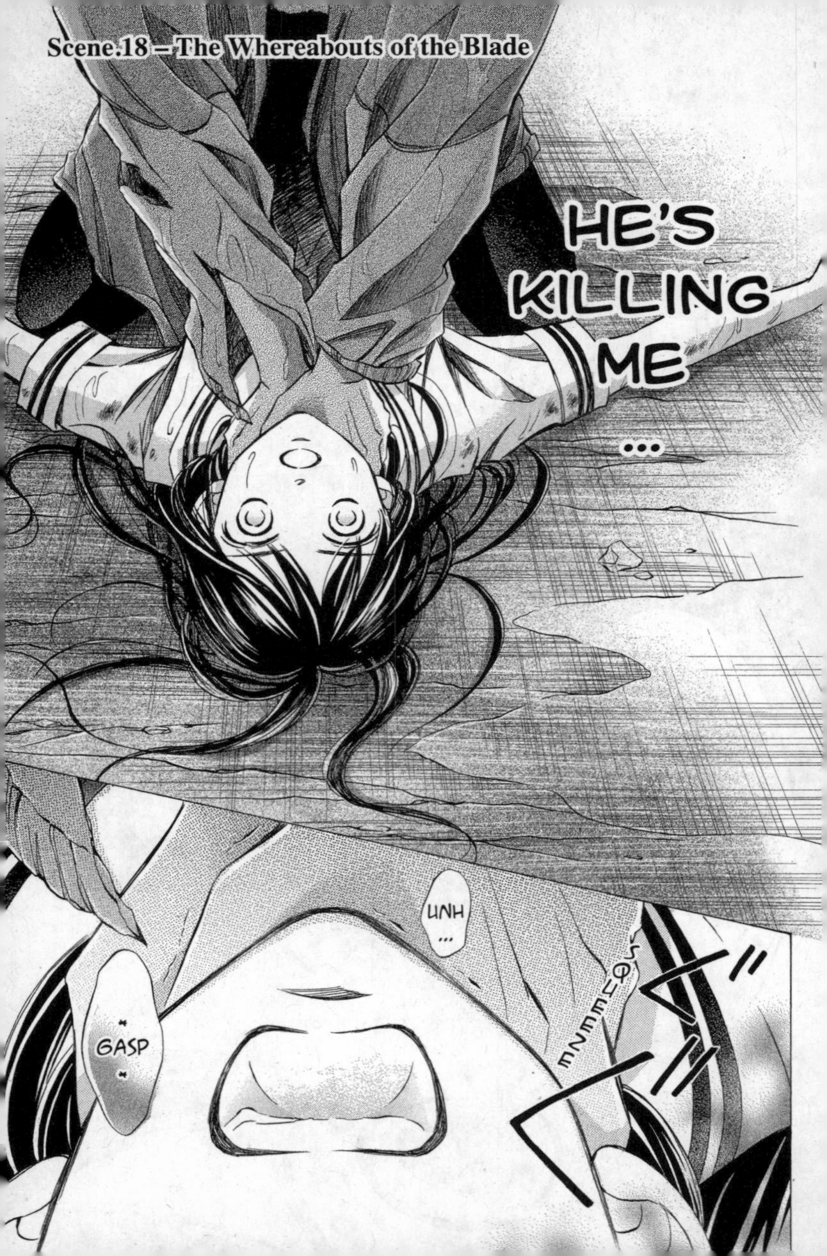
HE'S KILLING ME ...
SQUEEENE
UNH ...
GASP

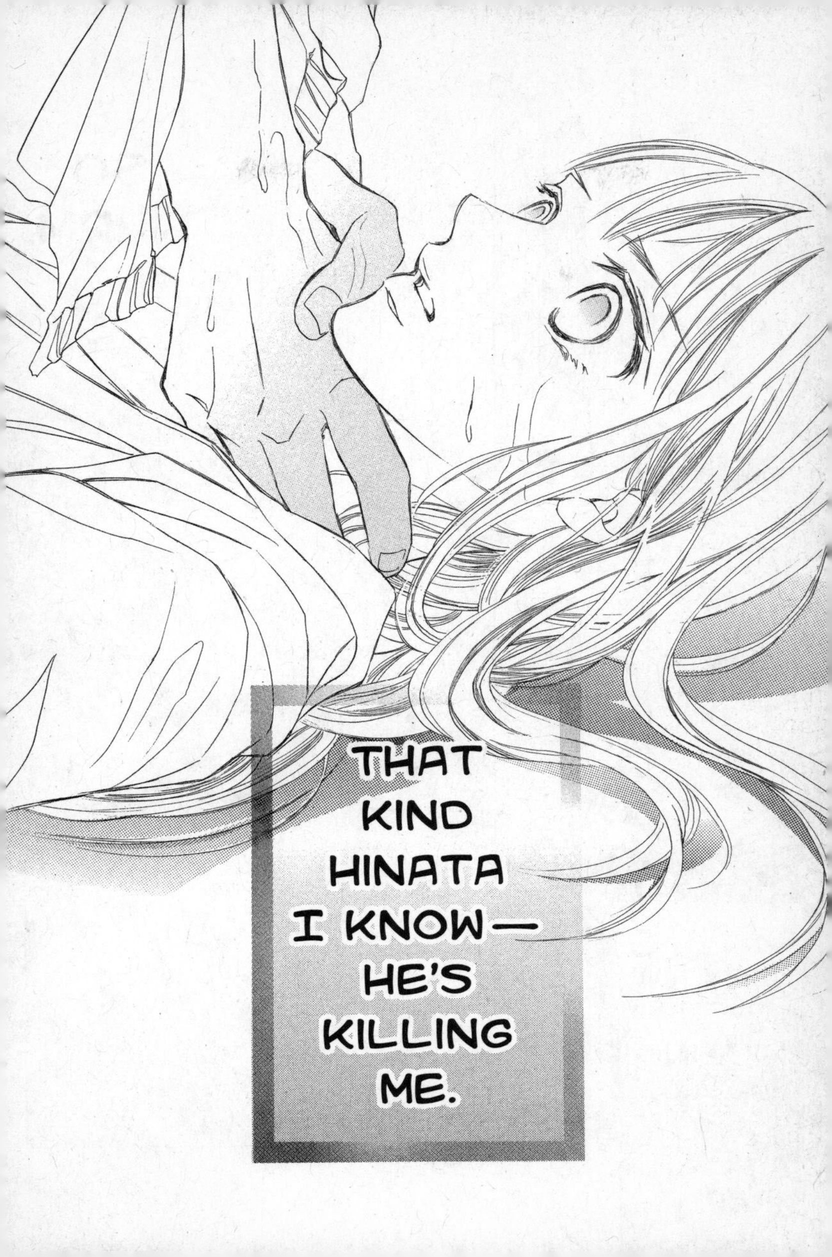
THAT KIND HINATA I KNOW— HE'S KILLING ME.

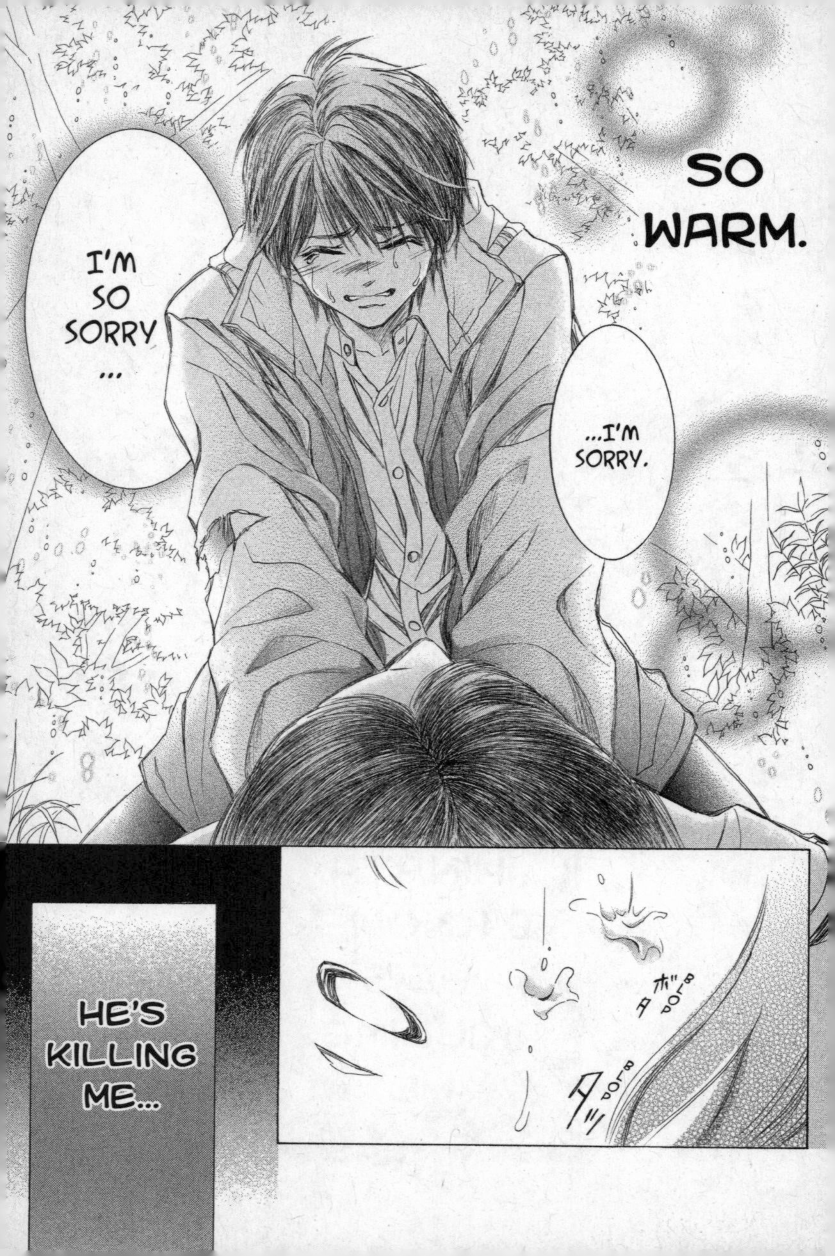
SO WARM.
...I'M SORRY.
I'M SO SORRY ...
BLOP
BLOP
HE'S KILLING ME...

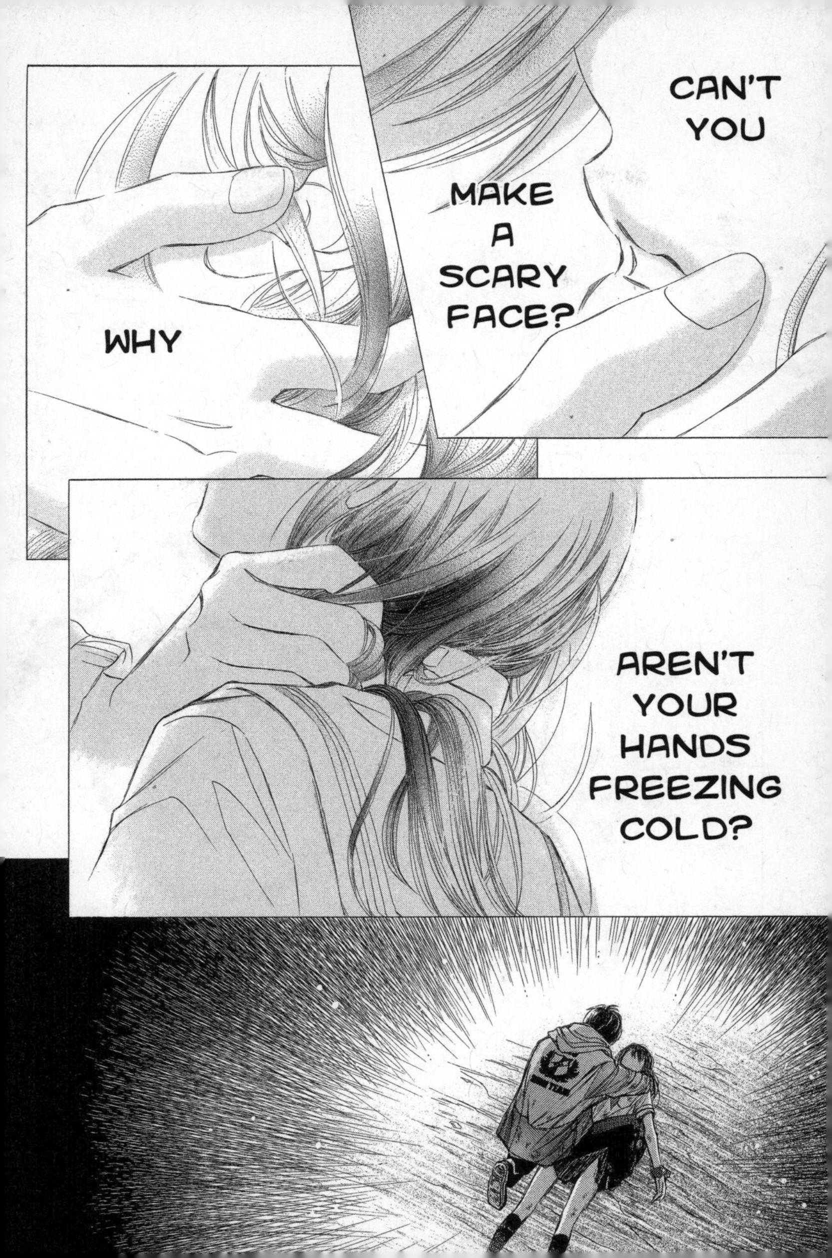
CAN'T YOU
MAKE A SCARY FACE?
WHY
AREN'T YOUR HANDS FREEZING COLD?

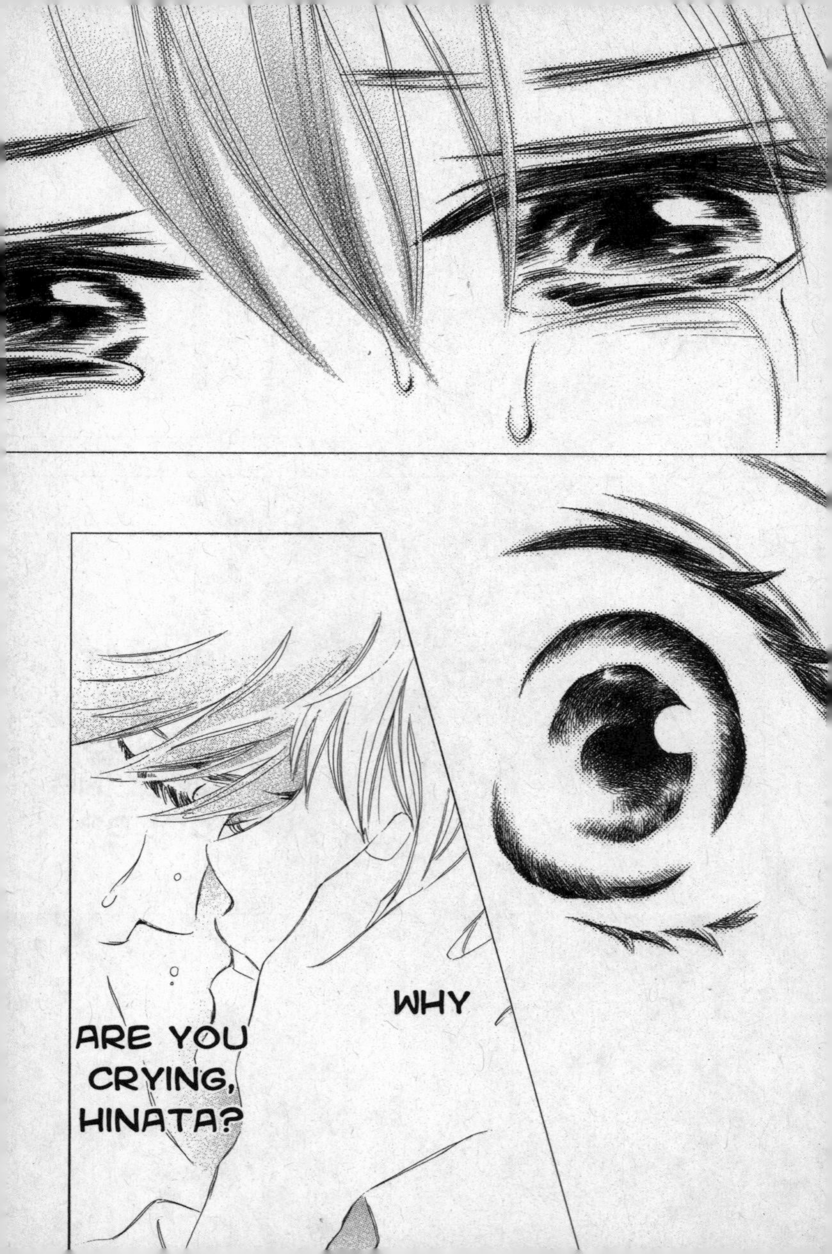
WHY
ARE YOU CRYING, HINATA?

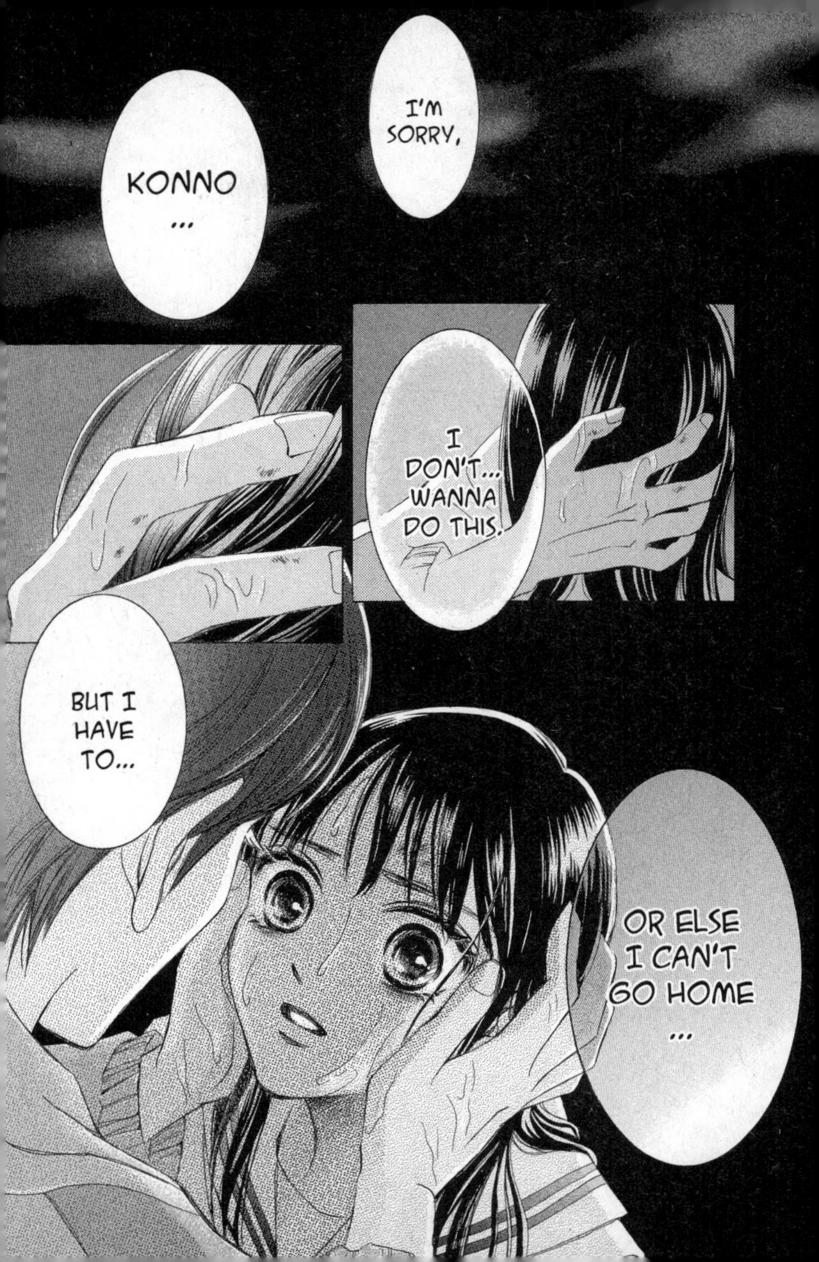
I'M SORRY,
KONNO ...
I DON'T... WANNA DO THIS.
BUT I HAVE TO...
OR ELSE I CAN'T GO HOME ...

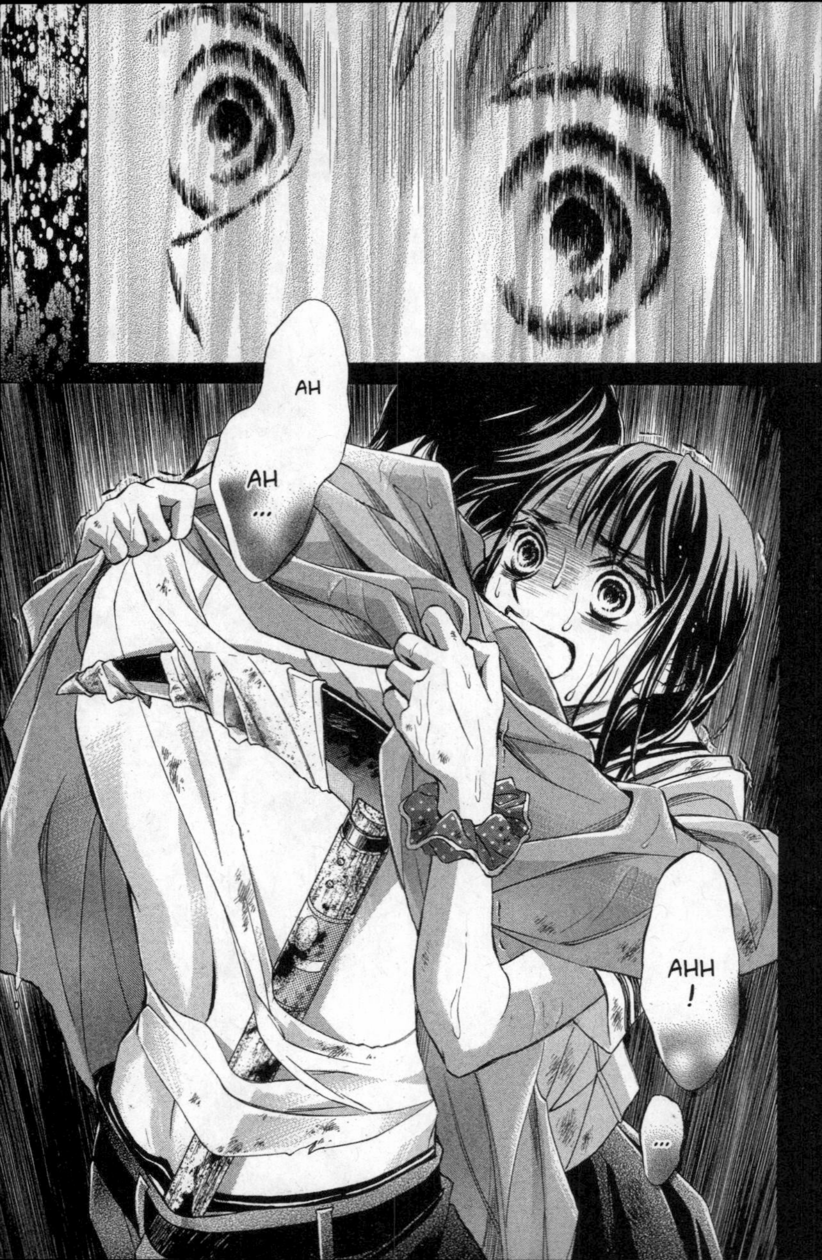
AH
AH
...
AHH!
...

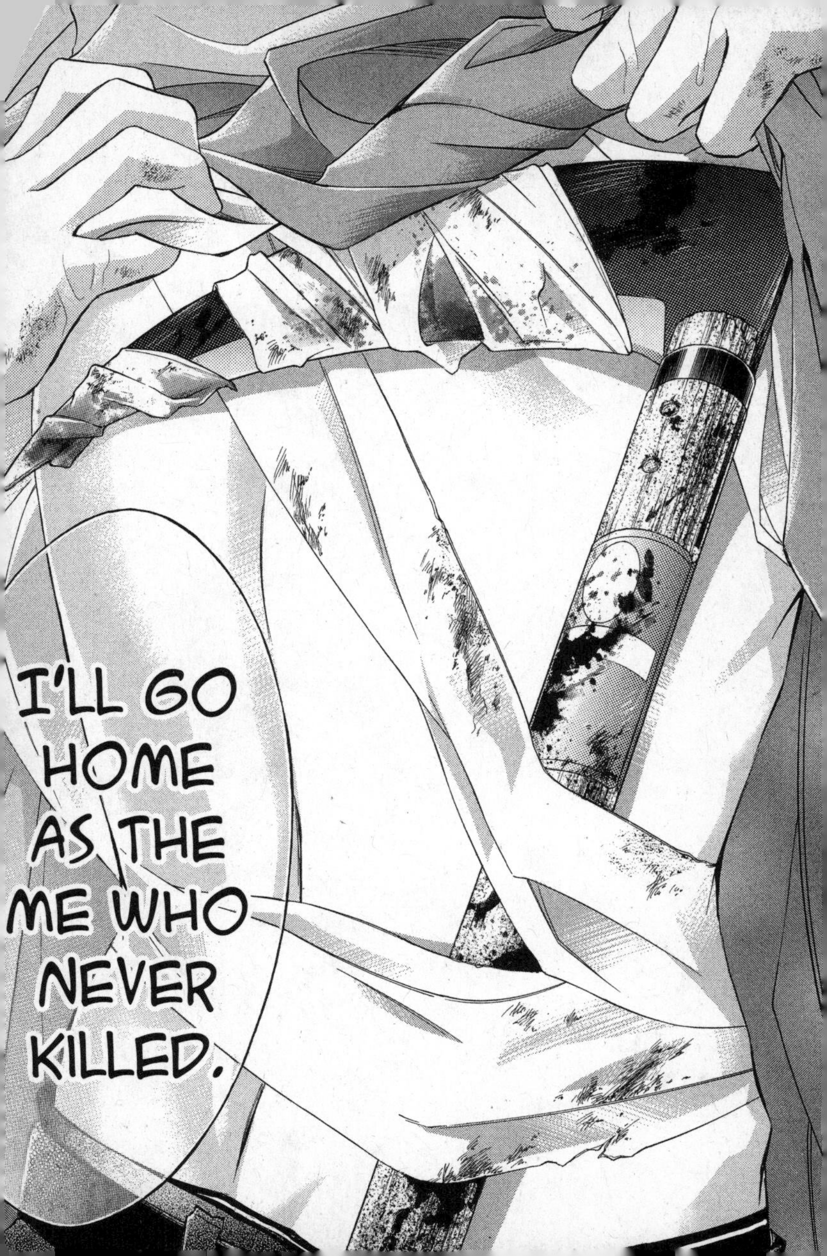
I'LL GO HOME AS THE ME WHO NEVER KILLED.

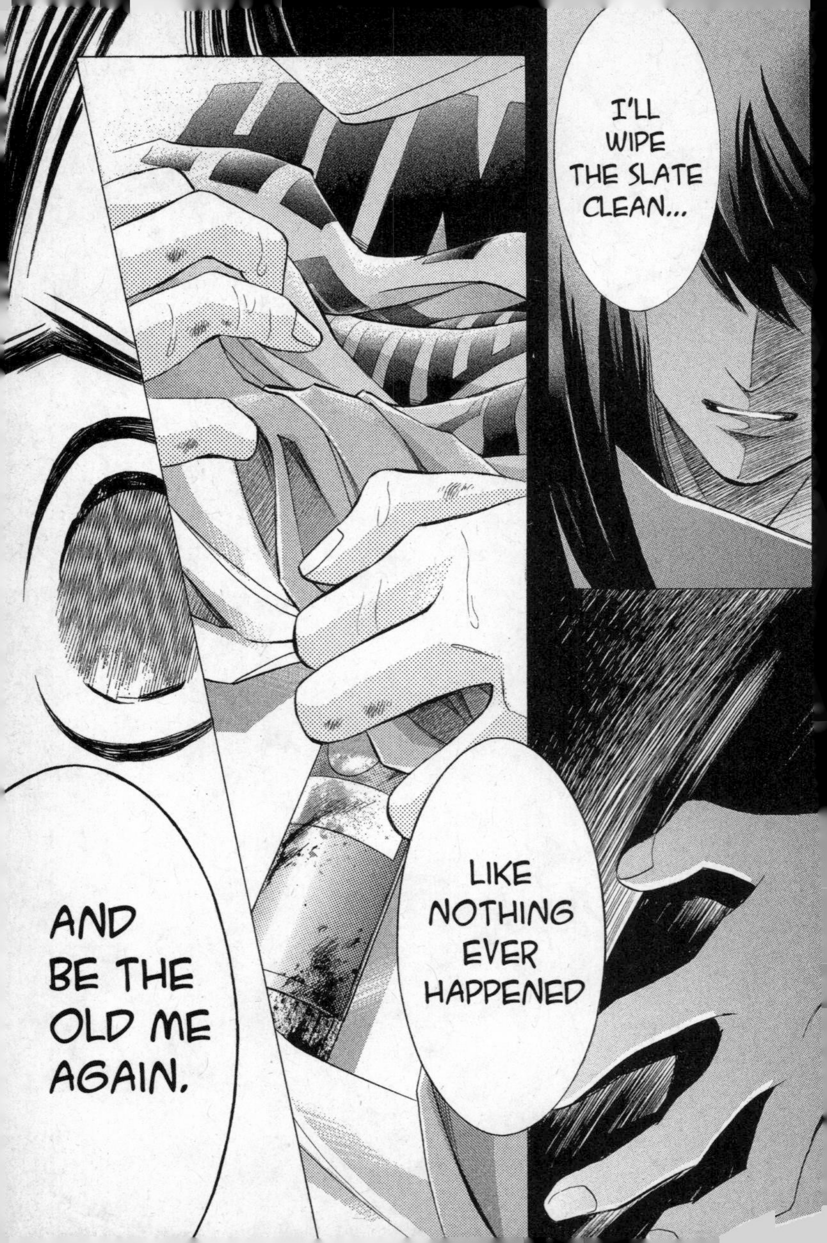
I'LL WIPE THE SLATE CLEAN...
LIKE NOTHING EVER HAPPENED
AND BE THE OLD ME AGAIN.

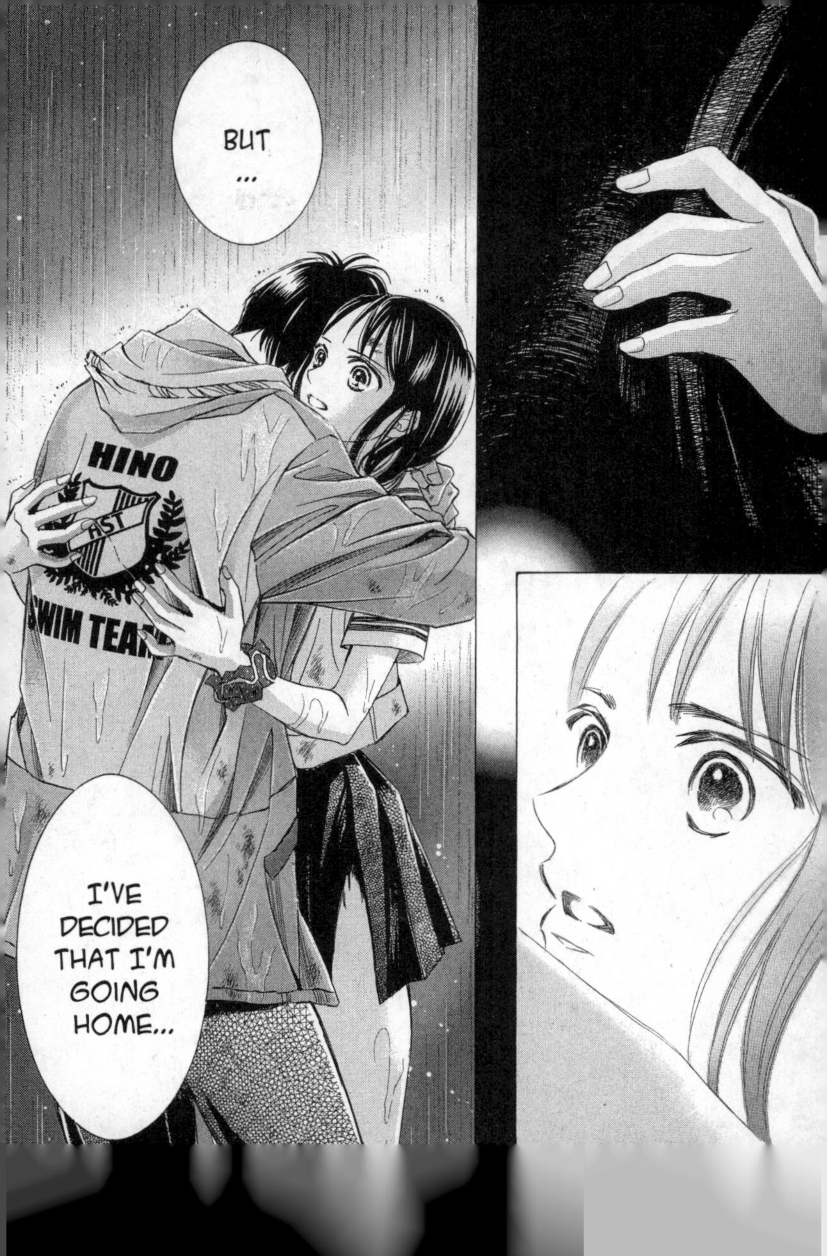
BUT ...
I'VE DECIDED THAT I'M GOING HOME...
HINO
HST

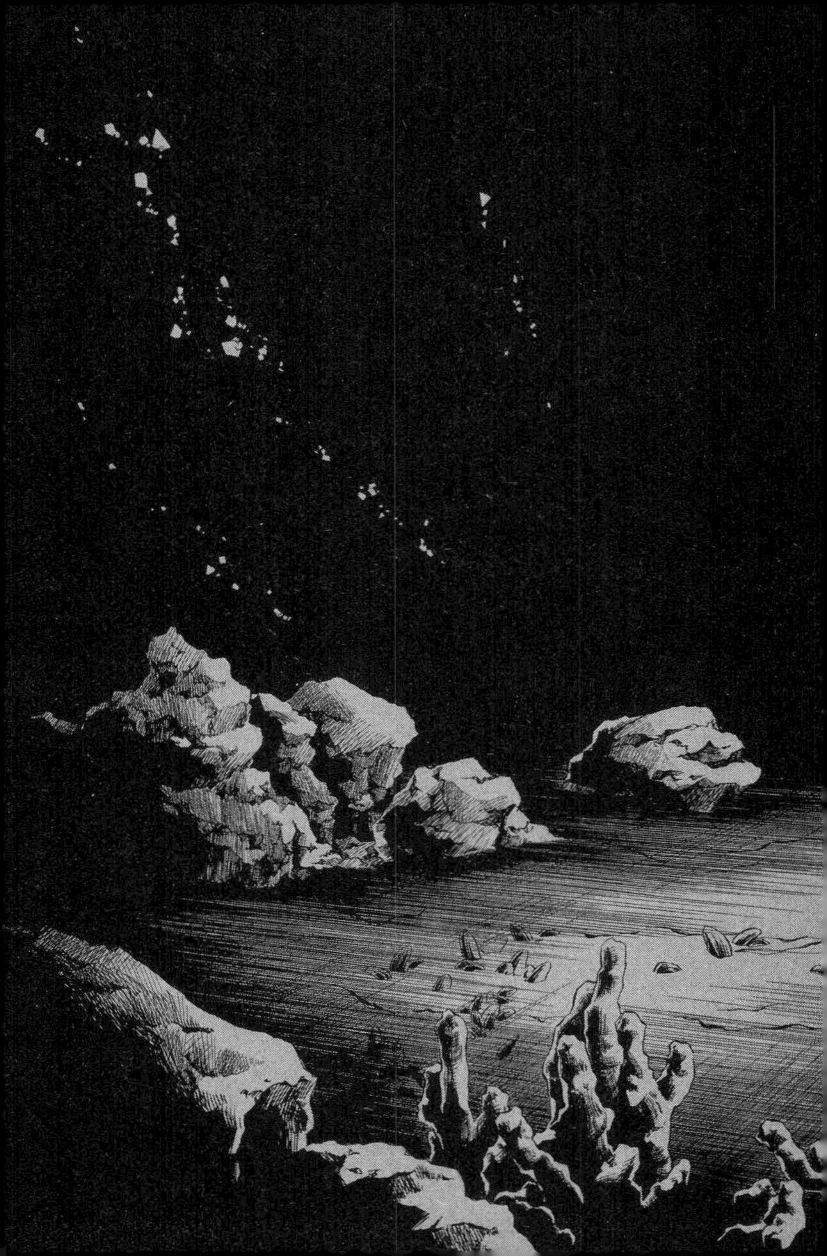

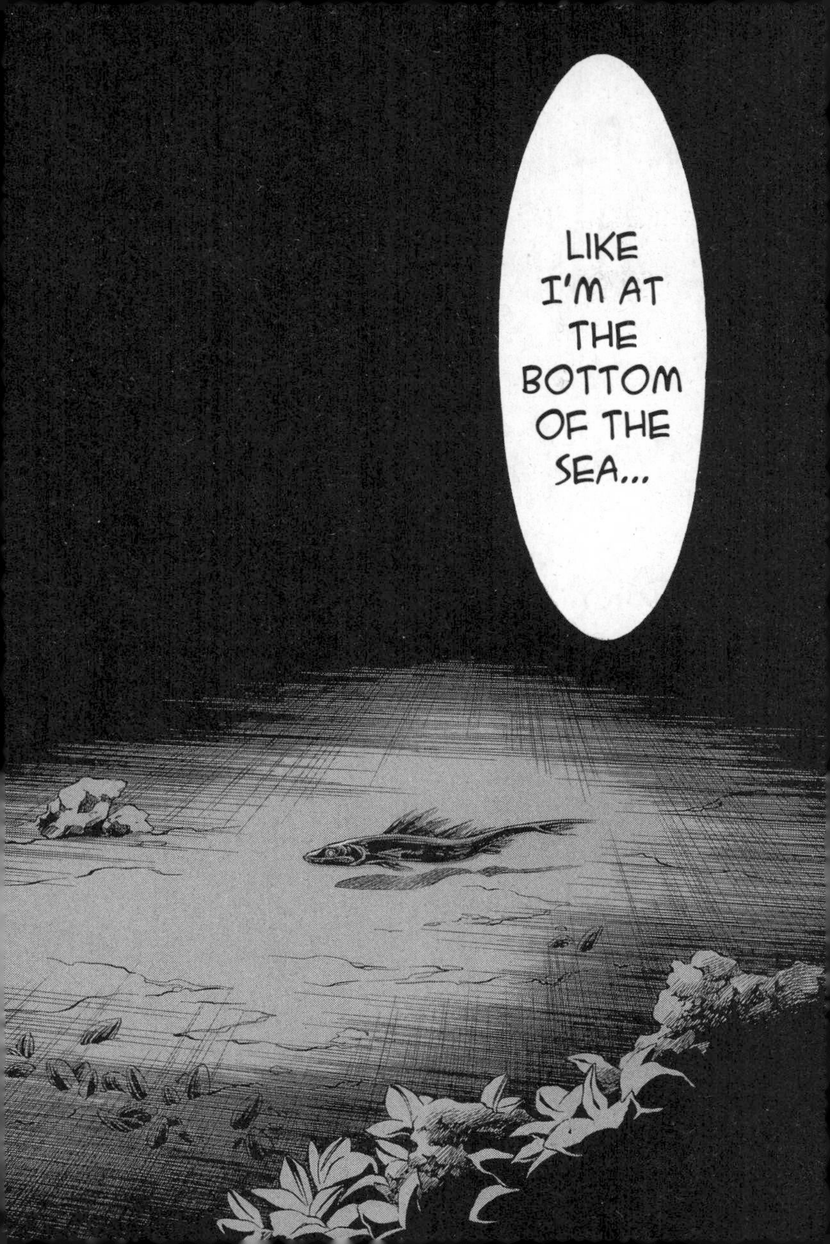
LIKE I'M AT THE BOTTOM OF THE SEA...

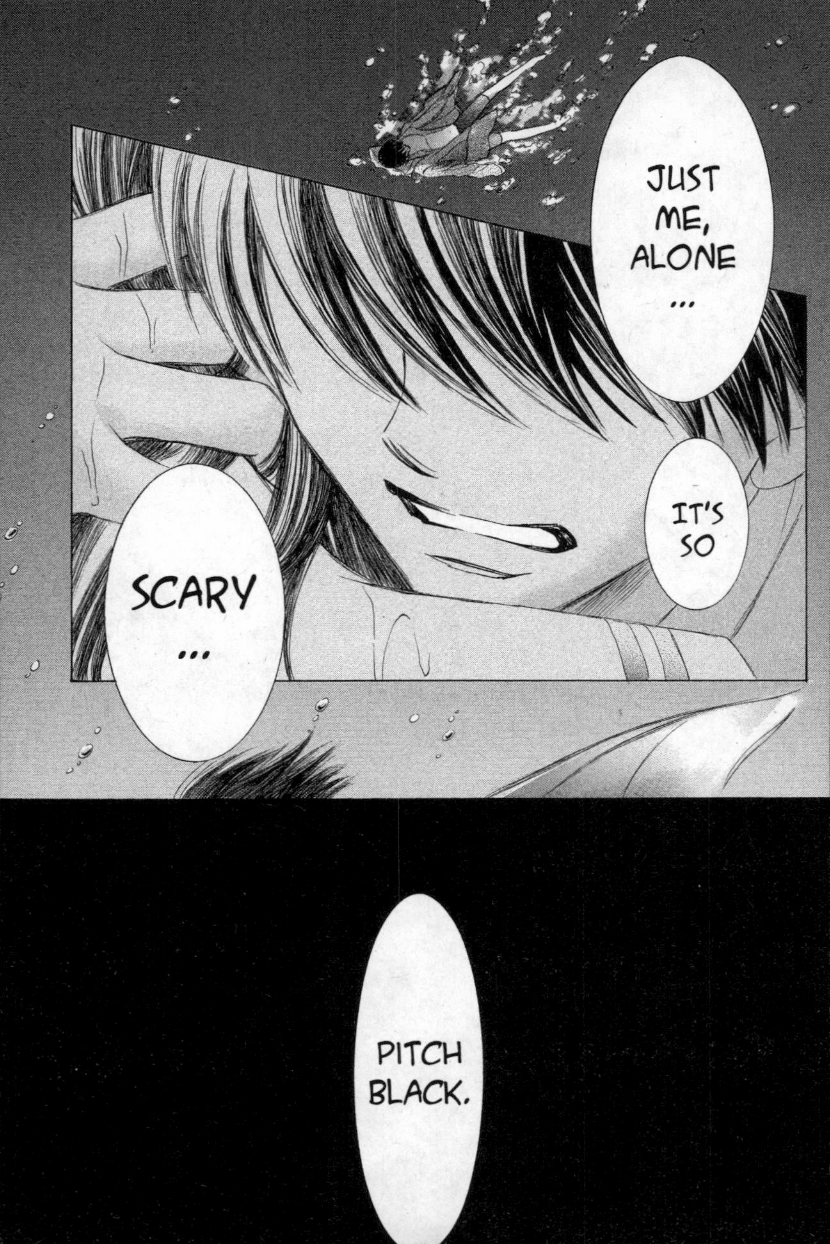

JUST ME, ALONE ...
IT'S SO
SCARY ...
PITCH BLACK.

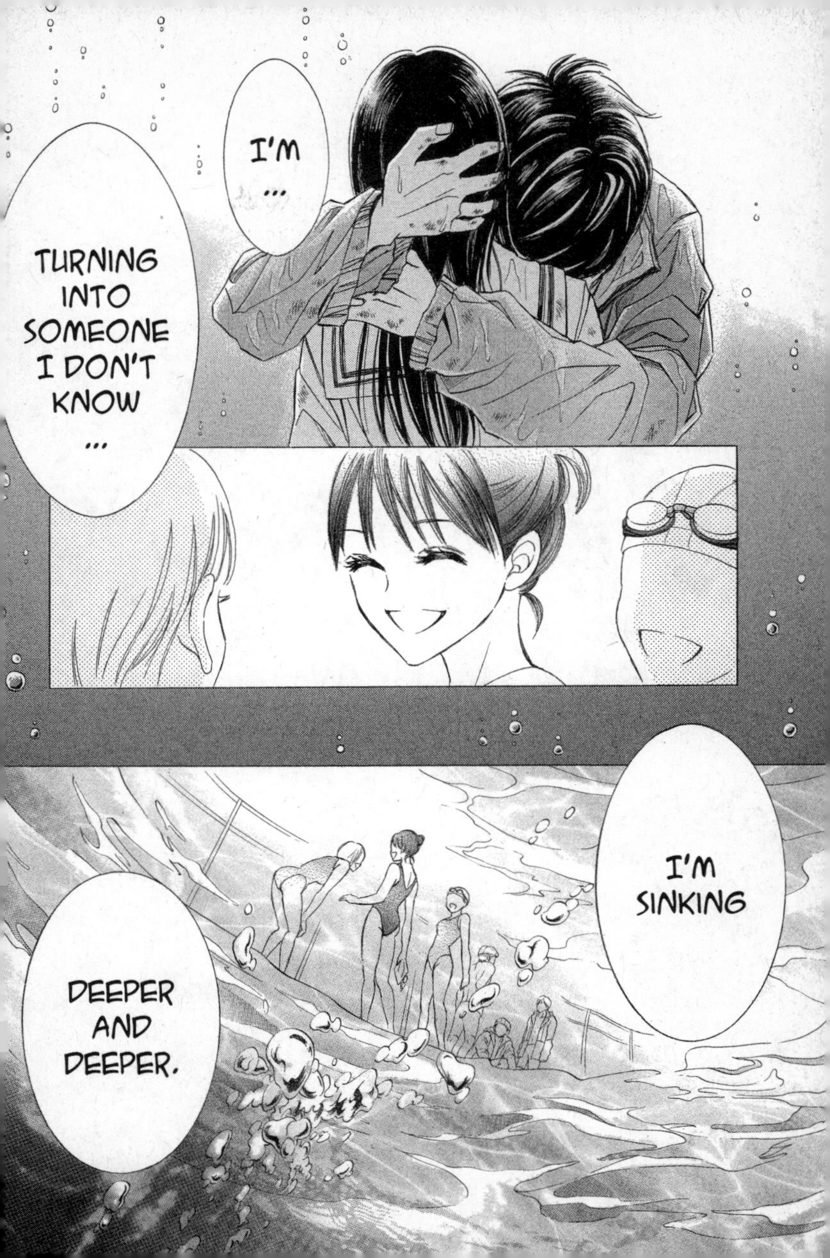

I'M ...
TURNING INTO SOMEONE I DON'T KNOW ...
I'M SINKING
DEEPER AND DEEPER.

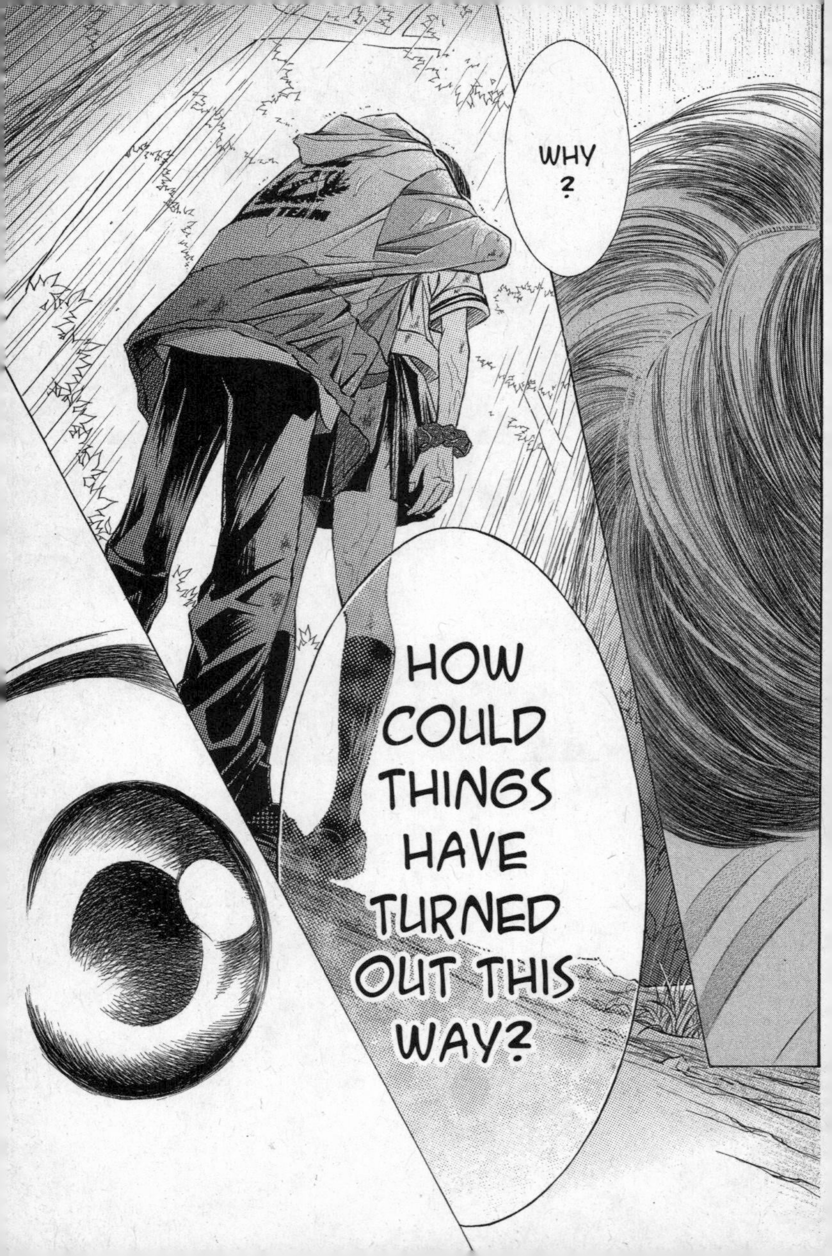
WHY?
HOW COULD THINGS HAVE TURNED OUT THIS WAY?

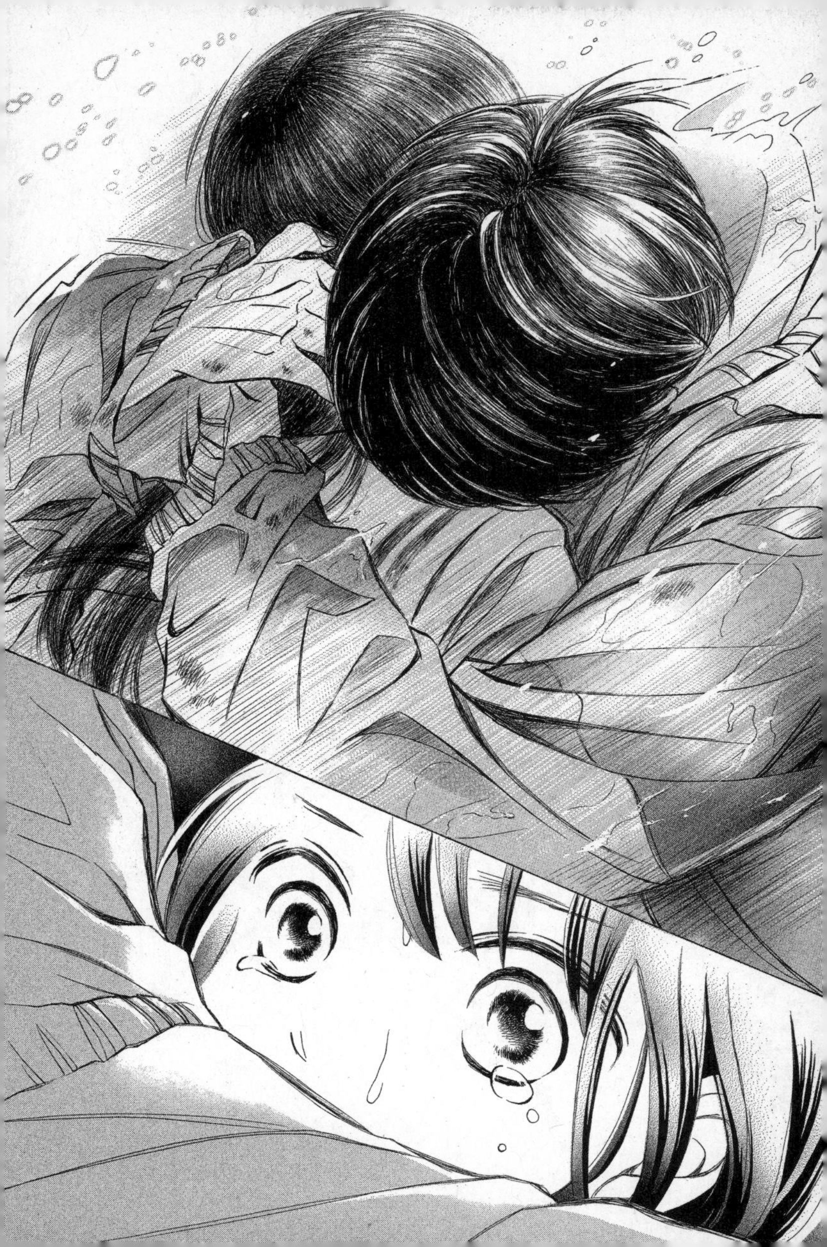

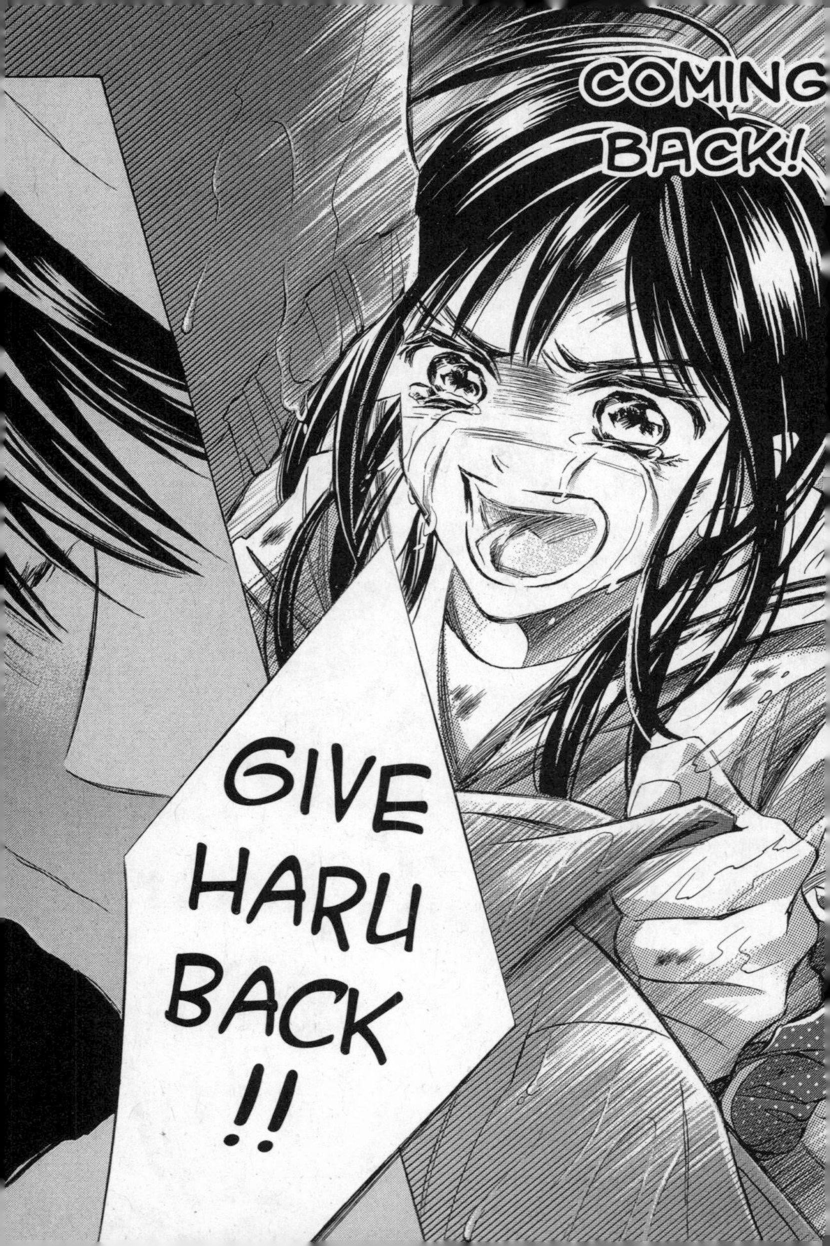
COMING BACK!
GIVE HARU BACK!!

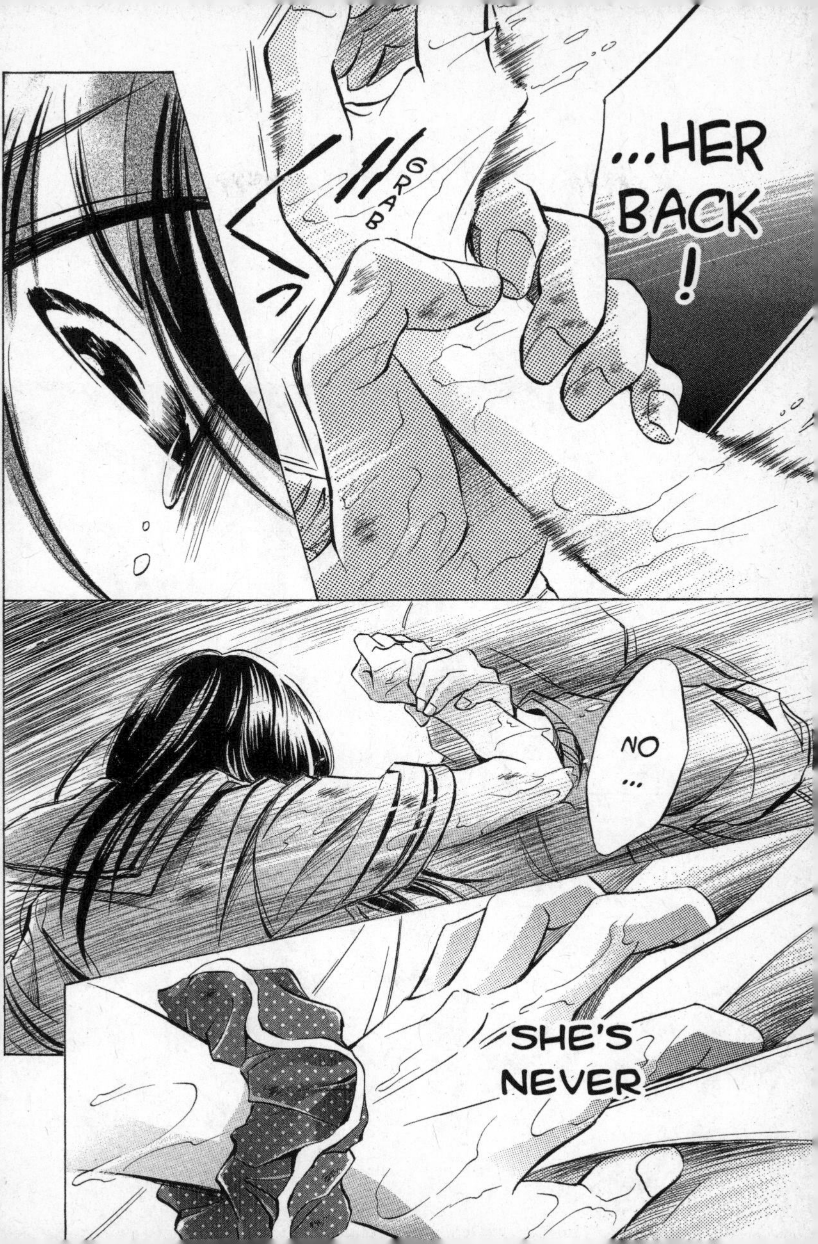
...HER BACK!
GRAB
NO ...
SHE'S NEVER

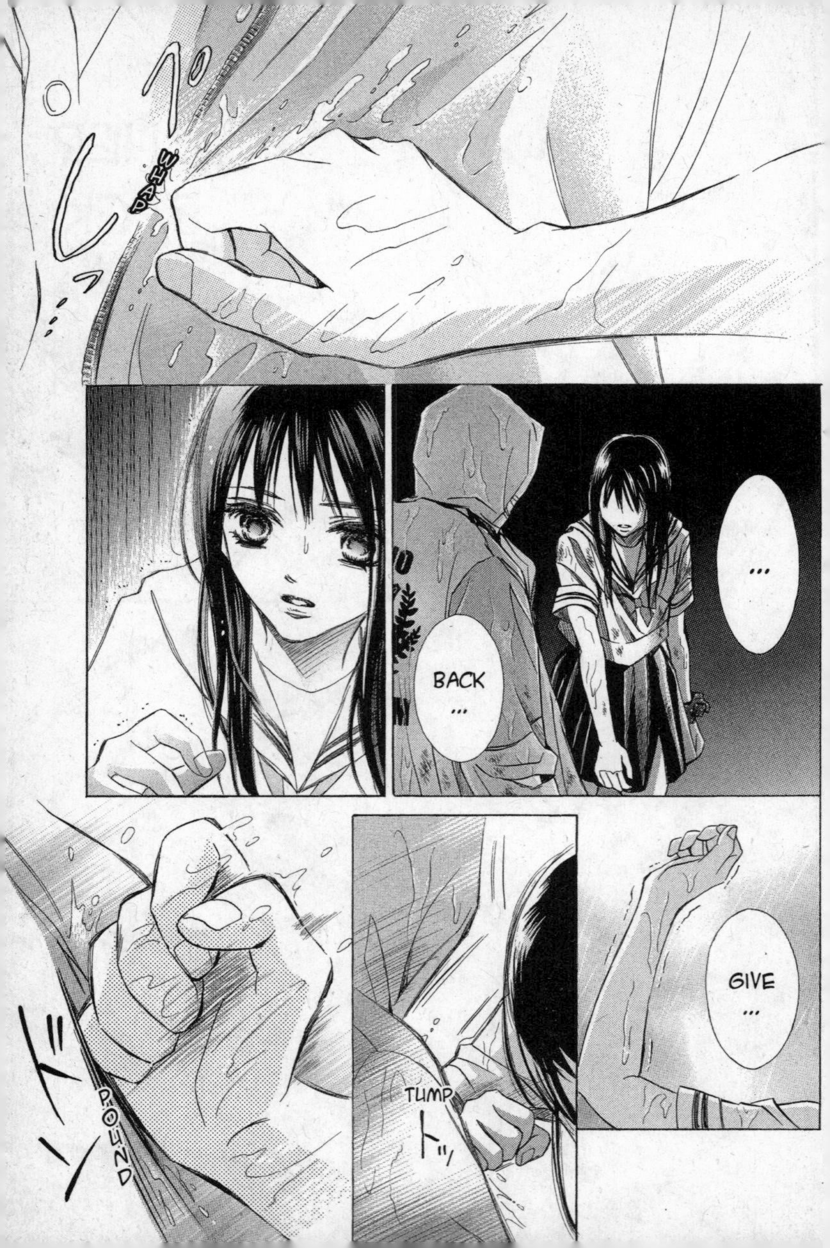
WHAP
...
BACK ...
GIVE ...
TUMP
POUND

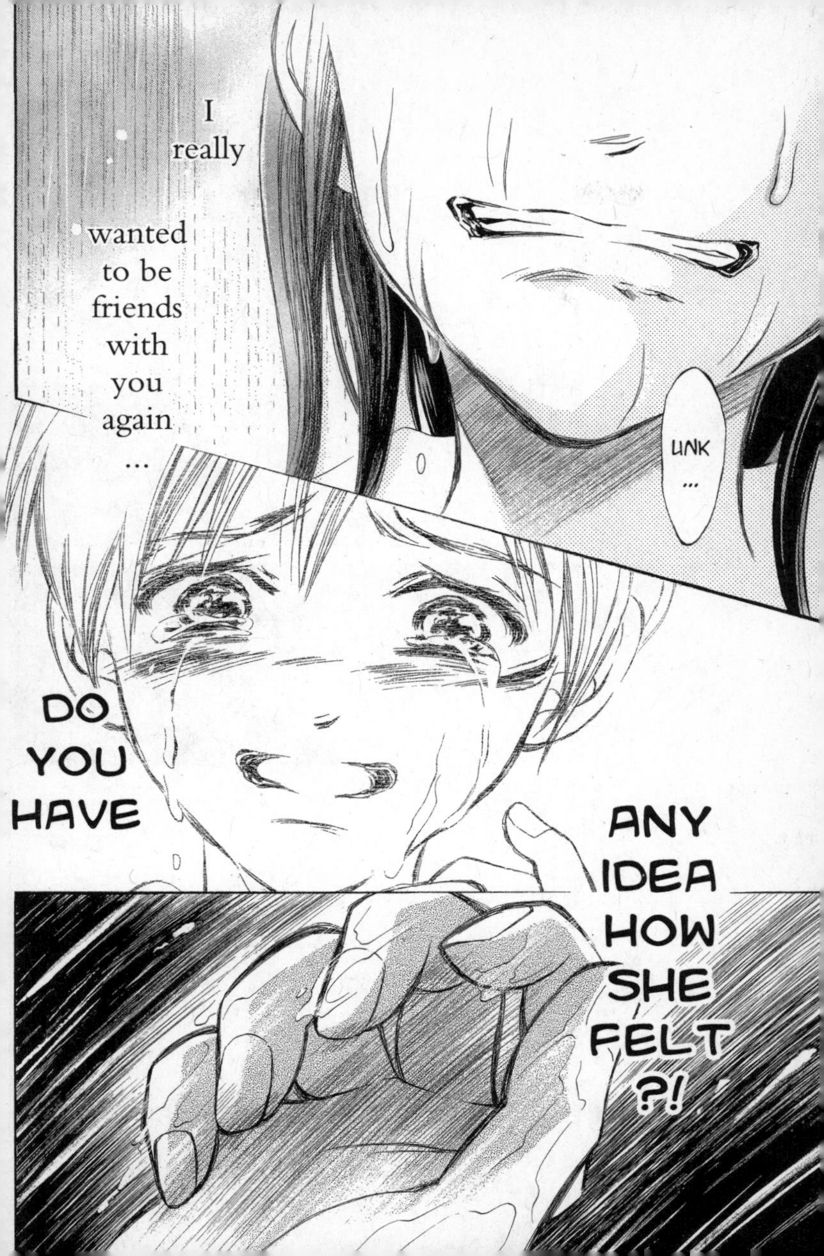

I really wanted to be friends with you again ...
UNK ...
DO YOU HAVE ANY IDEA HOW SHE FELT ?!

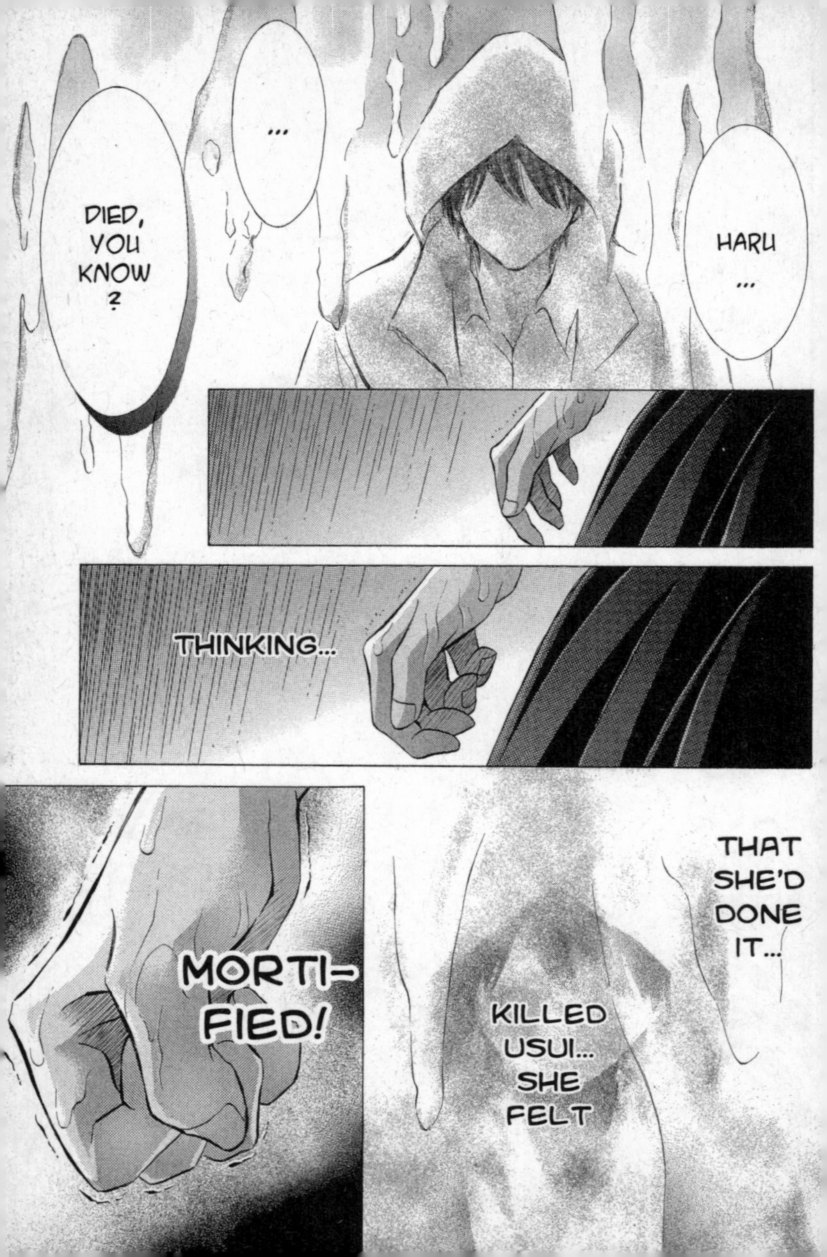
HARU ...
...
DIED, YOU KNOW?
THINKING...
THAT SHE'D DONE IT...
KILLED USUI... SHE FELT
MORTI-FIED!

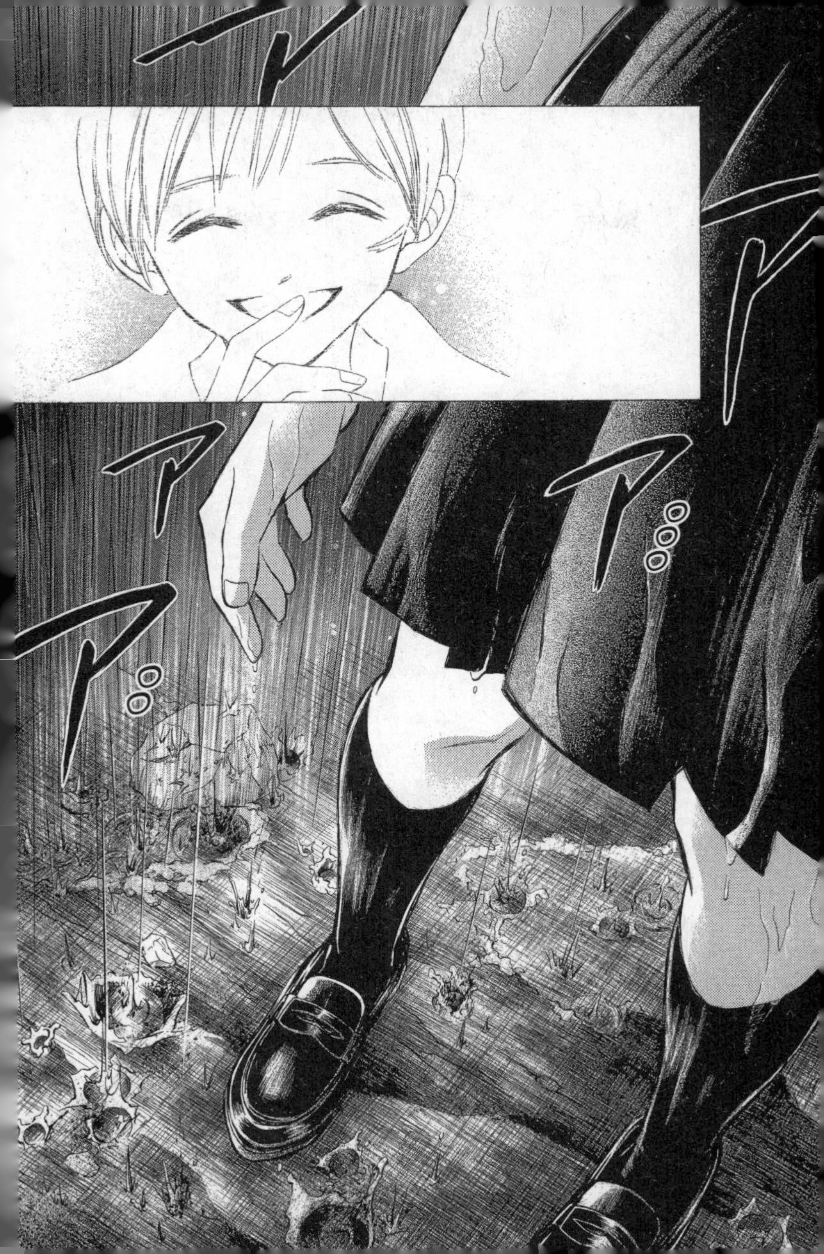

アア…
アア…

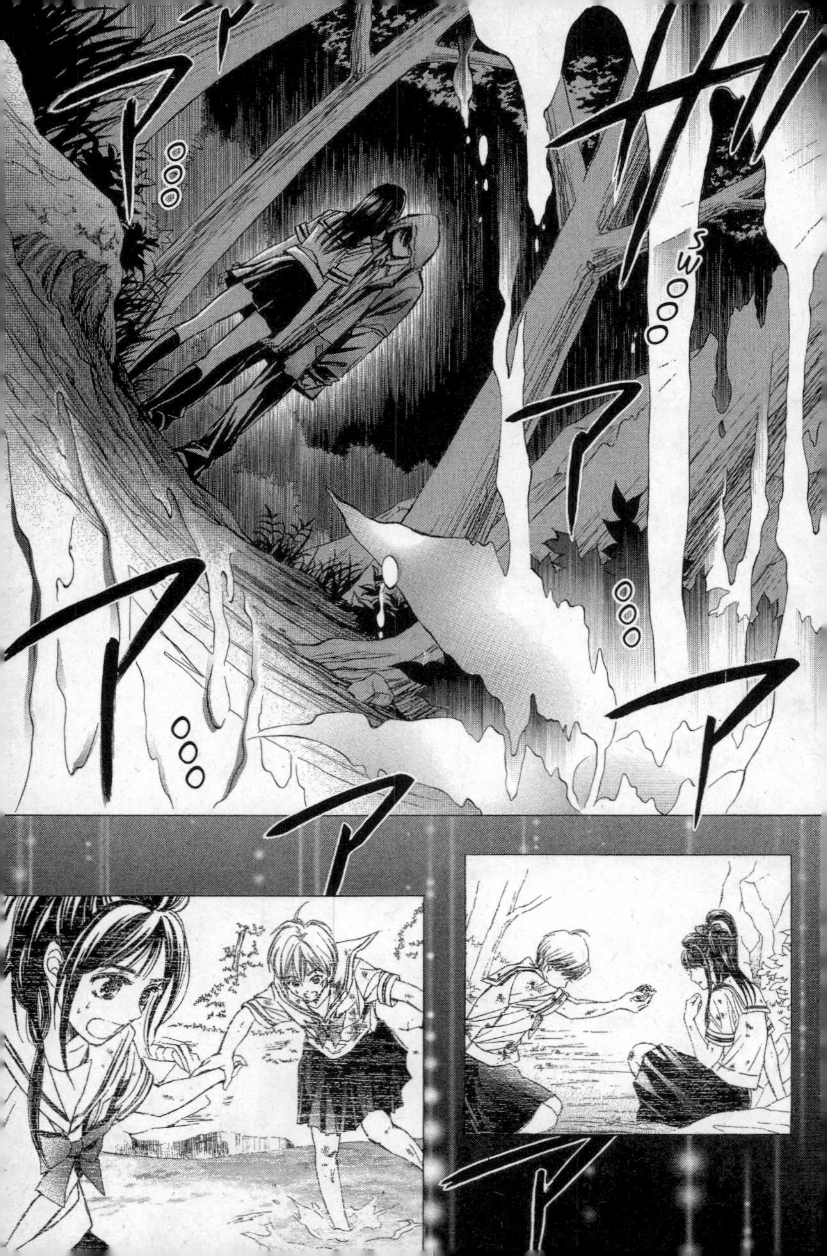
SWOOOO

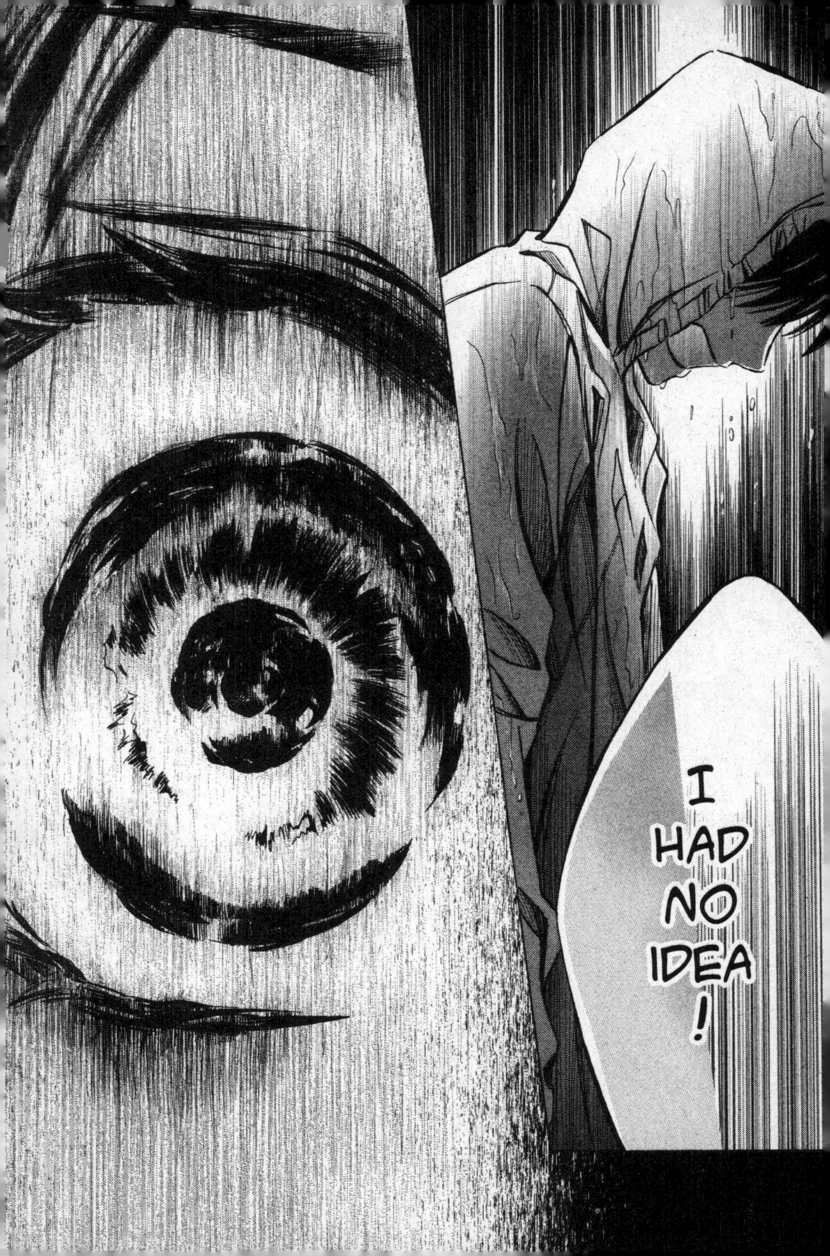
I HAD NO IDEA!

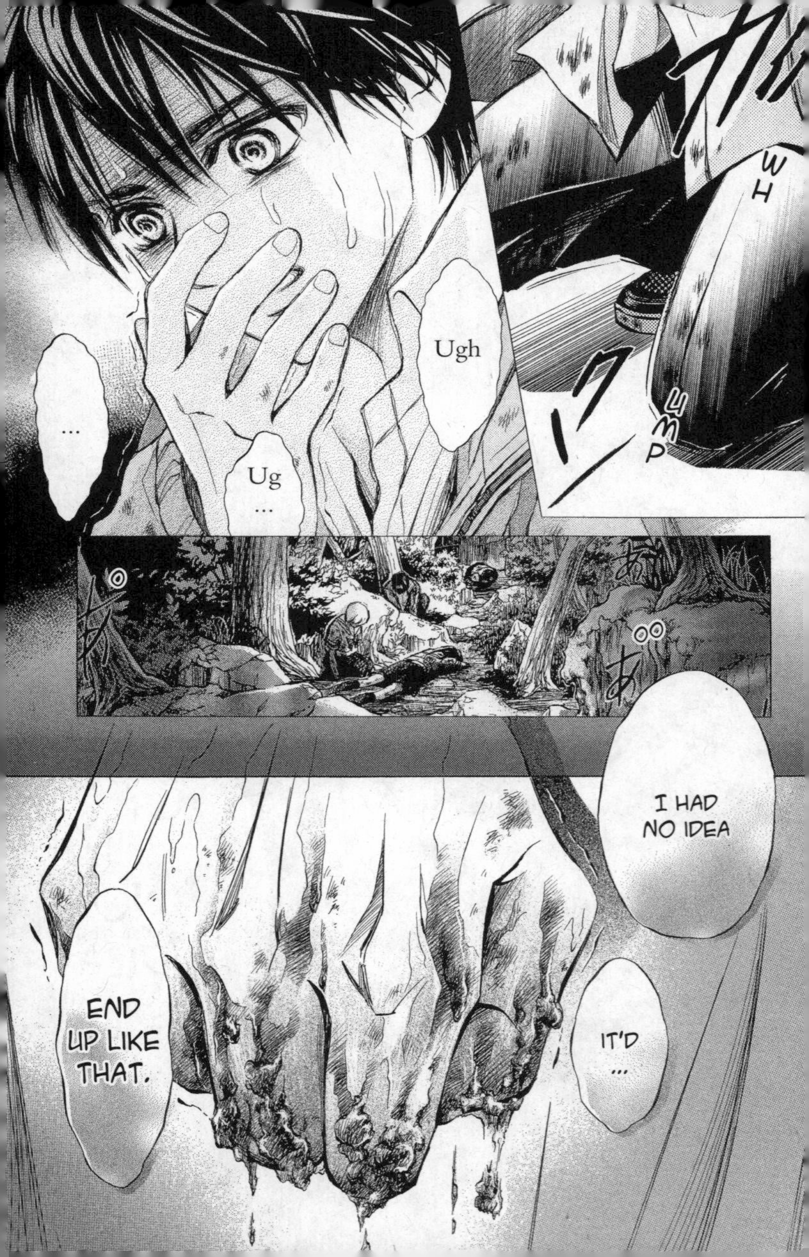
WHUMP
Ugh
Ug ...
...
I HAD NO IDEA
IT'D ...
END UP LIKE THAT.

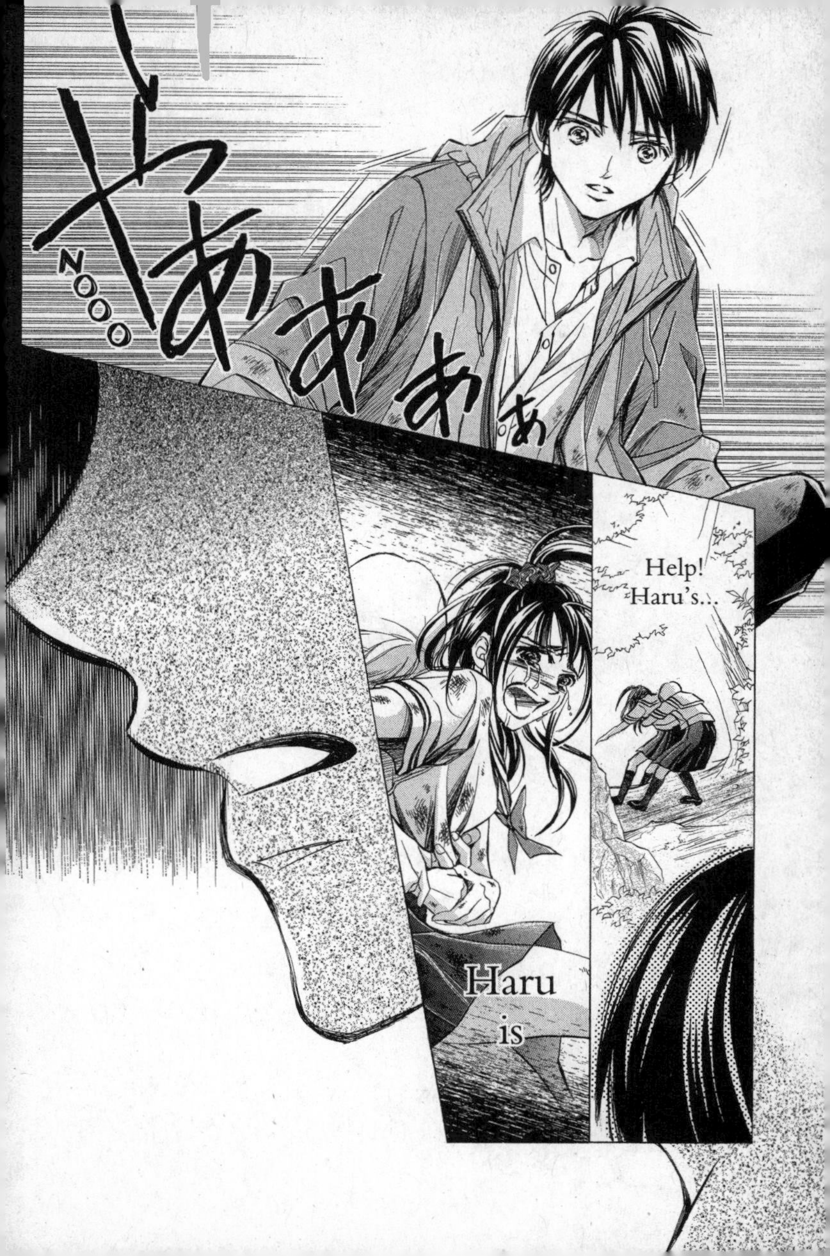
NOOO
Help! Haru's...
Haru is

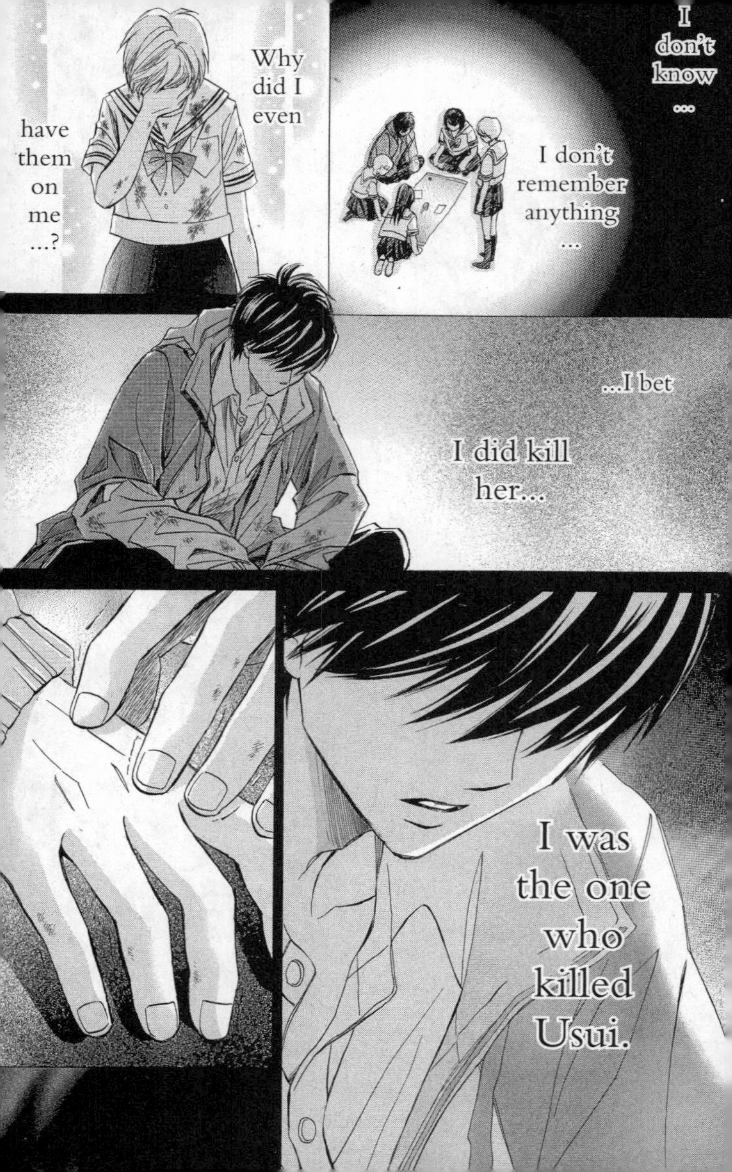
I don't know...
I don't remember anything...
Why did I even have them on me...?
...I bet
I did kill her...
I was the one who killed Usui.

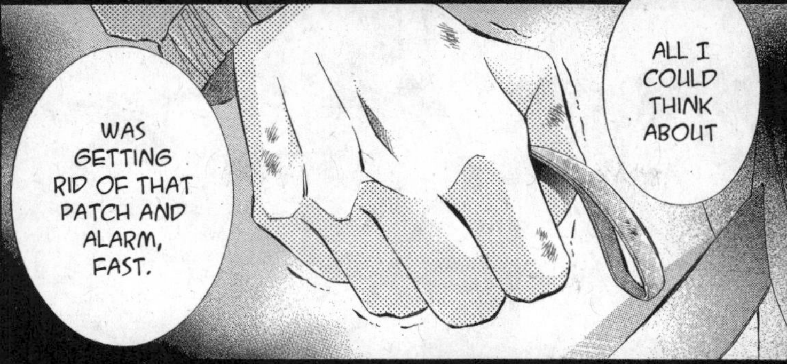
ALL I COULD THINK ABOUT
WAS GETTING RID OF THAT PATCH AND ALARM, FAST.

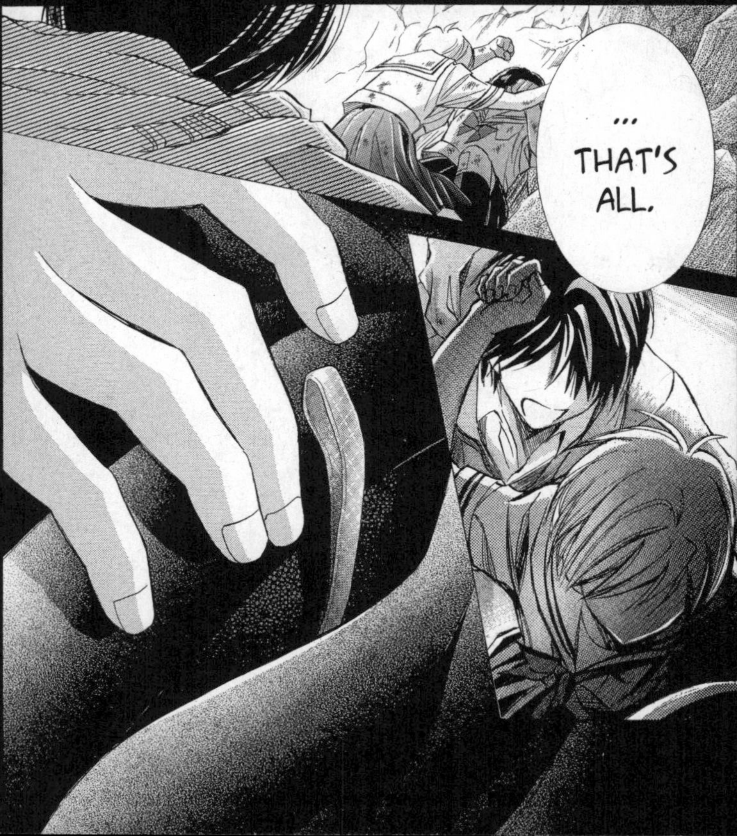
... THAT'S ALL.

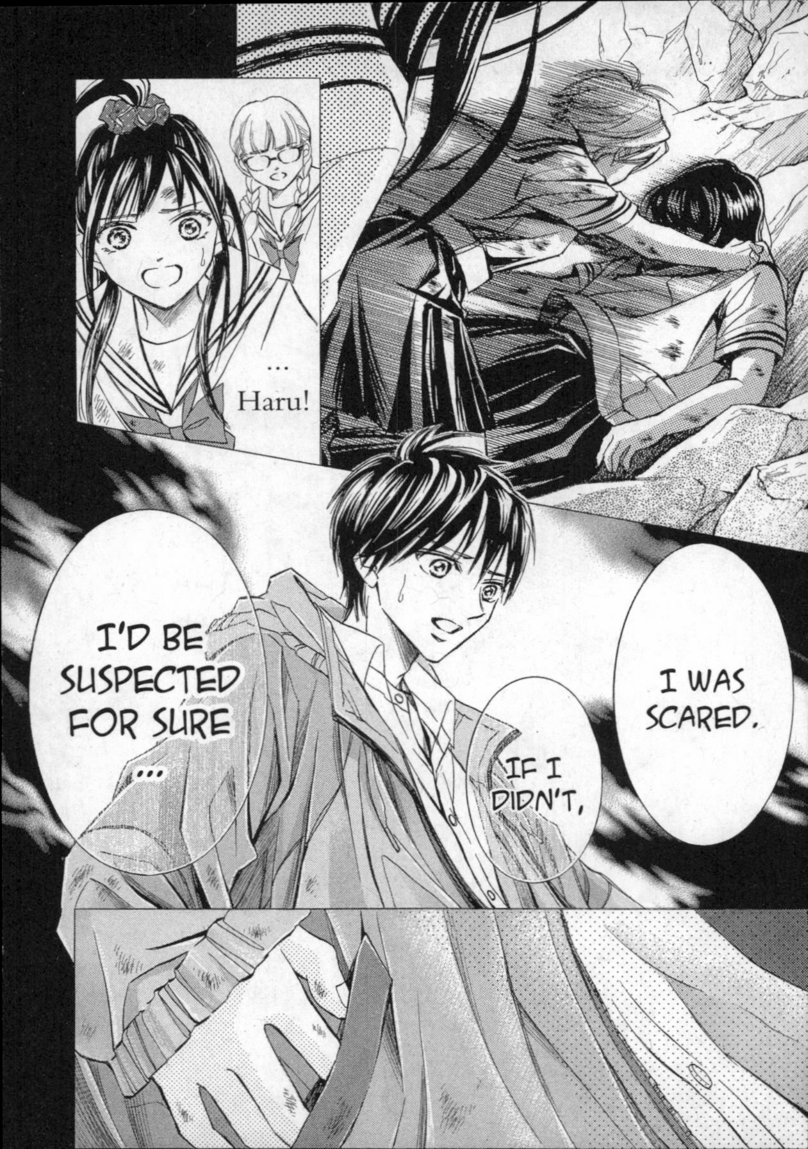
...
Haru!
I WAS SCARED.
IF I DIDN'T,
I'D BE SUSPECTED FOR SURE
...

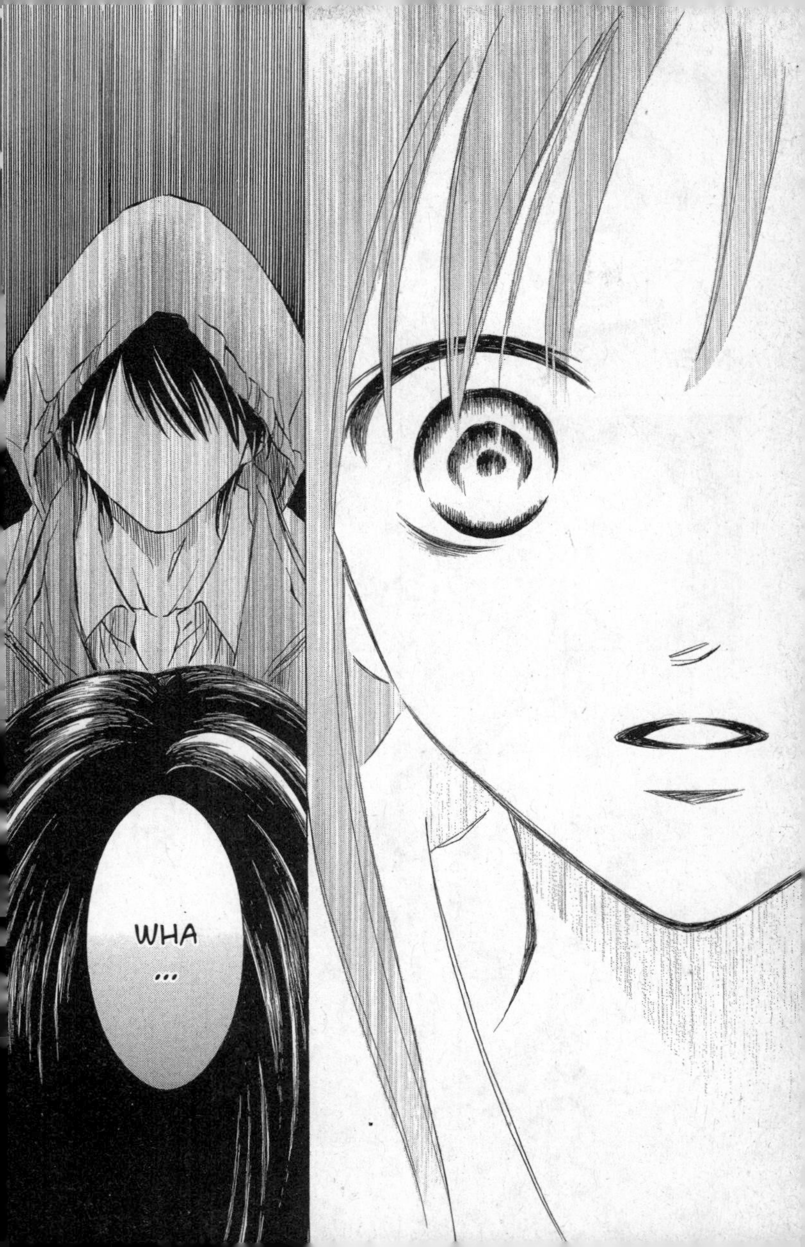
WHA ...

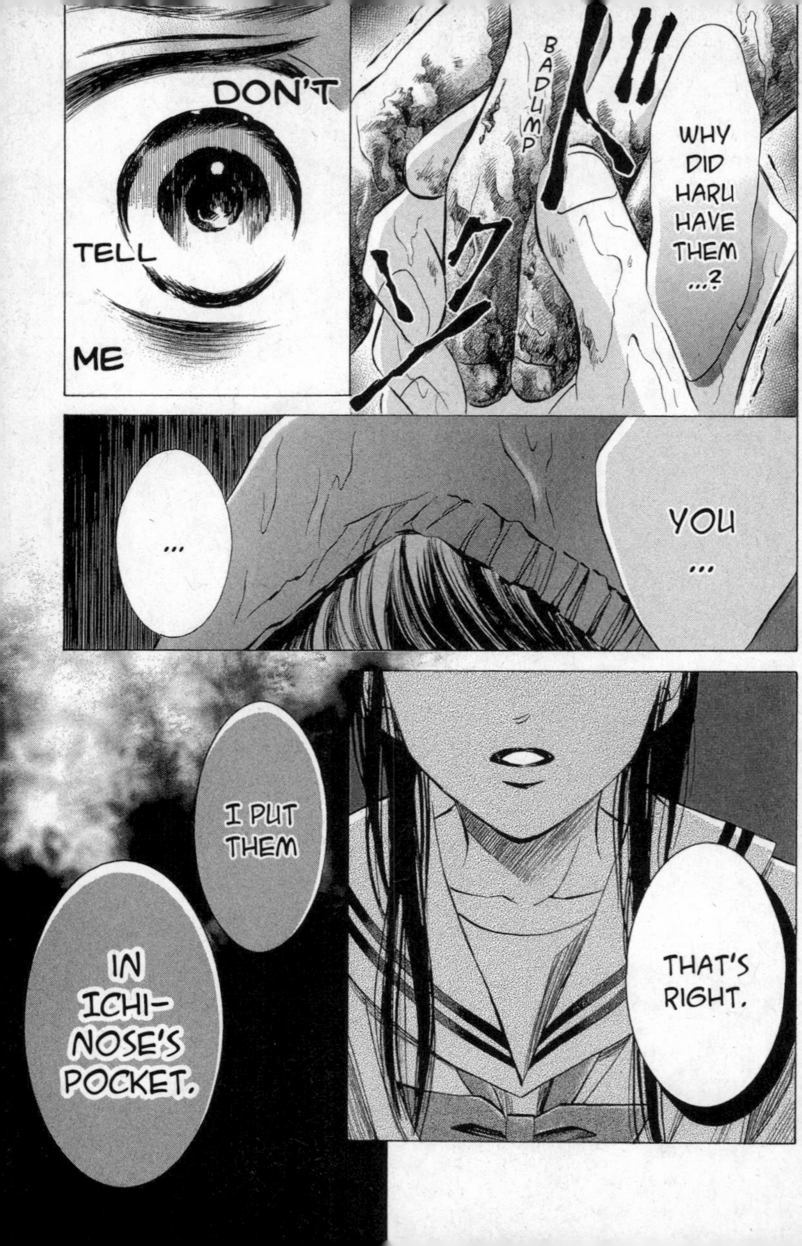
BADUMP
WHY DID HARU HAVE THEM ...?
DON'T
TELL
ME
YOU ...
...
THAT'S RIGHT.
I PUT THEM
IN ICHI-NOSE'S POCKET.

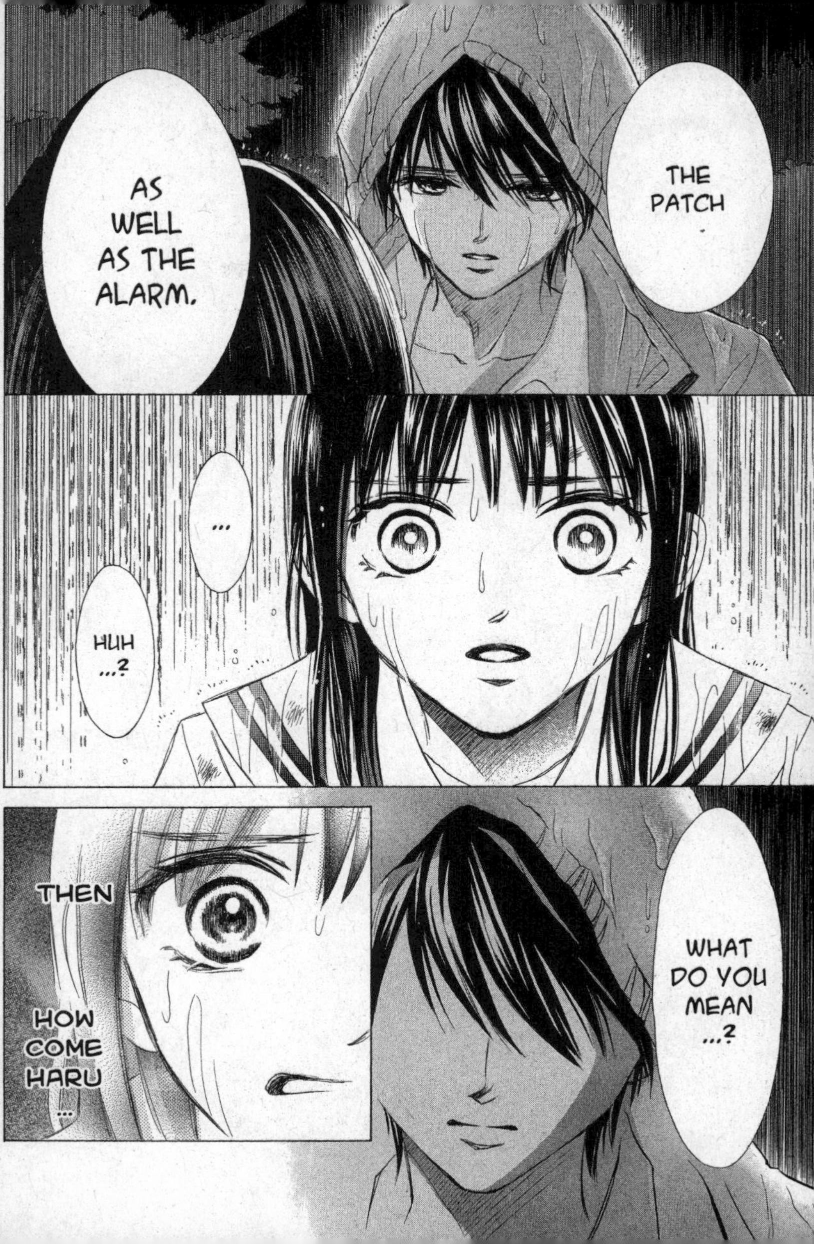
THE PATCH.
AS WELL AS THE ALARM.
...
HUH ...?
WHAT DO YOU MEAN ...?
THEN
HOW COME HARU ...

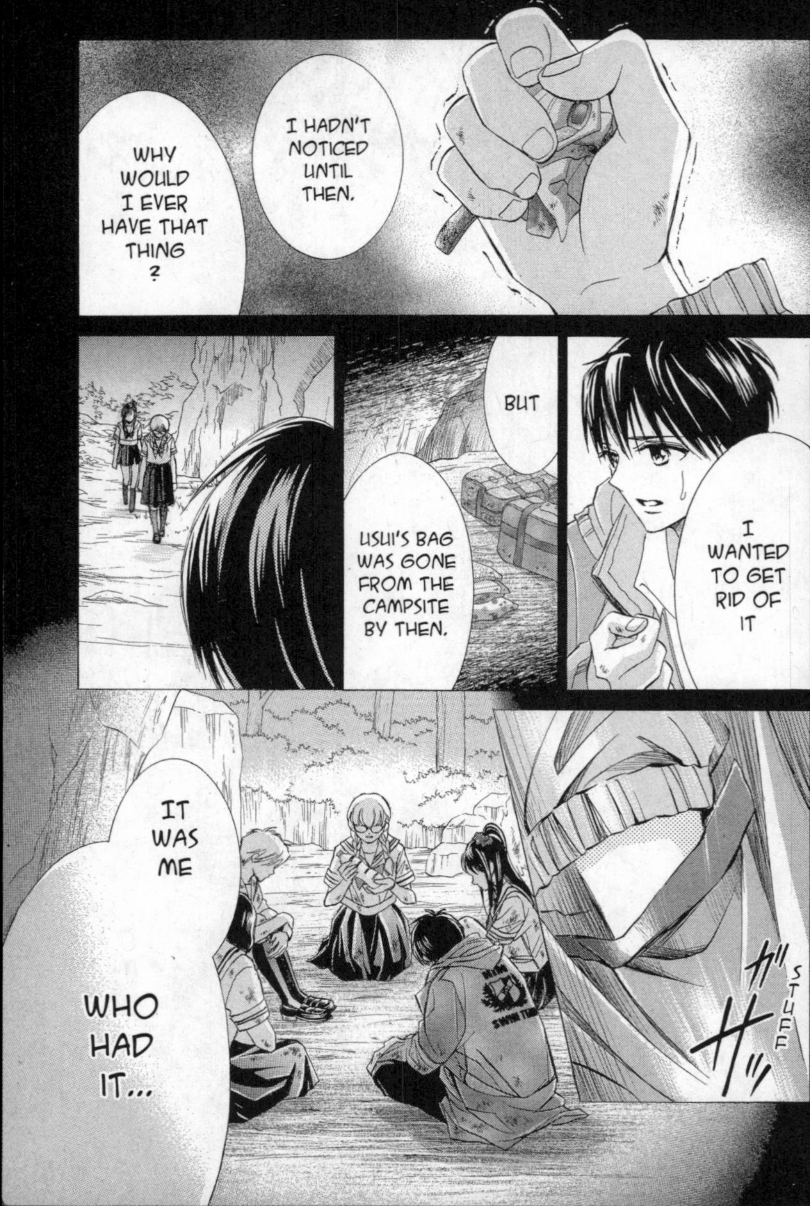
I HADN'T NOTICED UNTIL THEN.
WHY WOULD I EVER HAVE THAT THING?
I WANTED TO GET RID OF IT
BUT
USUI'S BAG WAS GONE FROM THE CAMPSITE BY THEN.
STUFF
IT WAS ME
WHO HAD IT...

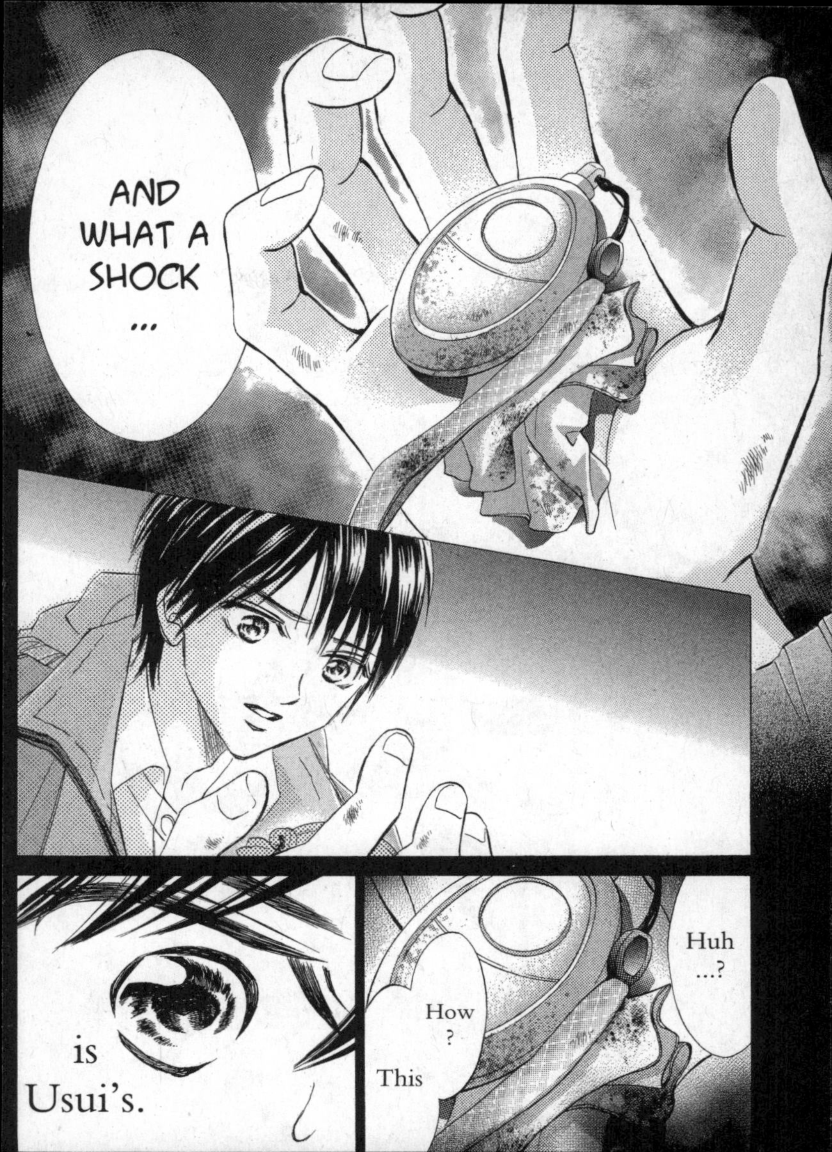
AND WHAT A SHOCK ...
Huh ...?
How ?
This
is Usui's.

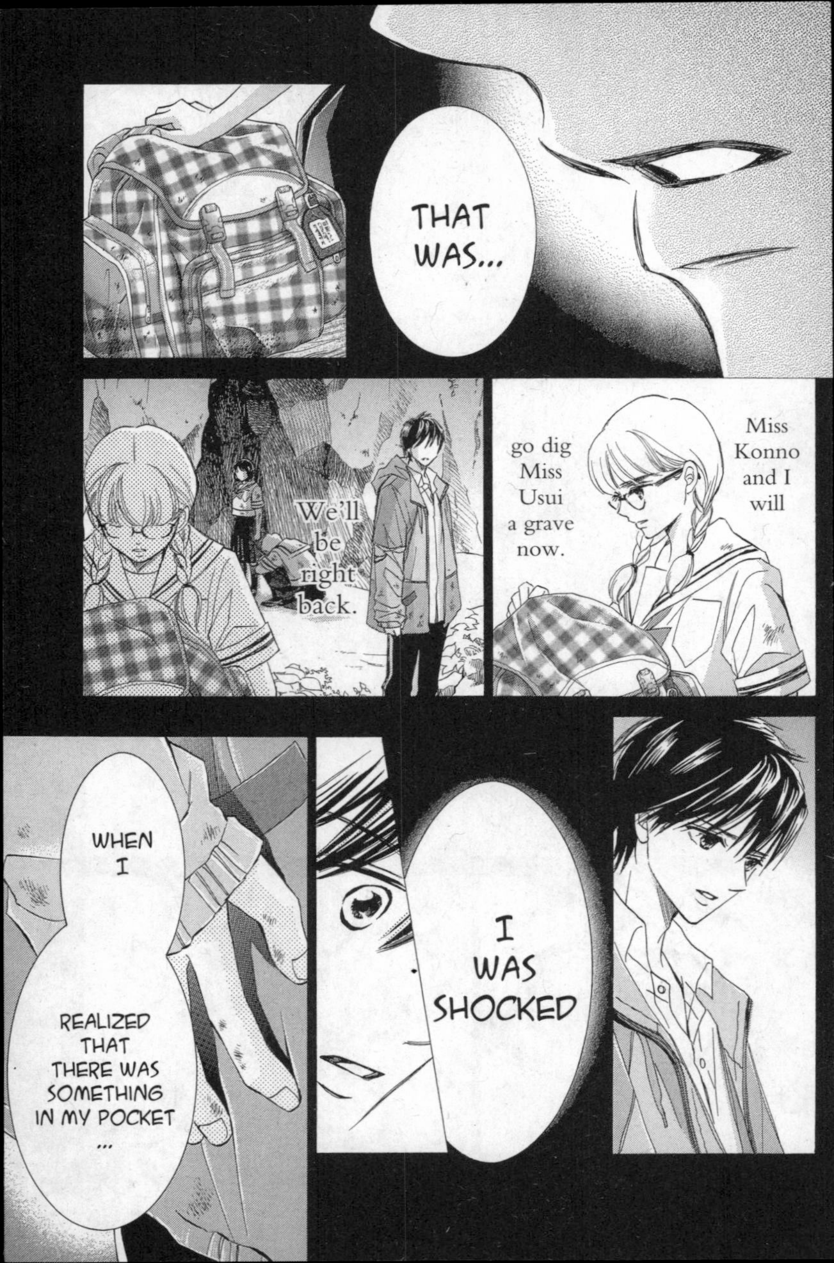
THAT WAS...
Miss Konno and I will go dig Miss Usui a grave now.
We'll be right back.
I WAS SHOCKED
WHEN I REALIZED THAT THERE WAS SOMETHING IN MY POCKET ...

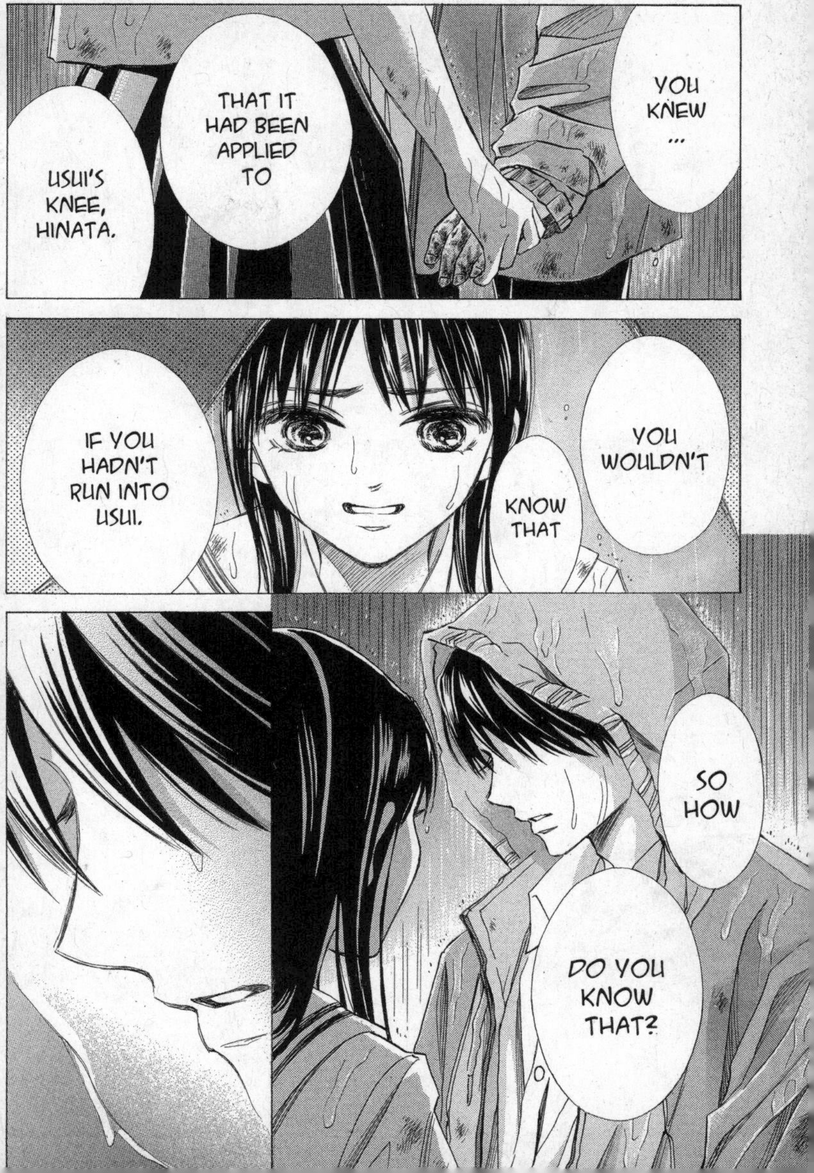
YOU KNEW ...
THAT IT HAD BEEN APPLIED TO
USUI'S KNEE, HINATA.
YOU WOULDN'T
KNOW THAT
IF YOU HADN'T RUN INTO USUI.
SO HOW
DO YOU KNOW THAT?

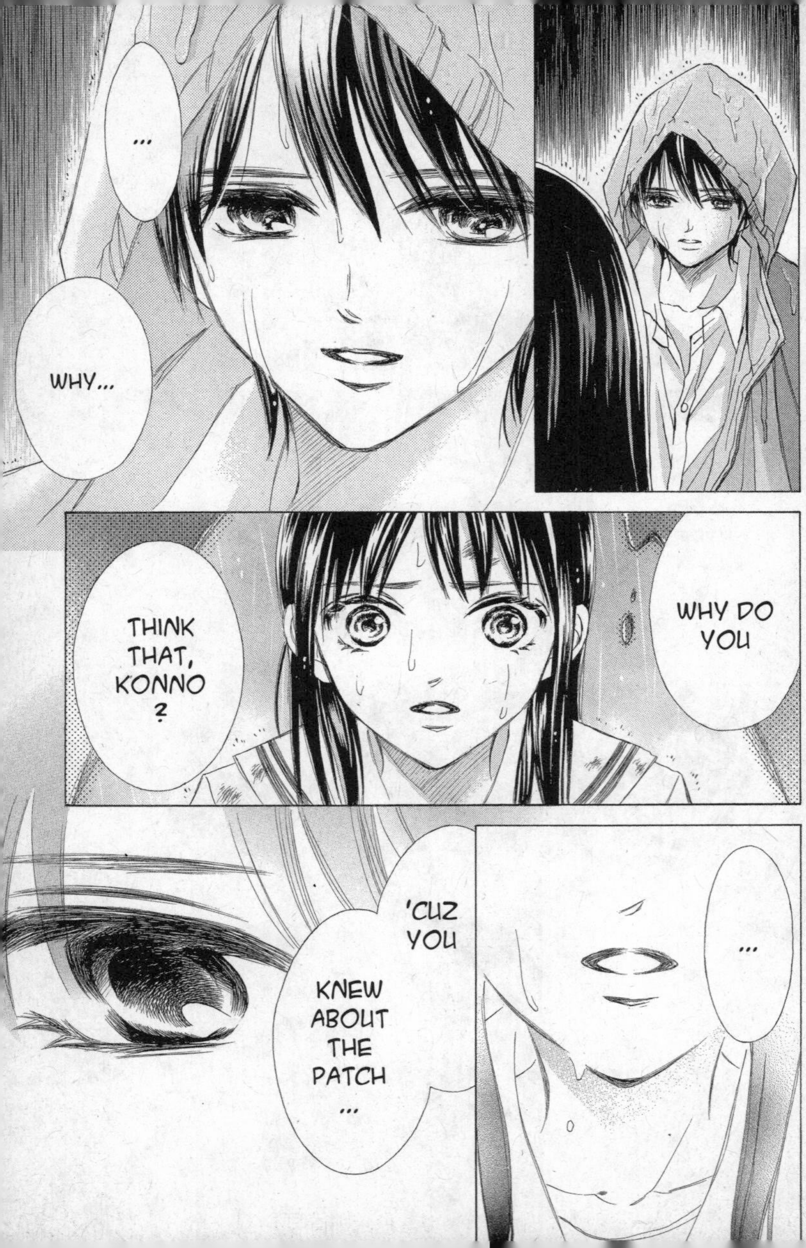
...
WHY...
WHY DO YOU
THINK THAT, KONNO?
...
'CUZ YOU KNEW ABOUT THE PATCH...

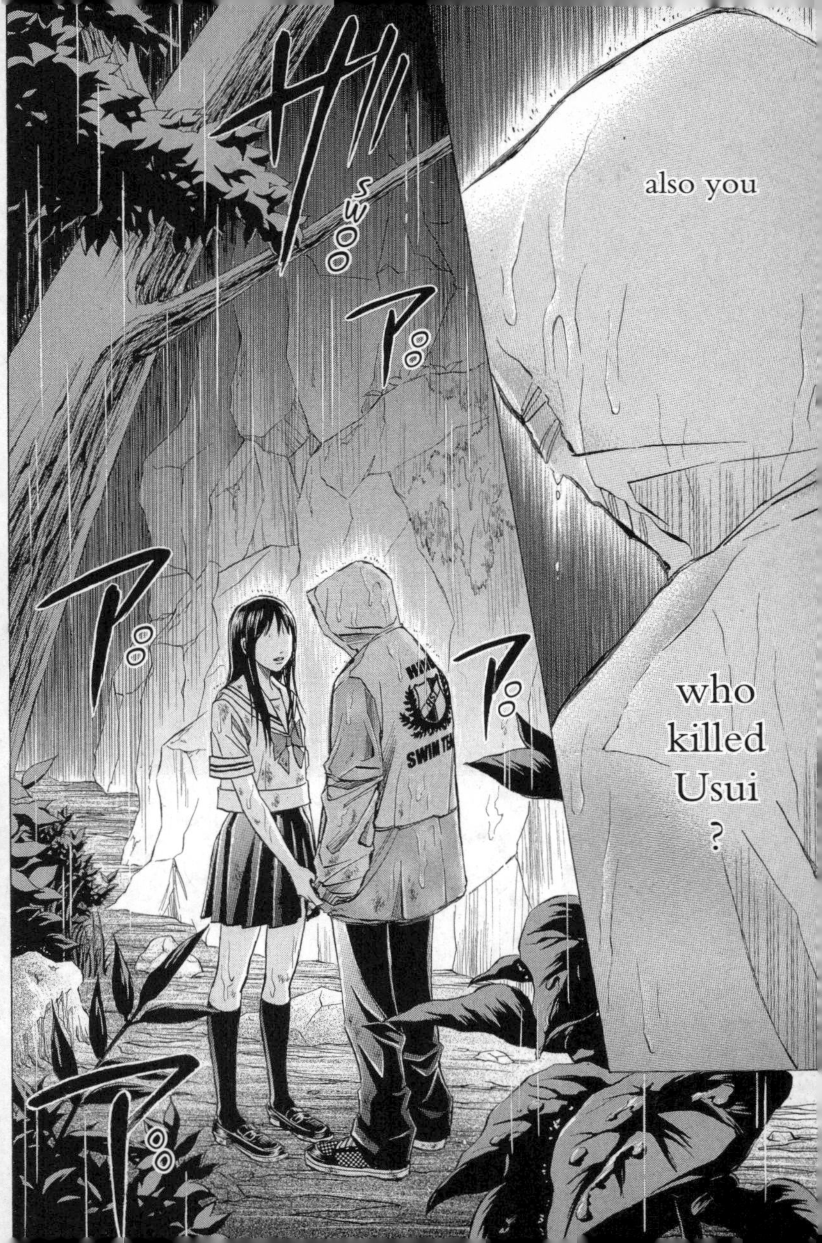
also you
ザ
swoo
ア
ア
ア
ア
who killed Usui ?

...But
the one

who
actually
ran away
from
Morishige
was you,
Hinata,
wasn't
it?

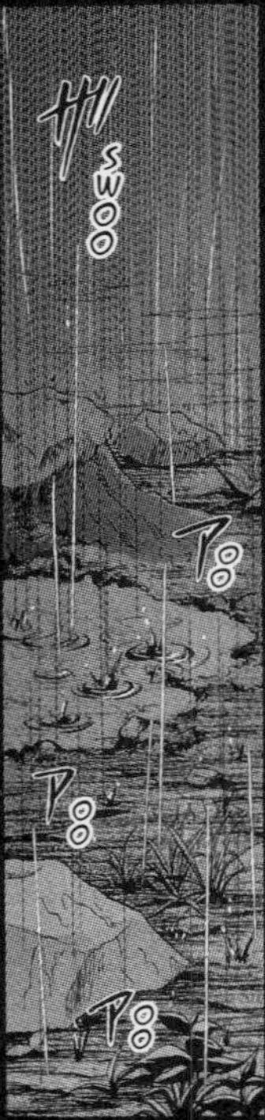
SWOO

And
wasn't
it...

Scene.17 – Deep Sea

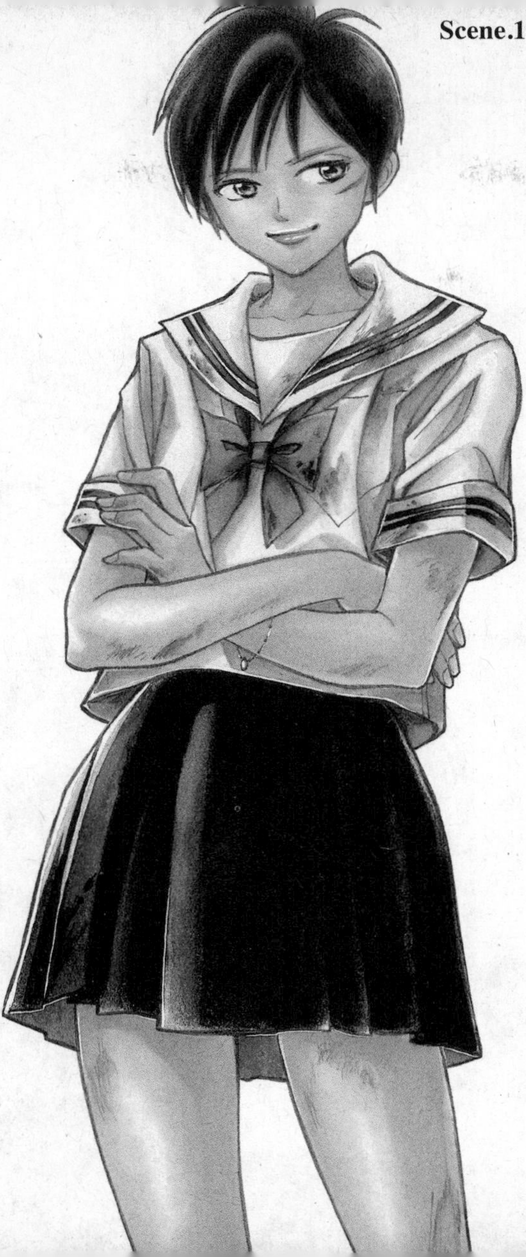

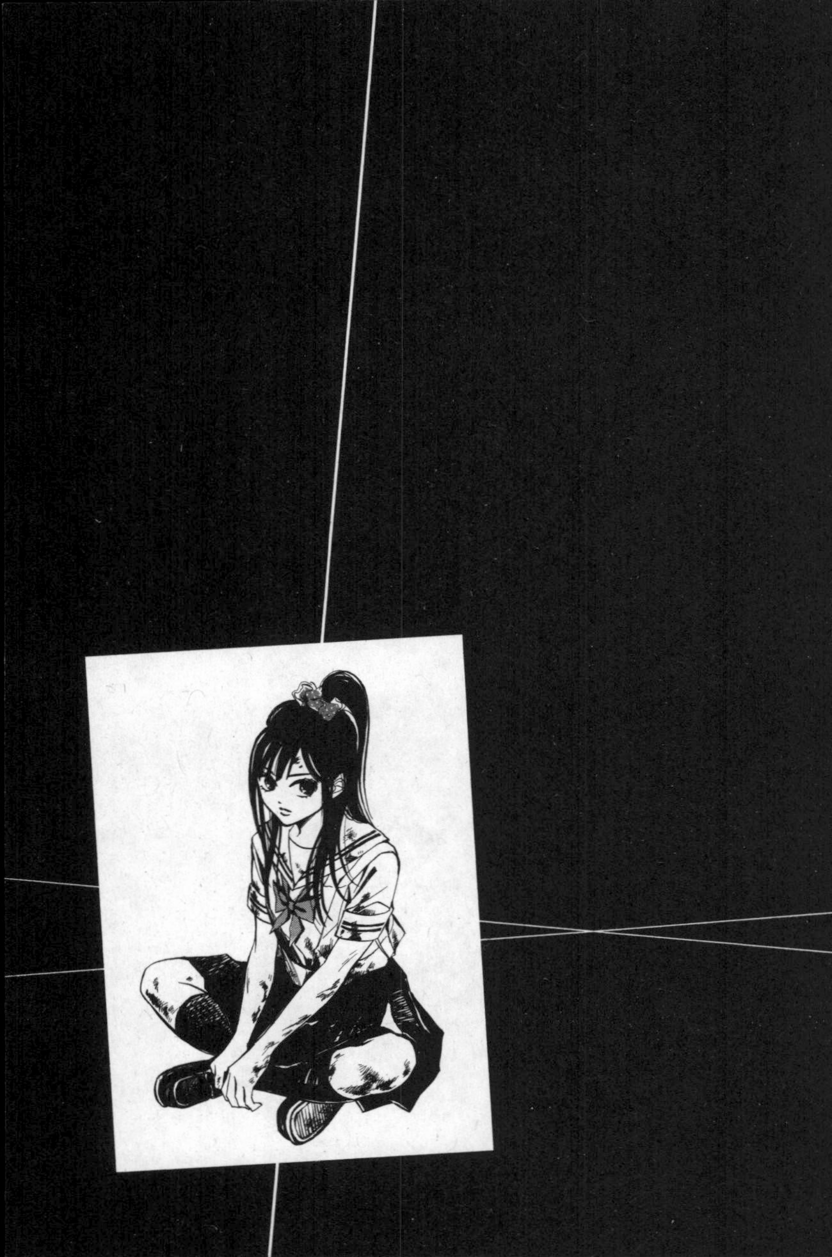

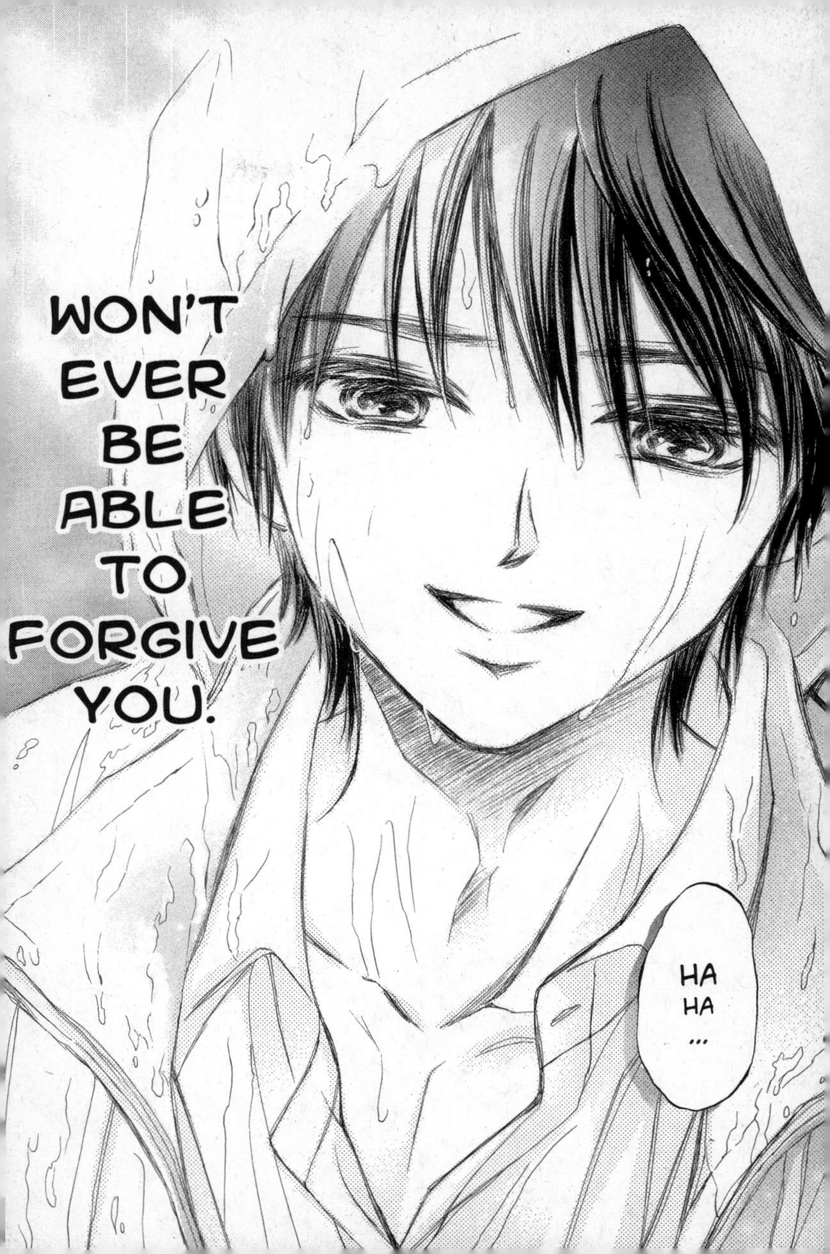
WON'T EVER BE ABLE TO FORGIVE YOU.
HA HA ...

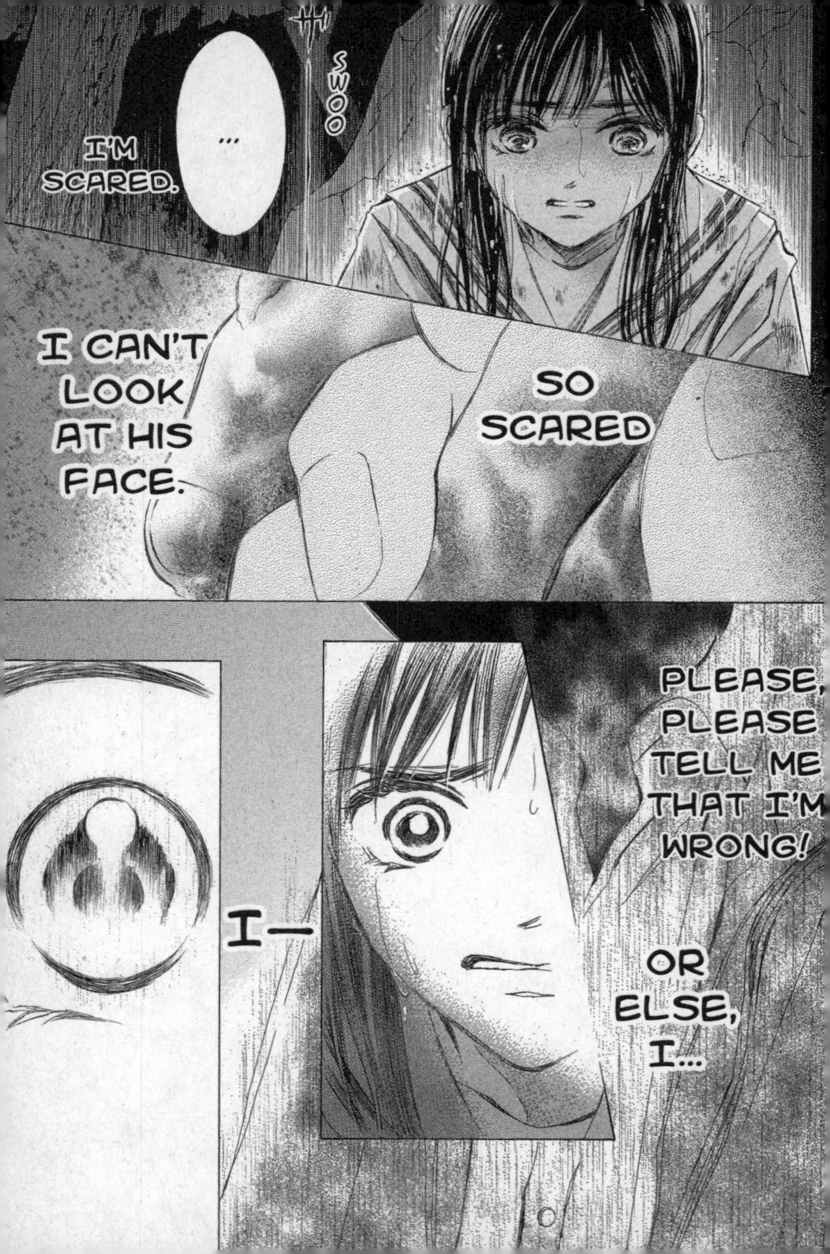
SWOO
...
I'M SCARED.
SO SCARED
I CAN'T LOOK AT HIS FACE.
PLEASE, PLEASE TELL ME THAT I'M WRONG!
OR ELSE, I...
I—

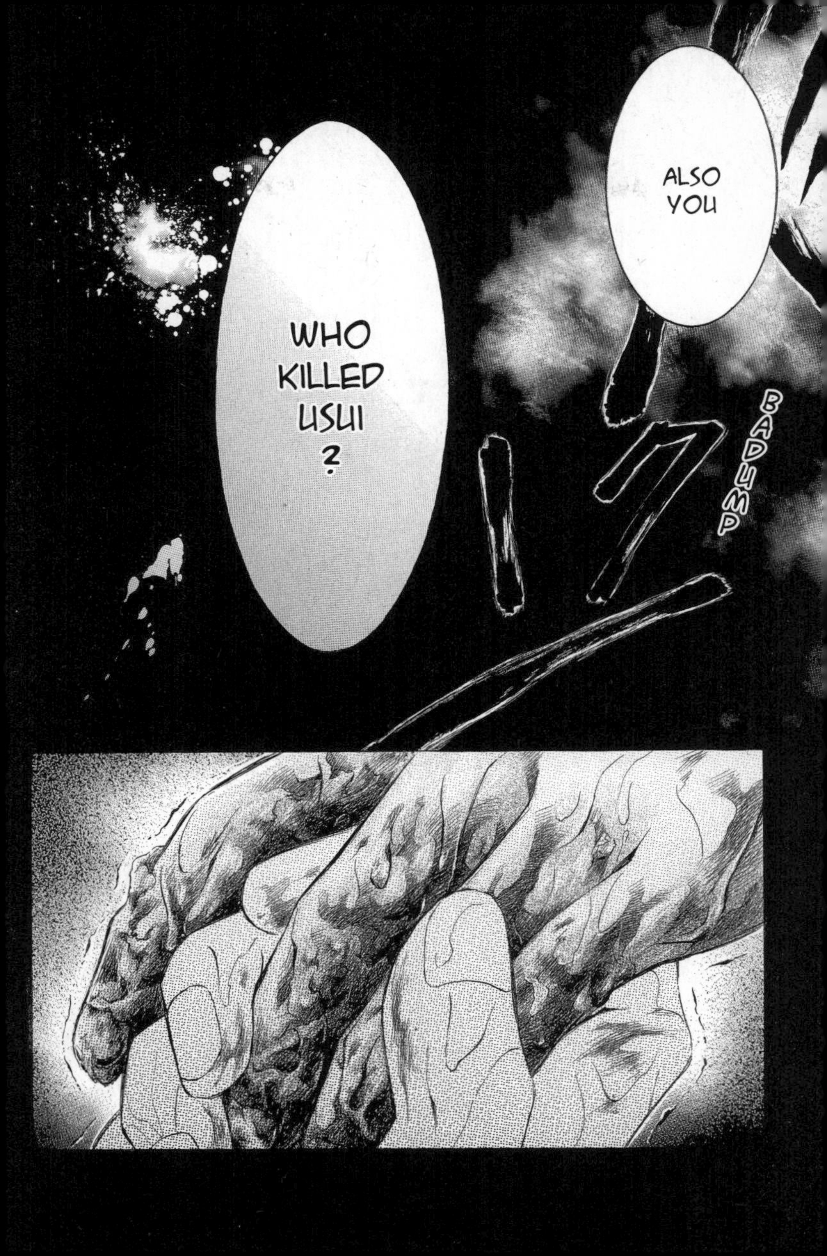
ALSO YOU
WHO KILLED USUI ?
BADUMP

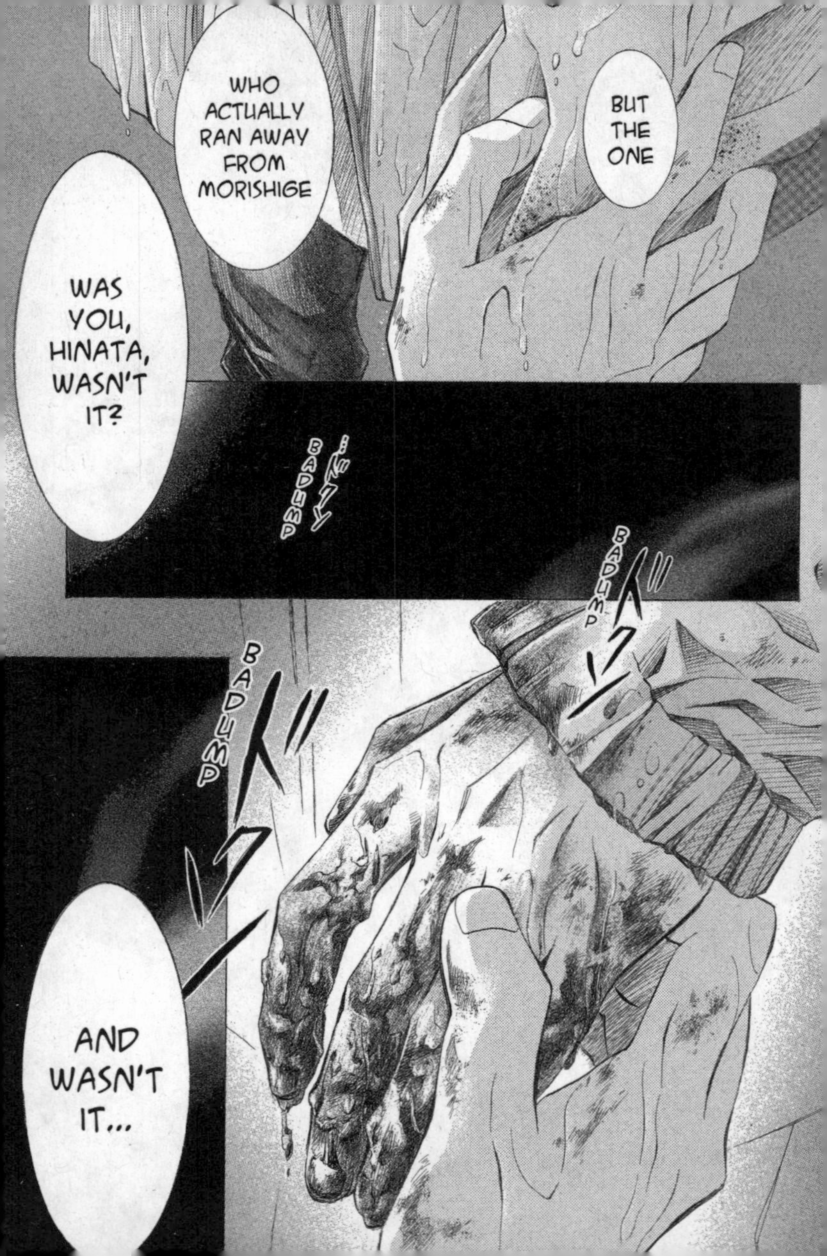
BUT THE ONE
WHO ACTUALLY RAN AWAY FROM MORISHIGE
WAS YOU, HINATA, WASN'T IT?
BADUMP
BADUMP
BADUMP
AND WASN'T IT...

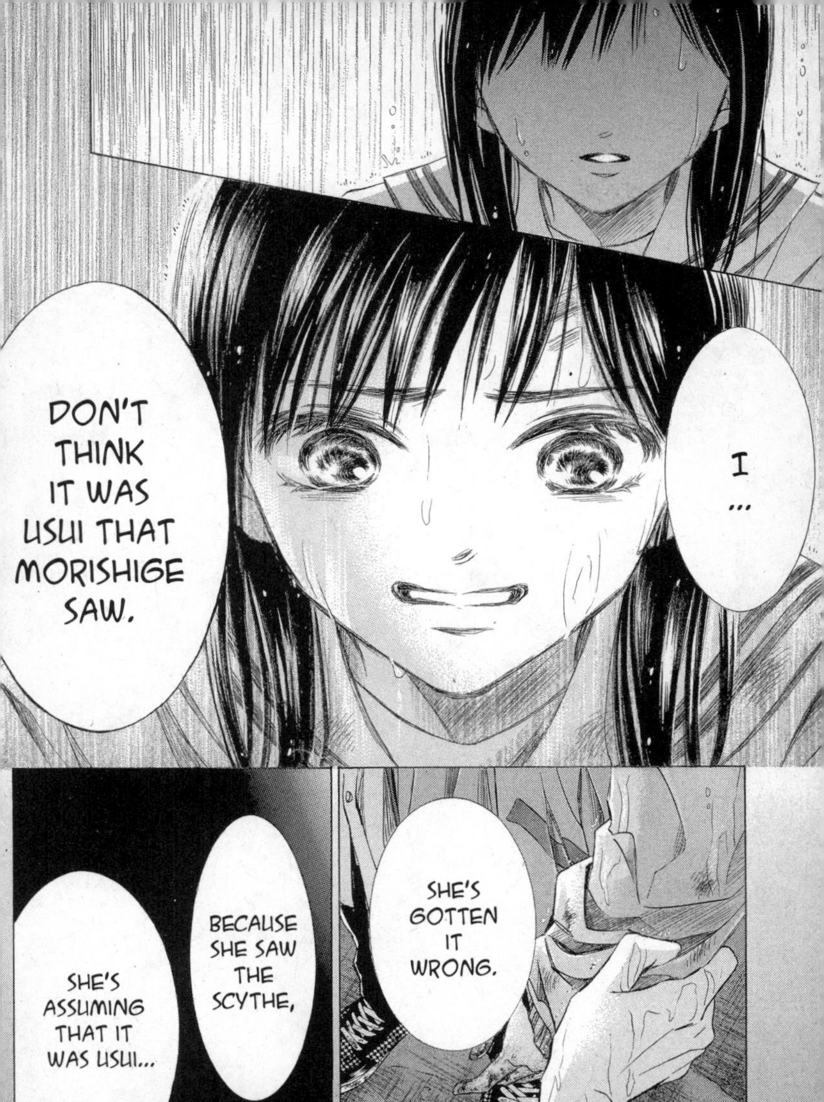
I ...
DON'T THINK IT WAS USUI THAT MORISHIGE SAW.
SHE'S GOTTEN IT WRONG.
BECAUSE SHE SAW THE SCYTHE,
SHE'S ASSUMING THAT IT WAS USUI...

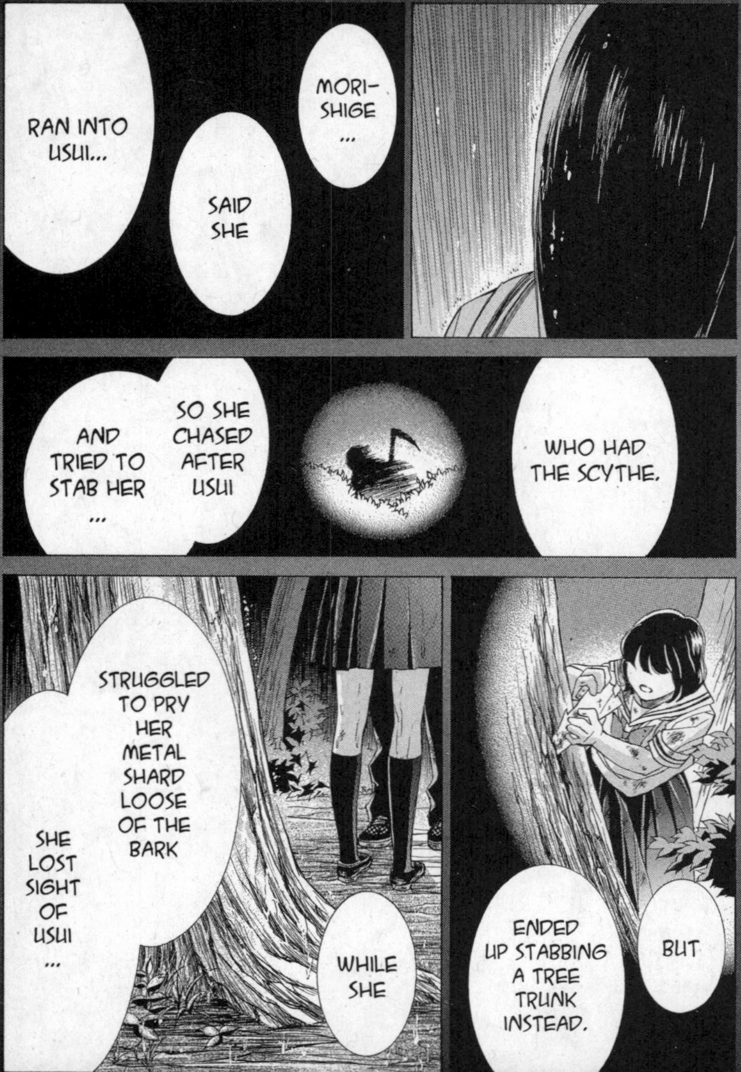
MORI-SHIGE ...
SAID SHE
RAN INTO USUI...
WHO HAD THE SCYTHE.
SO SHE CHASED AFTER USUI
AND TRIED TO STAB HER ...
BUT
ENDED UP STABBING A TREE TRUNK INSTEAD.
WHILE SHE
STRUGGLED TO PRY HER METAL SHARD LOOSE OF THE BARK
SHE LOST SIGHT OF USUI ...

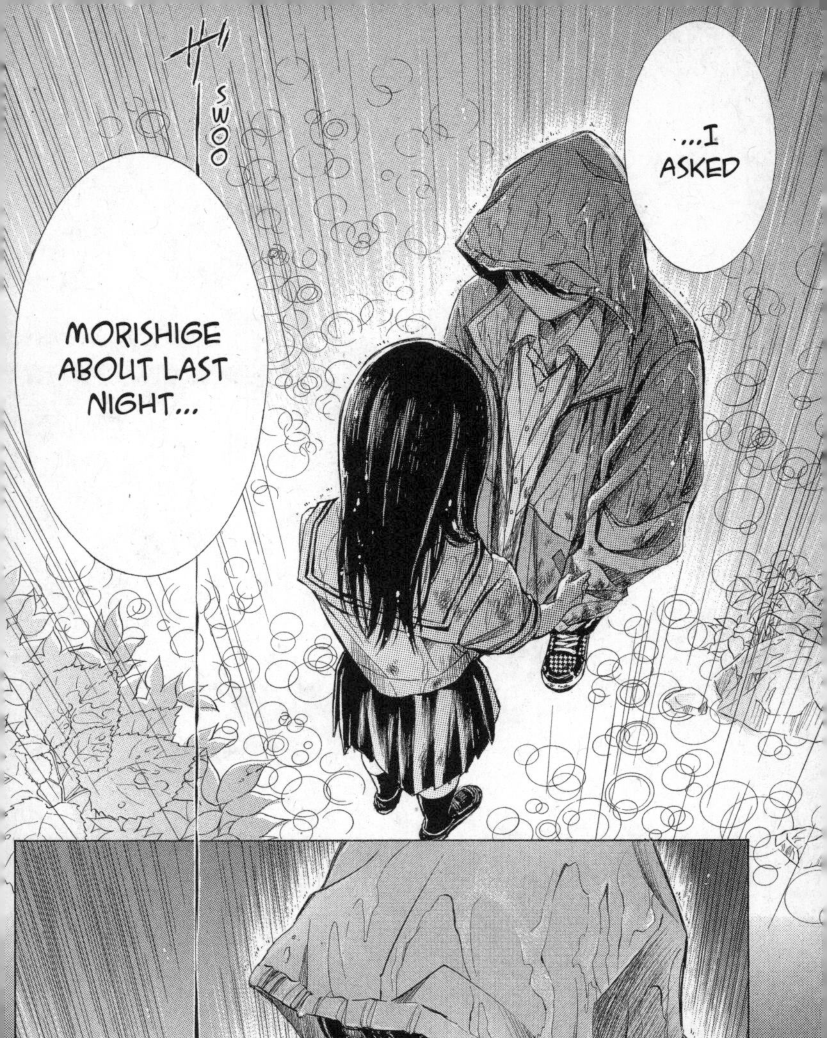
...I ASKED
MORISHIGE ABOUT LAST NIGHT...
SWOO

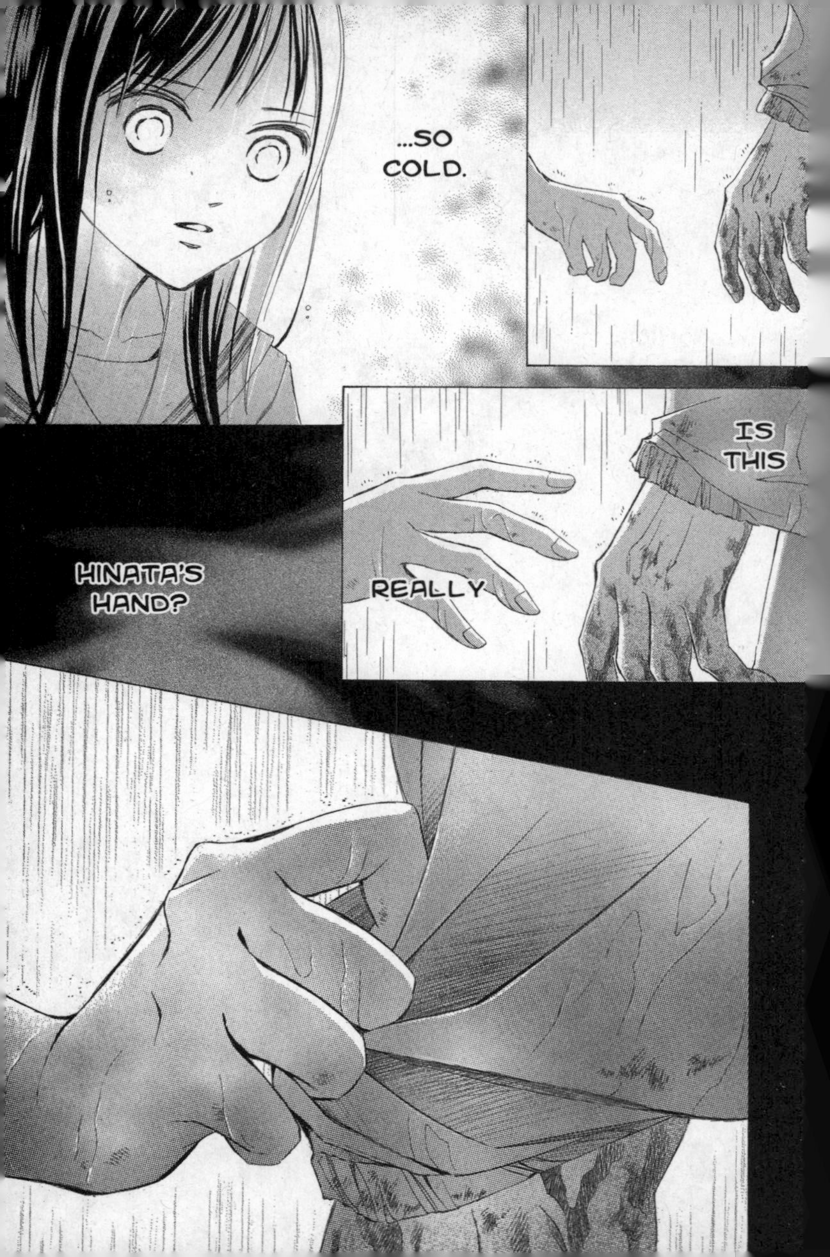
...SO COLD.
IS THIS
REALLY
HINATA'S HAND?

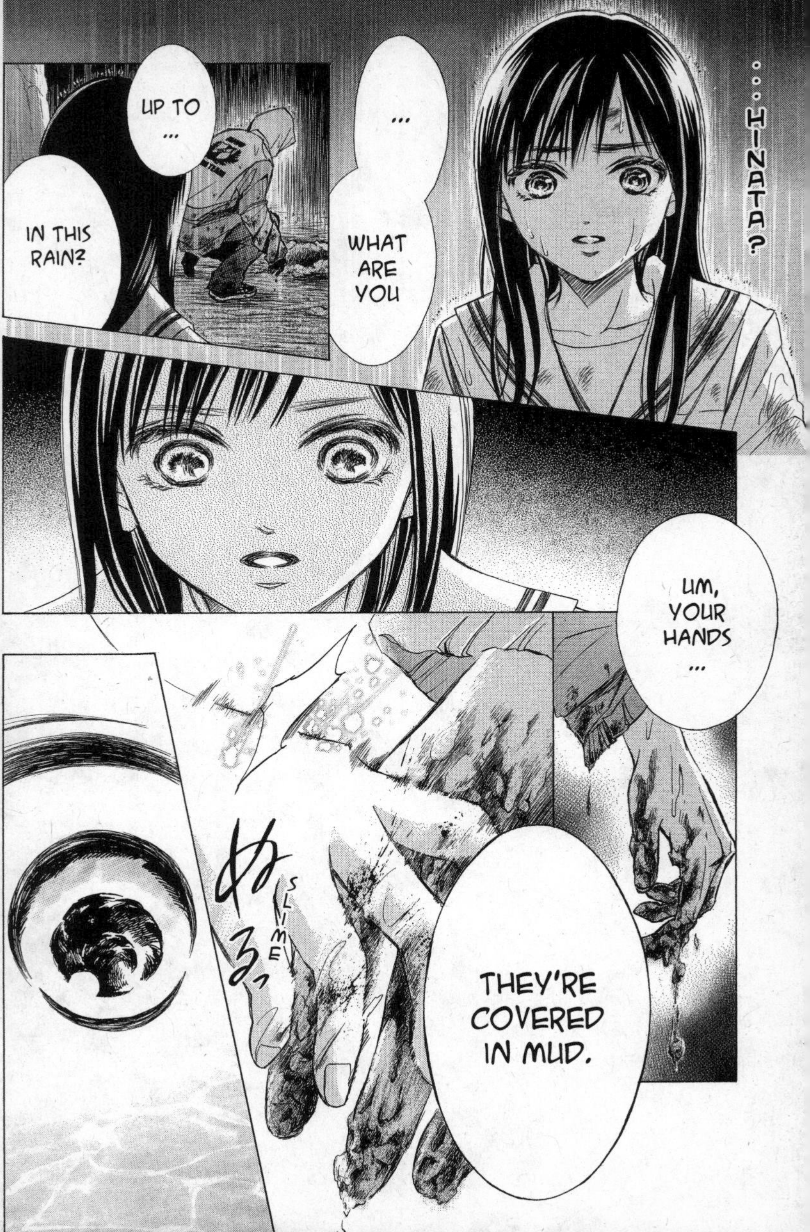
...HINATA?
... WHAT ARE YOU
UP TO ... IN THIS RAIN?
UM, YOUR HANDS ...
THEY'RE COVERED IN MUD.
ぬるっ
SLIME

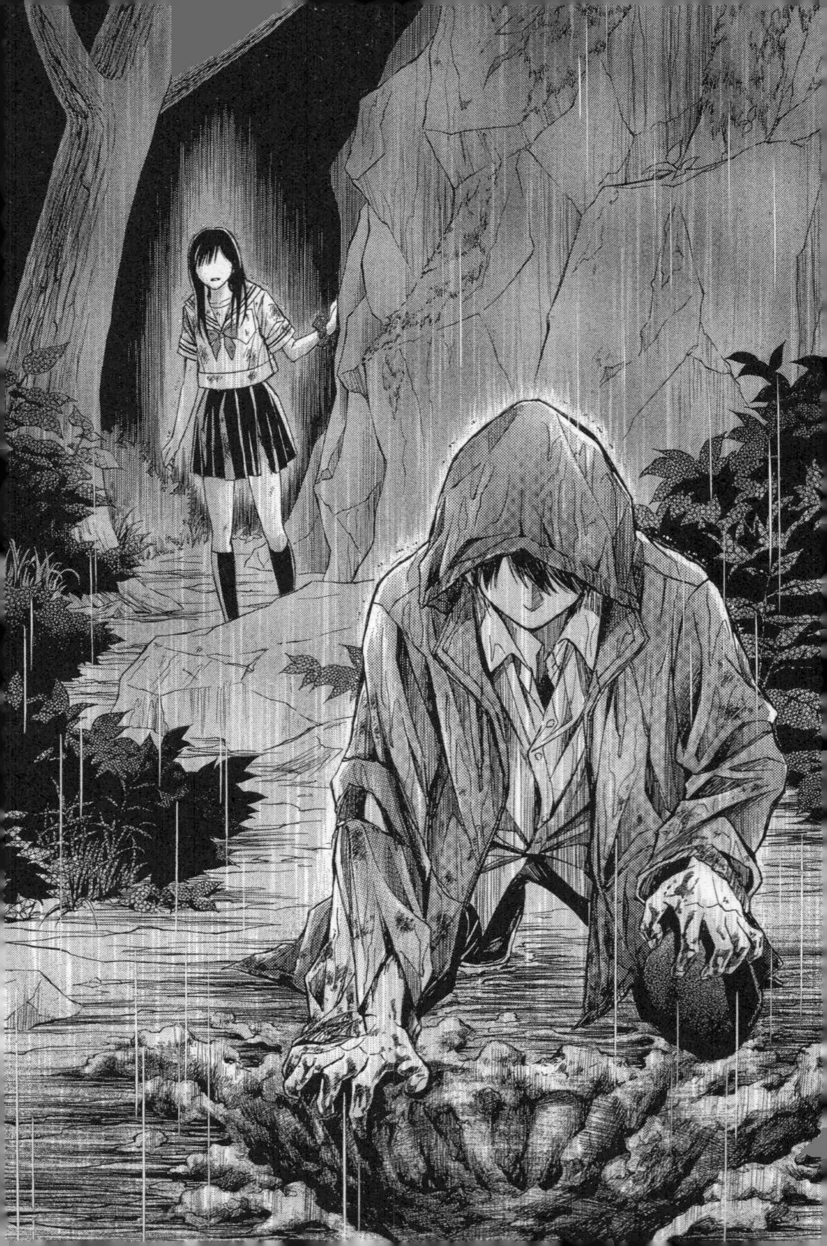

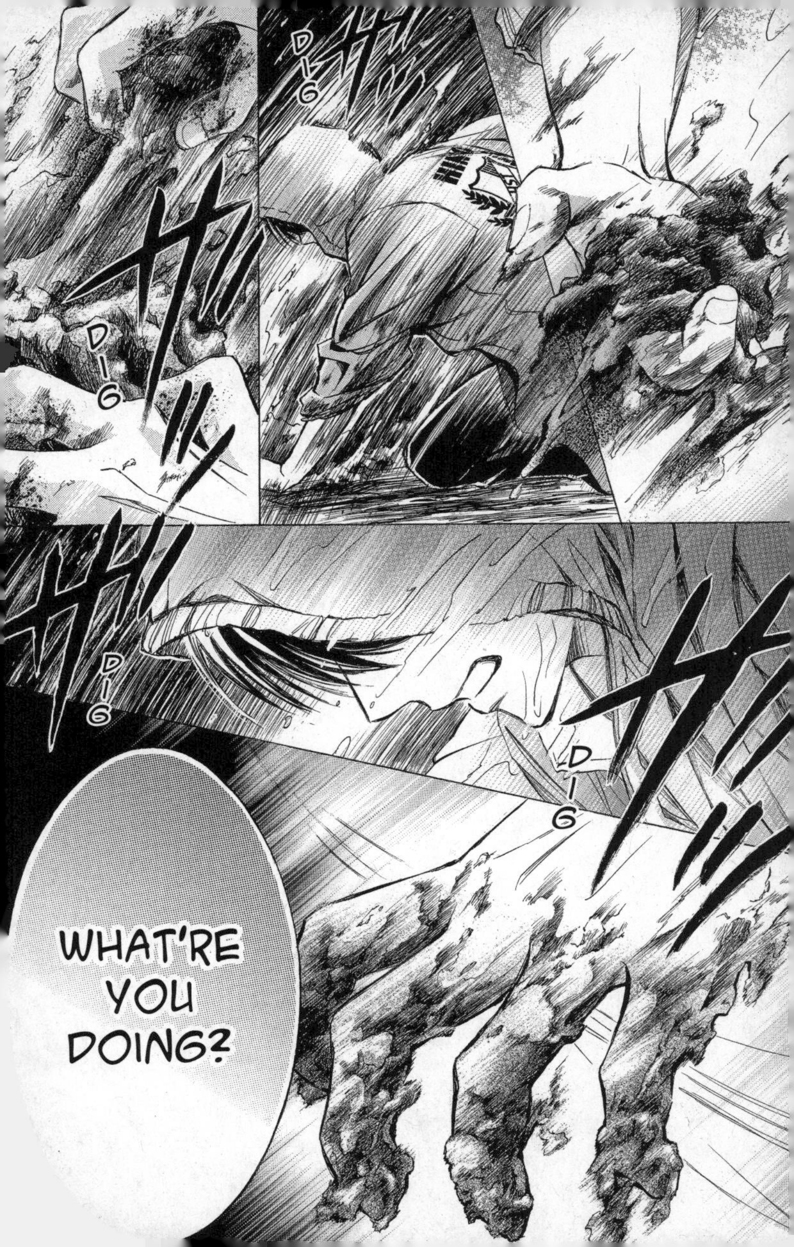
DIG
DIG
DIG
DIG
WHAT'RE YOU DOING?

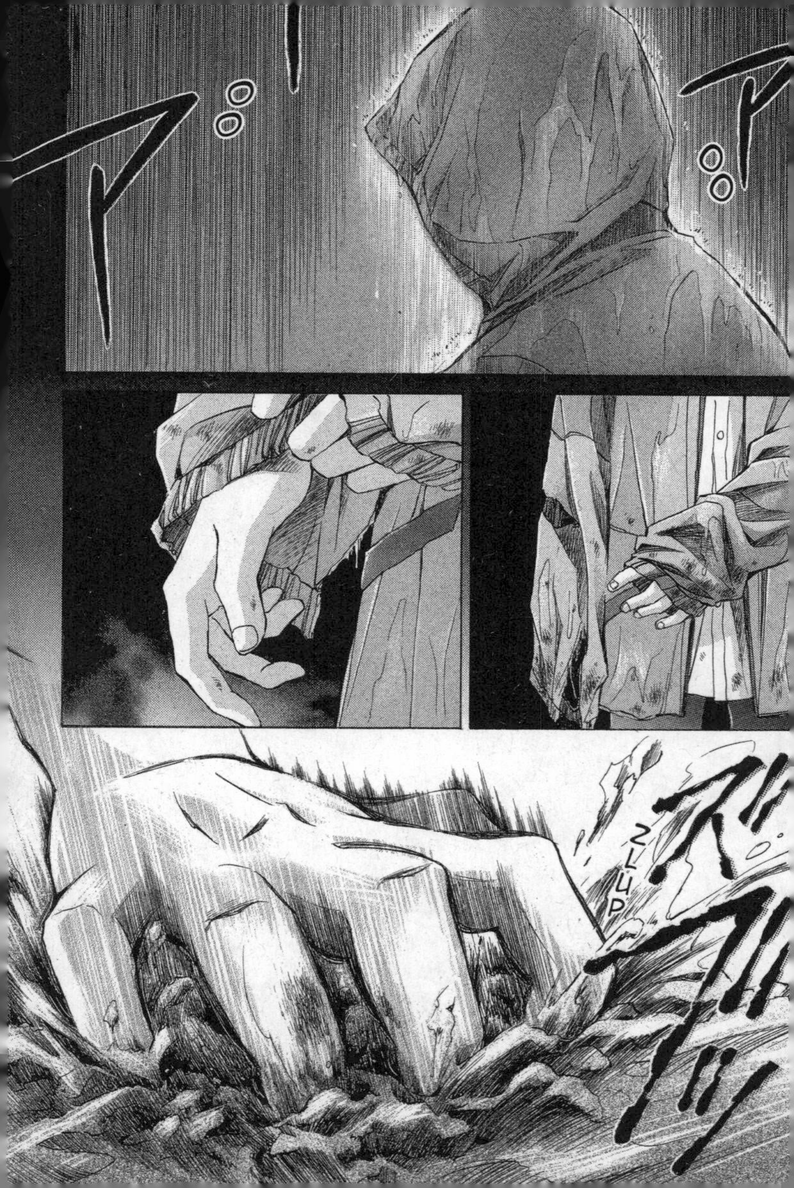
ZLUP

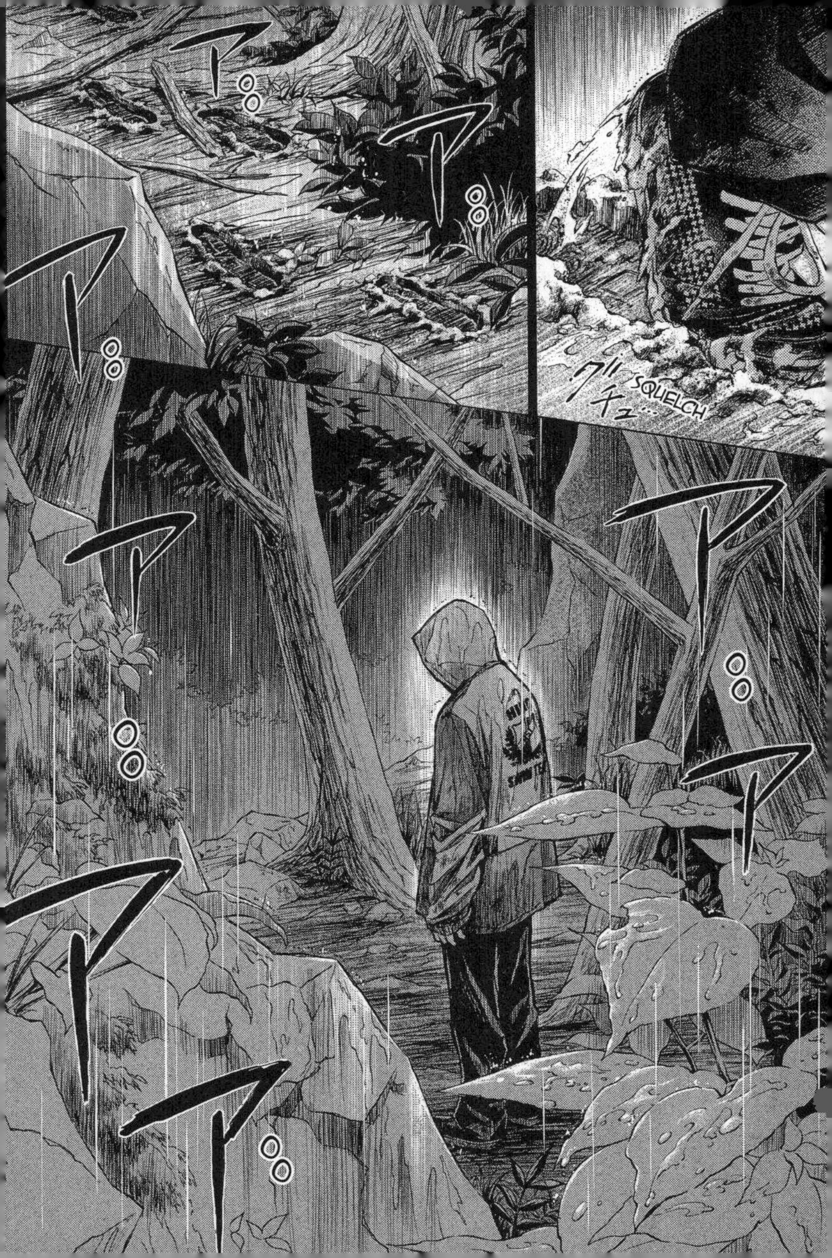
SQUELCH

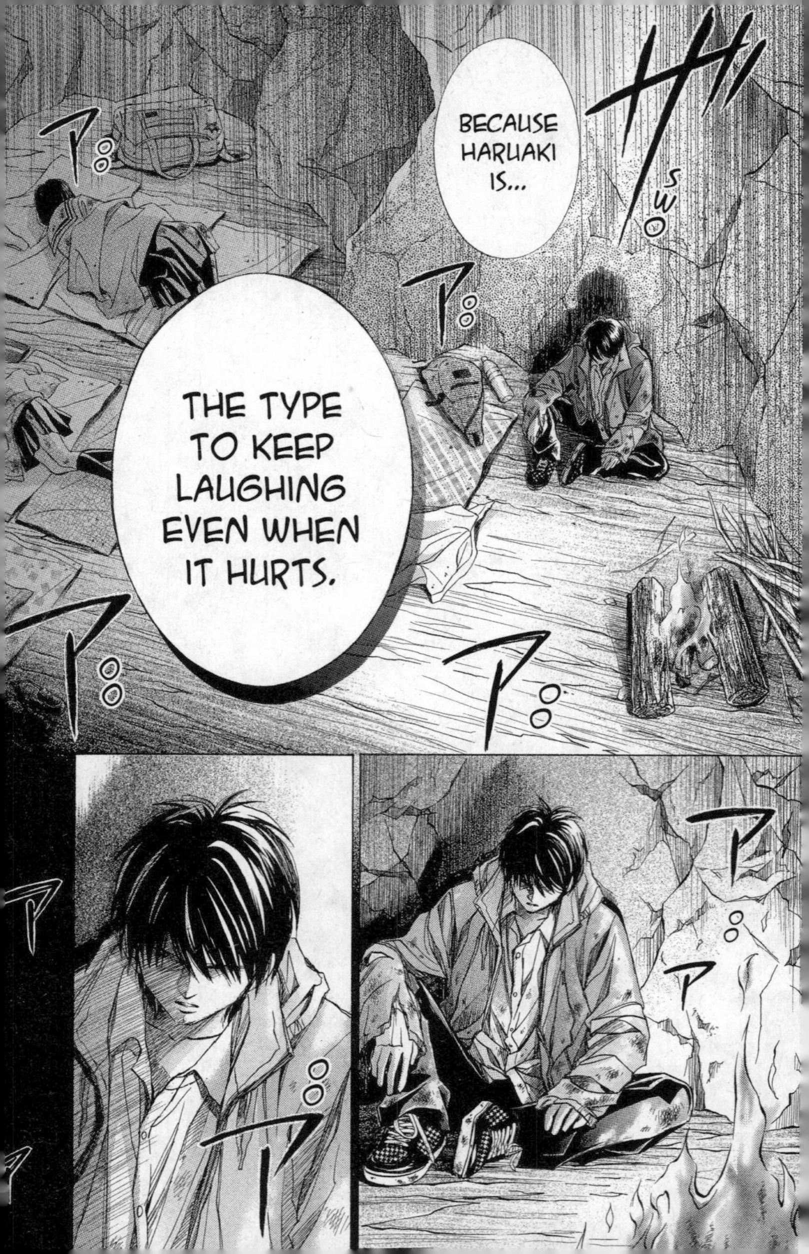
SWO
BECAUSE HARUAKI IS...
THE TYPE TO KEEP LAUGHING EVEN WHEN IT HURTS.

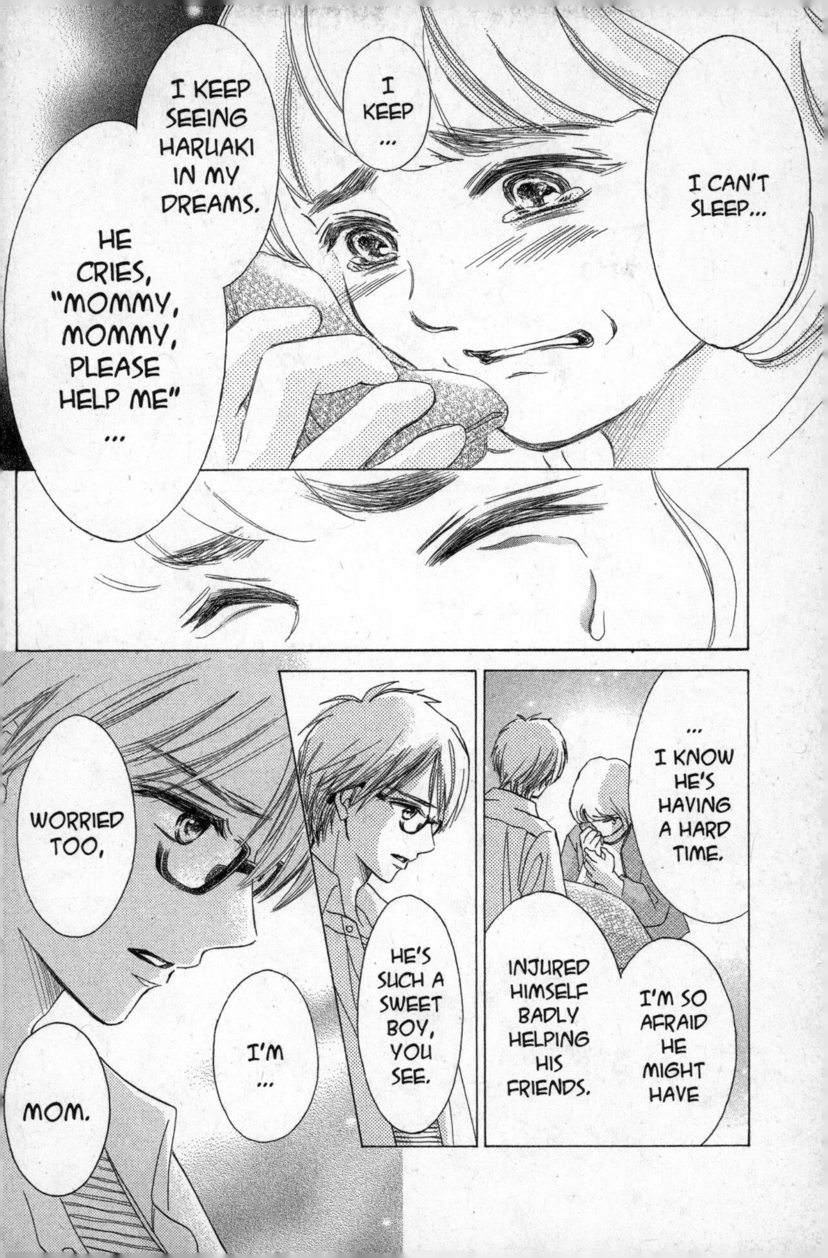
I CAN'T SLEEP...
I KEEP ...
I KEEP SEEING HARUAKI IN MY DREAMS.
HE CRIES, "MOMMY, MOMMY, PLEASE HELP ME" ...
... I KNOW HE'S HAVING A HARD TIME.
I'M SO AFRAID HE MIGHT HAVE
INJURED HIMSELF BADLY HELPING HIS FRIENDS.
HE'S SUCH A SWEET BOY, YOU SEE.
I'M ...
WORRIED TOO,
MOM.

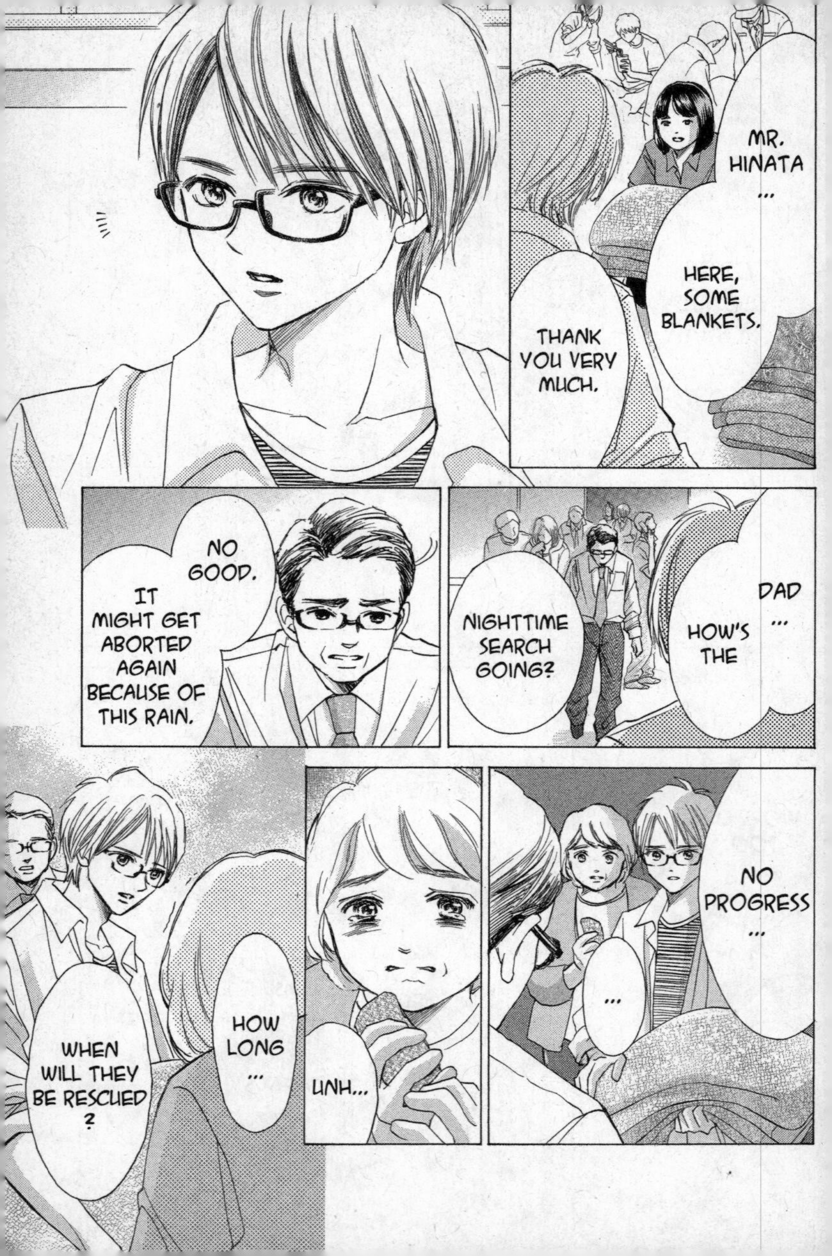
MR. HINATA ...
HERE, SOME BLANKETS.
THANK YOU VERY MUCH.
DAD ... HOW'S THE
NIGHTTIME SEARCH GOING?
NO GOOD.
IT MIGHT GET ABORTED AGAIN BECAUSE OF THIS RAIN.
NO PROGRESS ...
...
UNH...
HOW LONG ...
WHEN WILL THEY BE RESCUED ?

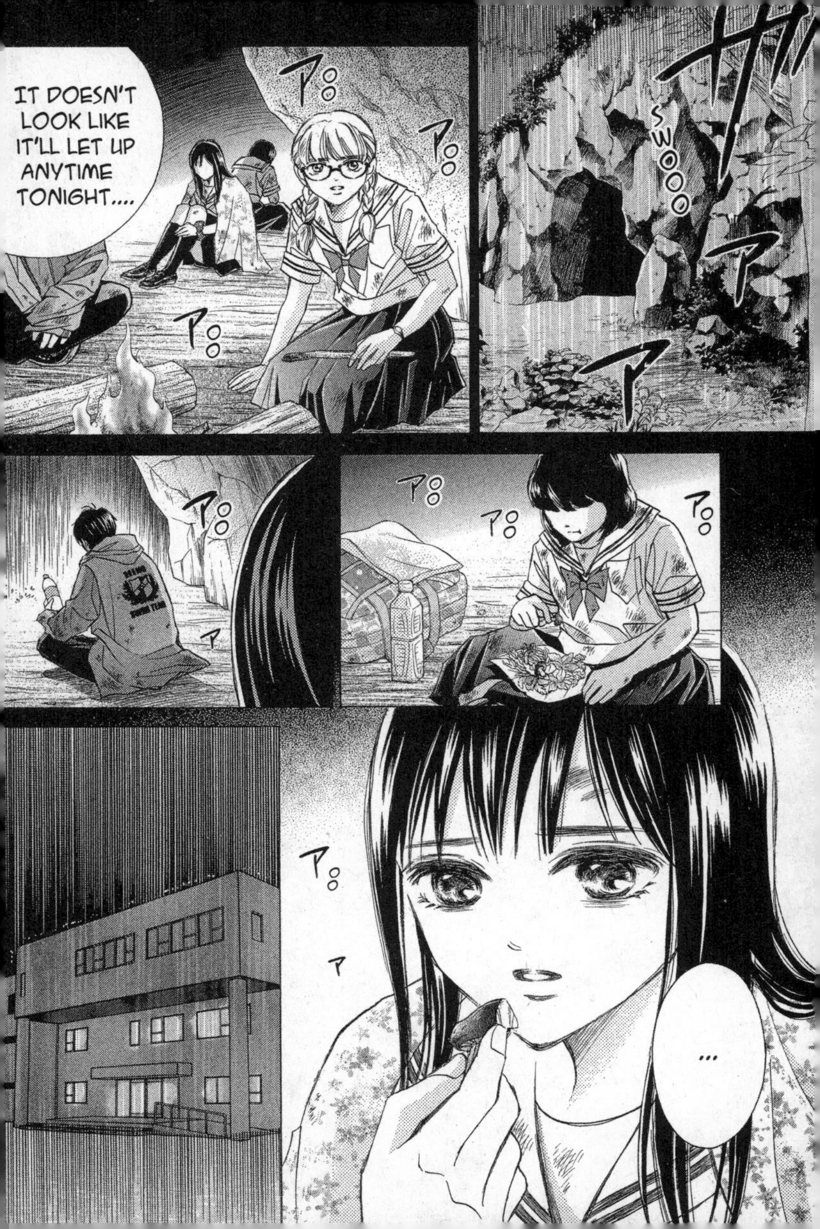
SWOOOO
IT DOESN'T LOOK LIKE IT'LL LET UP ANYTIME TONIGHT....
...

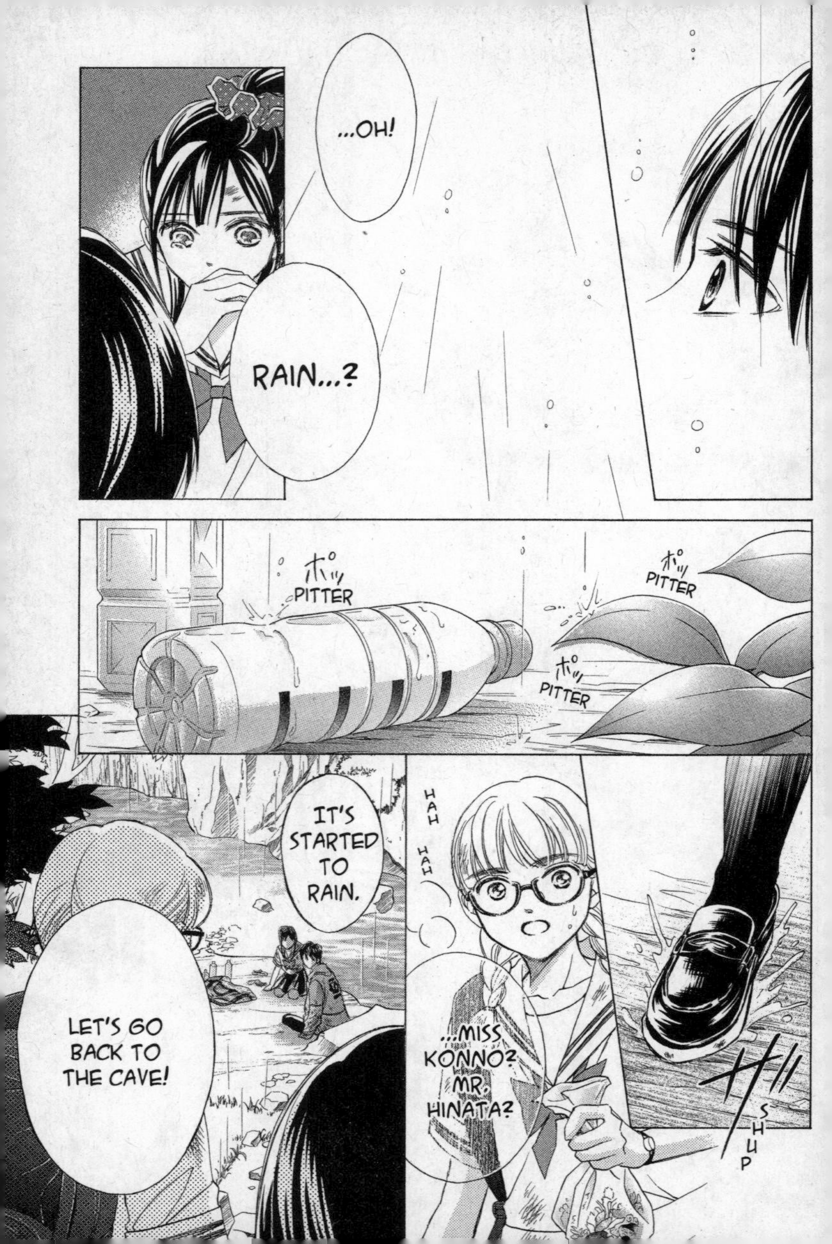
...OH!
RAIN...?
ポッ PITTER
ポッ PITTER
ポッ PITTER
SHUP
HAH HAH
...MISS KONNO? MR. HINATA?
IT'S STARTED TO RAIN.
LET'S GO BACK TO THE CAVE!

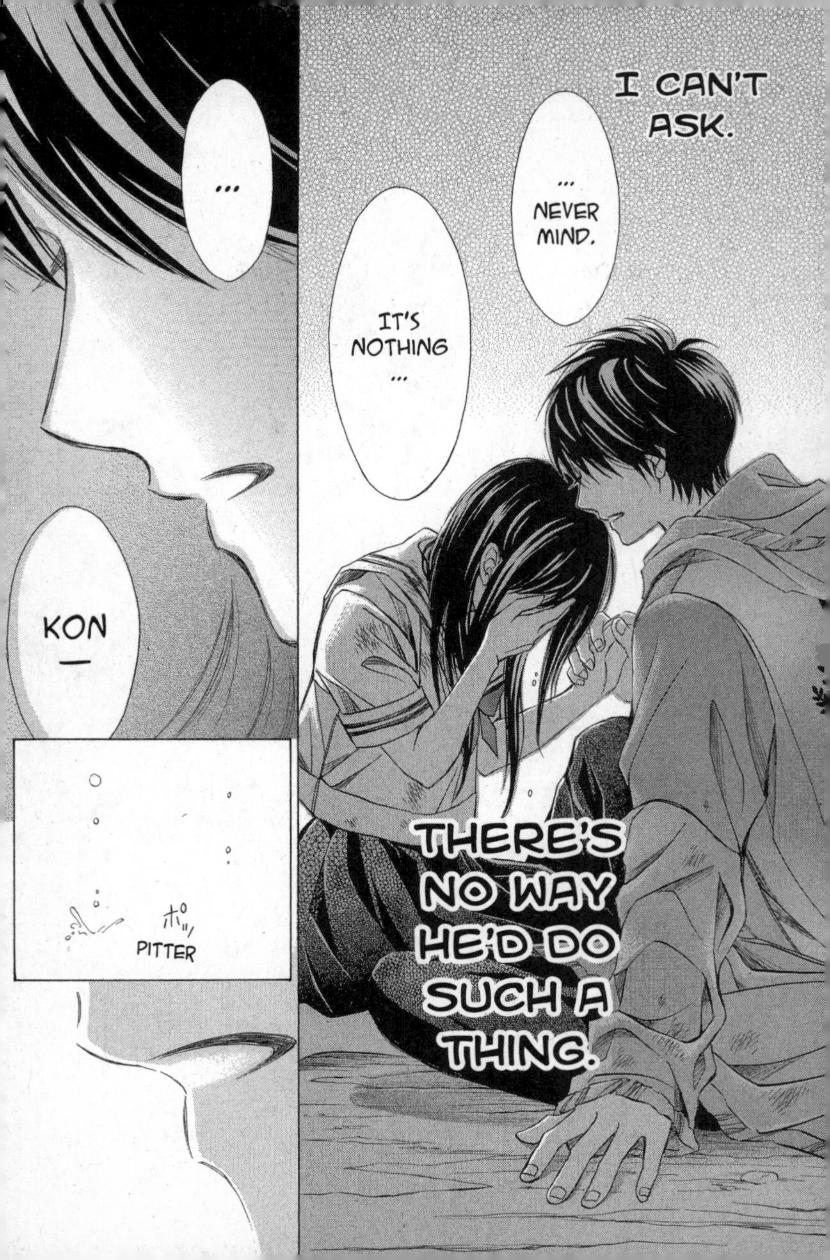
I CAN'T ASK.
... NEVER MIND.
IT'S NOTHING ...
THERE'S NO WAY HE'D DO SUCH A THING.
...
KON —
ポ
PITTER

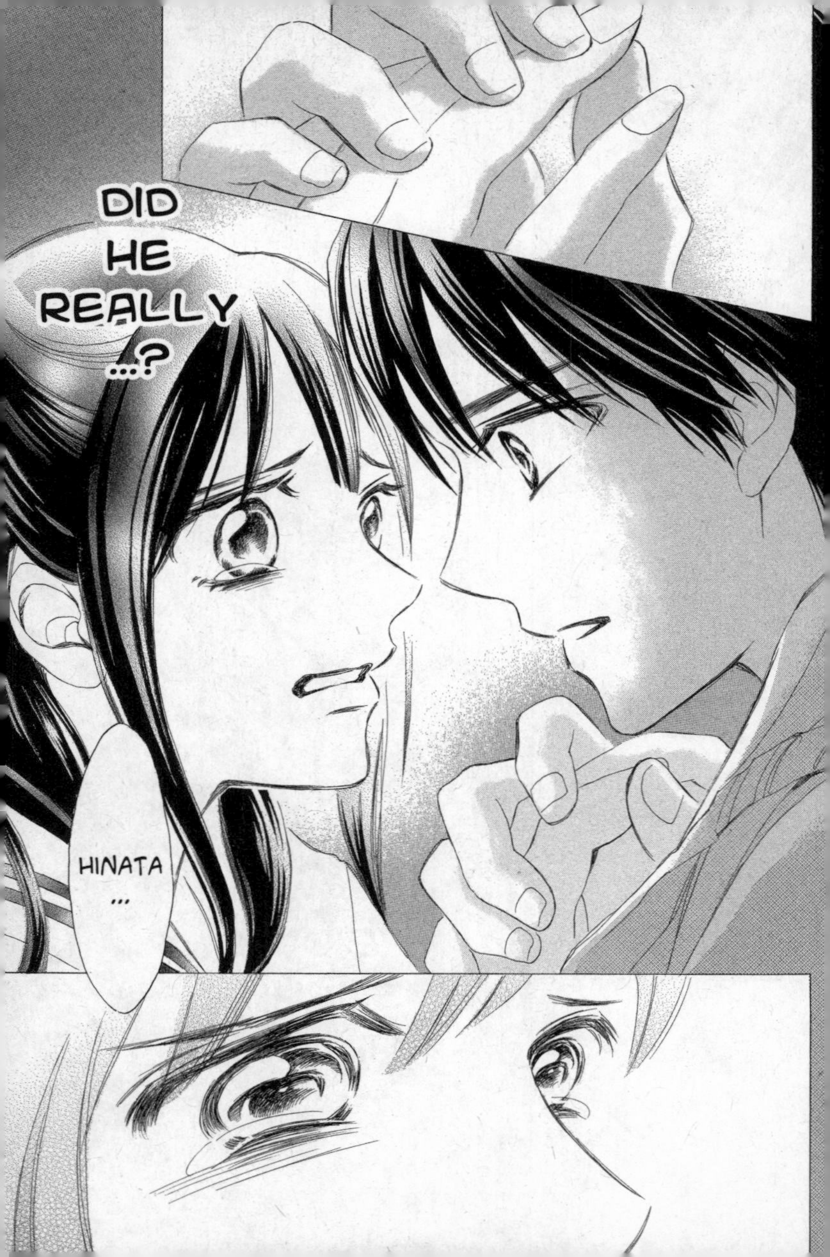
DID HE REALLY ...?
HINATA ...

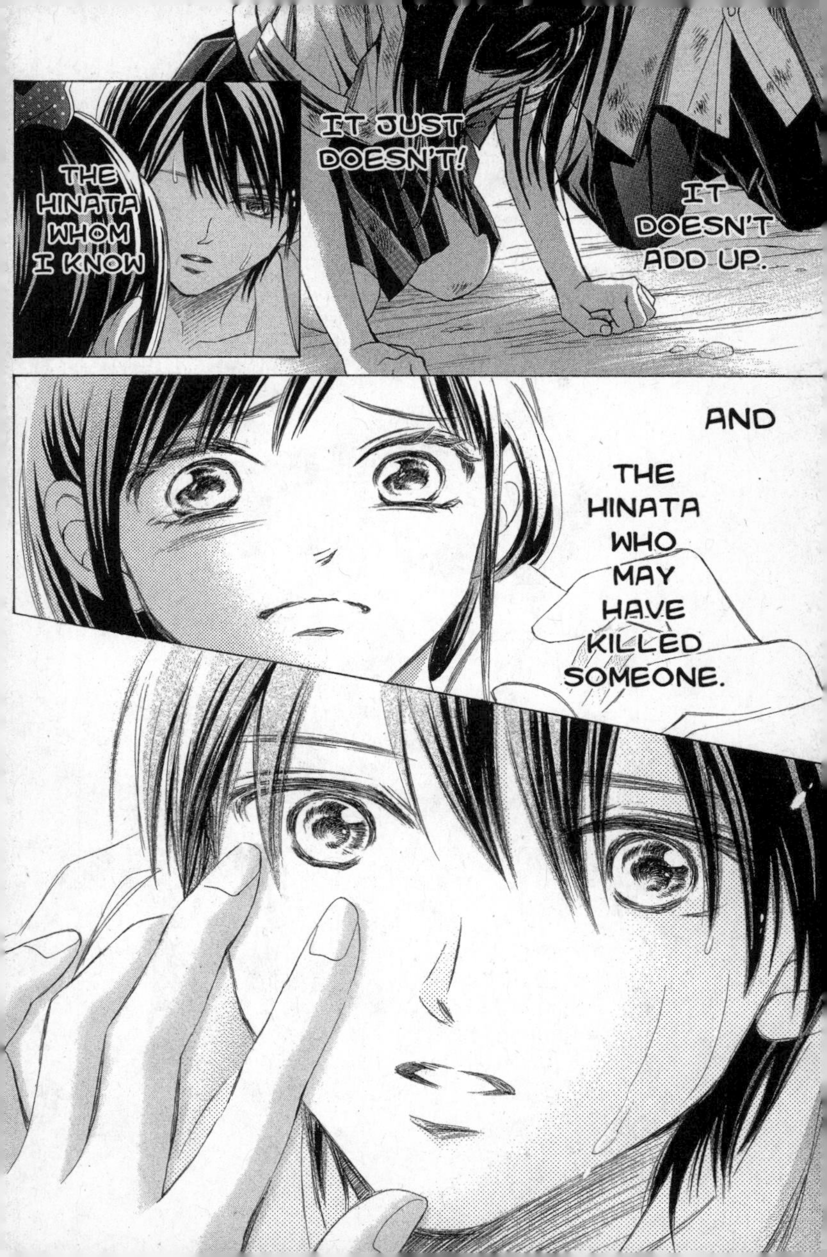
IT DOESN'T ADD UP.
IT JUST DOESN'T!
THE HINATA WHOM I KNOW
AND
THE HINATA WHO MAY HAVE KILLED SOMEONE.

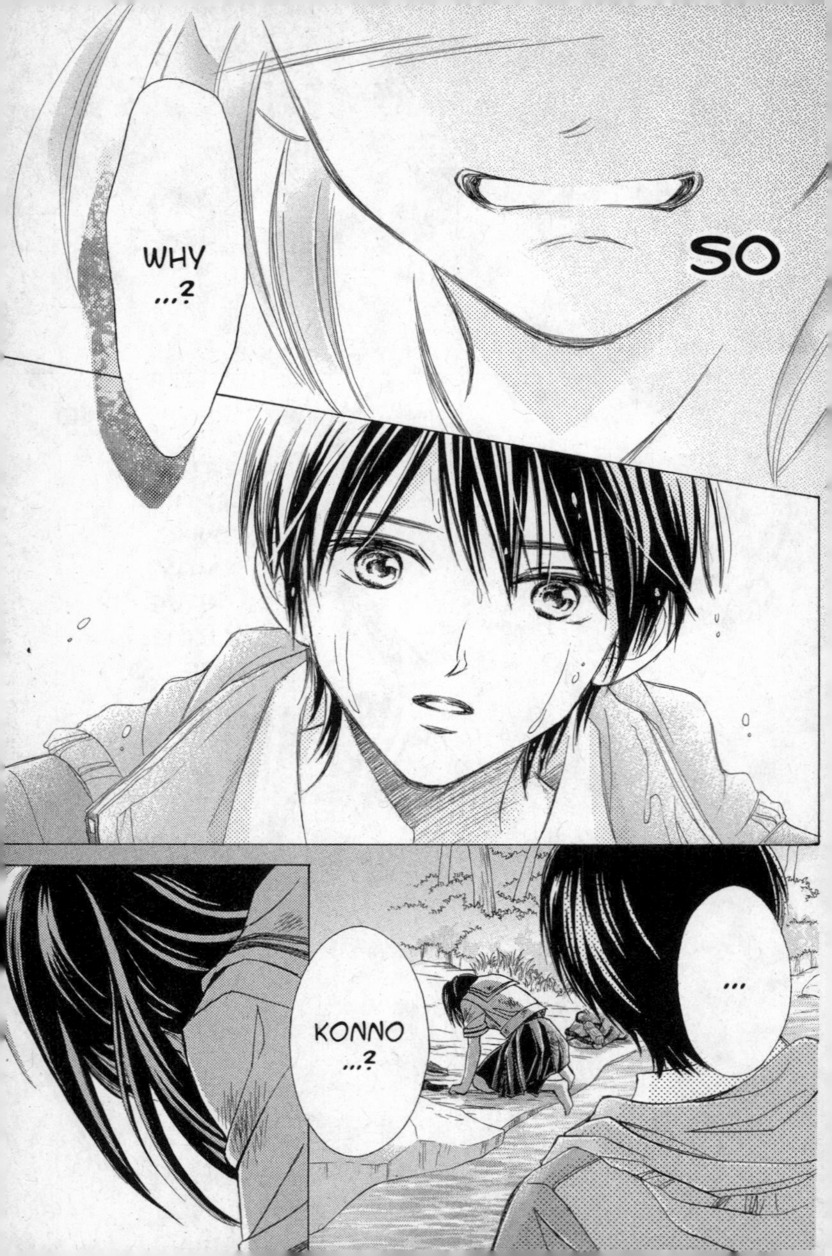
SO
WHY ...?
...
KONNO ...?

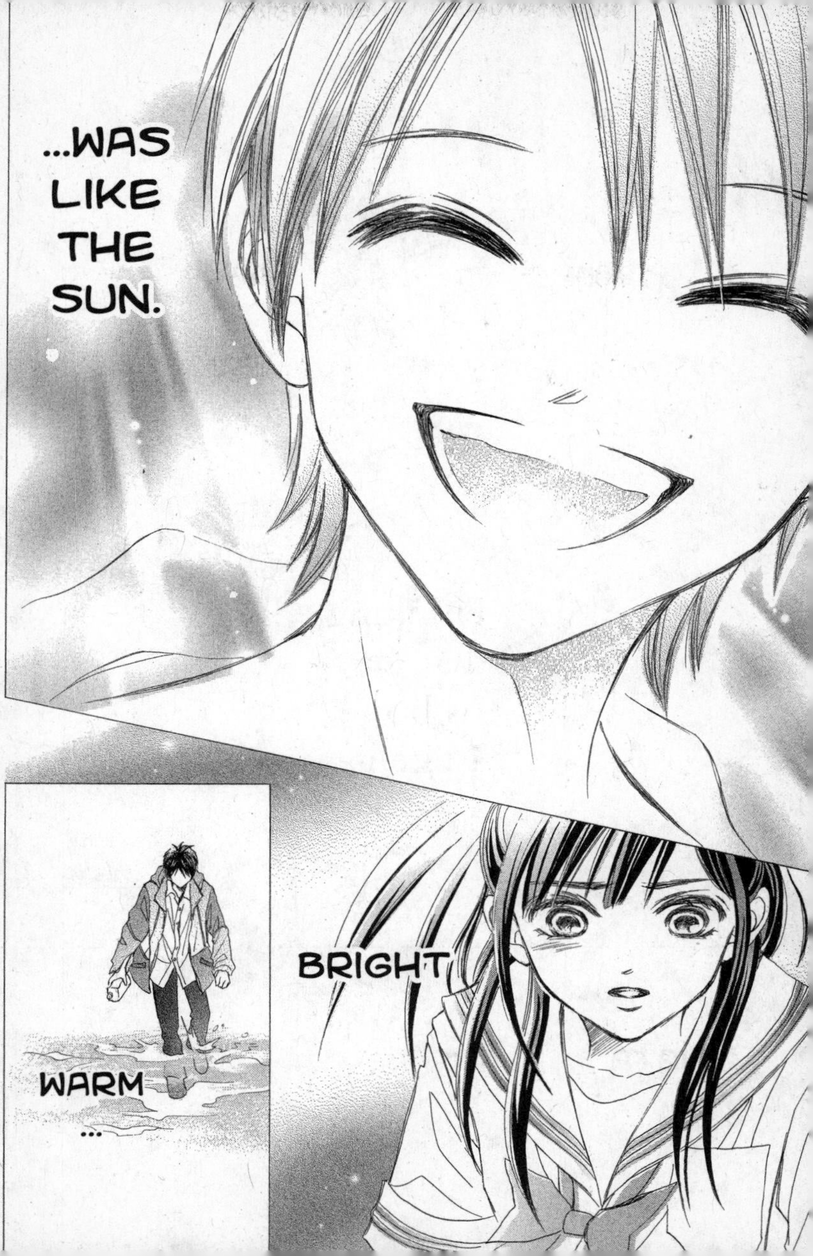
...WAS LIKE THE SUN.
BRIGHT
WARM
...

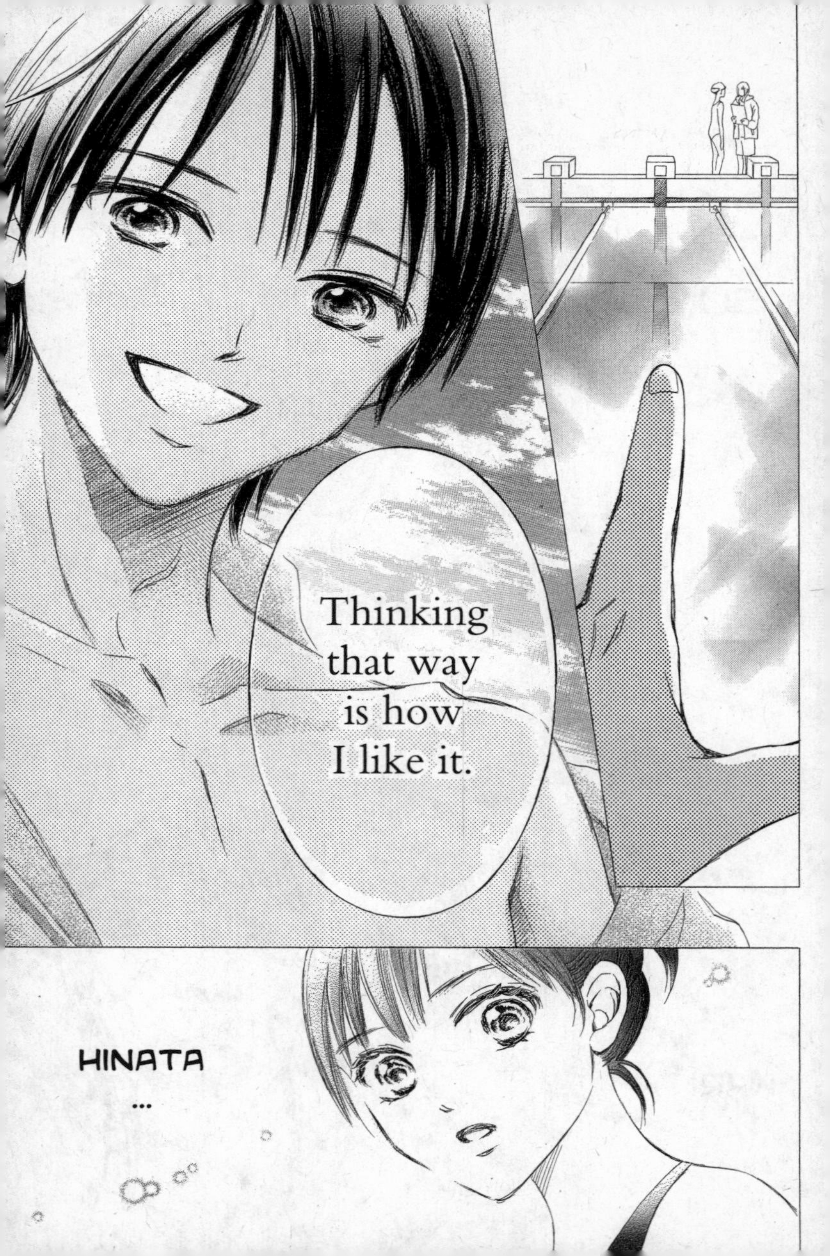
Thinking that way is how I like it.
HINATA ...

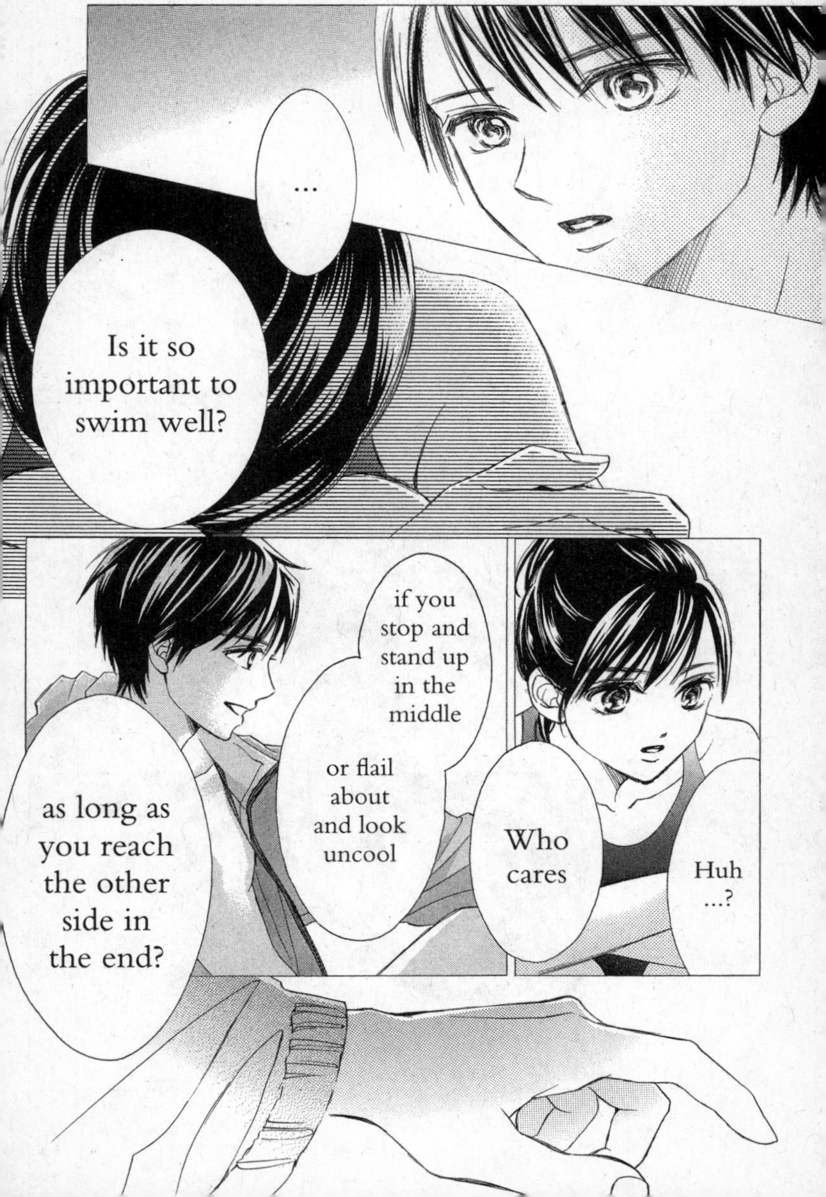
...
Is it so important to swim well?
Huh ...?
Who cares
if you stop and stand up in the middle
or flail about and look uncool
as long as you reach the other side in the end?

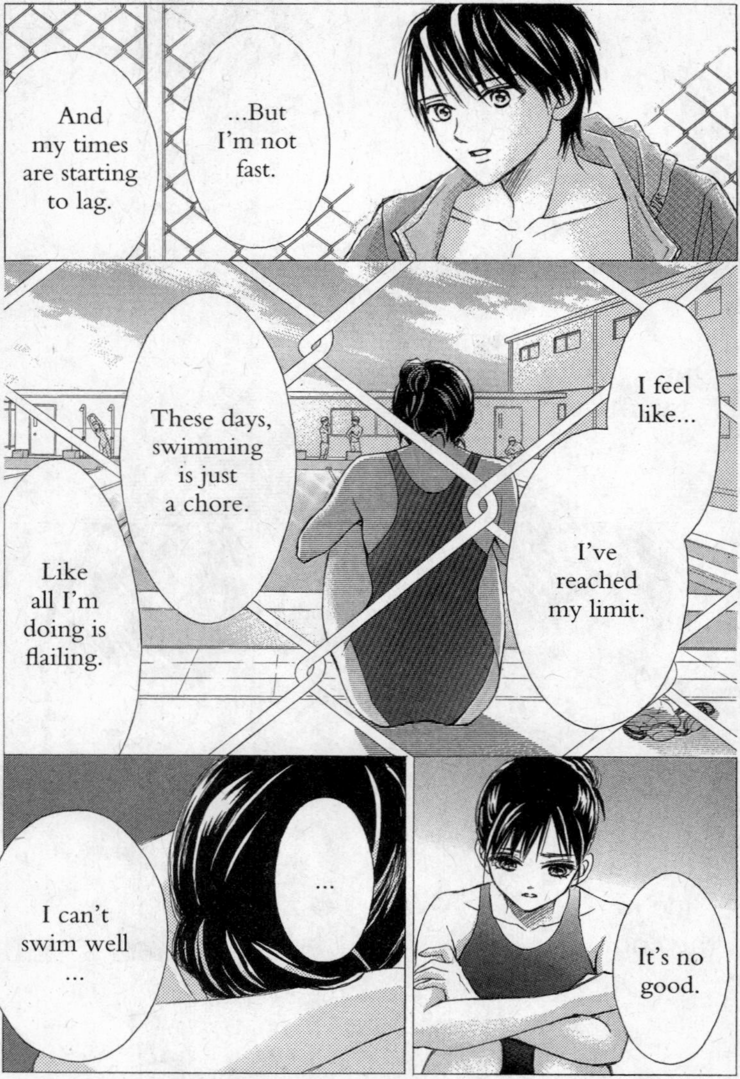
...But I'm not fast.
And my times are starting to lag.
I feel like...
I've reached my limit.
These days, swimming is just a chore.
Like all I'm doing is flailing.
It's no good.
...
I can't swim well ...

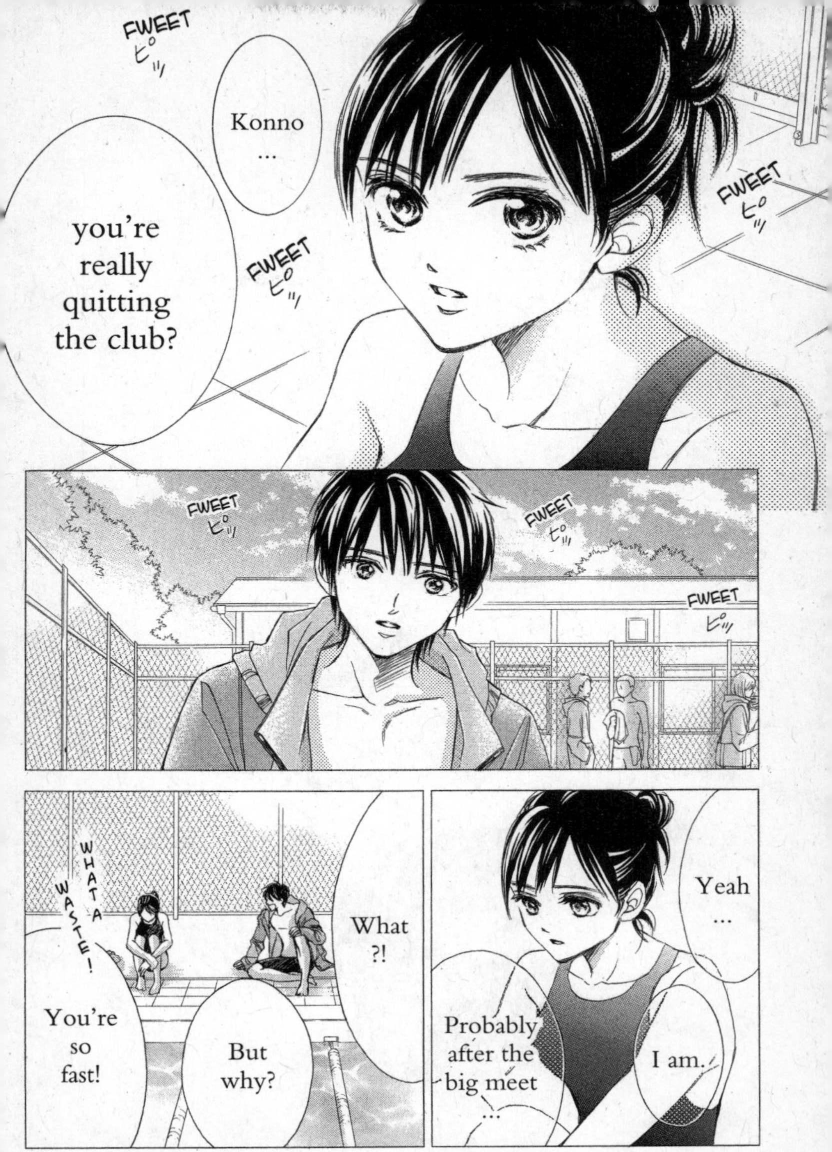
FWEET ピッ
Konno ...
you're really quitting the club?
FWEET ピッ
FWEET ピッ
FWEET ピッ
FWEET ピッ
FWEET ピッ
Yeah ...
I am.
Probably after the big meet ...
What?!
But why?
You're so fast!
WHAT A WASTE!

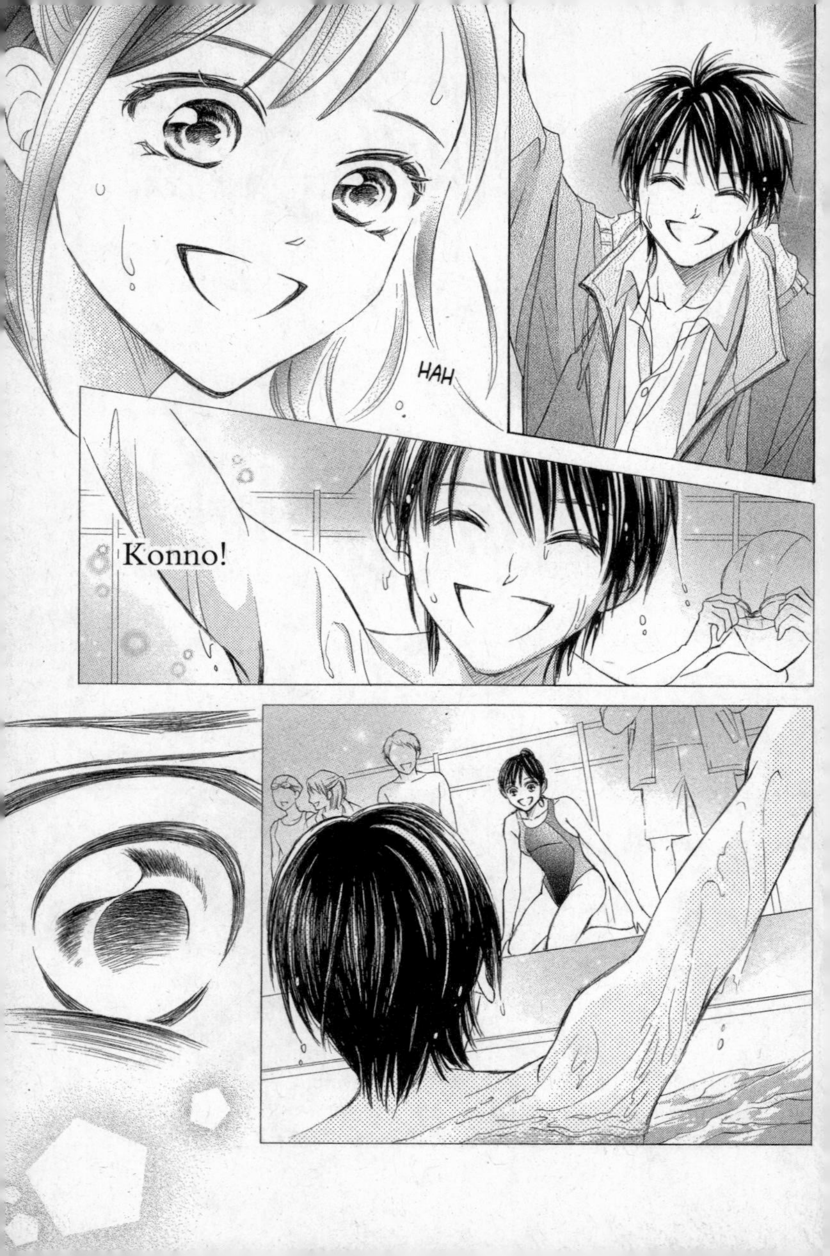
HAH
Konno!

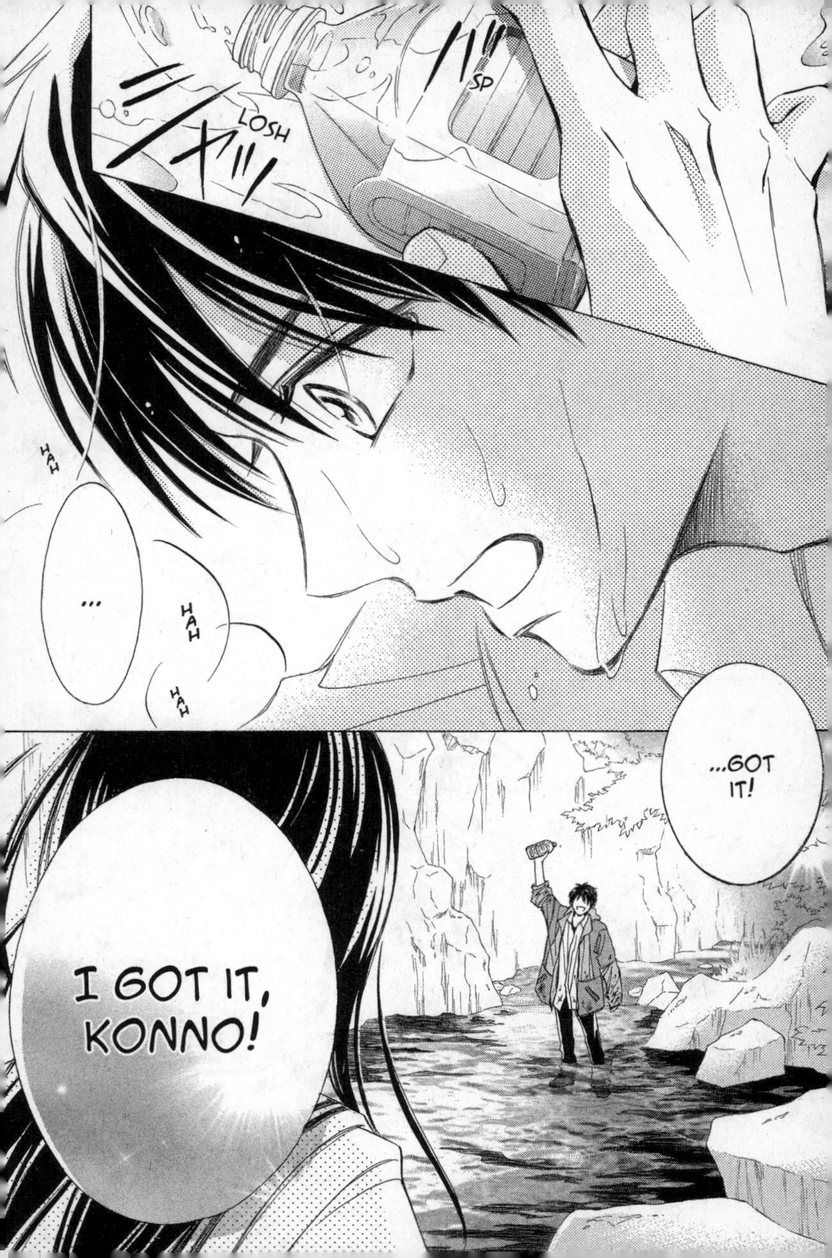
SP
LOSH
HAH
...
HAH
HAH
...GOT IT!
I GOT IT, KONNO!

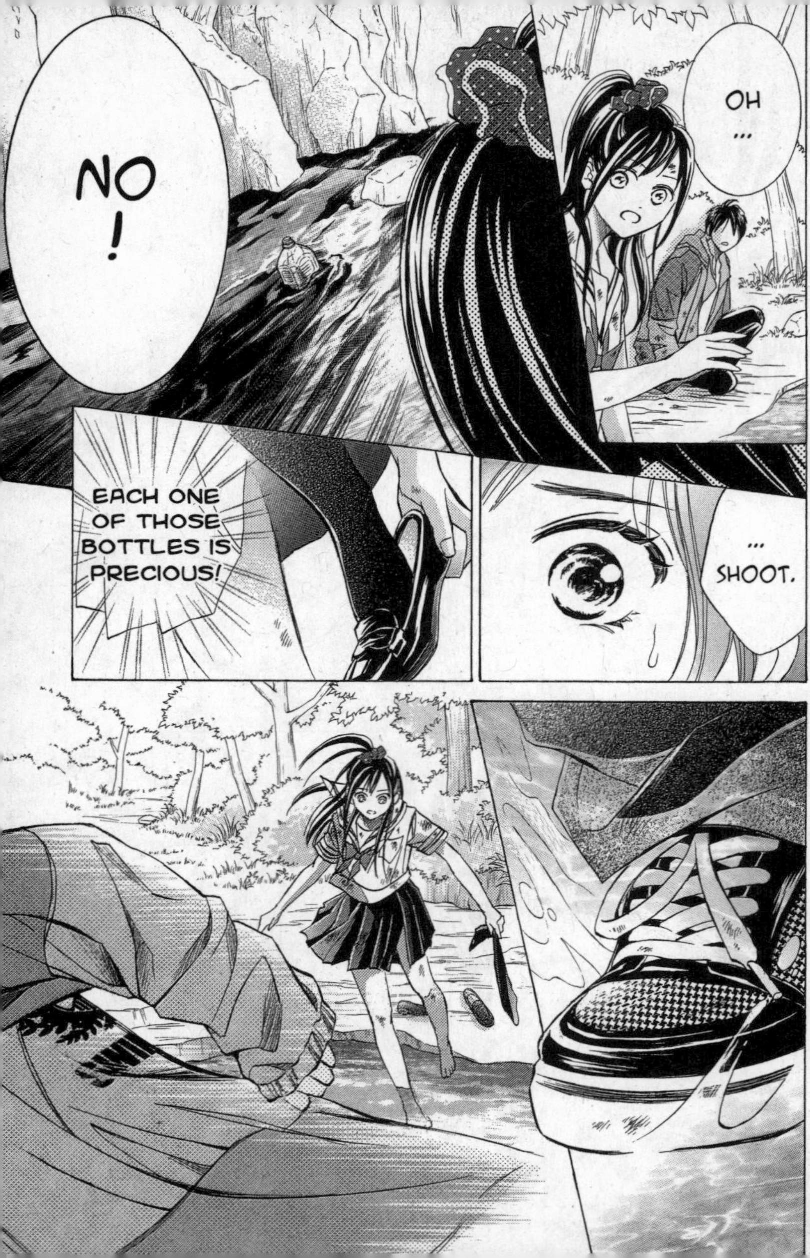
OH ...
NO !
... SHOOT.
EACH ONE OF THOSE BOTTLES IS PRECIOUS!

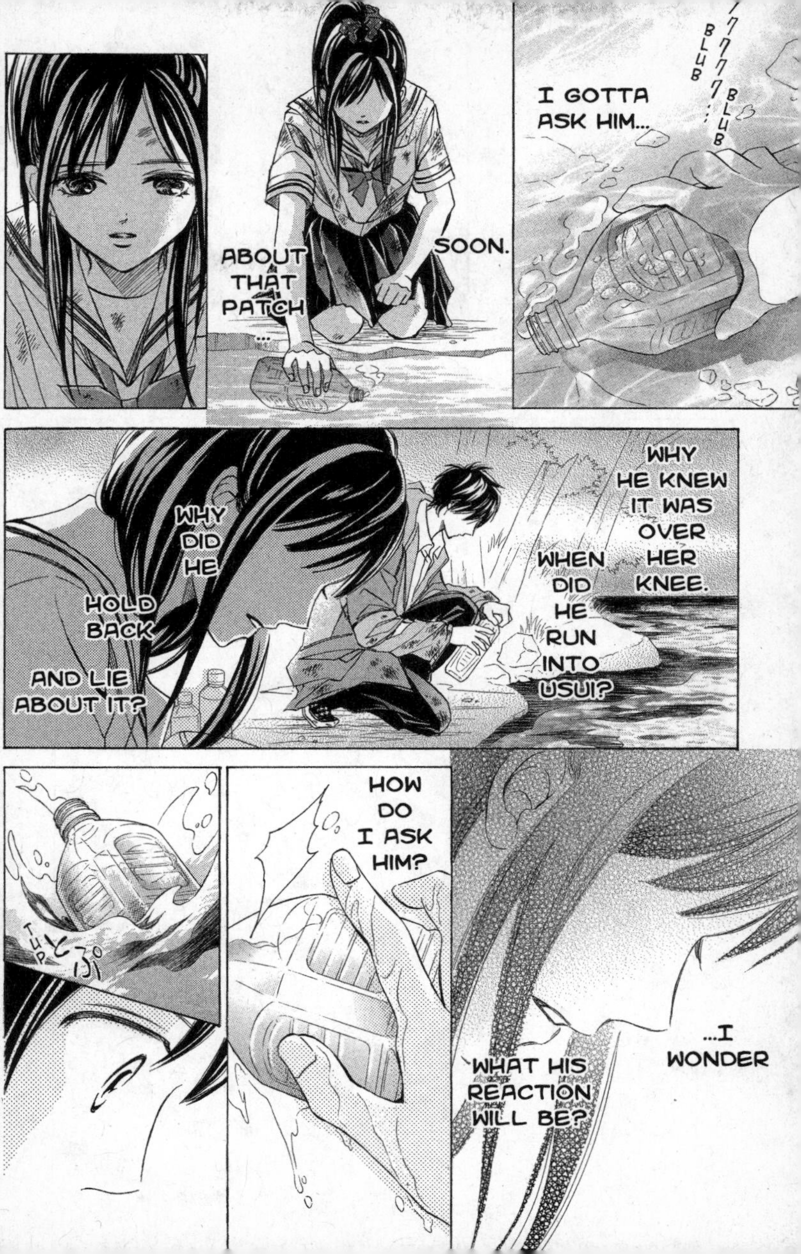
BLUB
BLUB
I GOTTA ASK HIM...
SOON.
ABOUT THAT PATCH ...
WHY HE KNEW IT WAS OVER HER KNEE.
WHEN DID HE RUN INTO USUI?
WHY DID HE HOLD BACK AND LIE ABOUT IT?
...I WONDER
WHAT HIS REACTION WILL BE?
HOW DO I ASK HIM?
TUP
とぷ

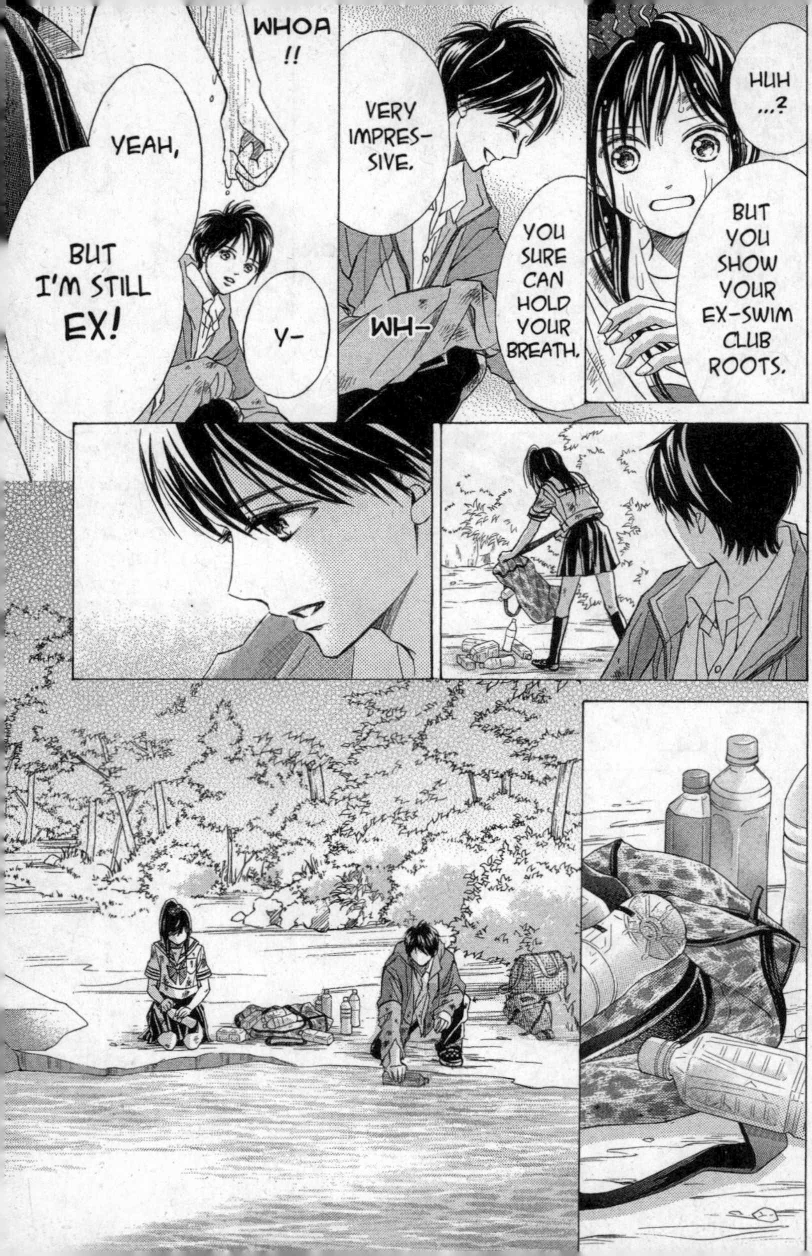
HUH ...?
BUT YOU SHOW YOUR EX-SWIM CLUB ROOTS.
VERY IMPRESSIVE.
YOU SURE CAN HOLD YOUR BREATH.
WH-
WHOA !!
YEAH,
BUT I'M STILL EX!
Y-

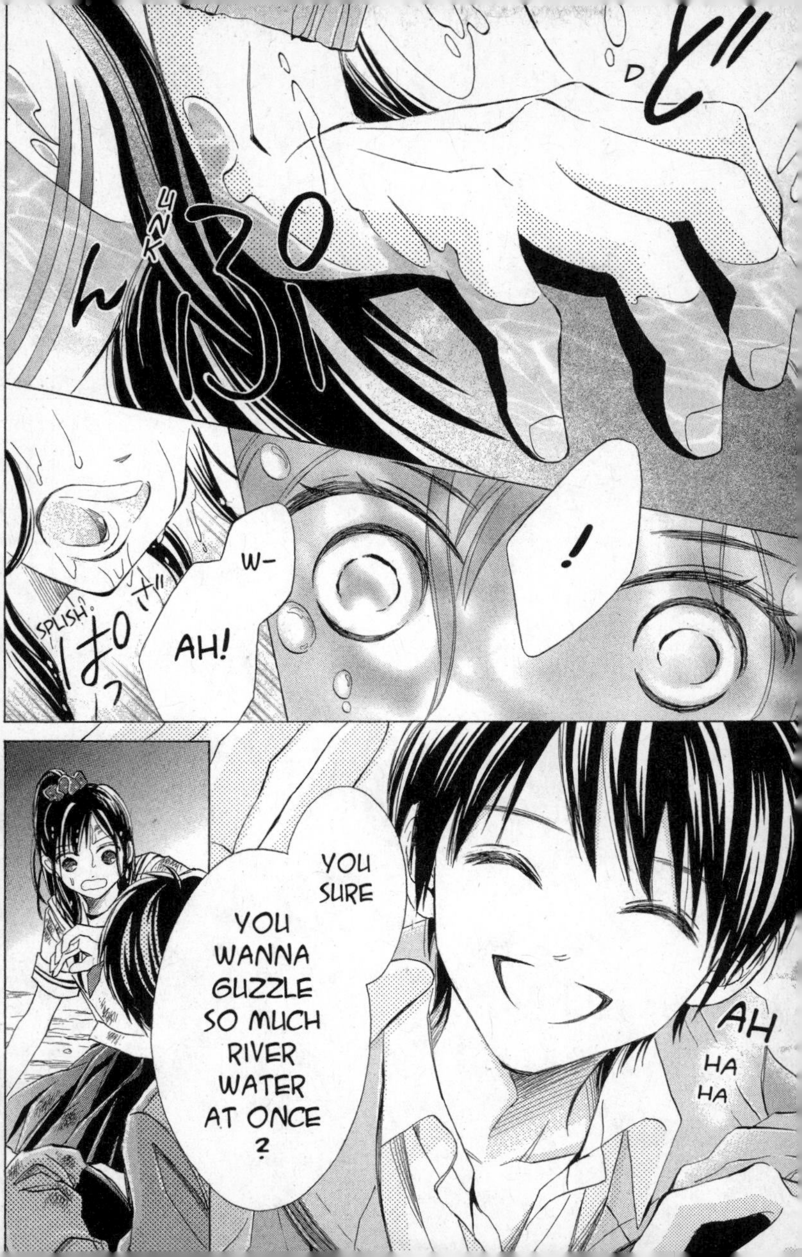
!
W-
AH!
SPLISH
AH HA HA
YOU SURE YOU WANNA GUZZLE SO MUCH RIVER WATER AT ONCE?

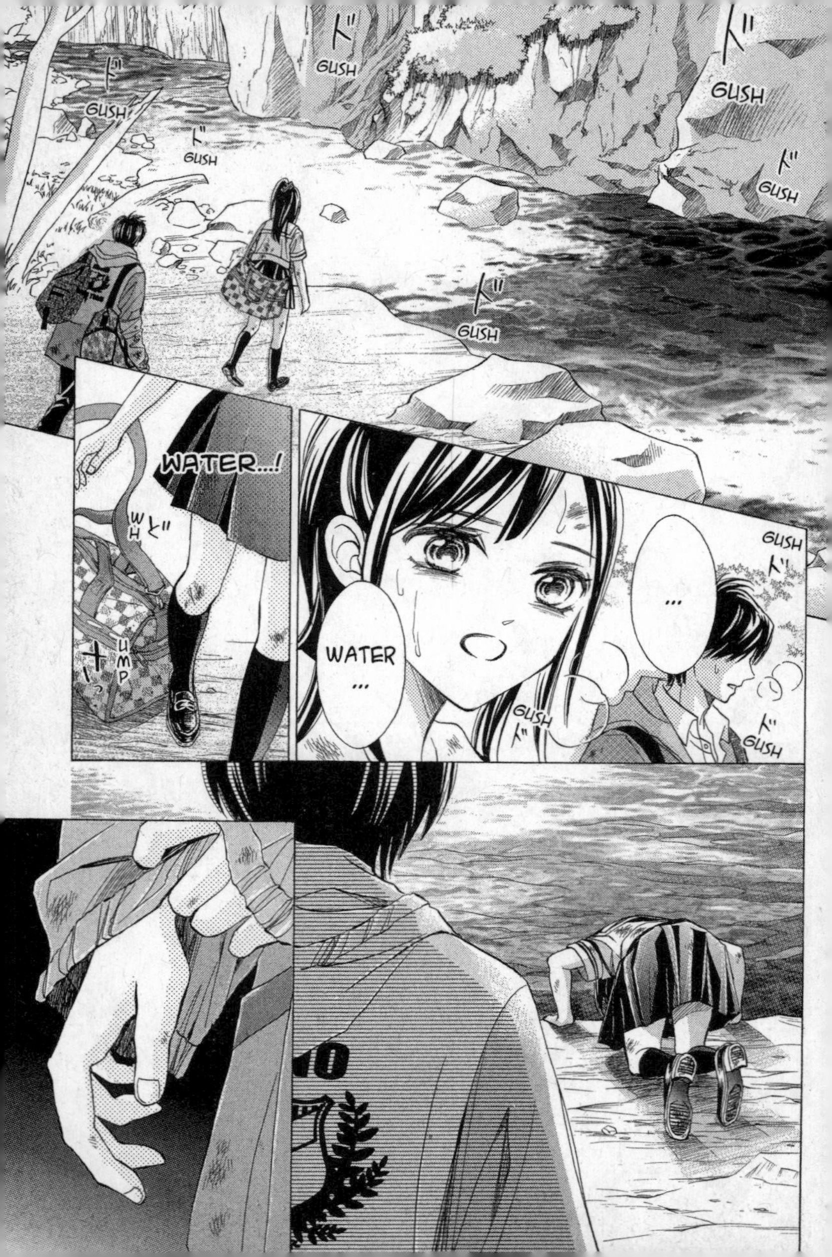
ド
GUSH
ド
GUSH
ド
GUSH
ド
GUSH
ド
GUSH
ド
GUSH
ド
GUSH
GUSH
ド
...
GUSH
ド
GUSH
ド
WATER
...
WATER...!
WH ど"
UMP

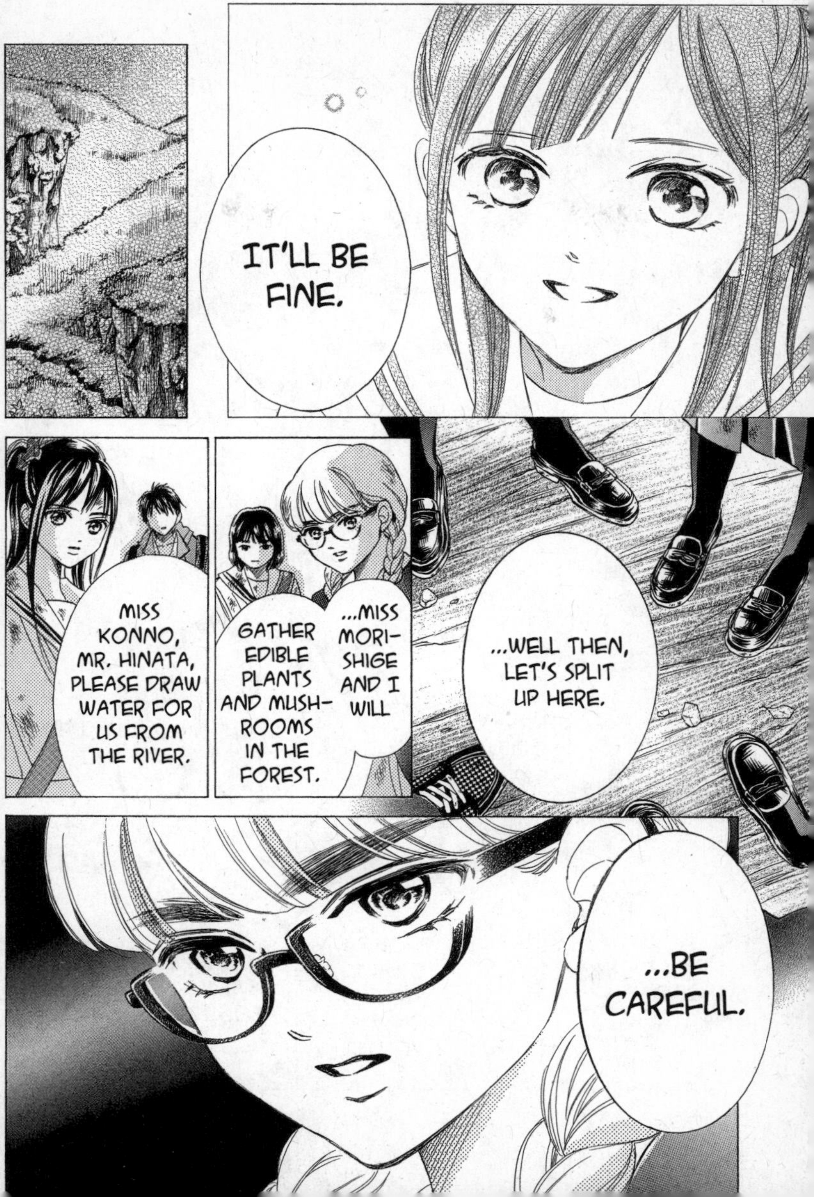
IT'LL BE FINE.
...WELL THEN, LET'S SPLIT UP HERE.
...MISS MORI-SHIGE AND I WILL
GATHER EDIBLE PLANTS AND MUSH-ROOMS IN THE FOREST.
MISS KONNO, MR. HINATA, PLEASE DRAW WATER FOR US FROM THE RIVER.
...BE CAREFUL.

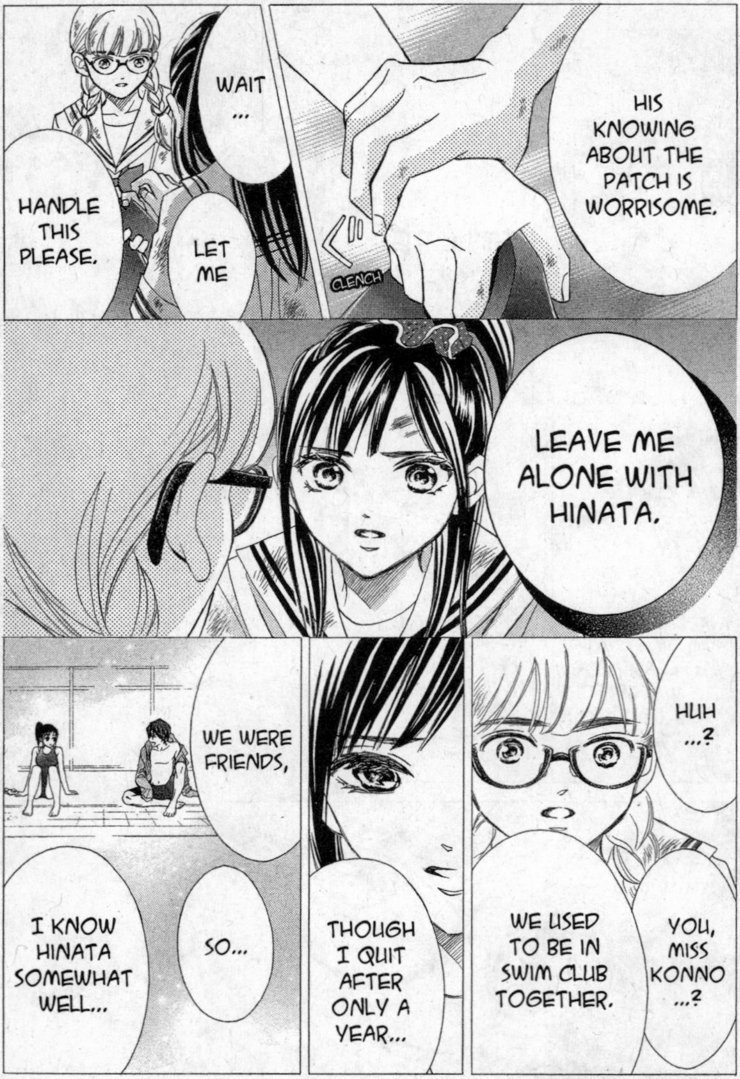
HIS KNOWING ABOUT THE PATCH IS WORRISOME.
CLENCH
WAIT ...
LET ME
HANDLE THIS PLEASE.
LEAVE ME ALONE WITH HINATA.
HUH ...?
YOU, MISS KONNO ...?
WE USED TO BE IN SWIM CLUB TOGETHER.
THOUGH I QUIT AFTER ONLY A YEAR...
WE WERE FRIENDS,
SO...
I KNOW HINATA SOMEWHAT WELL...

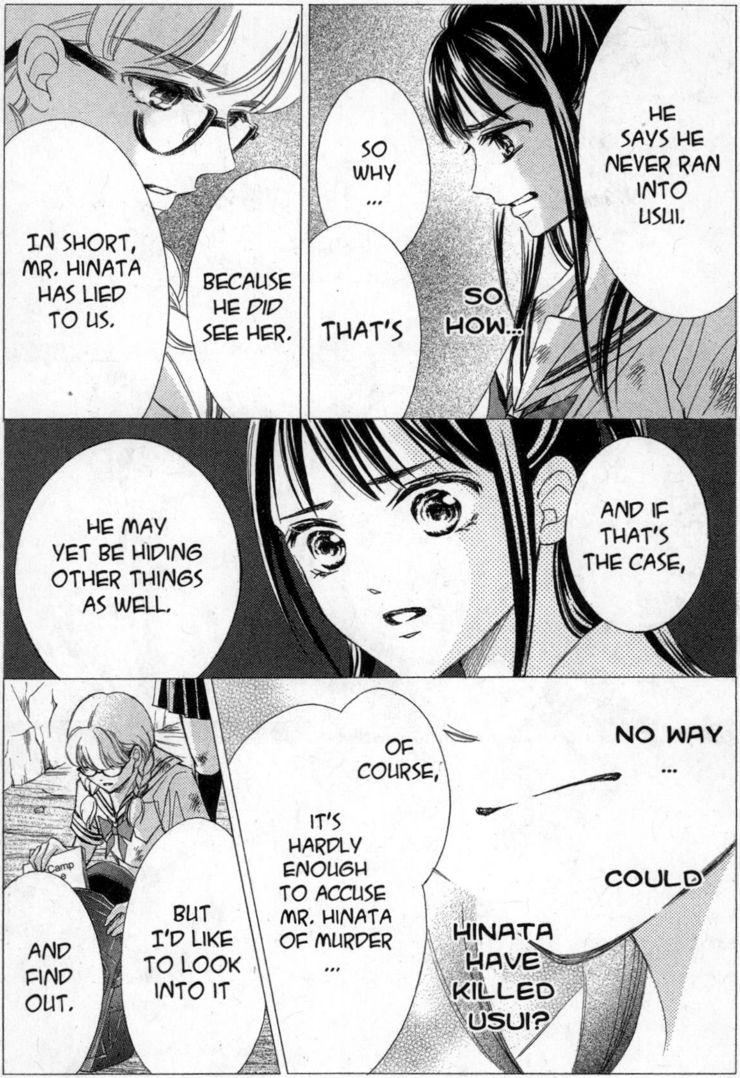
HE SAYS HE NEVER RAN INTO USUI.
SO HOW...
SO WHY ...
THAT'S
BECAUSE HE *DID* SEE HER.
IN SHORT, MR. HINATA HAS LIED TO US.
AND IF THAT'S THE CASE,
HE MAY YET BE HIDING OTHER THINGS AS WELL.
NO WAY ...
COULD
HINATA HAVE KILLED USUI?
OF COURSE,
IT'S HARDLY ENOUGH TO ACCUSE MR. HINATA OF MURDER ...
BUT I'D LIKE TO LOOK INTO IT
AND FIND OUT.

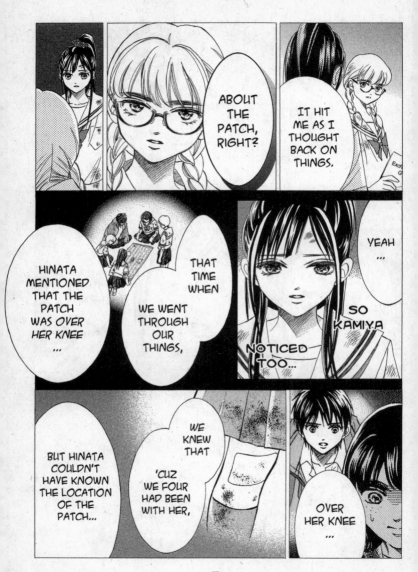

IT HIT ME AS I THOUGHT BACK ON THINGS.
ABOUT THE PATCH, RIGHT?
YEAH ...
SO KAMIYA NOTICED TOO...
THAT TIME WHEN
WE WENT THROUGH OUR THINGS,
HINATA MENTIONED THAT THE PATCH WAS OVER HER KNEE ...
OVER HER KNEE ...
WE KNEW THAT
'CUZ WE FOUR HAD BEEN WITH HER,
BUT HINATA COULDN'T HAVE KNOWN THE LOCATION OF THE PATCH...

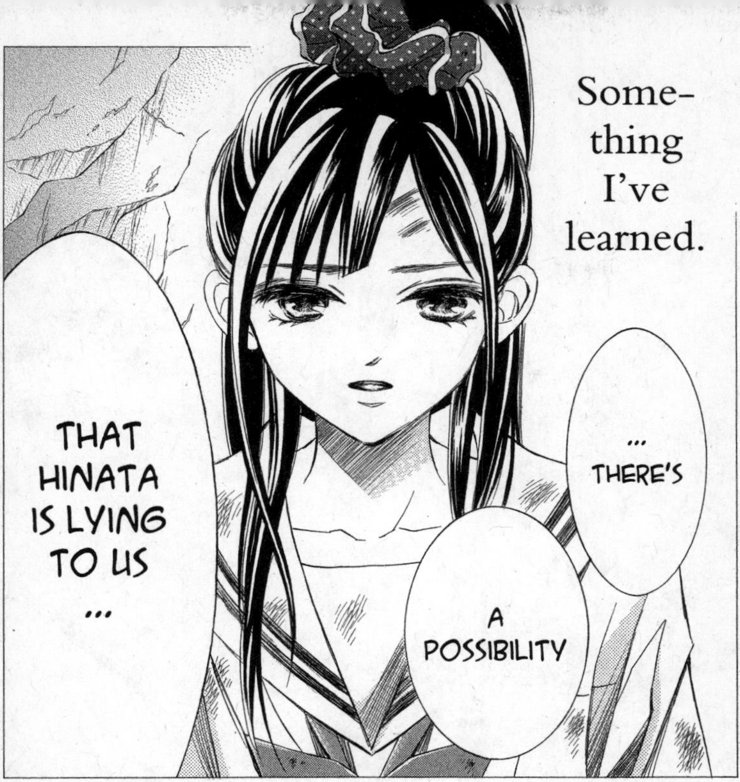
Some-thing I've learned.
... THERE'S
A POSSIBILITY
THAT HINATA IS LYING TO US ...

LIMIT

Scene. 16 Sullied Hands

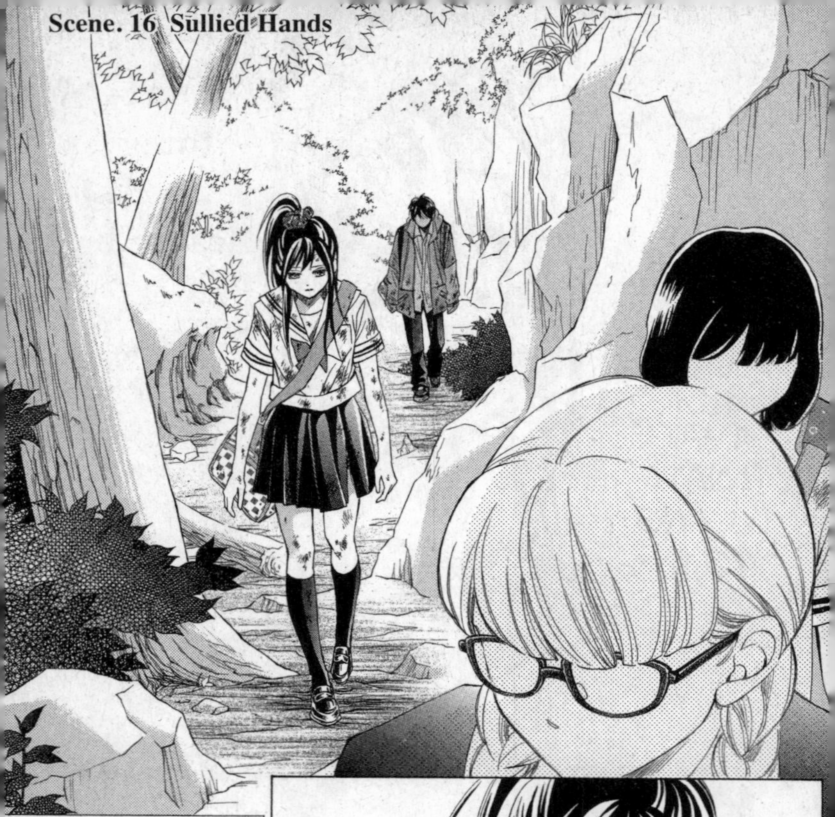

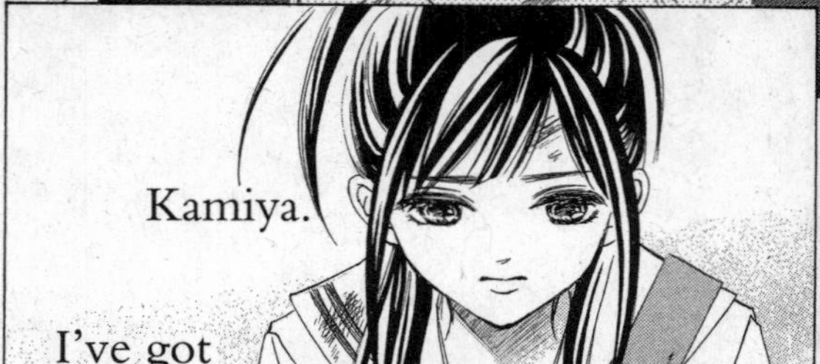
Kamiya.
I've got something

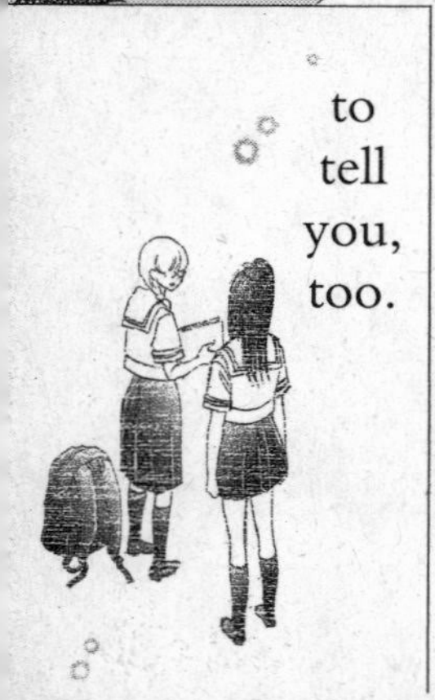
to tell you, too.

contents

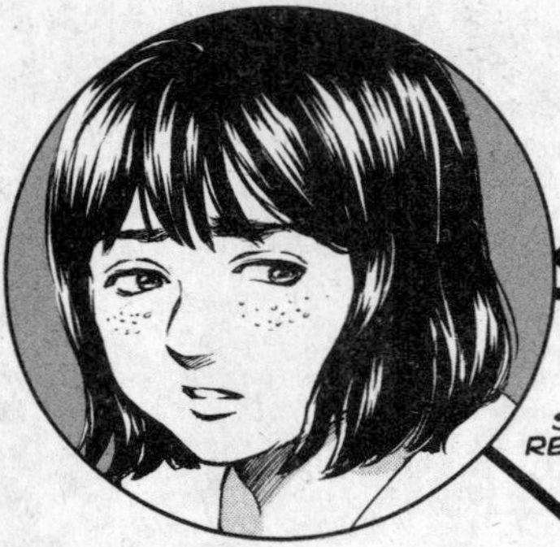

ASHAMED OF HAVING RIDICULED HER

SLOWLY OPENING UP TO HER

STRONG REVULSION

ARISA MORISHIGE
WAS A SUBDUED PRESENCE IN THE CLASS AND WAS BULLIED. AFTER THE ACCIDENT, SHE REVERSES HER STATUS AND REIGNS OVER THE OTHERS, BUT HER HEART IS WAVERING NOW THAT KONNO BELIEVES HER.

A SUDDEN BUS ACCIDENT THAT OCCURRED ON THE WAY TO AN EXCHANGE CAMP CHANGES EVERYTHING. THERE ARE ONLY A MERE FIVE SURVIVORS, ALL GIRLS. KONNO'S PERFECT, ORDINARY LIFE THAT WASN'T EVER SUPPOSED TO CHANGE COMPLETELY CRUMBLES AWAY.

"SCYTHE" IN HAND, MORISHIGE RULES THE FIELD THROUGH FEAR. ALTHOUGH THE SITUATION INITIALLY IMPROVES WITH THE APPEARANCE OF THE ONE AND ONLY BOY, HINATA, A HUNT FOR A PERP BEGINS AFTER USUI IS DISCOVERED DEAD. HAVING SUSPICION CAST UPON HER, HARU IS SHAKEN AND FALLS DOWN A CLIFF. KONNO HARBORS DEEP DESPAIR BUT THEN REALIZES A CRUCIAL "FACT." MEANWHILE, HINATA SPIES A RESCUE CHOPPER BUT KEEPS IT TO HIMSELF, QUIETLY HARDENING HIS RESOLVE WITH THE WORDS "I CAN'T GO HOME YET"—

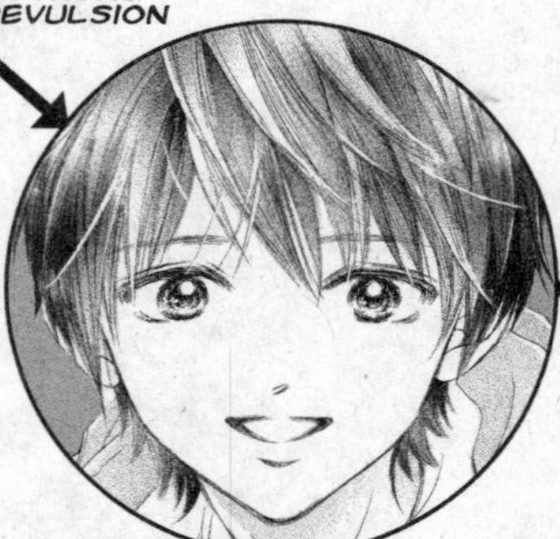

HAV

HARUAKI HINATA
HIS POSITIVE ATTITUDE HAS GIVEN THE OTHERS COURAGE. HOWEVER, HE ENGAGES IN ENIGMATIC MOVES SUCH AS CONCEALING THE SIGHTING OF A RESCUE CHOPPER.

RESISTANT AT FIRST,

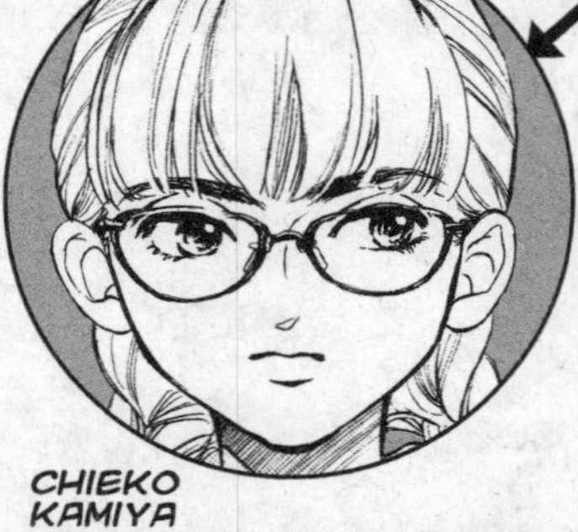

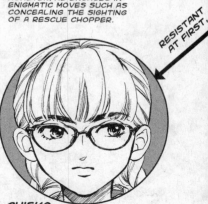

CHIEKO KAMIYA
HAS AN ABUNDANCE OF KNOWLEDGE REGARDING NATURE AND RESCUE. HAS HAD A COLDHEARTED SIDE, BUT IS SLOWLY CHANGING.

Keiko Suenobu

LIMIT 5

VERTICAL.

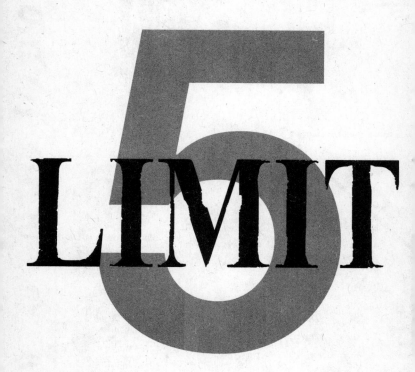

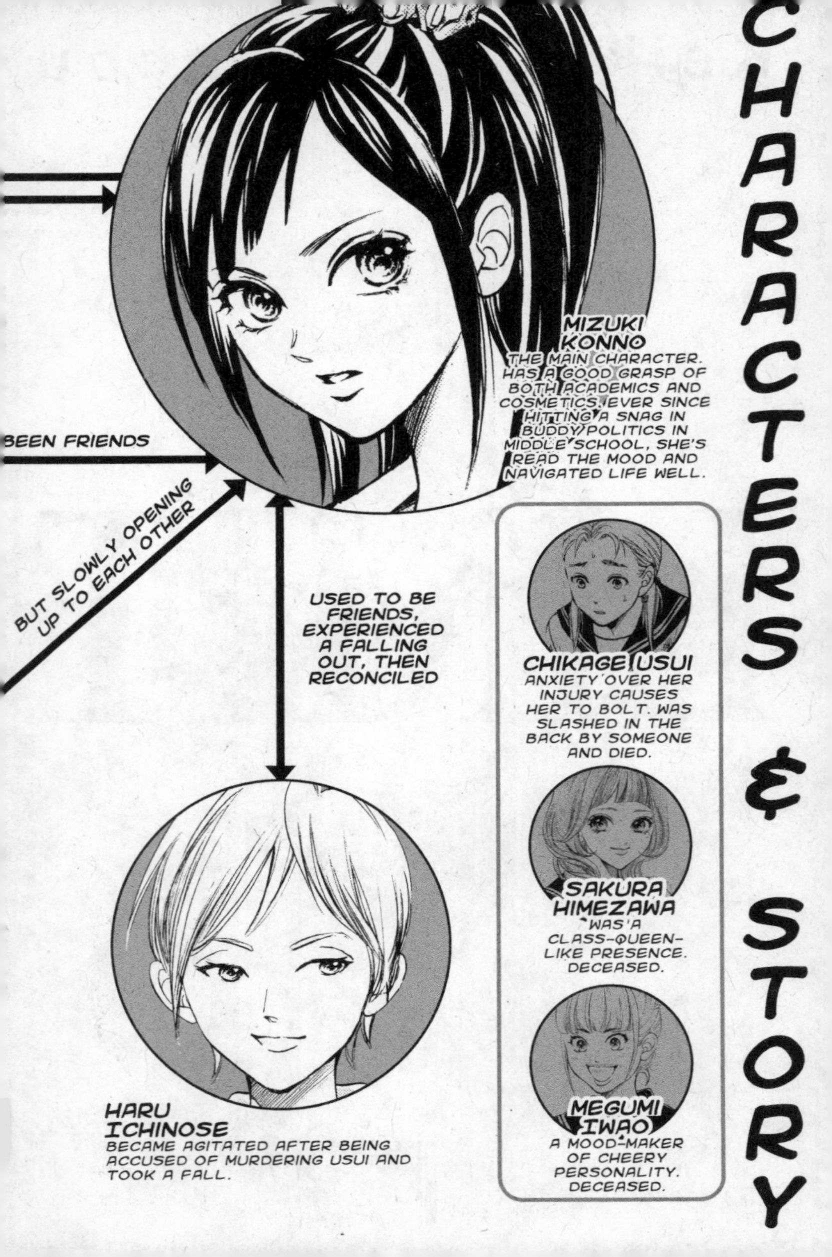
CHARACTERS & STORY
MIZUKI KONNO
THE MAIN CHARACTER. HAS A GOOD GRASP OF BOTH ACADEMICS AND COSMETICS. EVER SINCE HITTING A SNAG IN BUDDY POLITICS IN MIDDLE SCHOOL, SHE'S READ THE MOOD AND NAVIGATED LIFE WELL.
CHIKAGE USUI
ANXIETY OVER HER INJURY CAUSES HER TO BOLT. WAS SLASHED IN THE BACK BY SOMEONE AND DIED.
SAKURA HIMEZAWA
WAS A CLASS-QUEEN-LIKE PRESENCE. DECEASED.
MEGUMI IWAO
A MOOD-MAKER OF CHEERY PERSONALITY. DECEASED.
BEEN FRIENDS
BUT SLOWLY OPENING UP TO EACH OTHER
USED TO BE FRIENDS, EXPERIENCED A FALLING OUT, THEN RECONCILED
HARU ICHINOSE
BECAME AGITATED AFTER BEING ACCUSED OF MURDERING USUI AND TOOK A FALL.